Tani Ruiz is an independent writer and editor who grew up in England. A determined globetrotter with a background in investigative journalism, she worked for a range of publications and news outlets before delving into the field of international development. This is her first novel.

To my beloved father, mother and sisters

Tani Ruiz

X in Provence

Austin Macauley Publishers™
London • Cambridge • New York • Sharjah

This is a work of fiction. Names, characters, businesses, places, events, locales, and incidents are either the products of the author's imagination or used in a fictitious manner. Any resemblance to actual persons, living or dead, or actual events is purely coincidental.

A CIP catalogue record for this title is available from the British Library.

ISBN 9781035816309 (Paperback)
ISBN 9781035816323 (ePub e-book)
ISBN 9781035816316 (Audiobook)

www.austinmacauley.co.uk

First Published 2024
Austin Macauley Publishers Ltd®
1 Canada Square
Canary Wharf
London
E14 5AA

Chapter 1

Saigon, the day before Christmas. Not that it felt Christmassy in the hot and sultry city, which was fine with me. I had come to Vietnam to escape the holiday fanfare in Hong Kong…and for adventure. And I had found it all right, in the tunnels of Cu Chi.

On the northern cusp of the city, this sprawling subterranean network had only recently been opened to the public, and it was as mysterious as it was revealing. Scrabbling on the hard-packed earth uncomfortably below sea level, I found it mind-boggling how the Communist-allied Vietcong forces had managed to sleep, eat and defecate in these multi-layered warrens, waging war against the American enemy. There was no earthly way to describe their powers of endurance. Now I understood how this vastly poorer and smaller country was able to beat its big and mighty foe. The Vietnam war had ended almost twenty years ago—we were in the early 1990s—but in these tunnels time stood still.

Dumbfounded by this lesson in history, I pushed on. It was impossible to stand up or even kneel in parts of this claustrophobic maze. In the last stretch of my private tour, I was reduced to crawling, the ceiling no more than a few inches above my head.

I was beginning to feel a bit queasy—and quite frankly uneasy—when I saw light filtering through the exit a few metres away. Thank bloody god. My guide went on ahead, ascending the ladder first in order to help me out. Then I sensed it, something ticklish across my back, moving over my t-shirt. I looked over my shoulder—and screamed.

A mob of cockroaches was scuttling over me and more seemed about to drop from the surface. These were not the small fry you find in Europe but the finger-long, mottled-brown marauders with spear-like antennae.

Ubiquitous in Asia and my number one phobia.

Horror combined with panic. As in a nightmare I wanted to scram, but I was rooted to the spot. Limbs jellified. I don't know what fate would have reserved if a voice behind me hadn't boomed:

'Down, you lie down.'

Without questioning the command I slumped onto my stomach, face turned sideways. I felt a weight against my legs and a firm arm on my back. A man's head lodged on my shoulder, his body contorted to enable him to reach his targets. I could just make out his hand on the surface, grabbing cockroaches and flinging them somewhere behind me. Then he quickly manoeuvred away.

'Go, you go now.'

I bolted forward on all fours, scrambling up the ladder and emerging into a grassy area in a sunshine haze that hurt my eyes. I sat on the ground feeling shivery despite the heat, pulse pounding, throat parched, tasting earth. I would have flung off my t-shirt were it not for cultural sensitivities. A few seconds later my rescuer emerged with rather more elegance than I had managed.

'You okay?'

He sat down beside me.

'Oh my god thank you, you saved my life in there,' I heaved, the residue of horror now tinged with embarrassment.

'It is nothing,' he said, as if he fended off cockroaches every day. He spoke with an accent. French I guessed.

'No, what you did was…unbelievably courageous, to pick them up like that. Those big cockroaches…' I bore down on the word, 'are my nightmare. It's ridiculous, I know, this irrational fear, but then all phobias are like that aren't they? Once, it took me two hours to muster up the courage to tip over an empty suitcase with a dead roach inside. I'd killed it with a whole can of insect spray, I mean, talk about…'

'What is your name?' He brought my babble to an abrupt end.

'Ravinia.'

Why mention my full name? I always just said Rai.

'Ravinia.' He rolled the r, more Italian style than French. 'Beautiful name. You want to drink something?'

I nodded, still digesting his daring and wondering how the devil he'd suddenly appeared at my rear, like a genie. I hadn't seen him in the segment of tunnel I'd been shown, where it was just me and the guide. His guide must have been behind him. Then again, I hadn't looked back, focusing only on my next step. My watch said eleven forty-five. Had I been in the labyrinth for only thirty minutes? It felt far longer. Nearby we found a tiny outlet selling drinks, with two plastic tables and a couple of empty chairs inviting us to sit. When my Fanta arrived, I poured it into a glass, gulped it down and ordered another, wishing I'd brought a spare t-shirt.

'Where you from?' he asked.

'From England.'

'I am French. My name is Alain.'

His English was rudimentary—traveller's pidgin—and my spoken French wasn't much better, remnants remembered from school lessons and holidays in France. Fortunately, we didn't need an extensive vocabulary to rave about the Vietcong and their wartime exploits in the tunnels. After repeated utterances of 'incredible' and 'how did they do it'? we moved onto some backpacker trivia: how long our journeys were, where we had been, where we were heading and where we were staying in Saigon.

With my hair mussed up and my face caked with dirt, grit and sweat from the rush of cortisol, I can't have looked good, not that I cared. But Alain was eyeing me in a very, how shall I put it, forthright manner. I was also sizing him up, as you do with someone who has just saved you from a full-on panic attack, if not heart attack. His features were dark and distinct. Brown hair, cut short and a slightly receding hair line. Almond-butter skin tone. Jellyfish blue eyes. The lips—how curious. His lower lip and chin jutted forward slightly, but the disorder that this brought to his mouth was balanced out by a captivating rise at one end of his upper lip. Over his toned torso he wore a light blue t-shirt and dark blue jeans. I might have gone weak-kneed in the presence of such a strongly Mediterranean, masculine face. But the silly way he was gazing at me, like a swooning adolescent, was a damp squib. It didn't sync with the deep-voiced Indiana Jones heroics he had displayed a few minutes before.

My glass long emptied, I made to leave. I craved a shower.

'I can see you tomorrow?' he asked in English as I got up.

'Yes that would be nice,' I replied politely, lying through my teeth. I had no wish for a get-together in the remaining time I had left in this heaving city. But needs must, gratitude and all that. After agreeing the details of where we would meet, I left him, still sitting at the table, to find my guide.

The following day, I half expected Alain not to show up but he appeared at the appointed hour at the rooftop terrace of my hotel, with a ready-made plan.

'We walk to the river? Maybe take boat?'

'Why not?' The Saigon River—I hadn't yet seen it.

Off we set at a leisurely pace, observing the action on the streets as we strolled past noodle shops and women in conical hats selling their wares, men idling on the sides of pavements and others rushing by with heavy packages in their arms.

It was peaceful by the river, where for a time we stood watching the green water hyacinths floating away with the current. Solicited by a gutsy private entrepreneur, we took an hour's cruise in a small pleasure boat. The two of us glided along, enjoying the gentle motions of the craft and the breeze. Alain was funny and flirtatious—in French, having abandoned all attempts to speak English. I didn't mind. It was easier to understand him in his mother tongue, which he spoke slowly and clearly. I just couldn't jest back. His interest in me was obvious and I wished it were mutual. But he was too comical a figure to pump up my sexual adrenalin.

'Would you like to come back to my guest house? I'd like to play you some songs I've composed on my guitar,' he propositioned as we disembarked onto the embankment. I hesitated. I didn't want to have sex with him if that's what he had in mind. But I was curious about his lodgings and music and besides, I was still really grateful.

'Okay yes, to hear your songs,' I emphasised.

We pressed back into the melee of the roads. He led me to a shabby, two-storied building in a back alley reeking of incense and exhaust fumes. His room was large but dilapidated and there was nowhere to sit but the bed. I parked myself on a corner of his mattress. He took up his guitar and began to sing. I noticed how clean and well-trimmed his fingernails were and realised mine still showed bits of dirt. I cupped my hands in my lap, fingers curled in.

'Oh Ravinia I have a big problem,' he strummed with a dreamy, distracted smile. 'I'm attracted to you, I want to make love to you, what am I going to do?'

Seriously? I'd never heard anything quite like it from a man's mouth before.

'*Peut-être tu es la femme de ma vie.*' Me, maybe the woman of his life?

Peut-être pas. It was all I could do to suppress the giggles and just shake my head at this slapstick attempt at seduction. He clearly had talent as a musician though so I stayed on a little while longer to hear him sing, enraptured by the song about his 'magical trip to Madagascar'. He didn't try to touch me, although his soulful eyes stayed riveted on my face.

At a pause in the music, I stood up to leave.

'Can I see you again?'

'I'm sorry. I'm busy tomorrow and Saturday morning I take the plane to Danang. But thank you for a nice afternoon...and saving me from the cockroaches.'

With a farewell wave I left him to his music, never expecting to see him again. But shortly after arriving at the airport for my early morning flight, who do I run into at the check-in counter but the Frenchman with his guitar.

'What are you doing here?'

'I thought it would be interesting to see Danang.'

I think he wanted me to believe it was a spur-of-the-moment decision but spontaneous, my foot. He'd have to have done his bureaucratic legwork since in that era you needed a special permit to leave Saigon. I didn't know whether I felt pleased by his presence or put out by his audaciousness and the assumption I'd be glad to see him, knowing there was no way I could avoid him. The only foreigners on the half-empty flight, we sat next to each other on the plane, an ancient Russian workhorse. Part of my armrest was missing, the safety belt wouldn't buckle and coils of wire poked out from under both of our torn and tatty seats, which provoked a great deal of laughter.

'If the seats are broken just imagine what state the engine's in,' Alain gestured to the front of the aircraft. Cause of more mirth, but I also realised why Vietnam Airlines was known then as Hang on Airlines. The approach and landing in Danang proceeded to do justice to the nickname. After a shaky and seemingly brake-free descent, the wheels hit the tarmac with such a bounce you would have thought they were giant springs ready to boing the plane back up again. I'd landed in hairy rainstorms and blanketing fog before and I did what I always do in such circumstances: screw my eyes shut, cross two fingers of both hands in prayer and bunch them up against my stomach so my supplication is not too obvious. Alain seemed blissfully unruffled as we rattled towards the ground even though he'd been the one to pan the plane's aeronautics.

'There's nothing to worry about. The pilot probably flew fighter jets during the war.'

The flight survived, we shared a taxi-truck to the same guesthouse in town. It was during the drive that I realised the click had happened, the attraction that once born, seems inevitable. Maybe it had to do with the absolute fearlessness he'd displayed in the air although, god knows, he'd shown more derring-do under the ground but such things weren't dictated by logic. When Alain asked me at the reception desk of the guest house, 'Shall we take one room or two?' I answered with a smile.

The door shut, we made a bee-line for the bed. Our lovemaking was memorable, although not in the way we'd intended. Even before I'd eagerly spread my legs to guide him inside, the sound track had started: clanging from the brass head board rails against the mottled wall and some high-pitched screeching from the Ho Chi Minh-era bedsprings. Once he started thrusting in earnest it was pure discordant symphony, the brass and strings competing for the title of worst offender. It was as if the bed was furious at being woken from a slumber. Which meant I was far from being in the moment. Alain, calling the clamour 'the locals serenading us', took it in his stride—perhaps because there were no other alternatives for coupling, certainly not the cracked, dirty floor.

'I bet you it's all a set-up to liven things up for the staff,' Alain joked after he damn near collapsed the bed with his climax. 'Or maybe it's part of intelligence gathering to keep track of who's having sex with who!'

I made up for the distraction over the next seven days when, as lovers and travellers, we spent every minute together. Hiring an old bus with a driver, we explored nearby Marble Mountain and China Beach. We also ventured further afield to the riverine village of Hoi An and the ancient capital city of Hue. Without him, it would still have been a riveting road trip but much more solitary. And chillier too, since we were able to warm each other up after the cold-water showers and threadbare towels and blankets that were standard at each stop—the climate being much cooler than in tropical Saigon. His compliments were an inextricable part of his humour—perhaps to make himself also laugh and distract from some of the decrepit interiors we stayed in.

'You're beautiful in the morning light, the afternoon sun and the twilight shadows.'

As he touched and kissed different parts of my body, he applied adjectives: 'Long luscious hair, the colour of espresso…deep brown velvety eyes, they reflect your soul…lips like a leaf…a smile like jasmine in bloom…nose straight as a bamboo stalk…stomach smooth like mahogany…legs for dancing…olive oil skin.'

Can you get any cornier? Unable to contain his ardour, Alain waved me kisses for all the world to see from his bicycle rickshaw as we were guided, in separate contraptions, around sleepy, leafy Hue; amid the ruins of ancient palaces he played chase, cornering me for a quick caress. I still found his exaggeratedly chivalric gestures clownish but at the same time I couldn't deny feeling uplifted by his potent desire for me. Comedic or not he was entertaining to be with, resourceful and a gentleman who insisted on carrying my duffel bag and paying for lodging and meals. He bought me a miniature ivory-inlaid perfume bottle and gave me a poem signed with a drawing.

'Don't lose this paper, it's got my address in France. Do you have a photo of you I can have?' he asked. I gave him a tatty passport snap.

Who really was this funny Frenchman? We didn't digress into details. I gleaned only that he was thirty-eight, did some kind of interior design work and was divorced with an eleven-year-old son. I let him know I was twenty-nine and a journalist from London working in Hong Kong.

'Let's celebrate in style,' he proposed on the morning of New Year's Eve. From our forays to the shops we managed to procure a bottle of red wine, a packet of bean cakes and a tin of Russian caviar. We consumed our feast in the best hotel we could find in Danang, which wasn't anything to speak of but at least the bed was quiet.

'To meeting in Saigon,' we toasted each other, clinking our glasses. Bleary-eyed, I said my goodbyes to him early on New Year's Day to fly back to Hong Kong, where I promptly forgot all about him. As edifying as it had been, it was only a holiday fling after all.

Chapter 2

For three years, I didn't give Alain a second thought, although occasionally I'd recant the details of my cockroach encounter, still wincing at the memory. I didn't think about him until the afternoon I combed through the photos I'd taken in Vietnam and saw his face, smiling at the camera as if he knew that one far-off day he'd come into play. Maybe it was subliminal, for it coincided with my fantasising about moving on from Hong Kong—France being one of the destinations I was toying with. It wasn't that I didn't like the city. These were fascinating times in Hong Kong, where the looming change of overlord from Britain to China eighteen months down the line was the sub-text of every major conversation—with a singular thrust. Were you sad that Britain was losing its money-spinning, world-class colony to a bullying Beijing in 1997 or happy that motherland China was finally getting its territory back? There was a fin de siècle feeling to the place, boom amidst gloom, the optimists braying against the pessimists and vice versa.

No, the city was good but I was in a slump. My partner, Liam, had headed back to Dublin ten months previously to care for his widowed mother after she'd suffered a debilitating stroke. At least that's what he'd told me. And that he wouldn't be coming back. He'd been a science teacher at an international school in Hong Kong, a great intellect with a sharply analytical mind, but divorced from his emotions, which had been the greatest buffer between us. When, over two years into our relationship, he'd broken the news about Ireland, I hadn't asked if I could join him and he hadn't posed the question. From the limits we'd bumped into, I'd known there was no point in persisting. Even so, his going was a very bitter pill. I couldn't get used to referring to him as my ex.

The success that seemed to elude me in my private life smiled on me professionally though. I had arrived in Hong Kong shortly after the bloody Tiananmen Square killings, already familiar with city. It was a short hop from Taipei where I'd studied Mandarin for a year in my early twenties. Just a junior in journalism, I'd been ballsy enough to persuade the shipping magazine I was writing for in England to send me to Asia as their Far East correspondent. A few years after settling in Hong Kong, I'd crossed the Rubicon into mainstream journalism, then fallen into financial reporting. When a British news agency had offered me a job as an economics editor, I'd found myself sharing a twenty-foot desk with a bunch of old-school hacks and two other outliers—that is to say, women.

Workwise I wasn't part of the FILTH—'failed in London try Hong Kong'—crowd though I had friends who were and were rightly proud of it. FILTHers were everywhere. Couldn't hook a good gig in the UK? Didn't get that well-deserved promotion? Maybe you'd been sacked or were incompetent or didn't have the right credentials for a chosen career. Maybe you were too young or not recognised for your brilliance and talents. Or there was too much competition. No matter, you just had to get yourself to Hong Kong, the land of golden opportunity, where a bit of gumption could propel you far up the corporate ladder. Language was no barrier. In those days, there was no requirement to speak Mandarin. It was common to hear stories about 'failed' Brits walking off the plane at Kaitak Airport in the morning and going on to land a plum job by tea-time.

At least FILTH was equal opportunity, applying to both sexes. Not so with FIHTL, a set I did belong to, apropos of relationships. 'Failed in Hong Kong, try London', or at least anywhere outside Asia. Men who—because they were shy, particularly sensitive, overweight, ugly or for a million different reasons—couldn't get a girlfriend or get laid in the UK found themselves instantly in demand in Hong Kong, able to have their pick of women and what women! Stunning black-haired beauties were the prototype. Why the local ladies were agog over Western men is subject to debate. I only know that for many Hong Kong-Chinese women, being with an expat was more desirable than being with one of their own and vice versa. For foreign men who'd always had luck with the ladies, Hong Kong tended to greatly exacerbate traits such as cockiness, arrogance and commitment phobia, which I'd experienced all too frequently first-hand.

I had an English friend who fell for and married a Hong Kong fellow. But this was pretty exceptional. Generally speaking, the Hong Kong Chinese men weren't interested in us and the feeling was largely reciprocal. Pin it on cultural differences, a lack of chemistry and maybe the fact that we were the colonisers.

In offices where I'd worked, I'd witnessed the ugly arrogance of British bosses treating their talented local staff as below-deck inferiors. It made me furious.

I had dated Western men in Hong Kong—all of whom turned out to be flighty. I'd lived with an Irishman who ended up leaving. No more did I harbour high hopes of meeting a committed special someone.

'Talk about feeling invisible,' I often groused to my closest girlfriends who responded, 'Yeah, it's a bummer for the old self-esteem, isn't it?' or words to that effect.

Being invisible did have its perks, though. I could walk the streets of the city at any time of day or night without the slightest anxiety, confident in my iron-clad safety. But FIHTL was boring into my consciousness. Failed in Hong Kong, try London. Or at least France.

When the image of the Frenchman reared up, it wouldn't let go. I remembered his ardent exuberance with a mixture of disbelief and nostalgia. I wouldn't mind a dose of it now—a perfect antidote to the cynicism that was creeping into my vocabulary about men. Why not write to him? I'd kept his address. Probably he'd moved or married. He could have died for all I knew. But it was worth a try.

'I don't know if you remember me, I'm the English woman you met three years ago in Vietnam,' I penned in my perfunctory French. I included a few details about my life and how I was thinking of moving back to Europe.

Four weeks later I received a reply in the post.

'Of course I remember you. I never forget wonderful moments in life. I still have the photo you gave me and sometimes I savour your smile, waiting to see it come to life.'

In French, Alain described his various travels, his sculpting in marble (so he was a sculptor!) and how he had found his fantasy house in the middle of vineyards and olive trees in Provence. Provence for god sake! There was no mention of a woman.

'Coincidentally, I'm travelling to Thailand this winter and would love to stop off in Hong Kong if you wouldn't mind showing me the sights.'

'I'd be happy to,' I wrote back. 'I have a tiny flat but it has wonderful views of the South China Sea.'

As the date of his arrival approached I veered between palpitating excitement and extreme apprehension. He was, for all intents and purposes, a stranger. What if I loathed him? I would have to put up with him for ten whole days in the apartment I rented, so small you could almost smell another person's bad breath no matter where inside they were. It would be intolerable.

When I caught sight of Alain in the arrivals hall at Kaitak airport, I had a funny sensation in the pit of my stomach. He was far more striking than I remembered, so striking in fact that I wondered how I could ever have thought him not so. Glowing from three sun-drenched weeks in Thailand, he was pure muscle in all the right places and his eyes, they were bluer than I recalled and his smile, what a charm, it could melt a glacier. There he was, all five feet ten of him, a poster boy for sexual magnetism. I was bowled over by it but also bemused. The man I'd spent a week travelling around with seemed like someone else or maybe I was the one who was different. Did I see him in this new and scintillating light because of my lovelorn loneliness? I hadn't a clue. All I knew is that when he took me in his arms, hugged me tight and said 'Ravinia, it is so good to see you again' in his deep and confident baritone, I was glad I'd written that letter. The intensity of my attraction to him was both heady and scary because it raised uncomfortable possibilities. What were Alain's expectations of me and would I meet them?

The initial signs were encouraging. During the taxi ride from Kowloon to Hong Kong Island he stared at me with that lustful look that, if I'm frank, had prompted me to write to him.

'Now it comes to me,' he was pleased to make the connection. 'You look like Geraldine Chaplin, the actress. Charlie Chaplin's daughter. You've probably heard that before.'

I nodded, my ego stoked by the compliment (I admired the actress). I just wished I'd had the foresight to learn French fluently since last I saw him.

Entering my pea-pod of a living room he stood there open-jawed. In retrospect, the walls must have seemed like cage bars to him, this child of nature, although the views of the sea from the windows gave his eyes some breathing space.

That afternoon he told me about himself, this man born of a Basque mother and Venetian father. Parts of his story sounded like pure fable, especially the bit about finding and refurbishing an old stone house where he planned to sculpt like a Michelangelo. There must be a woman in all this I kept thinking and sure enough, he related with furrowed brows and hints of wretchedness how eleven months before he had suffered a devastating break-up with his girlfriend of two years. She had betrayed him. He appeared to be still smarting over her although he took pains to stress that he was now very much a free agent and looking forward, not back.

We sat on my indigo-blue batik cushions, making our way through a bottle of French red, roasted cashews and Italian biscotti placed on a low black coffee table. With each minute that passed, I grew more restless. When would he make a move? What was holding him back? Timidity was not something I could pin on him and my body language was obvious. Now it was I who wanted to say 'Alain I have a problem. I want to make love to you, what am I going to do?' I was on the verge of doing something when he leaned into me and stroked my hair. He kissed the soft dip just above my clavicle and the back of my neck. In seconds, we were on top of each other on my living room floor, tearing off clothes and finally giving into what my body had screamed for the second I'd seen him. After showering, we headed to my bed where, against the backdrop of ocean and giant container ships disappearing to the horizon, we explored each other slowly.

'A woman as lovely as you, why aren't you married?' he quizzed during dinner at a restaurant that night. It all flashed through my mind—Liam, other past loves, spurning and being spurned. It was an impossible question, not that I faulted him for asking it.

'I suppose because I haven't met the right man yet. I'm…' what was the French word for fussy? '*Particulière*.'

He seemed to like my simplistic response. 'So am I.'

The headiness of the days that followed was tempered by frustration, for I could express in French only a fraction of what my overheated brain wanted to say.

'Don't change your schedule because of me,' Alain insisted, so I brought him to my erstwhile living room, the famed Hong Kong Foreign Correspondents Club; to the beach at Repulse Bay, the market in Stanley, and to the Peak to gulp in the high-altitude air and the visual collage of harbour and hills. Oftentimes I would catch him looking at me more than the sights at hand. When I left for the news agency in the mornings he properly explored the city, which he hated, finding nothing redeeming in the crowds, the concrete and the giddy towers in the sky. He talked of whisking me away.

'Let's fly to Thailand, I'll take you to a beach.'

'I'd love you to, but I have to work.'

'Take some time off.'

I couldn't, so I had to think up a ruse. 'How about this. We'll go if you can bring me a white horse that can fly, bearing tropical weather.'

When I returned from the office the following day, I was greeted by a 'horse', the head and body cut from white strips of paper. It was flapping wings and blowing a hair dryer. We never made it to Thailand, settling instead for a weekend in Macao, an hour away by high-speed ferry. Lodging in a luxurious Portuguese pousada, we dined on grilled sardines, sipped glasses of the local wine and had sex like we were the first to discover it. His greedy stares and exaggerated gestures, in Vietnam so off-putting, were now a turn on.

I marvelled at his capacity to concoct aromatic dishes from my minimally equipped kitchen, from which had never emanated anything more complex than chicken stir-fries. Cooking had never been a priority although I loved to eat. But Alain, he had a winning touch with ingredients.

'Where did you get all these?' I looked in wonder at the potpourri of fresh prawns, long-stalked vegetables, herbs and spices he set before me one night.

'At your local market.'

When we kissed goodbye at the airport bus stop in Central, he told me how much he already missed me.

'I promise I will visit you in Provence,' I left him with. I didn't say what I really felt. I was in love with him. It wasn't just the potent physical attraction. There was an emotional connection that had mushroomed over the days and nights we'd spent together.

'So, what was it like with the Frenchie? I've been waiting all week for the scoop,' my Australian friend, one of the two other women on the economics desk, egged me on that night over a cheer-up drink at the Foreign Correspondents Club. The two of us were at the bar, unexpectedly crowded for a Tuesday night. I leaned in close and kept my voice down to make it harder for eavesdroppers. It was amazing how some journalists could listen while talking.

'Well, I'm happy to say he's not the FUFO type'—as in I fuck you and fuck off.

She laughed, as I knew she would. Thirty-five, single and with a string of rebuffs under her belt, my friend had helped me coin the acronym. It was crude, but to the point. We'd spent hours together, she and I, bemoaning and sometimes hooting over the Western men in Hong Kong, or rather the lack of any compassionate and committed ones.

'Not FUFO you say? Based on what evidence?'

I had my pick of examples.

'For one thing,' I said, 'he's truly considerate. Not ordinary considerate mind you but creative considerate. I mean I'm not used to someone using guided meditation and singing me to sleep when I have the odd bout of insomnia, which I had with him—probably a combo of stress and excitement.'

'What do you mean he sang?'

'Yeah, don't laugh, a lullaby, in French.'

'Frere Jacques? That's the only one I know.'

'No, Claire Fontaine. Highly effective I might add. He told me later I fell asleep minutes after he stopped.'

'Maybe he had insomnia too.'

'No, I can assure you not.'

'Lullabies, huh, that's a first. So far so fabulous. Sense of humour?'

'Is the Queen British?'

'Eh, I think her origins are German.'

I shook my head, chortling.

'Humour's his second name.'

'Let's go back to considerate. What else did he do?'

'Ran me baths with some gorgeous-smelling bath salts that he conjured up from god knows where. Cooked me fabulous meals. Oh, and he transformed my poky apartment into this sort of mini Taj Mahal. Okay, I'm exaggerating a bit. But god, the candles, the flowers, the…repositioning of things…seeing possibilities where I see nothing. Talk about artistic flair.'

'He sounds irresistible.'

'He is.'

'Sure he's not a closet FUFO?…Stop with that killer look, I was only joking. Happy for you honey but try to go easy on him. He's not exactly living around the corner.'

Which is why I didn't admit to her I was in love with him. Not because I feared a negative reaction but because of the timing. Here I'd gone and (re)met someone and the irony of it was that I was no longer thinking about leaving Hong Kong because I was about to trail-blaze into television. It had all happened so quickly. An American business news channel was setting up shop in Hong Kong and had hand-picked me and a few others for coveted posts as reporters. Several weeks previously I had handed in my notice to the news agency. The influence of my ambitious colleagues had rubbed off on me. My new aspiration was to become a financial news anchor, quizzing the experts on the markets and macroeconomics. Although I was petrified of failing, I was proud of this enviable new job, which gave me a foot in the door of financial TV.

Before starting, I had a two-week break, which I seized to fly to Provence, emboldened by Alain's unrestrained messages on my answering machine: 'I can't stop thinking about you, when are you coming here? Spring is already in the air, all that's missing is you.'

Chapter 3

It was strange and wonderful to see him on his home turf, in something other than traveller's garb, driving a car and bringing me to the house he had depicted in such glowing terms. I didn't think it could possibly live up to its reputation. But it did. The place was every bit as magical as he'd described, a jewel against land and sky.

'That's Mont Ventoux.' Alain pointed to the mountain that formed a cinematic backdrop to the house. It was a signature sight, clearly visible as we turned off the Route de Mirabelle into a narrow driveway about four hundred metres long, which ended at a gravely entrance. He'd told me a little about the house's history. But now I saw for myself, the sturdiness of the stone used to construct it one hundred and thirty years ago, the architecture a testament to another time, when, Alain lyricised in French, 'the furnace-like heat of summer and the chill-wind cold of winter needed to be kept out'.

Even so, the interior had been in ruins when he'd bought it. Inch by inch, he had resurrected the property with a team of black market labourers, most of them friends.

'I had to install everything, new electrical wiring, plumbing, roofing and heating.'

Clearly, it was a job of considerable proportions requiring unstinting amounts of time and money—certainly not for the faint-hearted.

The interior consisted of four large bedrooms on two upper floors, and at ground level the kitchen, a massively long living room and a smaller, though still spacious, study. These all coalesced into one another, white-washed, Mediterranean-style portals dividing the rooms where once there had been doors. One thing that immediately struck me was the scarcity of furnishings. The interior reminded me of a cathedral where the structure itself, the divinity of earth, stone and wood, constitutes the main richness. Alain's sculptures, carefully placed in strategic spots, had the space practically all to themselves.

Along with the piano. Alain hadn't mentioned anything about a piano in Hong Kong, where he'd seen the specimen I rented, squashed into what was billed as a second bedroom, but in effect was little bigger than the bathroom. His black upright was the first thing I spotted in the living room and I dashed over to it.

'You didn't tell me you had a piano.'

'It's a leftover from my musician days. I tinker on it from time to time.'

I ran a hand up and down the smooth white keys, the combination of notes I struck attesting to the instrument's quality.

'You promised in Hong Kong you'd play for me. No excuses,' he said, although his arms encircling my waist just then indicated he'd let me off the hook.

'I'll play something later, I promise,' after I've had a private warm-up, I thought.

Piano was a passion that had never wavered, right from the time I was twelve and begged my mother for lessons. The fact that my elder sister Julia was a child prodigy at the piano should have put me off for infinity, but strangely it had the opposite effect. I was inspired by her playing, her renditions of Beethoven, Schumann and Debussy the soundtrack to my childhood. Not that I had anything of her genius. But I did have determination. No one ever had to tell me to practice.

Next to the piano stood several tight-skinned African drums, a guitar and a few other instruments. The 'formal' dining area lay just beyond the kitchen, essentially a wooden trestle table with some iron-rattan chairs. At the opposite end of the living room, next to French doors opening to the garden, was a raised wooden platform as big as a matrimonial bed, draped with colourful fabrics and mirrored cushions. This Indian corner constituted the only surface in the room in which to sit, apart from the chairs. The ceiling was eye-catching, criss-crossed horizontally by wooden beams. In between these struts were faux beams, painted vertically like strips of bacon.

'I didn't want to put in full bathrooms, because that would have meant knocking down a lot of walls,' Alain explained that first morning, playing tour guide. 'Instead, as you can see, I've installed a sink and shower in each bedroom.' In the master bedroom, up stone steps to the first floor, he had created a touch of the tropics. Under a cover of straw thatch resembling a beach bungalow roof, he had put in a bath and sink. The first time I sat in the tub I was mesmerised by Alain's clever touch in bringing Mont Ventoux into the bather's field of vision. A glass partition on one side of the bath gave onto the vast atelier whose floor-to-ceiling windows showcased the mountain in full splendour: dangerous for a view junkie like me.

It was the atelier more than anything else that had immediately appealed to Alain, who was not looking to buy a home but a place to sculpt. Jutting out from the back, it ran the entire length of the house, serving originally as a workshop for the production of silk.

The turret-like terrace outside his bedroom was another masterful addition. From atop its low walls—the colour of honey and apricot—you could see cherry orchards, fields, rows of vines and that immovable mountain. The old *mas* was a monument to hardiness, of seasons come and gone and livelihoods earned, and yet there was something extraordinarily ethereal about it.

We covered quite some kilometres during my two-week holiday. Alain brought me to Gordes and other ancient Provençal villages that dotted the craggy countryside. He even took me—four hours away by car—to Genoa in Italy to meet his mentor, a sculptor called Vicenzo. Before a lunch of tortellini and seafood, we strolled along a pebble-strewn beach, Vicenzo and his girlfriend a few steps ahead of us. When his friends caught us kissing, they cackled, 'i due piccioncini' (the two lovebirds). Endearments, even corny ones, sounded sweeter in Italian than even French.

At the house, Alain plied me with champagne and home-made delicacies and read excerpts in French from Khalil Gibran's philosophical masterpiece The Prophet. The appearance of this book in his hands struck a deep chord. I had a treasured English copy of it at home. Gibran's odes on the human condition, on life, love and death, were fonts of wisdom and beauty to me. This criss-crossing of minds seemed far more meaningful than, say, sharing the same taste in food, films or other hobbies, not that these were trifles. But we shared a philosophy of the soul. How about that?

Together we watched the setting sun, the crepuscular light filtering through the windows of the living room and bathing his marble sculptures in a buttery glow.

The sex was urgent and often, right from that first frenzied fuck on French soil. We did it on the kitchen table, my ass on the edge, my jacket still on. I was beginning to covet the things I knew I shouldn't get used to, like those blue eyes boring into mine, the lively mouth, the ever-ready phallus.

'You know, sensuality is something that is essential to me in a woman, something I really prize,' Alain said several days into my visit, after we'd made love and were luxuriating in bed. The way he emphasised sensuality, the way he enveloped me in his arms as he said it, I took to mean that he saw it in me. I turned to face him, touching his cheeks and lips before kissing them, wondering if he knew how wonderful his words made me feel. How valued. Visible. Delectable.

One night, Alain went downstairs to fetch glasses of water, returning to the bedroom minutes later with a tray on which there was also a bowl with a spoon. 'Close your eyes,' he said, before I could peek inside. Draped across the bed, I felt drops of something cold, viscous and sticky on my nipples. Impossible not to look.

'Thought I'd give you a taste of the local lavender honey, on its own, so you can really savour the flavour.'

He set an example, slowly sucking the sweetness dripping from my nipples.

'Our bees make the best honey in the Vaucluse you know. Some live right here. In summer they nest high up in the plane trees. Lie back, I haven't finished yet.'

With his tireless tongue he removed the trail he laid along my stomach to just above my pubic hair, driving me crazy. When it was my turn with the spoon, I did likewise, drizzling and licking, driving him crazy. It was a good thing I loved honey.

I was flabbergasted at how much more substantial, metaphorically speaking, Alain appeared on his own terrain. I'd seen his fearlessness and resourcefulness on the road, his creativity in full regalia in Hong Kong, Even so, I'd never have believed this man to be possessed of so many exceptional skill sets. I mean what couldn't he do, this dynamo? Talented sculptor, composer and chef, tick. Gifted at commerce, tick. A pro at capoeira, tick. The captivation of capoeira…I'd heard about this Afro-Brazilian martial art but had never seen it performed. He soon rectified that.

'I was taught by a master in Salvador de Bahia. He learned it on the streets, as many still do. One day I'll show you the film I took, which captures him and his…magic. Come, sit here,' he said, pulling me up a chair from the living room table.

To a percussive, hypnotic beat emanating from the stereo, he began with slow, side-long sways, accelerating into gyrating bends and turns, arms akimbo.

These were followed by some fleet-footed acrobatics, his limber limbs lifting off the floor in swift, precise kicks. After a few minutes, he seemed to enter a trance-like state, which came over me too as I watched. I guess being good at Capoeira was a part of his resourcefulness and versatility. Or was it the other way around?

He had a knack for turning the ordinary into the exciting. Like a ride in his Fiat to a restaurant or the épicerie, the way he jumped into the car, turned the ignition with a flourish, grabbed my hand while driving—eyes on me as well as the road—squeezed into tight parking spaces with dizzying speed yet with great panache. Merely the way he selected wine from a wine list and groceries from shop shelves revealed him to be master of his life and decisive, a trait I highly valued because I could be insufferably indecisive about little things.

Not that he didn't have flaws, of course. His English was poor and he'd never once stepped foot in an Anglo-Saxon country. He disdained electronic gadgets—there was no TV, for instance, in the house—and didn't believe in sofas, suits or racket sports.

Flaws and all, I knew after five days I wanted to live with him. But I resisted the urge to reveal my feelings—certainly not before he did. It was only during a candle-lit dinner in the kitchen two days before I was due to fly back to Hong Kong that Alain confessed.

'*Je t'aime*,' he whispered, running his fingers over mine.

'*Je t'aime aussi*,' I echoed, relieved to unburden myself of those words.

'I want you to live here, in this house, with me, in Provence. *C'est fou, eh*?'

'Yes it's crazy. But I want the same.'

We had a lot to reflect on that night, not just the mutual confessions of love but our desire to live together. The following day, at breakfast, we delved into specifics.

'What do you think we should do then?' Alain began. 'When could you move here?'

Initially we were sensible.

'How about I work at my new job for six months then I come over? I mean, I should at least give it a try. I signed a contract.'

'Six months…yes okay. That seems fair.'

It sounded good, it sounded right. But even as I spoke, I wasn't buying into it. Neither was he because the next minute he said, 'but half a year's a long time for us to be apart. What about if you work for three months?'

Less viable but still somewhat sensible. I mulled it over.

'Three months? Yes, I can do that.'

But could I? Starting the job, passing the probationary period only to quit? Deep down I struggled. I didn't want to wait. It was Alain, however, who buried the notion of sensible, rational planning.

'It sounds like a real cliché but we have only one life to live…Let's not waste time. Why not pack up and move now?'

I studied him for a second. His face conveyed what I needed, love and reassurance.

'Well…' I kept him in suspense. 'What the hell,' I said in English. 'I'll move here as soon as I can.'

To celebrate our momentous decision we drove to an outdoor café on the windy, snow-tipped summit of Mont Ventoux, which had a rocky, lunar-like quality. Below us the Vaucluse lay in all its magnificence, swathed in hopscotch patches of shadow and sun. Splotches of cloud drifted above us in a cobalt blue sky.

'I told you in Vietnam that maybe you were the woman of my life,' Alain exalted as we as huddled together against the wind. 'I've never said that to anyone before. And it's true. I knew it then.'

I reflected on Alain's words, how utterly ridiculous they seemed at the time and how prescient they now appeared.

'I have a lot of love to give,' he kissed me.

But not as much as me.

Saying our goodbyes at Avignon central station, he pressed me to come as quickly as I could, reassuring me all the while it was what he wanted.

'I may be a little crazy but I'm not irresponsible. I've given this whole thing a lot of thought. I want you here. I know you're giving up a lot in Hong Kong to be with me.'

Giving up a lot was right. But he was worth it. I was in heaven on the long trip back to Asia, feeling my life had taken the most rapturous turn. But once in Hong Kong I was assailed with doubts. Was I insane to abandon a new career? To move continents for a man I hardly knew and couldn't express myself properly with?

There were parts of his past I was uneasy with. Alain had been honest enough to tell me that, unhappy in his marriage, he had left his wife and three-year-old son to devote his life to music-making, a pursuit he had dropped a few years later. He'd had three live-in relationships since his divorce and lord knows how many sexual encounters. '*J'ai beaucoup aimé les femmes,*' is how he characterised his womanising, while in the next breath assuring me that all this was in the past and he was a happy convert to monogamy.

'You're the woman of my life. I don't want anyone else. I love you.'

But could I trust him? Would he be faithful to me?

The day after I returned I phoned up my father in New England.

'Dad, what do you think I should do?'

I presented the choices without mentioning my misgivings about Alain. My father and I had an indelible bond. I valued his opinion. After the loss of my mother from brain cancer when I was sixteen, he did an excellent job of stepping into her shoes, becoming protective twice over, although he never attempted to assert his will over mine. With my either-or question, I had selfishly put my father in a quandary. There was a long pause at the other end of the phone. My father, not normally one to stall, responded haltingly.

'You must do what you feel is right. If you love him and want to be with him, then go.'

Subliminally what he was saying was: stick with the job. But my closest friends came down firmly on the side of *l'amour*.

'Listen honey, I'd go for the man. You can always come back to Hong Kong if it doesn't work out, no one will judge you,' is how my gutsy Australian friend put it. 'That said, I think you're better off in Europe if marriage is part of your life plan.'

I wavered like the pages of a book blown by a changeable wind. Love or career, heart or head, it was a gamble either way. I wanted to experience the peaks of my potential, but I didn't want to harbour regrets for the rest of my life that I hadn't given Alain a chance. I knew that my loneliness and longing for a partner were blind spots. Loneliness and lust, to be frank. Back and forth I went: What if I regret passing up this job in television? What if I take it and end up being alone? What if I never meet a man as plain damn incredible as Alain? What if I go to France and it turns into a bust? What if…what if…what if…

Somewhere between brushing my teeth and switching off the bedside light, it became obvious. Starting a new career or picking up an old one was less daunting than finding a special someone. And for all my doubts, I sincerely believed that Alain was that someone. I loved him. He loved me. And I'd had my omen. At the very same time that I'd written to Alain, he'd been thinking of knocking—'surprise surprise'—on my door in Hong Kong (I'd moved doors but that's beside the point).

On the designated Monday morning, instead of heading to the television studios I sat down in a chair and punched in a number.

'I have something to tell you,' I stammered to the woman who'd hired me—an executive with the network. 'I'm extremely sorry but I won't be coming in this morning…or ever. For personal reasons, I have to leave Hong Kong immediately and can't assume the job.'

My hands were slippery with sweat and my voice shaky. I had not slept the previous night, devoured by anxiety over how exactly I would deliver this bombshell. The voice at the other end switched from a surprised 'What?' to a hammer of hardness.

'You can't do that. You've signed a legally binding contract. You are obligated to start work.'

'I know I have. I'm very sorry, but I'm unable to honour that contract. It's imperative that I leave Hong Kong.'

I argued my case without a legal leg to stand on, forcefully but politely, against her shocked indignation. She ended the conversation with, 'I'll have to talk to our lawyers about this.'

In the end, the television channel let me go with a stern reprimand but without retaliatory measures although I knew that forever after I would be persona non grata with that organisation. I phoned my dad in America to tell him the news.

'I really feel that moving to Provence is the right decision. I see a future with Alain. I mean, life is a gamble isn't it, you've got to take risks. That's always been one of your mottoes.'

'Well, if that's what you've decided, I wish you the best. I hope it works out how you want.'

I didn't need to seek my father's approval because he gave it freely, even if he didn't agree with my actions. Which I knew he certainly didn't in this case. The fact that he never voiced his disappointment about me dropping the job in television before I'd even started might be seen as laissez-faire parenting—or just proof of his unconditional love. He'll be reassured once he sees how happy I am, I thought.

I gave up my flat, sold whatever furniture I could, packed valued possessions in boxes that I shipped through the post office, closed my bank account and said my farewells. My Australian friend waved me off at the airport.

'Bon voyage, and don't forget to invite me to the wedding.'

'Very funny. Just wish me luck sprucing up my French.'

Hurtling through the air, I slipped into a reverie about Alain and his incantations of 'you're the woman of my life'. It was hard to imagine now what had occupied the space inside me that he did. Loneliness and lust had driven me to get on that plane. But I also felt a spiritual and cerebral connection with Alain. And the house, the vines, Provence—these also played a part. When slivers of doubt poked through about giving up a career for a context I couldn't be sure of I reasoned philosophically. Life isn't a set of fixed algorithms but a series of random events and chances. Within that we have choices, we can listen or not to our voices. And mine was tuned into Mont Ventoux.

Chapter 4

Disembarking from the TGV at Avignon station, I scanned the platform. Alain was nowhere to be seen. I expected him to be waiting for me with open arms. What if he's changed his mind? Sick with anxiety, my stomach in knots, I lugged my two suitcases and laptop slowly towards the exit. Then I spotted him. He was hastening towards me, waving an arm, his blue eyes waltzing, a smile as big as the day. Talk about a shift of gravity. The bags now seemed like weightless packages as I floated towards him. From that point on, it panned out as I'd imagined.

'My beauty, you're here,' he murmured, and kissed me as if he were about to strip me. Goodbye old life, here's to love, I said to myself, in thrall to the fact that for once, reality was imitating fantasy. The intensity and immensity of it all. I'd followed my heart and here I was. It was hard to believe.

As we set off from the station in the last glow of afternoon light, I thought this seminal moment deserved some kind of statement to capture the onset of this new, and I hoped forever, chapter of my life. But I couldn't think of anything meaningful to say, or rather the right way to say it in my choppy French. Alain focused on the road, every now and then shooting me a look that was intense and incredulous. Maybe he needed a few quiet moments to let it all sink in. He broke the silence by asking how I'd been these past few weeks.

'Busy as you can imagine.'

I mentioned some of the nit-picky details of the move, saying nothing about the doubts that had plagued me. Now that I was here, to a rousing welcome, these seemed like an anachronism. As we sped along the motorway in the heart of Provence, I found the words.

'I don't think we should have high expectations of each other.'

I wanted us to start our cohabitation on a realistic note to avoid a crashing of hopes in the future.

'No no no, on the contrary,' Alain gushed with Gaelic emotion. 'We should expect the greatest things of our life together. We have everything it takes to be happy: love, time, money and a dream house.'

Shit shit shit, why'd I say that? I cursed myself for sounding so negative.

'Yes. You're right. We have everything for a great life.'

It was a sincere volte-face, expressed with passion, and it made Alain laugh.

'*Alors* that's the spirit my darling. How lucky we are to have found each other.'

Steering with one arm he reached out with the other, brought my left hand to his mouth and kissed it. Tearing my eyes from him I gazed out the window as we left the motorway, drove through Carpentras and entered a smaller rural road running through fields and pasture-land before skirting the local village, Mazan. Here I was, come to be the mistress of an idyll in the rolling vineyards of the Vaucluse. Incredible.

'*Mon amour*, we'll be home soon, your home, our home,' Alain's husky voice cut through the thread of my thoughts. It was five weeks to the day since he'd first brought me to the house. I calculated the time in my head, only then realising what date it was: first of April—April Fool's day. I smiled. Just the universe being humorous.

Having made the move, I can't say I hit the ground running. In fact, my feet didn't touch the ground much in the first two weeks, partly because I stayed in bed a lot. Though elated, I was supremely exhausted from the move and freezing. In that big belly of a house draughts escaped from all directions and I shivered everywhere but under the duvet.

'I don't remember feeling this cold in February,' I remarked to Alain the morning after my arrival, puzzled because it was no longer winter.

'That's because I had the central heating turned on all the time. But darling, that's not a permanent, or cheap, solution. Now that spring's here a good fire should provide enough warmth. Your blood will soon thicken to the colder climate.'

He forgot to mention that the mistral, that notoriously glacial wind native to southern France, hadn't made an appearance in February but it was now howling ghoulishly outside. As a concession, he turned the thermostat back on for a few hours in the evenings, joking that if he didn't, I'd head back to Hong Kong.

Still, some things couldn't wait. My third day there I determined to build a solid, sustainable fire on my own, my motive also being to prove to Alain, you see, I fit right in here. I'd never been a member of the girl scouts and I couldn't recall ever putting to work a single chimney in London, Hong Kong or New York, where I'd also lived. But how difficult could it be? A pile of twigs and several logs were piled by the kitchen fireplace, which was deep and wide, providing room enough for a family of copper pots that must have been the cooking modus operandi in the previous century. To my humiliation, I soon realised that this task was beyond me. Alain had given me the benefit of the doubt but after I'd wasted nearly a whole box of matches in my failed attempts with the kindling he decided it was time to intervene.

'You're missing a key ingredient,' he said cryptically, before going off to find some bits of paper that he scrunched into balls. Methodically, he manipulated these, some twigs and logs into a sculpted pyramid, which burst into flames on the first match strike. This was the first of many lessons to come, some in subjects I never dreamed would become priorities.

Alain made it easy for me to stay in bed, firstly because that's where he served me breakfast every morning for a week. The aroma of toasted *pain de campagne* reached me from the kitchen even before he brought the tray up. I couldn't remember ever feeling so pampered, well, apart from my holiday here. Onto the bread I spooned generous portions of chunky apricot jam and there was no resisting the lavender honey—no longer simply honey but an erotic accessory. Starving, I ate everything, including the colourful fruit he cut up, oranges, pears and kiwis that had never touched plastic. The guilt-free pleasure of breakfasting in bed was followed by a guilt-free period of lingering in bed. Unclothed, I was either swaddled by him or the quilt. Sometimes both. Whichever way, Alain couldn't stop gazing at me with his fluorescent eyes and whispering:

'*Ma beauté*, what a vision you are, I can't believe you're here.'

My beauty. Liam would have pooh-poohed that. He'd been sparing with sweet talk. Maybe coming from him it would have sounded silly or insincere. Not from Alain, who in that one word expressed more emotion for me than Liam was capable of doing using thirty, because he found it hard to do feelings.

Ma beauté. I needed to hear it, just as I needed time to decompress, readjust, be still in my skin, acclimatise to the cold, think without having to act. I was eager to jump into this new life I'd chosen, to create new routines, carve out a role for myself, do Alain proud, do myself proud—only not quite yet. It came as a relief, then, to be allowed some slack, the environment also not conspiring—as it did in Hong Kong—to get you up, showered, dressed and out the door in 20 minutes. An entrepreneur with his own business, Alain had the luxury of being able to schedule his time off.

That first morning after we awoke—and every morning thereafter—Alain flung open the green wooden shutters to let in bright sunlight and my first glimpse was of vines emerging to life after the dead of winter and the two large plane trees that stood in front of the house, their boughs thickening with spring foliage. Three rows of neatly planted vines fronted one end of the garden, a part of which lay on the far side of the driveway. The air smelled deliciously of fresh grass and wood smoke.

On day five of my new life, after another arduous morning in bed, Alain cast aside the duvet. 'Come on, let's take a walk to Mazan. The mistral's gone and left a beautiful sky. Time to show you the charms of our local village.'

I needed no goading. Leaving through the kitchen door, we joined the stony path at the back of the house that led directly to Mazan, a half-hour walk away. I loved how Alain often stopped to pick up a pebble or a wild flower so I could have a look, or so I could admire the views of fertile farmland fanning out on either side, or so he could rub my hands warm under his leather jacket.

'Shut your eyes and count to fifteen, then come find me,' he suckered me into playing hide and seek. I found him behind a tree at the edge of some private terrain. He came to me, arms spread wide, shouting into the April air, 'This is the woman I love and she's come from across oceans, deserts and Siberian tundra to live with me.'

It was a gift, this way he had of garnishing the ordinary so that it became, if not extraordinary, certainly more colourful. Maybe, though, it was simply that he knew how to live in the moment. Call it chemistry. He opened my eyes. With him, I felt alive.

Our first stop in Mazan was the Café du Siècle on Avenue de l'Europe. We chose a table placed sun-side under the wide awning. The balding waiter who came to take our order greeted Alain with a friendly pat on the back and asked, 'How's life, *mon gars*.'

'Not too bad, Gilles my man. I'd like you to meet Ravinia. She's come all the way from Hong Kong to set up house with me in this backwater…eh, I mean the best place on earth.'

The waiter and I beamed at each other.

'Welcome to the best place on earth,' he said, bowing for effect. 'Some citron pressé for the two of you? Or something a bit stronger, on the house?' he winked. We graciously declined that offer.

In the two other places where Alain made introductions, the nearby boulangerie and *magasin de tabac*, I received the same hearty reception. There I stood with a half-moon grin growing butterfly wings, fluttering on the niceness of being warmly welcomed as the amour of one its acclaimed denizens. Acclaimed because the baker, with noticeable deference, referred to Alain as 'the greatest artist living in our midst'.

Arms linked, we ambled along Mazan's narrow lanes—lingering vestiges of its medieval origins—passing pretty churches and fountains. Mazan had a post office, a driving school and several restaurants catering to its population of about five thousand. It also claimed the eighteenth-century Château de Sade, where the father of the writer best known for his sadism was born.

'Ah, here we go,' Alain said when we reached the Rue Napoleon. He pointed out the chateau with a certain pride and admiration, as if its presence in the village was a badge of honour. It was then being used as an old age home, so perhaps he had a point.

'The Marquis de Sade lived mostly in Paris but he spent periods of time at his chateau, staging some of his plays. In fact, he is said to have put on the very first theatre festival in France, right here in Mazan.'

'That's really interesting Alain, I had no idea.'

But I grew a little indignant when he launched into how some people called the Marquis 'the freest spirit who ever existed and a man ahead of his time'.

'Ahead of his time in what? Sexual cruelty and sadism? That's what he's famous for, at least in England. I wouldn't want to be around someone like him, that's for sure.'

Alain chuckled at my reaction. 'Ah the prudish English! In France, he has a better reputation, in fact he's something of a cult figure among the literati.'

After a fortnight in Provence I was still freezing, even with several layers on, but emerging from the tiredness, which, I think, had also been a protective shield. Stupendous as they were, the turn of events seemed unreal and I was processing them in fits and starts, sometimes feeling scared by my good fortune, sometimes overwhelmed and a bit of an alien, but always confident in the decision I'd taken.

Inevitably, the bed-lolling-honeymoon-of-a-kind period came to an end, but not before my official coming out. On a Friday morning, we set off to see Alain's brother, Pierre, the first member of his family I was to meet. It wasn't a social call though.

'He has the cauldrons we need to cook the chilli con carne for the party in your honour tomorrow night.'

The way Alain explained the visit struck me as odd. If one of my sisters lived in the vicinity, we'd be in and out of each other's houses. At the least, she'd have raced over to meet my new partner. But no sibling relationship is alike and what did I know about brothers?

All I knew about Pierre were the basic facts that Alain had disgorged. 'He lives on the outskirts of a village called Baume-de-Venise. He's an engineer, he's divorced, he doesn't have children. And he's much younger than me.'

Maybe because of the emphasis on 'much', I imagined Pierre to be smaller and slighter than Alain, with the same dark hair and eye hue and for some reason, wearing glasses.

Twenty minutes or so after leaving the house, we made a turn-off from the D21 road leading to Beaumes-de-Venise proper and pulled into Pierre's driveway. A nice touch, I thought, taking in the pots of bougainvillea that rimmed the limestone brick exterior of his two-storied cottage. Alain rang the bell.

'*Enchanté*,' Pierre greeted me at the door with three pecks on the cheek.

'I hope you're settling down well in the Vaucluse. It must be a big change from Hong Kong.'

Doing an indiscreet double-take, I must have come across as strange or rude as I sized up the man in front of me against my imagined version, momentarily losing my tongue. Pierre was much taller than Alain, well over six feet. He was also sturdier, with lighter skin colouring and dusty brown hair—lots of it. He had hazel eyes set in a youthful face and there was no sign of glasses. I would have guessed him to be in his twenties, not thirty-three. Alain would never be caught dead in his preppy corduroys and collared white shirt.

'Nice to meet you', I hurried out, finally finding my voice. 'Yes it's a big change from Hong Kong, but really great, what a lovely place you have and what a beautiful area you live in.'

We followed Pierre to the kitchen, where he served us peach grenadine in tall glasses. I looked around. The furnishings were modern, off-white porcelain floor tiles, two large stainless-steel sinks and an L-shaped granite worktop. This was no disorderly divorcé's pad. There were no dirty dishes lying around. Cookbooks were stacked neatly in a corner of the worktop. A silver-framed watercolour of boats against a seascape hung on one wall. Some glass figurines in the shape of deer and dogs sat on the window ledge.

'How's work going?' Alain asked his brother.

'Good thanks. The same as ever. What about you? How's business?'

'Business is fine. All is good.'

'So, you're preparing for the party?'

'Yes, a chance to introduce Ravinia to people in the community.'

I noted immediately how strangely the brothers talked to each other. Not with the slovenly familiarity of siblings but with the kind of wary politeness you reserve for a customs official. Pierre took pains to include me in the conversation, even if it was to ask if they were talking too fast. I liked how he addressed me, tilting his head down and to the side with a straight-on look that conveyed curiosity as much as camaraderie. His Provençal accent was much more pronounced than Alain's, more typical of his countrymen and thus harder to understand.

'The cauldrons?' Alain said brusquely around fifteen minutes into our visit.

'Of course.' Pierre fetched them from a cupboard.

'Will you come to the party tomorrow Pierre?' I asked before we left.

'Ah, these parties are not for him,' Alain intervened. I thought Pierre looked relieved.

'Well then, come and eat lunch or dinner with us soon,' I offered.

He nodded absently.

Back in the car, the two cauldrons in the boot, we reconnected to the main road and headed into Beaumes-de-Venise proper. Alain wanted to show me this curvy, hilly market burg whose tiny population made Mazan seem metropolitan. We parked and took a stroll around the main square splayed out around its stone fountain, afterwards climbing up to a higher elevation for a broader perspective.

'This is a great place to live if you like wine cultivation and a bit of craggy nature,' Alain said, pointing out the jagged line of the Dentelles de Monmirail on the heights above the village. They loomed up dramatically like the teeth of some prehistoric creature.

'Does Pierre like craggy nature and to cultivate wine?'

'I'm not sure about the wine, but he likes nature.'

'I hope it's okay to ask, but what happened between him and his wife? Why did they get divorced?' Alain took some time to answer, as if combing through memories.

'They were married for about…I don't even think it was three years. It was a mutual break-up. The details of it all, I don't know. He hasn't spoken much about it.'

'What was his wife like?'

'She struck me as someone very practical. Not much of a talker. But I only met her a few times. She was an accountant. I think they met in Toulon or was it Marseille? Anyway, she found a job in Orange, and Pierre was lucky enough to manoeuvre a job transfer there. He's the one who bought the house in Beaumes-de-Venise so she's the one who moved away when things didn't work out. I thought he should have sold it and moved on, but he loves the place.'

'Pierre doesn't live far away, do you see him often? I noticed you seemed a bit strange with each other.' I wanted to say 'distant'. I was thinking of my own two sisters, the cacophony when we were together.

'He works long hours and isn't home much. But the truth is, we're not particularly close. We don't have much in common. Remember, he's much younger than me so I didn't grow up with him like I did with Tristan (his elder brother) and Sylvie (his sister). He was more like an only child.'

'He was a surprise for your mother?'

'An unplanned baby you mean? Probably. At any rate, they're very close to each other.'

And with that, the conversation was closed.

From Beaume-de-Venise we headed to Leclerc supermarket in Carpentras, where we combed the aisles, stocking up on dozens of tins of garbanzo beans, tomato purée and slabs of beef for the chilli con carne that would fill stomachs at the following night's social do. When Alain had first mentioned throwing a party to celebrate my move to the Vaucluse, I imagined something quite intimate, a buffet of main dishes, desserts and wines, a night of razzle dazzle followed by a quiet day of clean-up. The more I gleaned from him, however, the more I realised this fete was an Alain institution and something entirely different.

'Darling, I just want to let you know more than a hundred people will be coming over on Saturday,' he told me a few days before the event. 'And not just from around here but also from Marseille, Paris and Nice. From Genoa too. Vicenzo the sculptor—remember him?—wouldn't dream of missing this party.'

'These are all your friends?'

'Actually not all. My friends plus their friends. The parties I throw are enormously popular. No one else I know has the room, the money or the desire to invite more than one hundred people over for a good time. It's one way I can share the house.'

I liked the spirit of generosity but the numbers not so much. But fine, I could deal with a big crowd. It was during our shop at Leclerc, when he started shifting bottles of wine and hard liquor from shelves into a separate trolley and stacking them up that not just the size but the scope of the event became evident.

'Wow, Alain, that's a lot of alcohol, even for the amount of people coming.'

'We need it. Didn't I tell you, darling, that my parties usually last for three days?' *Three days!* '…usually around twenty people stay over, mostly those coming from a distance…' *twenty people!* '…don't expect much sleep. It'll be quite crazy, but you'll see, it's enormous fun…' *Fun!* '…and a perfect opportunity for you to meet everyone.'

This was all a bit out of my comfort zone, which in itself was an uncomfortable truth to own up to. Not that I would ever fess up to Alain, whom I'm sure would not be charmed by such an admission. While the chilli simmered for hours on oversized gas cylinders—the pungent aroma of spices perfuming the whole house—I had no choice but to give myself silent therapy. Okay so you're not thrilled about a three-day bash, a massive sleepover with people you don't know and won't be able to talk to properly. But Alain expects you to be adaptable and to throw yourself in. Sure it's a challenge. But it's a great learning experience, a growing experience. A test of your mettle. And you are going to rise to the occasion. No complaining. You're going to show Alain you're a good sport and a good hostess. So damn well get over yourself and try and enjoy it.

Alain was a master organiser. He'd had plenty of experience in catering for an army, so I didn't need to figure everything out or indeed anything, apart from my costume. These parties, Alain told me, always had a costume theme and tonight's was the onset of spring. Revellers had been told to come as a flower, plant, fruit or insect. At eight o'clock, the first arrivals appeared in the driveway that I had spuriously named New Delhi Drive because with the rain it turned into a sodden, muddy bog—reminding me of the drenching monsoonal downpours in India. Luckily there was no rain that night. In another hour or two, cars would form a continuous line along the drive, reaching right to the road.

Weird forms started coming through the door, sprouting leaves, roots, rinds and wings. My decorative necklace of orange peel and an orange taffeta skirt were rather insipid next to some of the inspired creations. There was an endless stream of people, many curious, I am sure, to meet the new English paramour of the artist-in-residence whisked in from the Orient. A medley of faces approached, each giving me three pecks on the cheek, announcing their names, looking me up and down—their outfits permitting—some asking a cursory question or two, before disappearing into the 'long room', my pet name for the living room. I couldn't remember a single name and the faces became a blur, but no matter. Pumped up by my pep talk I felt proud to be the mistress of this mansion, proud also that, judging by the way guests greeted him, Alain was hugely popular in this community.

I moved into the mass and tried to strike up a conversation or two but what with the language handicap and the noise I soon gave up in frustration. Sensing this, Alain frequently waddled over in his banana-skin wrapper to plant a kiss on my lips. On one of those occasions he tantalised with, 'I have a secret to tell you.'

'Tell me, tell me. At least, give me a hint.'

'Well, it concerns you and me.'

I could squeeze nothing more out of him but his provocation left me light-headed. It must be about marriage—him and me. A few days before in the kitchen, a sly smile etched on his face, he'd asked: 'Do you like the idea of marriage, you know, in general?'

Like the idea? This was my kind of lingo. But I couldn't display my elation at what he'd clearly intimated. I needed to play it cool because appearing too keen might be off-putting even though he was the one asking. But it was hard to find the cool-keen balance.

'Well, my parents had a good marriage, it was a good model for us children, but, you know, it's important to be independent, and have your own interests and things. People need to respect each other. Talk to each other. And give each other space.'

God, what was I saying? Bringing my parents into it? Later I regretted waffling on, realising I should have simply said yes. But he got the message.

While Alain mingled I surveyed the crowd, a glass of champagne in hand. I'd drunk more champagne in Provence during these past few weeks than I had in my entire life. Even so I had my limits. Anything more than three or four glasses of bubbly or wine usually led to nausea, dizziness and vomiting, which tended to rob the whole experience of pleasure. It could be such a drag, this kink in my DNA. Being seen as a loser by my work colleagues because I couldn't hold notable quantities of alcohol might reflect badly on them but it still rubbed me raw. For that reason, I had sought to keep a low profile at the mandatory Friday night marathon guzzling sessions at the Hong Kong Foreign Correspondents Club. It would be interesting to see if the same views regarding booze prevailed here.

Standing and sipping, my eyes settled on one woman in particular: Danielle, Alain's former girlfriend. She was not in disguise but draped in an indigo dress that clung to her like cling film. Even before I'd met Danielle I'd formed a picture of her in my mind, naked, it has to be said, because that's the image that stuck with me when Alain had related the sordid details of their break-up. Disaster had struck one morning in winter.

'I'd just finished a sculpture. I was very excited about it and drove over to share the good news with my friend Jacques. When I walked into his house, there was no sign of him downstairs so I went up to the bedroom, which was also empty.'

That's when he heard noises emanating from the bathroom. He opened the bathroom door and what he saw was his undoing:

'Danielle was making love with Jacques in the shower.'

Alain rushed out of the house, shattered by the vision of those two interlocking bodies.

He'd recounted all this, cloudy-eyed, as we sat on my living room floor in Hong Kong. He and Danielle had lived together in Carpentras for most of the two years they were lovers. Alain had bought the property with her in mind as its mistress. After the discovery of her betrayal, he'd ended the relationship even though he was still painfully in love. He'd sworn to me that he was over her and they were now just good friends. And he'd made a point to prove it. Only two days before, he'd told me that while they were still together, he'd started carving the torso of a woman. He hadn't intended it to turn into a faithful replica of Danielle but that's how it'd evolved. He'd placed the sculpture securely against a wall before leaving for Thailand and when he'd returned (that is, after our reunion in Hong Kong) he'd found it mysteriously smashed to pieces.

'When I saw that I felt completely healed. It was like an exorcism had taken place. I was freed from the pain and suffering.'

I might be a facts-are-everything journalist but I also believed in things you couldn't see or explain. So I took Alain at his word, applauding his openness to extract meaning from inexplicable phenomena.

But then he uttered the words that would echo relentlessly in my brain.

'Our relationship was only about sex.'

Only? It had to have been the obsessive kind, which is the best, no, the worst kind of all. The voraciously spectacular kind that eats you up and spits out your soul. Whereas Alain had managed to root out the vision of her unfaithfulness from his mind, it took up residence in mine. Only instead of seeing her with Jacques, I pictured her with Alain, right from the second I'd first laid eyes on her when she had popped over one morning during my February holiday, much to my surprise.

'So pleased to meet you. Alain's told me all about you,' she'd said, smiling a charm. She'd asked about my work in Hong Kong and I'd told her about my new job in television.

'This is a holiday before I go back and start.'

'Well, you're in great hands here. Alain will show you the best there is of the Vaucluse.'

So friendly, I'd thought, not what I'd expected from an ex. She'd put me at ease, even as she'd held me transfixed.

Danielle was not conventionally beautiful but oozed a potent sexuality that was like golden syrup dissolving on the tongue. I suppose it is one of those inborn qualities that some women have and others might strive for but never attain. She was the primordial Eve, the incarnation of carnality. Her shoulder length, dark-brown hair was not special in and of itself, but the way her fringe fell almost to her eyes—flamenco-flashing dark eyes—was playfully provocative. Her lips manoeuvred into the most seductive formations. She smoked cigarettes as if she was kissing, feigned upset with a Lolita-like pout, laughed with a playful throatiness that you could never ignore. Equally hypnotic were the movements of her long arms, hands and fingers, adorned with rings and bracelets, which she shook in wide-angled gestures to illustrate a point. She liked to wear short skirts that showed off her shapely legs whose poses seem designed to draw eyes. She was the epitome of a femme fatale. All this, on top of her extrovert, attention-seeking personality meant that she dominated any gathering.

Was I imagining it or did she, at the party, cast a perennial eye out for Alain, even as her boyfriend Jacques chain-smoked silently next to her?

I felt the first dreadful stirrings of jealousy.

As the hours passed, the consumption of alcohol rose and heavy house music replaced samba and rock. What began as a party devolved into a rave. Feathers and skins fell off and outfits disintegrated along with the ability of individuals to stand up straight. At one point, Alain left on a suicidal mission to drive home a friend who had drunk even more than he had. When he reappeared, I begged him off more driving. Around five in the morning I started to clear up, a way to keep myself busy and cheery. Into sturdy garbage bags I dumped empty bottles and mounds of cigarette butts clumped in paper plates and on the floor. I wiped up spills and even a puddle of vomit (not my own). People kept offering me joints, which I had to refuse because smoking hash or weed just made me paranoid. I didn't see anything stronger around, not that I'd have been a taker. I'd been well and truly inoculated against the hard stuff.

I was two months into my master's degree programme in journalism at Columbia University in New York City when I met my boyfriend. He was studying for his MBA at the business school. Like me, he didn't smoke cigarettes or drink much and I took it for granted he wasn't into drugs. How out of character it therefore appeared when he accepted a line of heroin offered by an acquaintance of his. We were at a party in some student digs in upper Manhattan when, half-way through the night, this person had ushered us over to a table in the corner of the room. I'd thought nothing of it until I saw him cutting some lines of white powder.

'Cocaine?' I'd asked.

I'd snorted it a handful of times. I loved the coke high but hated the comedown so I wouldn't have been tempted.

'No, it's heroin—China white. Much better than coke.'

I was astonished he could so casually whip out an opiate at this gathering of graduate degree seekers where nothing stronger than spliffs were circulating. I was doubly astonished when my boyfriend blithely took the straw proffered and snorted the powder, like it wasn't worth a second thought. Heroin for crying out loud—the stuff you didn't mess around with or did at your peril. It suddenly occurred to me that I'd never asked him, had no idea, whether he'd taken this, or any drug before.

'First time with heroin?' How bizarre to be asking the question. He nodded his head and indicated, nonchalantly, that I should follow suit. 'Be a little adventurous,' he said. You must be joking. I reeled from my boyfriend's thinking that I could be roped in. I felt ready to dump him. But then subversive thoughts crowded in, why not…to be on a level with him. You can try anything once, even heroin. So, adding even more astonishment to the evening I accepted the straw, snorted half a line—the sharp tangy taste of the powder dripping from nasal passage into mouth—and in minutes felt myself flutter into a universe of sleepy, weightless, cloudless peace. I didn't even mind the throwing up (I had to make several trips to the toilet). So this was heroin, the big bad drug so smashingly good I knew there could be no second time leading to a third. It was hours later, at dawn, when we were at my boyfriend's place and the drug's effects had pretty much worn off, that we talked about the experience.

'I guess I don't know you as well I thought. I'd sort of assumed you weren't interested in drugs, not to mention hard drugs.'

'I'm not. Look, it was completely spontaneous. He happened to offer it and I was just curious about something so many people talk about, that's all. I wanted to see what all the fuss was about.'

'So do you? Because I do,' I said before he could answer. 'I get it now when people say that it only takes one time to get you hooked. No repeats okay, can we agree on that?'

'Okay sure,' he vowed. So that, I thought, was that. We didn't see this particular acquaintance again and there were no more encounters with drugs. Months passed. We moved in together to a run-down railroad flat between Broadway and Amsterdam. Everything seemed fine, we were happy and I was heavily into my books. But there were little things: he would often return late, saying he'd been at this concert, that lecture or with this friend, sometimes sounding suspiciously vague. Plus, he was always short of money, even though his wealthy parents were helping him out—his father was a plastic surgeon, his mother a patron of the arts. In fact, a few times he even asked if he could borrow from me. I was living on a shoe-string, surviving with a student loan plus earnings from a part-time job as an administrative assistant for a travel agency. Then one night—the clock read two forty-four a.m. to be exact—I awoke for no particular reason and automatically noted the empty space next to me. Where was he? I got out of bed, went to the living room and saw what I will never forget: my boyfriend slumped in a chair, eyes shut, a syringe on the floor and paraphernalia on the table. Thinking he'd overdosed I rushed over and shook him. When he opened his eyes, I was so relieved I just stood there and cried. Having been caught red-handed he didn't bother to deny anything.

Turns out he'd been using heroin since that first sniff, graduating from snorting to injecting. He'd done a masterful job of hiding his addiction, from keeping his stash out of sight to shooting up when I wasn't around or when I'd gone to bed or when he was out. He'd cleverly disguised the track marks on his body, complaining of eczema. I was incredulous. He, of all people, into heroin? How could that be? He was a Columbia Business School graduate student, a serious lad, the product of a patrician family and parents with high educational standards. But appearances had deceived. I found out that his father had piled on the pressure (he was the youngest of three sons) to choose a 'career with a good price tag' when what he really wanted was to study philosophy and play the drums. The parent's marriage was a shambles and his mother had been stingy in her affections with him, yearning for a daughter. His grades had plunged and he'd all but stopped going to class. He'd pretty much chucked in Columbia.

It was he who agreed to a fortnight's schedule for getting clean and going to Narcotics Anonymous meetings. Plan A was weaning off with methadone, Plan B was rehab, which I assumed his parents would pay for. I believed him when he said he wanted to quit. But the two weeks turned into a month, then two months then four, during which time he repeatedly lied about his using and we fought and it became intolerable. How I came to hate the heroin. It was evident he hadn't hit bottom and, at my wits end, I left him. I moved back into my father's apartment, a little older and much wiser about the ravages of hard drugs.

We made it to bed around seven in the morning, only to be woken a few hours later by the sound of thrumming from the living room. Franco, Alain's best friend and an avid musician, couldn't keep his hands off the African drums. I felt like throttling him. But I held my calm and served strong black coffee and croissants to the twenty or so people who'd crashed out wherever they'd found a space, including one right by the piano. I was impressed when Alain organised an efficient clean-up, realising I hadn't needed to mount a solo effort. Teams were formed, one to scrub the floors, another to gather the rubbish, a third to do the washing up and so on. It was good to have order restored.

Afterwards the party continued on a mellower note. The stereo was turned back on, and drinks and joints reappeared along with friends who'd left only hours before. People lounged in the tree-shaded enclave in front of the house and in the garden beyond, slowly getting sloshed while exchanging rollicking reviews about the previous night.

'We came back as soon as we could,' announced a jaunty Danielle accompanied by Jacques.

As the day wore on, it became much more wearing. I was spent, not so much from the lack of sleep but the effort of trying and failing to join in slang-rich conversations, feeling cut off from everyone except Alain. But so what if I was grumpy and tired. So what if I just wanted to reclaim our space. I'd vowed to myself I was going to play merry and I kept to that, smiling a lot, nodding my head and making sure there were plentiful nibbles. The only concession I allowed myself was a little break. In the late afternoon, I slipped away to the pebbly path behind the house that led to Mazan. I found a boulder and sat, contemplating the tepee tip of Mont Ventoux. Alain noticed my absence, taking me aside when I returned to ask if I was okay. 'Fine,' I assured him. 'I just felt like a little walk.'

That evening Alain ladled steaming pasta into bowls for the revellers, the most hardened of whom didn't depart until Tuesday morning. When it was all over and I took stock, I concluded that the party had taught me two lessons: I had coped and kept my cool. And I needed to become more easy-going, flexible and go-with-the-flow, like Alain. Yet even Alain had sighed with relief after waving off the last straggler.

'The party was a great success but I'll admit it's good to get back to the quiet, and to you,' he said, grabbing me with suction.

'Truthfully, I'm not that keen on big parties.'

The confession had slipped out. Shit. Surely he'd see this as a character weakness.

'I'm sort of glad you aren't because that's in such contrast to Danielle.'

His response was a surprise—and a vote of confidence. With her hanging around, I needed all the votes I could get.

Chapter 5

After the fete, reality of a sort set in. For one thing, I had to relearn how to drive and Alain had to resume his work. To earn a living he sold high-end, hand-crafted kitchens. These rustic units with all the gadgets were fashioned out of hard wood and decorated with motifs in the glorious pastel watercolours of Provence. Two models, one green, the other pink, were on display in his very own shop, La Belle Cuisine, along with a few of his sculptures that added an arty, exotic touch. The lighting was enticing; no ugly electrical tubes but track lights that cast a soft glow on the handsome surfaces. I admired his kitchens. Perhaps if I'd had one of them I'd be a better cook.

Above the door the catchy nameplate in Toulouse Lautrec lettering tempted passers-by to stop and peek inside. The shop was located along a well-frequented road in Carpentras, the nearest town to us of any size. Carpentras had the usual pedestrian-friendly quaint old quarter along with modern hypermarket behemoths around the periphery. Alain went to his shop only when needed; he preferred to phone and arrange meetings with interested browsers—those who stepped inside and were greeted by none other than Danielle, his secretary at La Belle Cuisine. She still worked part-time for her former lover, who had given her the job when they were a couple. When Alain had told me about this during my first trip to Provence, I'd laughed it off. I laughed no more. I was irate. The job gave her legitimate excuses to contact him, come over and insinuate herself into his life.

Alain also sold kitchens on behalf of other retailers, a lucrative niche which earned him hefty commissions. A scatterbrain who lost every bit of paper that came into his hands, he was a stickler about noting down appointments in his agenda; and for being on time for a rendezvous.

As for me and the driving…One of the biggest shocks I faced was going from total independence to near total dependence on Alain. Going anywhere apart from Mazan required a car and stupidly, I had forgotten how to drive. Only a few months after finally passing my British driving test I had moved to Hong Kong where I had never once driven. I might just as well never have learned. To open a bank account in Carpentras I needed Alain. To buy a hair dryer I needed Alain, ditto to go to a doctor. I couldn't even fill the fridge without his help and it galled me, as it did him.

As quickly as I could I arranged lessons with the driving school in Mazan. Twice a week a bespectacled, avuncular instructor picked me up at the house in a white Renault and thus began my re-education in the driver's seat. I vowed to get my confidence back and be mobile in a month, max two.

Yet, my biggest bête noire was something else. Call it a slide into linguistic quicksand. I'd gone from talking as an adult to communicating like a child, sometimes even a toddler, only I couldn't have the tantrums I sometimes felt like having from the sheer exasperation of not being able to say what I wanted to Alain and others. A million times a day it was: What's the word for…? What's the verb for…? What's the gender of…?

So I set myself a goal: six months to become properly conversant in French. Alain began making enquiries for a student or anyone qualified as a tutor. In the meantime, I arm-wrestled him into taking me to an electrical goods shop so I could buy a TV 'to help me improve my French'.

A television was a big deal in our house. Alain disliked TVs, part of his overall antipathy towards electronics and technology.

'Gadgets compromise creativity and lead to complacency and sloth.' This was his conviction—and perhaps his heresy. He was proud of the fact that machines always broke down in his presence and even that he had trouble fixing them, as if that raised his standing as an artist. Curiously, he never had problems with his car, the link to his livelihood. Personally, I was having none of it. As well as a television I bought a fax machine.

'You are not to touch these,' I instructed Alain, 'in case you break them.' Both were installed in the room on the top floor that Alain anointed my study. Alain's friends teased him mercilessly about the television, but the Luddite in actual fact liked it. For it was he who would suggest from time to time that we watch a documentary. Like the one we saw about the life and work of the iconic James Joyce.

'Really excellent programme,' I told my sister Julia on the phone. We spoke to each other regularly, she from the Manhattan apartment that she shared with her husband. She'd long ago abandoned the piano but had kept the gleaming black Steinway grand given to her as a child.

'Alain and I both have Ulysses on our must-read list…talking about which, I have my very own, Ulysses I mean.'

'Alain? So what dragons has he slayed?'

'Well, he almost wrung the necks of some big-shot yacht owners in Nice the other day.'

We'd headed south to the Mediterranean city for some meetings Alain had scheduled with potential clients. In the car, he'd asked me what I planned to do while he was wrapped up with work and I'd joked I would go down to the harbour to spot the big yachts and find myself a millionaire.

'Don't you ever say that to me, not even in jest,' he'd countered with vehemence. Touché. Nevertheless, I was careful not to run to him like a lap dog when I heard his car pull into the drive, even if he'd been away for hours in meetings, even if I yearned to. I was determined to keep myself active during his absences, adhering to my own schedule of self-study in French, piano playing and exercise. Often I went for walks, exploring the paths that branched out from the back of the house, wandering past the odd residence or farm, crunching over stones, gorse and wild grass. Sometimes I meandered to Mazan, past the Chateau de Sade, the greying hulk that now housed the aged and sick, trying to imagine the antics of the Marquis and his stable of willing accomplices—or victims. The chateau looked worn and withered. Once it must have appeared grandiose.

The next challenge presented itself not in Provence but Paris. It was the second week of May and we'd embarked on Alain's annual pilgrimage to sell kitchens at the home furnishings fair at the cavernous Porte de Versailles expo centre.

'Darling I don't want to leave you alone in the house, I really want you with me in Paris,' he'd sought my accord, not that I needed persuading. I was thrilled at the prospect of going with him to arguably the world's most *romantique,* foot-friendly capital. Nothing could dampen my spirits about the two-week trip, not the warnings we wouldn't be able to spend the days together or about his 'difficult' boss, Marc, who he described as a greying, pot-bellied, wealthy, gay, forty-five-year-old Parisian, highly possessive of his sales staff. It didn't take long for this to manifest, for as soon as we arrived in Paris there were problems.

‘This hotel room isn’t big enough for one person let alone two,’ Alain fumed when we squeezed into the closet-like space that his boss had reserved. ‘I’m sure Marc did this on purpose because I brought you.’

We couldn’t change rooms because the hotel was fully booked so we left the place near the trade venue where Marc and his team were staying and found better accommodation elsewhere. This infuriated Marc who insisted we return, which only further stoked Alain’s anger and I feared things would escalate all because of me. Thankfully after one night’s sleep they both calmed down—about that issue anyway—and we stayed put.

A routine was quickly established: In the mornings when we awoke, we couldn’t wait to mate, coming together like magnets, prised apart only by the door knock signifying our room service breakfast. After the fruit, yoghurt, croissants and coffee Alain would shower and shave and leave for the exhibition hall. An hour or two later I would put on my walking shoes and lose myself in the streets, museums and cafes of the capital, in the evening meeting up with him and the sales team—Marc and three other men—at a bistro in Rue St. Charles. Reunited with Alain, I was happy to listen as they talked shop, describing the foibles of some of the customers, the successes and disappointments of the day. Alain’s colleagues were collegial, but Marc, I quickly realised, resented me.

His deliberate snub came on evening number five. We were at our usual table in a corner of the busy bistro, nursing pre-dinner drinks. Jacket around his chair, Marc wore a light blue shirt that was strained at the shoulders. Aureoles of sweat were visible around his armpits, on his forehead, between his fat chin and thin lower lip and on his slightly bulbous nose. He had an unhealthy pallor. The fingers of his right hand—his hands were small I noticed—drummed on the tablecloth, his left hand scratching his ear. Casting his beady eyes on Alain, who was sitting opposite him (I was next to Alain) he said point blank so that everyone could hear:

‘These dinners are a team affair and should remain so. No partners. It’s always been that way. She shouldn’t be here. Nothing personal. Just business.’

In shock I looked at Alain, wondering how he’d respond.

‘Actually, I do take it personally.’ Alain spoke calmly with a bionic confidence, sort of like the Mafia don in the Godfather.

‘Ravinia is made to feel welcome and stays. Or I go.’

His colleagues drained their glasses in perfect synchronicity, suddenly captivated by the blue and white chequered tablecloth. I held my breath, expecting a blow-out, but instead there ensued a battle of stares. The first to deflect was Marc.

'Okay, the point's conceded,' he said quietly.

Relief registered in everyone's eyes as they looked back up. But I was mortified. The last thing I wanted was to be a troublemaker even if I didn't like Marc's manner. Marc knew what Alain's riposte would be so he likely never had any intention of pressing further. Communicating his message to me loud and clear was victory enough. He certainly didn't make me feel welcome but Alain let it go—'occupying the higher morale ground,' he told me later. Revived with food and more drink, his colleagues resumed their anecdotes but I barely listened, wishing I was somewhere else.

Marc's outburst didn't stop me, though, from heading to the Porte de Versailles the next day to see Alain in motion. It was quite a job to find him inside that voluminous structure. The crowds, the paraphernalia on show and the harshly lit interior criss-crossed with endless steel rafters made my head spin. Marc's stand was one of forty in the kitchen section. I wondered how on earth Alain managed to sell any of the units, which didn't come cheap. Yet sell he did. This was one of Alain's juiciest jobs, the reason why he came back year after year and put up with Marc's shenanigans.

'My love, I've missed you so much today.'

Alain embraced me in front of his colleagues and Marc, who glared at me odiously before stalking off. Even under the harsh artificial light, Alain's blue eyes retained a rawness, conveying desire. The first few days in Paris, he'd phoned me at the hotel before I set off simply to say 'I love you,' leaving me with a smile as big as Les Tuileries. But that evening and the next he turned quiet and dour, refusing to join Marc and the sales team for dinner. I felt relieved and admired him for standing up to Marc, but our dinners together were sombre affairs where I did most of the talking, his silence, the absence of laughter or smiles, revealing a changed mood.

'What's going on?' I finally asked him on the second night. 'You're obviously upset. Is it Marc?'

'No…well yes. I'm exhausted. Being around that pain-in-the-ass, putting up with his snide insults and the non-stop sales pitch, it's getting to me. Sorry if I'm taking it out on you.'

I understood. Alain was used to being his own boss and not taking orders from anyone. Even so, his abrupt mood change, revealing an aspect of his personality I'd never seen before, made me anxious. I tossed and turned for those two nights, finally reading between the lines. I realised he was upset about boycotting dinners with Marc even if he wasn't keen on them, riled at feeling obliged to take a stand. And I was the cause, usurping some of the energy he needed for work. My presence here was part of the problem—only he didn't want to admit it.

It was then that I decided to visit my eldest sister Lilly in London. Alain needed a break, so did my feet and there was a new niece to meet. When I told Alain the next morning—before I'd even asked my sister—about my trip he put on a bit of a hangdog look but I could tell he was relieved because, to my disappointment, he said nothing to dissuade me.

'It'll be good to see your sister. When are you leaving?'

'Today. Soon as I can.'

I took some solace in his '*bon voyage*' caresses. As soon as he left I called Lilly, who knew I was in Paris with Alain.

'Mind if I come over for a few days?'

'Mind? I'd be over the moon.'

'I can't wait to see Maggie. She's what, twelve weeks now?'

'Going on fourteen.'

'How are the brothers taking it?'

'No problem so far, they're much more interested in the dog.'

I headed to the Gare du Nord, hoping to catch the next Eurostar train. I was in luck, a seat was available. This modern technological wonder had only recently opened, slicing hours from the Paris-London journey that before had involved a stomach-churning ferry crossing through what always seemed to be gale force winds. I sat in my comfortable window seat with the café au lait and brie baguette I'd purchased and before I knew it, the train was whizzing through the Channel Tunnel and I was peering at vistas of English countryside stretching to the horizon. Before my eyes passed mellow cows, rich pastureland and tidy hedgerows, not really so different from those of northern France but symbolising something tangibly familiar and reassuring. I didn't even mind the crowds at Waterloo station or on the Tube, whose labyrinthine lines and stops I'd spent hours and hours memorising as a child. I had flown into England on my last visit a year ago, making more or less annual trips from Hong Kong to see family and friends and occasionally for work.

It was late afternoon when I rang the bell of Lilly's four-bedroom, semi-detached house in Muswell Hill. The arrival of Maggie had added a few more degrees of mayhem to their madcap household, although it was hard to say who contributed more to it, her three and six-year-old sons or their year-old, shaggy, Irish red setter. I made a point of coddling my two nephews, who peppered me with kisses when I gave them the chocolate I'd bought at the Gare du Nord. In between breastfeeding and meal preparations—her au-pair helped with the school runs, dog walking and tidying up—we snatched our moments.

'So, is life glorious with your Provençal prince?'

'Alain's totally wonderful. I can't wait for you to meet him. I still can't believe that he and Provence aren't some kind of illusion, my mind playing tricks on me.'

I decided not to mention his crotchetiness in Paris. That would mean dwelling a little on Marc and besides, it would all be over soon.

'He's really been there for me. But, you know, there's a fair amount of culture shock. Totally normal I guess. After five and a half years in Hong Kong and New York and London before that, living in the country takes a bit of adjustment I guess. I've just got to find my moorings, make my own friends. I don't want to be dependent on Alain. And of course I need to get to grips with the language. To be honest, I sometimes feel like a fish out of water.'

'Well, to be in Provence, I wouldn't mind feeling like a fish out of water. I'd put up with being a fish out of anything.'

Lilly, four years my senior, was a little envious of me because she had a thing about France, Frenchmen and country houses. From time to time, she'd indulge her nostalgia for the budding actor she fell madly in love with at seventeen while working as an au pair at his house in Versailles, a town on the outskirts of Paris. Their romance petered out when she returned to London and their lives took off in different directions. He went on to become a big screen star in France. My last skip to Paris, for a long weekend a little over six years before, had been with Lilly.

'How are the driving lessons going? Making progress?'

'You'd have to ask my instructor though you might not get what he says. His accent does my head in, trying to figure out his directions, which isn't the safest thing on the road. Thank god he's got a sense of humour. I'm also racking up time in Alain's car. He's insisted I drive it alone on the empty back lanes. So far I haven't crashed it.'

‘And Alain, is he keeping you in the style to which you want to become accustomed?’

‘Lilly! I plan to work and make my own money, as I’ve always done. Living together doesn’t change any of that.’

‘Yeah well. You say he’s making oodles of dosh. Let him spend some of it on you. You need to discover what fun it is to be spoiled.’

My winsome, wacky, captivating sister. She could talk you under the table and her observant eyes missed nothing. She was quick on her feet like no one else I knew. As an adult there was a lot I admired about her, like her spontaneity, free spirit, gregariousness and stage presence, things that when we were children I’d resented her for. Okay, I still sometimes resented her for. Her entrance into a room sparked a charge, she generated buzz. I could never hold the attention of others like Lilly or tell a story with her flair and effervescence. People gravitated to her as naturally as they sensed my innate reserve, although I did my damnedest to it cover up. Bigger in personality she was but at five feet five, she was two inches shorter than me. Her lean face was framed by leonine hair reaching to her third or fourth vertebra. Like Samson, she seemed to derive strength from it and wouldn’t dream of lopping any of it off.

I bought only when I had to but Lilly was a born shopper, using credit cards as if they had nothing to do with credit. She’d amassed a vast collection of antique knick-knacks, her hobby since adolescence (in which era I’d gone on the occasional scout with her to Portobello Road). But she was also disposed to give you the shirt off her back or anything she was wearing if you merely mentioned you liked it. ‘Take it, it’s yours,’ she’d offer, removing said item. A Led Zeppelin-loving hippie, her wild coke days were behind her although she loved to relax at night with a joint. The hash, though, was on hold while she breastfed.

I drooled over her baby, watching as she slept in her wooden cot by her parents’ bed, wrapped in a white onesie and cottony baby blanket, a long-eared bunny and a brand new cuddly bear placed on either side. When her eyes opened, able to focus on this unknown face above her, her little lips puckered into a ball and a cry issued forth. I picked her up, nestled her against my chest, and closed my eyes. She stopped crying and all was peaceful—except for inside me. A maelstrom began to rage, feelings of intense tenderness for this little being mingled with a horrible sense of envy of my sister for being a mother thrice over. It was a painful explosion of broodiness.

I had always assumed I would have my own children one day, but that day seemed distant. Even when the idea of motherhood gained more traction after I turned thirty, the balance was still more towards my career than caring for a new-born. But now, it was demanding attention, priority. Alain was the catalyst for these profound baby blues, hardly something to celebrate. A baby was still a fantasy because I hadn't even broached the subject with him. On my first trip to Provence when we took the momentous decision to live together, I was afraid the mention of children might scare him off. Now I regretted that I hadn't been bolder, in fact that I'd made a monumental blunder. Not to know his mind on this essential issue—was he open to the idea of having kids with me or not?—after moving half way round the world to live with him seemed incomprehensively foolish.

Lilly and her husband Nick were devoted parents and big on family building. When they'd married six years before, she was already three months pregnant. As an only child Nick, an entrepreneurial market boy from Stepney, said he wouldn't mind spawning a sports team. And so, even with baby number three, they were not yet finished.

Candles burning in ceramic holders at the head of the bed, a bottle of champagne and two glasses on the table. A red rose in a vase. I noted these with glee as I stepped into the hotel room, entering with my key. There was a muffled noise of running water from the bathroom. The door was open. Alain was rinsing after a shave.

'The lady is back from London.'

Our eyes clicked through the bathroom mirror and in the time he took to swivel, I'd closed the distance. Chin still wet, he wrapped his bare arms around me. I was the one to pull away, to wash train-grimy hands. I was thinking of a shower, maybe a glass of champagne, as prefaces to the erotic interplay I'd envisaged on the early evening Eurostar back to Paris. But waiting wasn't his thing. Pressing against me, he lifted my hair, slack against my neck and shoulders, and nuzzled the skin. In one graceful movement, he pushed up my top, freed my breasts, and grazed my nipples, while untying the knot fastening his drawstring trousers, exposing his shaft that was three quarters the length of a classroom ruler and equally as wide. Now desperate for him, I tore off my jeans and panties.

'*Ma chérie,*' he murmured, turning me around so I could lean against the sink. Bending his knees he pushed inside, his thrusts indelicate like seismic shocks. When he came, he gripped my waist with those powerful hands that had so nonchalantly disposed of the cockroaches. Not that cockroaches were in my mind just then, only how good it felt to be pressed against him—my man who I had missed to distraction, and it had only been three days.

'I missed you,' he said, drawing feather-light circles on my stomach as we lay on the bed after another round in the la-la land of lovemaking. 'And just to think, I was about to ask you to go on a mission because I thought you'd be bored in Paris and I didn't want to subject you to anymore of my grumpiness. I know how much you love to travel and go off the beaten track.'

'A mission?' I perked up 'What mission?'

'Curious eh?' he laughed. 'Well, it's to do with Tristan, my elder brother.'

'But I thought he was dead.'

'He is dead. Sadly that's the point.'

I knew a bit of his background. Tristan, two years older than Alain, had travelled to India at the age of twenty-seven. There, he'd had an epiphany. Once he'd inhaled the polluted Indian air, the meaning of his life was revealed: this country was his spiritual home, not France. Thus began a rather incredible story. Tristan had sold up in Provence and headed back to India, where he'd found deliverance as a sadhu, a holy man who lives by the vows of poverty and chastity. He never returned to France. Twelve years later and precisely twelve days after he'd been anointed the guru of a community, he'd keeled over and died on the grounds of his ashram. He was just forty-one. The official autopsy had pinned the cause of death on a brain aneurism—the sudden bursting of a blood vessel—but according to Alain, that wasn't the truth.

'He was murdered, poisoned. At least that's what his most devoted disciple, a man called Arjun, told me. And I believe him, although there's no proof.'

'Who does Arjun think killed him?' I'd asked.

'Apparently, the suspect was a fellow sadhu at the ashram—Tristan and he had the same guru. When the guru died and Tristan was chosen by the elders of the community to succeed him, the other sadhu became extremely jealous and plotted his revenge. He felt that because he was older and a true blood Indian, that he should have been first in line for the honour. He also resented how popular Tristan was. How Tristan was adored by people in the community. How he attracted the most disciples. The sadhu could have slipped something into the food that Tristan ate at lunch, dhal and some fruit. That's what Arjun said.'

The point was, this same Arjun was organising a Bandera—a festival of prayer and celebration—on the third anniversary of Tristan's death.

'Arjun lives in a village close to the jungle in Uttar Pradesh, where Tristan spent a large chunk of what turned out to be his last years. He wrote to me saying he needs money for the Bandera. The problem is he doesn't have a bank account so I can't do a transfer. The only way to get money to him is to actually give it to him. That's where I thought you could come in.'

When Alain had first told me about his brother I was floored. I had been to India four times, I had seen sadhus, I had visited ashrams. But never had I heard of a foreigner attaining the status of a guru.

'Don't you think he's a unique case in all of India?'

'Maybe. What I do know for sure is that he was completely devoted to his guru.'

Would I have jumped at the chance to deliver money to a man I'd never met in a remote corner of India? Very possibly. But all thoughts of travel were aborted by the workings of bureaucracy, or rather our naive thinking—and we both considered ourselves globetrotters. When the following morning I turned up at the Indian Embassy on Rue Dehodencq to enquire about a visa, I was told it would take ten days to process. Forget that. I wasn't going to wait around in Paris while Alain returned to Provence. The mission never got off the ground but it had given me an idea.

Chapter 6

Alain couldn't wait to see the back of Paris, all those hours spent cooped up indoors around Marc in a city he disliked taking their toll. The morning after the glorious night of my return, I wasn't surprised to see him revert back to a mass of crotchety frowns and complaints—about the food, the crowds, the concrete and pollution—at the end of his tether with a dictatorial Marc, notwithstanding the bounty he was accruing from record kitchen sales. He was hardly any cheerier at our celebratory last-night dinner at a bistro in Montparnasse.

'This is the last time I'm working for that bastard,' he swore, followed by, 'You shouldn't have come to Paris.'

His words stung. The fair was finished, his pockets were full and he should have been happy. Exhaustion didn't have to mean moroseness. Morose myself, I counted down the hours to our departure, those first fabulous days in Paris overshadowed by these last.

The minute we boarded the TGV Alain's face decompressed into a colossal smile and his humour reappeared, along with his boundless energy and eagerness to please ('What would you like for dinner tonight darling, champagne and grilled salmon? What shall we do tomorrow my love, anything you like'). It was a stunning metamorphosis. By the time we arrived in Avignon he was a different man, or rather the same man who had left for Paris two weeks before. I wouldn't miss the urban Alain that's for sure.

Back from Paris, not only did I resume the driving lessons. I threw myself into the French grammar and conversation lessons I started with a twenty-something university graduate who worked part-time in an office and tutored languages and maths on the side. Alain had fortuitously found him through some teacher friends of his in Carpentras. Our coaching sessions on Mondays, Wednesdays and Fridays took place in the back office of La Belle Cuisine when Danielle was on her lunch break. At first, Alain drove me or I took a taxi. All that changed when I finished the driving lessons, passed my theory test, obtained my French license and bought my first car, a second-hand Honda from a garage. By the end of June, I was driving myself to Carpentras. I'd reached my goal. I was independently mobile.

Every time I turned into New Delhi Drive the luminous, orangey peach exterior of the house dazzled like a fairy tale setting come to life. Really though, Alain's house represented an idiosyncratic leap of faith, considering he had been looking for a simple space in which to live and sculpt. When the local real estate agent showed it to Alain and Danielle one morning in August before closing up shop for the requisite midday break, they had had very different reactions.

It had been love at first sight for Alain but not for Danielle, who'd been dead set against the purchase, proclaiming the rebuilding would consume their entire lives.

'I dropped her off at home then came back alone and sat and thought and dreamed. I had visions. I saw the house completed and breathing; I felt its powerful aura and its chapel-like tranquillity. I decided then and there to acquire it. By the end of the week, I'd signed the mortgage papers and the deal was done.'

The pair had calculated that reconstruction would take about a year, at which point they planned to move in. But six months later, on the fateful day when Alain had found his woman in flagrante delicto with his close friend, everything changed. On a freezing February morning, Alain had moved in alone. Only one bedroom and the kitchen were habitable.

The kitchen had a natural, inviting charm, heightened by the wooden beams that covered the ceiling and the light that poured in through the glass door that led directly onto the driveway, the garden and the rows of vines, whose colours and volume seemed to change weekly, if not daily. The kitchen's décor was minimalist, which was ironic, considering what Alain did for a living. A simple set of white stucco shelves against the wall held plates, cutlery and glasses. Alain's pride and joy was his convection oven although his marinated lamb cutlets—his trademark dish and my favourites—he grilled in the fireplace directly over the embers. The stone floor here, as everywhere in the house, was kept in its original rough form, merely touched up with a coat of cream-coloured lacquered paint.

Alain was finicky about furnishings and kept them to a minimum, part of the multiple contradictions of his character that I was discovering daily, sometimes to my consternation. Although he made an ample living and was used to spending as he pleased, he viewed money as 'the root of all evil' and fulminated on how it corrupted people and led to sleazy lifestyles. But I liked money. It was greed that corrupted people not paper bills. One morning he awoke in a sweat.

'I dreamed you had put carpets all over the house. *Quelle horreur*.'

'What's wrong with carpets? The house I grew up in had lots of them. A different colour for each bedroom. Mine was blue.'

'Call it an artist's sensibility.'

'You mean an artist's arrogance,' I corrected him with a kiss.

'Carpets are stifling. They stop a house from breathing. And a house needs to breathe. Hell is a place of wall-to-wall carpets.'

'Carpets keep the heat inside. I think the ancient Greeks would have put carpets in their homes if they had existed then.'

It was a nonsensical and rather immature defence of happy childhood memories of my hyacinth-blue bedroom but at least he let me have the last word. Yet, I had to admit his superlative taste in aesthetics, in creating a magical, mellifluous ambiance, as essential to him as water. In the evenings, he turned off all the lights in the house and lit dozens of small white candles carefully placed on every step up to our bedroom, around the living room, the Indian corner and next to his sculptures. The blackness of the night outside accentuated the cathedral-like ambiance of the inside. A subtle aroma from incense sticks suffused the air. And the music...often hallowed, achingly soulful Gregorian chants or the syncopated, sexy rhythms of Brazilian samba. And the food...dishes of the freshest ingredients consumed by the flames of a fire.

The pleasure I took in all this was accompanied by some self-critical assessments. I realised I hadn't given much thought to creating an ambiance *hors pair* in the places I'd called home. Was it because I was lackadaisical about my environment, too lazy to go the extra mile or because I lived in my head much more than through my senses? Maybe all three. To make nice, you didn't need a fancy house or expensive art and ornaments. In Hong Kong, Alain had transformed my tiny flat with his nifty touches. No, you needed consciousness, effort and eyes. Alain had big eyes, in a manner of speaking, because as well as being into detail he was a big-picture kind of guy. Maybe these twin talents—paying attention to the little stuff and the big—is how he excelled simultaneously as an artist and commercial salesman. I thought success at one automatically precluded success at the other. Not so.

With Liam and other past loves, I couldn't remember forever wanting to look at them. With Alain, I couldn't stop looking: as he shaved, standing over the sink in our bedroom, muscled arms over broad chest; as he ate his muesli and fruit in the mornings; as he dressed for work in a white shirt, black bolero and trousers, dashing like a Castilian matador; as he glided gracefully through the rhythms of capoeira in the long room; beat his African drums in a hypnotic trance; blew into his Indian conch shell; cut chunks of bread; chopped up onions and garlic, and seduced clients on the phone with a meaty depth to his voice.

A pencil became a tool of wonder in his hands, producing a love poem, a sketch of a kitchen, a profile of my face. I kept the poems and portraits. Mundane, everyday tasks were imbued with meaning. Every action, from percolating coffee on the stove, brushing teeth at the sink to hanging up wet sheets on a clothes line he executed with precision, flamboyance and purpose.

Purpose was something I struggled with. We had glossed over what I would do in Provence in our heated tête-à-têtes about my moving continents. Having abandoned my career for him, I was hell bent on finding a pursuit I could dive into—apart from learning French—but what? A local job was out of the question. That required language fluency and besides, I had no legal right to work because I held an American passport. At least I had some savings to fall back on, so money-making could be delayed for a few months. I spent many hours pondering before the realisation hit. When I told Alain I would like to try my hand at writing a book, he was rhapsodic.

'*Mon amour, c'est une idée géniale*. I've always wanted to live with another artist. You have all the space and privacy you need.'

Indeed I had my very own garret that I furnished with a desk, a sofa bed and some shelves, paid for with my savings. The room had a sloping, wood-beamed roof and two windows that looked onto the iridescent fields and vineyards in the direction of Mazan. There was a shower and sink in one corner, and just outside on the landing, a toilet. I had my refuge. I had the time to write. And I had a brainstorm about a book.

I continued to grapple with culture shock because although I was a European at heart, Asia was where I felt most at home. In terms of priorities—and much else—Hong Kong and rural Provence were as alike as meat and melons. When I read in a survey while still living there that Hong Kongers placed attainment of wealth above love in terms of what is most important in life, I flung up my hands in disgust. But even so, I admired the strong work ethic of the populace that spoke of a sense of discipline and responsibility.

In Provence, amongst Alain's clan at any rate, work was something you might just have to consider if the government checks stopped arriving. The sense of entitlement from the state was so ingrained that it didn't seem worth the effort to look for a real job. Granted in France there were strong incentives against hiring, such as the hefty social charges for employees, but from what I saw people preferred to tap into the bubbling black market. It was a parallel economy soaking up all kinds of skills and services, from the harvesting of grapes to the building of houses. As an entitled individual you could pocket cash on the side and still sponge off the state. Perfect.

Milking the system is how Franco, Alain's good friend, managed to spend most of his life playing the drums for pleasure and partying in his own house in Vitrolles, a grim suburb of Marseille, for which, admittedly, he paid a pittance.

In Provence, I was discovering that what mattered most were food, wine, sex and parties, not necessarily in that order. Carpe diem baby: a cliché but true. Life was about taking the time to indulge, to wring out of each day as much self-gratification as you could, which, as a theory, wasn't bad at all only in practice it tended to, well, make people lazy about earning a living.

The decision to write a book restored some of my confidence, diminished as I discovered that the things I'd been good at, like being a journalist, dissecting the news and navigating in urban jungles, counted for nothing in my new environment. Not that Alain didn't appreciate my skills. He liked that I was cut from a different cloth from the women in his circle. He liked that I had lived in different countries, spoke other languages, had years of a career. These carried weight with him but admittedly, what seemed to take precedence was something I was no expert at: primping and priming myself for the greatest sensual impact. I knew how important sensuality—in all its forms—was to him and so I wanted to cultivate it, seed it, flower it in myself. A new goal to add to the others.

With prompting from Alain, I binned my underwear, the bras and panties that didn't flatter, at least as much as they could or should.

'I'm taking you shopping,' he zapped me with one day, rushing me to the car. In the chic lingerie shop in Cavaillon where we were the only customers, I paraded one skimpy item after another, Alain either nodding to signify he liked it or shaking his head and scouring for another size or style. I walked out of the shop with an entire drawer-full of new lingerie. Perhaps to make up for his bad mood in Paris, he also gifted me a bottle of my favourite Givenchy perfume, a pair of silver-studded earrings, the complete set of short stories by Guy de

Maupassant and a beautiful art-deco desk lamp for my study. Lilly's right. Feels good to be spoiled.

Never one to invest much time in the details of preening, I took a leaf out of Alain's book. He groomed himself meticulously on a daily basis, removing the hard skin from his feet, cleaning, cutting and filing his nails, and attending to his cropped, chocolate-brown hair with slavish devotion.

'You like watching me doing this don't you?'

It was mid-morning. I was lying on the bed naked, propped up on one side, completely absorbed in how Alain was filing his nails at the bedroom sink.

'It's your fault,' I teased, 'you make it look like art, like you're sculpting.'

'Darling, I hope you don't mind my suggesting this but have you ever thought of shaving it off?' He pointed to my pussy. 'We could still leave a little triangle on top.' I looked down at my mound of pubic hair. I'd often given it the scissor treatment but shaving it off completely had never occurred to me. No man had ever asked and frankly, I considered it a protected zone, like a UNESCO world heritage site.

'I thought that was something only porn stars did.'

I attempted humour to cover up a sudden feeling that I was behind the times. Alain laughed.

'Come on, let's do it now. The results will be worth it.'

'Eh, well, I suppose…'

Before I could finish the sentence, he sprang into action. Manipulating scissors, razor and non-scented shaving cream, Alain took less than fifteen minutes to craft my new style, then perched on the bed to admire his handiwork. The sight of bare skin where there had been bush looked weird to me, at least at first, but I took solace in the neat little triangle that remained. The 'royal jewels', Alain baptized my private parts. Not even the aloe vera cream carefully applied to the skin to stop any redness or itching could prevent him from tucking in with his tongue. The rawness I felt after the razor was soon zoned out by my first pubic hair-shaved orgasm.

I made sure to keep my triangle in mint condition and my labia shorn. It was another item added to my grooming list, along with military-schedule shaving of armpits and legs and preventing, god forbid, a single strand of hair from sprouting between mouth and nose and above my eyebrow line. It was all new, this consciousness about haute body maintenance that I supposed was standard practice for the French female. It took time, but I had time. Liam hadn't been particular about appearance—mine or his. He'd taken plenty of showers but I don't remember ever seeing him properly scrub his feet, and his shoe-polish black hair received just a few cursory comb strokes after his morning milky tea and buttery toast. I couldn't recall him ever noticing when I'd had a haircut or worn something new. He'd been more concerned that I knew the origin of things, scientifically speaking.

'Science was his passion. So was biological anthropology,' I explained to Alain, who'd asked about my former live-in lover. 'I learned a lot from him.'

'Such as? Tell me one thing.'

'Well, for instance, I didn't know there were other human species around hundreds of thousands of years ago. It wasn't just us homo sapiens and Neanderthals that lived on this planet. You know what he used to call me? "My English Sapiens". He was my "Irish Sapiens".' I pronounced these terms in English.

'How romantic.' I detected a note of sarcasm. Okay, so they weren't lovey-dovey but all pet names that sweethearts call each other tend to sound silly to others. Serves me right for wanting to impress Alain. A bit on the defensive, I made a point of accentuating Liam's down-to-earth qualities.

'It wasn't all science of course. He loved art films and exhibitions…and sports and exercising.'

Liam had been particularly fond of rugby, like half of expatriate Hong Kong. He'd sometimes played it and regularly jogged. I hadn't been fond of rugby or jogging, but I'd loved to be entangled in his long limbs. Frustratingly, his libido hadn't matched mine, but with Alain, what a contrast. His desire for sex was not just daily but often hourly and it was contagious. Soon I was in lockstep, running my hands over his torso, kissing his lips, licking the outer lobe of his ear…switching my attention to the bulge in his trousers. The house offered a rich menu of settings, many of the fucking spots in view of Mont Ventoux, appearing through our windows like a totemic breast.

Speaking of appetites, Alain was more than happy to prepare our succulent meals that I was ravenous to eat, knowing of course that cooking was not my forte. A trip to the market or the épicerie with him to buy ingredients was, at first, an educational affair. I had no eye for picking the choicest produce.

'This tomato is the perfect ripeness, see?' Or 'these asparagus stems are too thin and stringy, but this bunch, thicker, with the dark green tips is just right.'

A whiff of a mushroom was enough for him to deduce, 'You can tell these were picked this morning.'

Alain was a stickler for gastronomic ritual. Lunches were never casual but lengthy, sacrosanct affairs. Today, like yesterday and the day before, he had stopped what he was doing at noon to wash, peel and chop for the mid-day meal—he did the cooking, I did the clearing. The menu was sautéed green beans, steamed dory and a salad garnished with his inimitable dressing of olive oil, mustard, crushed garlic and lemon. Yesterday we'd eaten tomatoes flecked with leafy basil and sea salt—the tomatoes so rich and juicy they seemed more like oranges—and braised chicken. We drank either wine or water depending on our mood. The culinary reverence extended through to the postprandial espresso, made in his metal stovetop brewer.

But ritual was never to be confused with routine.

One of the first things he had said to me barely after we'd entered the house on that first day of April—even before we'd had our welcome-to-your-new-home fuck—was this:

'Darling, I meant it in the car when I said we have everything we need for a great life together. I just don't want it to be a banal life.'

'Me too,' I said, thinking he was referring to the evils of boredom and bickering, a common enemy of *la vie à deux*. I certainly didn't think banal applied to the simple stuff, such as waking up in the presence of someone you love and being comfortable in mutual silence. I hankered for the hundred humdrum details of everyday life shared with a mate—which I didn't consider banal.

In truth, I couldn't relate the word to my own life. Born in Buenos Aires to adventurous, risk-taking American parents, I had grown up in London in a minimally boundaried and highly non-conformist family: My mother, with more chutzpah than Hercules, had driven a black taxi around London, preferring this to any normal vehicle. She'd sometimes given lifts to pedestrians who flagged her down, not out of braggadocio but a genuine good-heartedness. She'd appeared to frequently conjure up out of thin air, or at least from a rather small fridge, four-course dinners in our Highgate home that heaved with luminaries from the worlds of art and entertainment. Our doors had always been open to friends and friends of friends from every-which-where.

She'd hoisted us into independence early, sometimes to my exaltation, but also to my horror. One summer, a few weeks before my tenth birthday, I was sent to Valencia on the east coast of Spain for a month to learn Spanish at the home of a girl around my age whom I'd met only once, a few months earlier. The encounter took place during a whirlwind Easter road trip around Spain with my mother and two sisters. It was our mum's whim to ferry us in her London taxi and alone at the wheel, she never batted an eyelid at the constant stares from astonished onlookers. The father of the Spanish girl was a chef in a restaurant where we had chanced to eat lunch. No one in the family spoke more than two words of English. I was miserable and pined for home for the duration of what felt like an exile. The only sweeteners were the omelette baguettes in the evenings and the sugar biscuits dunked in carnation milk at breakfast.

In London, we'd been fed a rich diet of music, culture and travel. My father was a trumpet player, my mother had plumped for the piano. My childhood in England had been followed by university degrees in New York, Mandarin studies in Taipei, extended globetrotting, a return to London where I'd found my feet in journalism and the job transfer I'd engineered to Hong Kong.

Settling down to me was a dream—in which repetition was most welcome.

Things looked promising when, in the third week of May, Alain and I embarked on a project to procure a *certificat de concubinage*.

'What's this certificate?'

'A piece of paper that will formally recognise us as living together.'

We hoped it would lead to that most precious of documents, a residency permit since I was living in France on nothing but a flimsy tourist visa. We were halfway through filling out the requisite form at Mazan's town hall when we realised that we needed two witnesses as co-signers.

'No problem, wait here.'

Alain dashed out, reappearing twenty minutes later with two of his friends, who were only too pleased to lend a hand, lapping it all up as an anecdote to tell later on. As it turned out that piece of paper was of no use. Rules were rules: To be eligible for residency, I had to be married to a French national. Back to square one it was.

One sunny Thursday afternoon at the end of May we drove to Avignon. We headed to the popular Place de l'Horloge and sat down at a café, a stone's throw from the elegant Hotel de Ville and its landmark clock tower. This pedestrian-only square, with its myriad outdoor restaurants and easy-going ambiance, was a perfect spot from which to gaze at a bird dipping into one of the tall plane trees, at amblers strolling by on the flagstones, or at other café lingerers. It was especially good for thinking about nice little nothings, in hugging proximity of a sweetheart.

Nursing a citron pressé, I was in a happily soporific state when Alain cut in:

'I've been avoiding the subject, but I think we need to talk about it. Babies, motherhood. What do you think? Do you want children?'

He looked at me, doleful and expectant. He's beaten me to it. I took the plunge.

'Yes I do. I've always wanted children—to be a mother. What about you? Do you want more children?'

His eyes diverted to the cobblestones before once again fixing on me.

'I have my son who I love very much, and he's enough for me. It hasn't been an easy path and experience has left its mark,' he paused. 'When I left him at three years old I was plagued with guilt and I still am. It's the one regret I have in life. Not leaving the marriage but hurting my son, who I know begrudges me for it.'

'And you're scared you will do this again with another child?'

'No no. I'm not afraid of repeating what I did. But at the same time I don't want to have another child to prove that I can do things differently…do things right. I'm happy with you, I want to spoil you, and a child would come between us. Plus there's my sculpture. All selfish reasons but true. Fathering. So much goes into it,' he trailed off. 'Your wanting a child, that weighs on me.'

The mood was shattered.

'But look, I don't want to seem like an ogre. Let's discuss it again in six months. Let's see how things evolve.'

He looked doubtful. A nuclear darkness engulfed me as I sat in that square, now slumped over, realising the choices I might have to make. That night and for the following few days I was unable to contain my sadness, shedding copious tears and withdrawing into silence.

'What's wrong with you my darling, why are you crying?' Alain asked tenderly, although he must have known.

'I want you to be happy.'

But from that moment on he made sure I took my birth control pills. And I…I comforted myself with the reality or fantasy that nothing was written in stone. He will change his mind, he will come around. He will do it for me.

Chapter 7

It was Alain's son Christophe who unexpectedly snapped me out of my funk. He came over that weekend for his regular twice a month visit when Alain had full claim to him. His dad went to fetch him, as was the custom, from his maternal home, a return trip of over two hundred kilometres. The first thing Christophe did after walking through the door was plonk his duffel bag down on the stone bench hewn from a wall near the kitchen fireplace. Then he looked me square in the eyes for the very first time and said, '*Salut,*' which I registered as significant progress. Even more surprising, he asked me how I was.

'Great,' I answered. 'What about you, how's school?'

'Blah,' he said with mock misery. 'Too much homework.'

'Which I hope you're doing,' interjected his dad, emphasising the last word. 'Because if you don't, my son, and you fail your exams, I'm sending you to the monks in Carpentras.'

It was an empty threat for I knew he had no intention of removing his son from his local lycée and cloistering him in a church school but it was enough to get him to hunker down to his books.

What a turnaround. Alain had told me with a certain amount of pride about his own stint from the age of seventeen at a technical school in Avignon, where he'd excelled at computer programming. He could easily have pursued it as a career. Instead, he'd flunked all his exams and failed to get a certificate 'on purpose', saying he'd made a choice to chase girls and have fun rather than study. But that was then. I couldn't imagine him counselling his son to make the same choices now.

Before, when Christophe had stayed at the house, he'd been reserved and cautious around me, a child of few words and no eye contact. I hoped this apparent emergence from his shell signalled an acceptance of me as a fixed presence. My clumsy French hadn't helped with the bonding. Nor did the awkwardness of adolescence—he was fourteen when I came onto the scene. I knew that for him, I was an unknown entity and one more in the stable of significant others that had trotted or cantered through his father's life.

Christophe was also a bit more outspoken with his father, asking during dinner if he could watch the television I'd bought, a request that was not granted—I assumed he didn't expect it to be.

'You spend enough time in front of that waste receptacle,' Alain railed, a stand I rather admired but kept to myself. Alain began to lecture his son about how he mustn't be a sheep and mindlessly follow the masses, whether it was eating at MacDonald's, buying plastic junk or seeing violent films.

'Don't follow the crowd because you're afraid to be different. Take risks,' he advised his son. Christophe said nothing, but when his dad got up from the table to get some water he flashed me a knowing smile—the equivalent of a wink—that I responded to in kind. For that wonderful moment, delighting in this new-found conspiratorial togetherness that I took to be a poke at his dad, I felt we were bonded.

I couldn't help but admire Christophe's boyish beauty. His finely chiselled face bore his mother's imprint: an aquiline nose, full yet delicate lips, and velvety brown eyes, a few shades darker than his hair. He really was a decent kid, not into drugs or rabble-rousing. His dad may not have been the best role model—flying the coop when he was just a toddler—but he had many redemptive qualities, one of which was opening up the world to his child. Once a year he'd spirited him off to a far-flung place like Thailand, Indonesia or Egypt for a father-son adventure. If ideological inculcation was a sign of paternal affection then Alain was indeed very affectionate, impressing on him his non-conformist views on religion, politics and psychology.

At around ten that night, I made a mug of hot chocolate and brought it up to Christophe's bedroom, which was opposite my study. Posters of rock bands and road-devil motorcycles were plastered on the walls and his wardrobe resembled a jumble sale lot. Christophe was lying in bed, dressed in a black t-shirt and faded striped pyjama bottoms, reading a football magazine only faintly illuminated by the antique lamp on his night stand, bought by Alain at the Sunday market at l'Isle sur la Sorgue.

'I thought you might like this—hot chocolate.' I placed the mug on the stand.

'Thanks.' His voice registered surprise. The truth is, I hadn't dared disturb him in his bedroom before, thinking he might find even this simple gesture too awkward or intrusive.

'Enjoy the magazine. Sleep well.'

I was headed out the door when he spoke. 'Wait, do you mind if I ask you something?'

'Of course not. Anything.' I turned and walked back to his bed, curious as to what would come.

'Is it true you met my dad in Vietnam?'

'Yes, we were on holiday there—we met in Saigon, or Ho Chi Minh City as it's officially called. Vietnam was just then opening to tourists.'

'And then you met again in Hong Kong right? And you were a TV journalist?'

'Yes, three years later, he visited me in Hong Kong.' I paused, not quite sure how to continue.

'I was a journalist, but not in TV…Well, just before your dad came to Hong Kong I was offered a job as a reporter for a TV programme but before I started…I, we, decided that I should come here instead.'

I didn't think I was imparting anything new although I realised just then I didn't know exactly what Alain had told his son about our brief history backdating Provence.

'So you never took the job in TV?'

'No, I didn't. But no regrets…I like it here,' I smiled.

'What was the programme?'

'News, for a financial news channel.'

'What would it have involved?'

'Talking to people, interviews about economics, investments, the stock market, that kind of thing.'

'Is it all done live?'

'A lot of it, yes.'

'Hmm. Sounds cool.'

I left him pondering my words, delighted by his curiosity and our conversation.

On Saturday morning, Christophe wasn't allowed a lengthy lie in. It was always that way. His father woke him around ten and after breakfast put him to work in the garden watering the grass and chopping wood in the woodpile into smaller logs. It was a modus operandi well established by Alain, who paid his son for the effort.

'He's got to learn the value of money, and manual work is good for him. I worked with my hands when I was his age.'

Alain had told me this the first time I'd seen Christophe—without complaint mind you—doing these paid chores. Looking at him now through the kitchen door I noticed how he didn't cut corners but dragged the hose to the furthest reaches of the garden rather than trying to water the grass at the garden's rim from a distance to minimise the effort. Alain's words to his son popped into my mind: 'And when you do something, no matter how small the task, focus on it, do it well and with precision.'

Before, when Sunday afternoon had rolled around and it was time for Christophe to leave, I hadn't felt much of anything. But this Sunday, when his mother, Marianne, came to pick him up, it was different. I wanted him to stay. There was no chance of that though, his mum being his primary carer. She and her son lived in a flat in a rather dreary housing estate in Miramas, a town on the water north of Marseille. Marianne, who worked at a local pre-school, remained on amicable terms with her ex-husband for the sake of their child, if nothing else. Perhaps her wounds had healed and she'd forgiven him. Teenage sweethearts, they were both twenty-three when they'd married, Alain fresh from completing his mandatory eighteen-month military service, which he went into frothing at the mouth, furious at having to cede a second of his time to the army.

Throughout his marriage, his job as an insurance salesman making morning and afternoon house calls had brought him untold opportunities to put his pecker in a lot of holes, to be crude about it, the ring on his finger no impediment to his libidinous ambitions. He was making good money, driving a BMW and living in a big house he'd bought near Apt, a famed market town at the foot of the Lubéron Mountain. His charm was enough to seduce a medusa.

'I thought my male organ was a bone until the age of thirty,' he once joked, to make the point that he had matured since then and didn't seek to cheat with subsequent partners.

Had Marianne been aware of his countless infidelities, I wondered? Had she just accepted his dalliances like a good French wife, with a shrug of the shoulders? Alain always spoke well of her, praising her sweet and lovely nature.

'She never gave me a hard time.'

But I know for a fact he'd given her a damn hard time. She was destroyed when he'd left her after seven years of marriage with a toddler to raise. She'd worshipped the man and her world had fallen apart.

‘It wasn’t easy for me,’ Alain had defended his actions. ‘My friends and family shunned me because of what I did. They were scandalised. But I had to do it. I couldn’t live a lie anymore. Even for my child.’

Marianne had never remarried but it seems she had found love again with a divorcé whose children lived with their mother in America. They didn’t share a home but saw each other on weekends. Whenever she came to pick up Christophe at the house she was always polite to me but guarded. I often wondered what she thought of my bedding her ex.

One Sunday in early June Alain decided that it was time I met Josephine, his mother. She lived in Arles, the town immortalised by Van Gogh and the ear that he cut off in one of its brothels. During the two-hour drive to Arles, I was a little apprehensive, unsure if I’d win her approval. Would she accept me, a foreigner? Or would I get the cold shoulder?

‘You have nothing to worry about,’ Alain soothed when I voiced my fears. ‘She’s not judgmental in that way. And besides, how could she not warm to you?’ Taking his eyes off the road for a second, he mouthed me a kiss.

Josephine’s flat was a walk-up in what looked to be a nineteenth-century building in a residential area whose roots I was told stretched back to antiquity. No sooner had we walked in the door than I felt at ease, for Josephine was as welcoming as could be, fussing to make sure I was comfortably seated and served an aperitif and some olive tapenade before lunch.

The big surprise was seeing Pierre, Alain’s baby brother. Alain hadn’t mentioned he’d be at their mother’s place that day. Pierre stood up when I entered the living room. His height made an impression—he was a head taller than his brother.

‘Nice to see you again,’ he said. We exchanged pecks on the cheek, he bending down slightly so I could reach.

‘You too. Alain didn’t tell me you’d be here.’

‘I’m not sure he knew I would be.’

I hadn’t seen Pierre since the morning we went to collect the two cauldrons for the spring fete.

In her flat that afternoon, Josephine clucked like a contented chicken as she moved around, short and a little thick around the waist, yet feisty and nimble. She was happy, I thought, to have her two sons around her even though they exchanged barely a word to each other. Their hellos had been cursory, a slight nod accompanied by '*salut*', displaying that same bizarre formality. There was a covert unease, a stepping on eggshells as if eliciting the slightest emotion would upend something. When Josephine disappeared into the kitchen to tend to lunch, Alain sank into an armchair with a book of poems by a local writer, Frédéric Mistral, plucked from a bookshelf back-ended on both sides by candelabra, choosing to read rather than converse with his brother—that alone told a story.

I sat next to Pierre on the room's single sofa, covered by faded chintz. The walls of the living room were peeling in a few places and the furniture was a little fusty but the room was filled with homey touches such as doilies, plumped-up cushions and framed photos.

I wasn't even looking at Alain when incongruously, completely unbidden, images of us that morning in the kitchen after breakfast flooded my mind. I saw him, spreading his legs atop the built-in stone bench as I pleasured him with my mouth, a dribble of semen still on my tongue as afterwards he repaid the compliment on me, my bottom on the edge of the bench, eyes closed, leaning back into the comfort of cushions. Normal it may be for hot-headed lovers, yet I still marvelled at how our lovemaking wasn't something to be programmed between something else but was the menu du jour, enjoyed as leisurely as the traditionally lengthy three-course French lunch; or sometimes as brief but explosive bursts throughout the day. I laughed inwardly at my delusional thinking that he and I did things no one else did. Did other couples think that way? Pleasurable thoughts of sex were never far from my mind, a different set of diurnal preoccupations from the time—which now seemed far away—when I was a news-obsessed journalist glued to a computer screen.

Enjoying the images, I nevertheless banished them to talk to Pierre, who was fiddling with his silver band watch. He was dressed more casually today in jeans and a Lacoste t-shirt, his hair combed to one side giving him an even more boyish aspect. His facial features offered less of a contrast than his brother's, although perhaps he was more wholesomely handsome, with a classically straight nose and portrait hazel eyes.

'Is it broken?' I asked, pointing to the watch.

'It's losing time, I think it needs oiling,' he replied, putting the timepiece back on his left wrist. 'I'll fix it later.'

'Alain told me you're an engineer. I admit, I don't know anything about engineering. What exactly do you do?'

'I'm what's called a structural engineer. I help design buildings, bridges, canals and things like that.'

'You studied this at university?'

'Yes, I got my degree in civil engineering in Marseille—at the University of the Mediterranean. And my first job in the field there too.'

'Why did you choose engineering?'

'Well, it seems I didn't inherit the artistic genes. No fiery passions. No tumultuous talents.'

There was no bitterness, just faint amusement in his voice. I thought his words sounded poetic—fiery passions, tumultuous talents. He could have used simpler, plainer adjectives.

'What do you mean?'

'My hands don't have magic. I can't sculpt, paint or draw, or at least draw anything other than linear structures.'

'Who is the painter?'

'Tristan. He wasn't a painter exactly but a genius draughtsman. Before he left for India, he worked for an architect who, it seems, had appointed him his heir apparent. He could do astounding things with a pencil.'

'Alain told me about him, how he could draw with his eyes closed.'

Pierre must have been in his teens when Tristan left Provence for India. I wondered how much he remembered of his brother. I asked him.

'Oh I have some memories. He used to come here for the odd Sunday lunch, and occasionally I would go to his chalet in Salon de Provence, where he lived. I used to love it, because he always had lots of friends around and good music. And,' he uttered, 'there was a great deal of hash.'

'You smoked hash?' I said, as if it were blasphemy, stereotyping engineers (as I'd once done with MBA students) as people who didn't do those sorts of things. He seemed to read my mind, blasting through the shallowness of my bias.

'Don't look so shocked. Engineers aren't all boring,' he laughed.

'I've since stopped the hash though. I have a hard time with the smoke in my lungs.'

'You could try Marijuana cookies.'

'There's a thought. Do you have any recipes?'

'I'm sure I could find some.'

I hadn't expected him to be so candid. Before I could dig any further, however, he broke in.

'I understand you're a journalist. Are you going to look for work in journalism here?'

'In French it would be impossible. No, I have my own project in mind.'

'Which is?'

'Well, I'm thinking about writing a book.'

'Would that be your first?'

'Yes. It's something I've always wanted to do.'

'May I ask what the book will be about?'

'About Tristan, your brother.'

When I'd broached my idea to Alain, he'd been immediately supportive. In fact, he'd loved the idea. It was he, after all, who had fed my fascination with Tristan with photos and tales of his two visits to India to see his brother. The first time Tristan ventured to India he'd very nearly been deported back to France for massively overstaying his visa. Back in Provence he'd worked hard to earn the cash to head east again. Only this time, instead of flying, he'd hopped on the much cheaper 'magic bus' to India, which crisscrossed Iran, Afghanistan and Pakistan. No doubt the hash he'd smoked on the road compensated for some of the bumps and scrapes that littered that infamous hippy trail.

'I'll never forget what Tristan told me,' Alain had reminisced. 'Only a few days after he got to New Delhi, all his belongings and money were stolen at Old Delhi railway station. He was waiting for a train and had fallen asleep. When he awoke, his bag was gone. His passport and a few rupees in his pocket were all he had left. He didn't panic or anything, but calmly walked to the bus station (the Interstate terminus at Kashmere Gate) and boarded the first bus that he saw. He handed those few rupees to the driver, using words and gestures to communicate: "Take me as far as this money will get me." At the driver's signal he got off. The village he found himself in was called Maksar.'

Maksar lies in sugar cane territory, about fifteen kilometres from the River Ganges on the Delhi-Lucknow road, although it wasn't on any map.

'It was here that he met his guru, Premdas, and was reborn as a sadhu about two years later.'

I was intrigued by Tristan's story, his renunciation of the good life in Provence for a sojourn of sacrifice in rural India. The project appealed on every level: the subject matter was spiritual, the message one of love and it would involve an investigative trip to the sub-continent. I wanted to portray his reincarnation as a sadhu and the apotheosis of his life as a guru—and who knows, find out for myself if there was any truth to Arjun's words. Was he really murdered?

Josephine wasn't shy about asking questions, fairly grilling me about my life in Hong Kong and what the Chinese were like during our delicious lunch of vegetable and saucisse casserole, baked artichokes and thick hunks of bread washed down by the bottles of Chateauneuf du Pape that Alain had brought. I had to search for the adjectives I needed to do my descriptions justice in French, and at times it was more self-conscious stutter that emerged than proper speech. I noticed Pierre was as interested in my depiction of the city as his mother and very much au courant about the impending handover.

'What do you think about the transfer of Hong Kong to China? Do you feel more positive or negative about it?'

It was good of him to ask but it meant translating my vociferous political views—sharply negative as it happened—into overly simplistic terms that reflected no nuance.

'My two eldest boys were the great travellers of the family,' Josephine remarked and I noticed her usage of the past tense. It was her first reference to Tristan. 'They had this great hunger to see the world.'

I thought she meant it as a compliment but Alain seemed to take offense.

'There's a big world out there to see, mother. Provence is not the navel of the universe,' he retorted rather aggressively. While I completely agreed, I wasn't going to say so, finding myself keen to defend Josephine.

'Yes, but this hunger can also get you into trouble. And cause grief.'

Ah, her true feelings. I wondered if this second reference to Tristan and his untimely death in India would elicit a sympathetic or curt response from Alain. But he said nothing and an uncomfortable silence ensued. It was broken, finally, by Roland, Josephine's live-in partner, who made some comment about a particular new goat cheese he'd just discovered, which he went to fetch from the kitchen. Roland was fifteen years younger than Josephine but you couldn't really tell the age difference, he looking older and she younger than her years.

I was curious to know more about Josephine's life—in her own words—but it wasn't the occasion to ask and besides, asking might have provoked painful memories. Alain had revealed to me the epic nature of her early years, not an easy story to hear. At the age of six during the Spanish civil war, Josephine had been wrenched away from her parents in San Sebastian in Basque country to the safety of France, along with an older brother. She never saw her parents again or her three other siblings who'd remained in Spain. I tried to imagine the depths of her suffering as a child, the terrible separation from her family, essentially forced orphan hood even if her parents had had her best interests and safety at heart. Her adoptive mother had been kind, but the father had made inappropriate gestures towards her, and so it was that she'd accepted the first suitor who came along.

Aldo heralded from a north Venetian family and at thirty-five, was seventeen years older than Josephine. After marriage they'd settled in Givronex, a village in the Bouche-du-Rhône and produced four offspring, a daughter and three sons. Alain was the third child, and the apple of his mother's eye—so I was told—the gilded son who could do no wrong. But they didn't see much of each other. Alain fiercely protected his privacy, drawing a cordon around his personal life even, or maybe especially, from his mother. I noticed that Sunday how obdurate he was with her, which wasn't like him at all. Or was it? I thought of him and Pierre. A similar yet different dynamic. With his brother he was subdued, his words and gestures measured as if under ration. Alain had told me himself, without a hint of ill will, that he'd inherited his mother's Basque pride and wilful stubbornness, not that these traits were particularly discernible in her on that first, or indeed subsequent visits.

In contrast, Alain only ever expressed deep love for his father. He'd died of a heart attack when Alain was twenty. Two years before his demise his furniture business had collapsed, plunging him into bankruptcy and gobbling up the family house and all his other assets. Moving his family to the flat in Arles, he desperately hoped to put the financial catastrophe behind him but his health took a turn for the worse. After his death Josephine, left penniless, was forced to seek work for the first time in her life, selling goods in the market to support Pierre, who was barely out of primary school.

Alain, normally articulate and apt to hold an audience rapt, sank into low-wattage mode at lunch, his body language communicating separation. At one point I whispered in his ear 'are you okay?' to which he just nodded and stroked my leg. I was seated next to him and opposite Pierre. The hosts were at each end of the table. It was Pierre who did most of the talking after that awkward silence, ensuring no repeats. I couldn't tell if the subjects he raised—a new pedestrian-only quarter, a change of mayor, road works on a major arterial route—really interested him or were pursued simply because they were neutral topics. There was an easy banter between Pierre, Roland and Josephine, who, if she'd momentarily lapsed into sadness about her dead son, had reverted to being charming and cheerful. Alain threw in a word or comment every now and then but it was spoken without his usual zest.

Driving back home from Arles, the early summer light obviating the need for tail-lights, Alain cut into my thoughts about his family, his free hand reaching out for mine.

'So, what did you think of my mother? I can tell she thinks highly of you, as I expected of course.'

It was how he said it rather than what he said that was uplifting, conveying, through his light-hearted tone, that her opinion of me mattered to him, although given his behaviour towards her I wasn't at all sure why.

'She's great, so lively and curious about things. And Roland…they seem happy together.'

Alain nodded. 'They are a good fit. They take care of each other.'

'But Alain, was something wrong? You were quiet and a bit strange at lunch. And a bit aggressive with your mother. Is something wrong?' I repeated. 'Do you have difficulties with her?' I wanted to say did she press your buttons?

His brow crinkled, his mouth forming a grimace.

'Nothing's wrong, I assure you. Sometimes we have our clashes. I guess that happened at lunch when she mentioned how travel can get you into trouble. Perhaps I did react a little strongly. I think deep down she disapproves of my adventures. I understand she's scared that something may happen to me after what happened to Tristan but life has to be lived. I've always been very independent. But I've nothing to hide. There are no mysteries about it.'

But was that true? His answer didn't explain the pronouncedly clipped tone I'd witnessed not just at lunch but all afternoon, which signified what, repressed anger? I wanted to delve into psychology, dig into his childhood. What type of mother had she been? How did he perceive her? Well I knew that this primal relationship was fundamental to a human being's emotional and social development, including my own. I mean, look at my relationship with my mother. I'd loved her, but I'd also harboured a great deal of anger towards her, mainly for being outrageously different from the mums of my friends. My mother had had few social scruples, none, at any rate, that had prevented her from being outspoken and, well, on the embarrassing side of eclectic. She'd dressed in bold colours and always applied lip stick and mascara in her taxi, usually during a traffic light stop. Her driving, moreover, had been downright dangerous. She'd spent half the time swivelling her head, chatting away to passengers in the back as if she was one of them. It used to terrify me. How she hadn't constantly crashed I don't know. I'd secretly yearned for her to be at home when I returned from school, greeting me with a cup of something warm and a biscuit and asking me how my day had been. But usually she'd been out doing something useful like picking up visitors from the airport, easing people away from the edge as a volunteer with the Samaritans, or scouting for sheet music for our lessons.

Much later, when it was too late, I came to value her differences and quirks but at the time I'd just felt upset and a host of other emotions I never admitted to. She'd seemed so outwardly confident but inwardly, as my father told me long after her death, she was riven with insecurities because of the love-hate relationship she'd had with her mother.

My domineering, selfish, grandmother had been needy. She'd put her wants above her daughter's needs, inappropriately embroiling her in the fights she'd constantly had with my grandfather who, as far I could gather, had been a meek man (he died when I was a baby). What's more, my grandmother had been highly critical of my mother, trying to dictate her choices in life, including her choice of husband. Thankfully my mother had rebelled, following her dreams like studying at the Sorbonne in Paris on a scholarship, learning languages and deciding who she would marry. This intelligence about my grandmother had been a complete revelation. As a child I never saw those sides of her, experiencing her solely as a homely presence who made delicious cakes for us on her frequent visits across the pond.

My mother had appeared the opposite of needy—certainly she never used her kids as any kind of a bulwark or sounding board for problems. Plus she'd had a good marriage. If anything, I'd wished she'd been needier, at least of me, devoted though she was to her family. I often wondered whether it was my mother's profound inner doubts about her self-worth and insecurities that I'd internalised. Lilly had her energy, Julia her artistic talents and I resembled her the most physically. Losing her at sixteen, when I was full of adolescent angst and ire, meant I never got to know her as a full-rounded individual, something other than a mum. The wound of her loss ran deep.

My mind drifted back to Alain and his mother. I began to stitch together some questions but then, brain-weary, decided to leave family dysfunctions for another day.

Alain was a hand-holder. He took the time to translate when I couldn't keep up with the drift of social parlance, a lot of it patois. But every so often he couldn't help having a dig at my naivety. The punch line about pastis was one of his favourites.

'It was the time she was visiting from Hong Kong,' he'd start off. 'I had to go out early one evening to see a client. When I came home, there she was in the bath, a glass half full of something by her side. "What are you drinking darling?" I asked. "Pastis," she replied. I looked at the glass. "Pastis? Did you add any water to it?" She shook her head. "Why, was I supposed to?" I grabbed the glass from her. It's lucky I came home when I did, otherwise I'd have found a dead body in the bath.'

There'd be laughter all round and I'd join in sheepishly, my expression conveying: How was I supposed to know that the stuff is forty percent proof? To me it tasted like liquorice, which I love, not liquor. Thankfully I'd only had a few sips.

I was surrounded by people who paid Alain fealty as if he was king of the court, which indeed he was, in a pseudo late twentieth-century version of Versailles and noblesse oblige. His friends popped over spontaneously and with great regularity. One of the reasons he had bought his big house was so that artists and others could congregate there and the '*coucou, comment vas-tu*' visits were never to be criticised, even if the timing happened to be terrible. Hospitality, no matter what the hour, was de rigueur, and there were no locks on any of the doors so it was easy for whomever to enter. Mostly I didn't mind the social calls but when I did, I tried not to show it. You've got to be more easy-going, flexible, go-with-the-flow, I reminded myself. The lesson from the fete.

A lesson exceedingly hard to apply when it came to Danielle. She was the *coucou* queen, driving over to the house whenever she felt like it, which was far too often for my liking. She was always friendly to me and easy to chat to, but my stomach started to churn every time I saw her with Alain. She was always buttering up to him: with looks that lingered too long, words conveying hidden meaning and even blatant flirtatiousness. It became obvious to me that she still desired him.

'Alain, I think Danielle still wants you,' I drummed up the courage to say one day.

'That's possible,' he said, without a hint of surprise. 'After we split up, she tried to get back with me.'

Apparently, six months after their separation she had come around to the house with a bottle of champagne and ideas of seduction.

'She drank a lot that night so she didn't want to drive home. Maybe that was an excuse. Anyway I made her sleep in another room. It was difficult because I still loved her.'

Every time I saw them together I couldn't stop thinking of them as lovers. Those words, 'it was only about sex', began to haunt me more with every passing week. I wondered constantly if he really was over her. There were no overt signs to suggest otherwise. On the contrary, when Danielle was present, he was particularly loving and solicitous, often drawing me into a tight embrace.

The man she had traded him for was a spectator next to Alain's flamboyant burlesque and bottomless charm. Jacques was soft-spoken and preferred to inhabit the shadows. At gatherings, he would sit quietly and chain smoke through nicotine-stained teeth, yet there was something sensual about him that must have captivated Danielle. He had a lanky torso and shoulder-length brown hair that fell over half his face although he sometimes tied it back into a ponytail. His eyes were blue-green, his look languid. He was comfortable, I thought, to let Danielle take over although I wondered how he felt about her constant flirting. At twenty-nine, he was two years younger than his girlfriend and twelve years Alain's junior.

What a long way those two men had travelled. From one of his best pals, Jacques had become a pariah for the sin of humping his lover. Alain, not prone to physical violence, had wanted to punch the life out him for his treachery but instead, had spent months purging the hate from his body and quite remarkably had expunged every last drop of it, or so he said.

'Two nights before I left for Thailand, I invited Jacques around to the house for the first time since the "incident" and we spent the evening drinking and laughing,' Alain recounted proudly. The fences were mended.

I liked Jacques. He seemed thoughtful, comfortable in his own skin and unassuming, not the type who had anything to prove. I don't think we ever exchanged more than two sentences together on any single occasion, reluctant conversationalist that he was. I just wished for his sake he'd stop smoking so much and get his tarnished teeth cleaned. He worked for himself, designing gardens, and drove around on a scary looking motorbike. I supposed he was making ends meet. He and Danielle lived in the modest house he rented in St. Didier, a village close to Carpentras. He didn't have the financial means to indulge her as Alain had, and I wondered if she missed that. Jacques seemed to adore Danielle and I certainly hoped that the feeling was mutual but it was difficult to tell. She was affectionate with him but then spoiled it all with her pouting, siren airs around Alain and quite a few others.

In key ways, Danielle was still intimately insinuated into Alain's life. Not only was she his secretary at La Belle Cuisine, she was also insured to drive his car, and signed his checks that were in her name for tax purposes. At the house, she would strut around the kitchen organising and arranging things as if she were the mistress, all this done not so much with a sense of arrogance as assuredness. Watching her I often felt deeply inadequate and humiliated. I wanted to yell at her, stay out of our lives. I wanted to erect boundaries, a Maginot line that she was forbidden to cross. But she was almost like family.

Once, when I confessed my jealousy over the fact that she was still so large a presence in his life, Alain looked at me intently and mouthed very distinctly. 'It's finished. Ended. I can't fire her from the shop because that would be complicated. Anyway,' he added as an afterthought, 'She's just a party animal, surface deep and only interested in having fun. You're worth a hundred of her.'

His reassurances helped, but her effect was insidious. It was as if, since she couldn't physically cosy up to Alain, she decided to invade the out-of-bound bits of my life. Her shadow began to follow me into the bedroom. I imagined her as this tsunami of sexuality, torridly, wildly seductive and uber-orgasmic. She and Alain had never copulated in this house—so I assumed—but that didn't stop me from imagining them, the sound of her volcanic eruptions bringing on his own. Once I even imagined her looking back at me in the mirror as Alain fucked me from behind, her voluptuous laugh slicing into my ragged breathing and taunting, he's still mine.

Chapter 8

It was a cool Saturday morning in mid-June. We'd just finished breakfast and were discussing the logistics of Christophe's visit the following weekend when Alain abruptly shifted the focus back to the present.

'*Chérie*, what do you think of going to a special club in Avignon tonight?' He posed the question as if it had just popped into his mind. 'It's a healthy place where men and women can explore their sexuality together.'

He began to elaborate on the activities that went on under its roof. It was fun, it was fantasy and it was safe.

'Safe? Are you sure about that? You and I are still getting to know each other. We're exploring here.'

I was utterly thrown off guard, wondering how long he'd been thinking of this intrusion into private territory. I didn't want to go.

'My darling, we will only do what you are comfortable with.'

So florid and reassuring was his description of how the club would bring us closer together that by the time we left the house I was prepared to give him the benefit of the doubt. We set off for Avignon at around eleven, after extensive grooming. That night he ensured that I was properly attired, which is to say, not attired much at all: fishnet stockings, a slinky black Spandex skirt, a décolleté top, high heels. I almost didn't recognise myself.

There was no sign of any sort outside the club, only an iron grill in front of the door, which was opened after a few knocks by a man who closely scrutinised us before letting us pass.

'Why this inspection?' I whispered to Alain.

'They don't let any unaccompanied men in, only couples and women.'

Inside was a narrow vestibule where Alain had to pay—a steep admission price I noted. Beyond that was a lavishly appointed bar and just ahead, a strobe-lit dance floor that gave onto a darkened lounge whose walls were hugged with sofas. On one wall was a large screen showing films of an explicit nature. We drank a glass of champagne, moving from bar to lounge, eyeing the women who gyrated snake-like under the strobes.

A few couples were discretely occupied in the corners. Nestled on a couch, Alain slid his hand under my show-it-all-skirt and into my ever-eager crotch. For a second, this registered as a racy thing to do in public even if it was a private venue. He removed his hand, put two fingers in his mouth, and slid them back. I reclined, letting his fingers do their up-down-and-around circuit, already wanting more. As I reached out to reciprocate, he grasped my hand.

'Let's go,' he mouthed, suddenly impatient that I see what this club was famous for. Upstairs we went, to a series of dimly lit rooms where figures were engaged in a no-holds-barred bacchanalia of caressing, licking, mounting and moaning. Bowls of condoms and boxes of tissues were laid out neatly on several low tables.

We placed ourselves on one of the sofas, Alain murmuring in my ear, '*Chérie*, let me see you enjoy yourself.' Soon I was the object of fondling, on my breasts, my thighs, around my ass and elsewhere by a man I had not exchanged a word with, only the barest eye contact. I felt oddly emotionless, somewhere other than in my skin as his hands played with me.

I caught Alain looking at me hungrily and I knew he wanted me to engage with those hands. For his sake, I writhed a bit as they roved over me. Then I saw him move to another sofa, doing to another woman what the hands were doing to me. She wore only stockings and a red lace chemise.

These *ménage à deux, trois, quatre, cinq* in various stages of progress all around us were not eye-opening. I had experimented with threesomes and a woman or two in the past but seeing my partner in the arms of a nameless third party, now that was new—and not one bit nice. I saw them kissing, man on top, and I froze, unthawing a little when he shifted to catch my eye. He must have sensed my discomfort for he left her and returned to me. The original hands on me had moved somewhere else and I was now the object of lustful advances from a woman whose touch I had to admit was considerably more artful and less gropey than the man's. Alain squeezed in beside me and soon it was just he and I together in the midst of those bawdily occupied bodies. Having him all to myself at that moment was the most sublime experience. I didn't care who was watching as we rammed into each other.

Afterwards we went downstairs for more champagne refreshment, ascending again for act two of what gave Alain such an inordinate thrill. He was in his element in this pleasure dome, whose ambiance was electric and whose rules of engagement were based on respecting the words '*oui*' or 'n*on*'. If you didn't like someone's touch you had only to say no and the hand would pull back.

'Darling what do you think? Did you like it?' Alain was glinting with satisfaction as we drove back home on the empty motorway just before dawn.

What did I think? A sincere answer would have required more vocabulary and complex sentences than I had the capacity for at that moment. It would have delved into how this was a whole new world for me; how my feelings were running amok. Part of me liked what I saw and thought I was lucky to experience such sexual diversity, but a little voice squeaked, why the need? Aren't I enough for Alain? How secure a partner is he? Will he want to do this again? My mind grappled with weighty questions such as how the club squared with monogamy and marriage. Could you go 'clubbing' as a mother to young children? I knew there were swingers' groups in England, but I'd thought this was mostly the preserve of long-married couples with grown-up kids seeking outside thrills, not lovers who couldn't keep their hands off each other. And yet…maybe I was being too prim and narrow-minded. Too quick to judge. What harm was there in a bit of fun? If that's all it was, he and I together, then why not? Easy-going, flexible, go-with-the-flow. Fucking strangers, now that's where I drew the line. I'd never do that. There was no denying the contagiousness of the club's orgiastic fervour though. My peaks of pleasure that night had been right up there on the Richter scale. So I wasn't lying when I simply replied, 'it was very exciting. I had a great time.'

Shortly after this outing we embarked on an excursion of a different kind. This time I had no idea of the destination as we pulled out of the driveway one cloudless morning, Alain revealing only that we'd be gone the best part of the day.

'It's a surprise darling. You'll find out soon enough.'

We drove past Cavaillon into the Bouche-de-Rhone countryside, to a village I didn't recognise. Alain pulled to a stop in front of a house on the corner of a narrow, tree-lined street.

'Welcome to Givronex, my home village. This is where I was born.' He indicated the house through the side window of the car.

Alain's childhood home was a large, two-storied structure whose exterior was the colour of a crunchy autumn leaf; its windows were hidden behind locked shutters. Here the clan had lived, the paternal grandparents included, until financial ruin had forced them out. Inside its doors Josephine had given birth to Alain, the only one of the four siblings to be born at home. The house was inhabited, although the occupants didn't appear to be at home.

After a few minutes, Alain restarted the engine. 'Time to see where I got married.'

Alain had pointed out the church before we entered the village, sitting atop a high limestone bluff. To reach it, we followed the road up a fairly steep incline, coming to a stop in a tree-shaded parking area. The sight of it caught my breath.

'This church is incredible,' I said in wonderment. Dominating the village from its perch on a peak, it was a spired sanctuary that was as beautiful as the idea of Alain marrying in a church was bizarre. But it was true. He and Marianne had had a traditional service, exchanging their vows under a vaulted roof, their family and friends packing the pews. It was a perfect Catholic wedding in a perfect spot, a funny thing for an atheist.

I too was an atheist, although my ethnicity was Jewish, my grandparents on both sides Eastern European Jews who had escaped pogrom in the old world hoping to find a better life across the Atlantic. Two generations later their offspring, my parents, had crossed the ocean in the opposite direction, taking my siblings and I to Western Europe.

'Voilà, la Monastère Notre-Dame de Givronex,' Alain announced as we began our stroll around the eighteenth-century chapel, taking in the surrounding sights that included the ruins of a medieval castle. The ample views encompassed the long stretch of woods where Alain and Tristan had roamed freely as children, losing themselves for hours under its green canopy. Alain recounted stories of his boyhood antics in those forests and I listened, thinking how utterly different our backgrounds were, my youth spent in urban vastness in a sophisticated world, his in rural spaciousness communing with nature. No wonder cities depressed him. They were beginning to depress me.

This ancient, austere village on the Durance River, with its ramparts, churches, castle and magnificent views of hilly, woody countryside had shaped Alain's youth. I was happy he wanted me to see it.

Leaving the Bouche du Rhône we drove to Mont Ventoux and parked in a spot more than half way up to the summit. On a grassy, deserted outcrop, we devoured the cheese and bread we had bought en route, staring at the panorama before us. Wiping away the crumbs, we sank back on the blanket we'd brought from the car and I closed my eyes. Just as I was about to doze off I felt a graze on my lips and then cottony light kisses on my neck. Aroused, my eyes sprung open. Alain had the taut, hairless midriff of a Greek statue, bronzed skin smooth as a taper, creaseless breasts like plated armour—a body made for loving. He interrupted his caresses to unzip his trousers. Freed from boxers his phallus glistened in the high-altitude air, straighter than the tree trunks at the base of the mountain, a favourite autumnal haunt for mushroom pickers. He removed my panties and felt the tell-tale wetness. Only perhaps the birds witnessed as he entered me and we fell into sync, the pleasure of our union vanquishing fatigue. Later, he leaned on his side, breaking the human silence:

'*Mon amour* you really are special you know that? *Tu es la femme de ma vie.*'

In that instance culture shock, and even Danielle, were relegated to minor matters. They were a small price to pay for a seat in paradise.

Alain loved tales; especially spicy Moorish and Arabian Nights tales. So when he heard about the wandering storyteller he just had to invite him over to the house, along with around fifty adults and children to share in the delights. The weather that June evening was uncooperative, but at least the rain held off. We managed to hold the first half of the session in the garden, moving inside only when the wind became a nuisance and started blowing away the paper plates and cups that held the food and drink we'd laid out.

The audience gathered around the star attraction in a wide arc, some people sitting on chairs, others on blankets and mats. As soon as he started a hush settled over the crowd. Of Lebanese descent, the yarn spinner was tall, with a thick mop of black hair, abyss eyes, luxuriant eyebrows, wide lips and a silvery voice that sucked you in like quicksand. His words sliced through the wind. The atmosphere was jovial but respectful for there was no drunkenness. In the middle of a story about Saracens in the desert, Alain disappeared inside, hurrying back seconds later.

'It's for you,' he kept his voice low. I hadn't heard the phone ring.

It was my Chinese friend Annie Leung, calling from Hong Kong. After a few preliminaries, she came to the point.

'I have the budget so it's decided. I want you to come to Hong Kong and China in late August to write a special report on shipping.'

Annie, who at one time had worked for the same corporate group that I had, published a maritime magazine in Hong Kong that was backed by mainland

Chinese interests. Would I be the magazine's English-language editor? she asked. I agreed to the work without hesitation. The title sounded grand but it wasn't a full-time job—more like one-off consultancies since she only planned to produce two or three issues a year—advertising from Chinese companies being her golden egg. It wasn't that I wanted a reprieve from Provence. I needed to replenish my savings, drained from all my recent purchases, the lessons and other expenses. I also needed to play it smart, keep a foothold in journalism, even if the circulation of Annie's magazine was to a small, specialised audience. When I told Alain about the trip, he was nonplussed.

'Darling, I'm not used to this, the love of my life leaving me.'

I laughed at his melodrama.

'You were ready to send me on a mission to India, remember? And besides, I thought you wanted a woman who was independent, who does her own thing.'

'I do, but…'

'But what?' I was enjoying this.

'It's just that it's happening a little too quickly and three weeks is a long time for you to be away.'

Let him suffer a bit. I wouldn't tell him how much I already missed him.

Chapter 9

Adapting to the non-rules, I had grown more relaxed about Alain's social open-door policy (notwithstanding Danielle). But when Alain broke the news that a group of five actors would be moving in with us for the month of July, I went into stress mode. One of the troupe members was Seline, whom he'd dated for a month the previous summer. She apparently still carried the torch for him. Our house was to be their staging post while they performed a nightly spectacle in Avignon, whose annual summer theatre festival was the most important date on its calendar. Alain had promised to lodge them months ago at the troupe's request—well before visiting me in Hong Kong. Even so I couldn't hide my upset at the prospect of sharing our home with a quintet that included his former flame.

'Alain, I'm not comfortable having her here. Even if you did finish it with her because she's neurotic and unbalanced. She'll probably be jealous of me, and it will all be so difficult.'

'Darling I understand how you feel but I can't go back on my promise to them now. Accommodation in Avignon is usually booked up a year in advance.'

He mulled it over for a few seconds before conceding: 'Tell you what. We'll keep this floor to ourselves so at least we'll have some privacy with everyone around.'

Christophe would also be staying with us for the whole of July, accompanied by his best friend for a fortnight.

We knew the day the troupe was due to arrive but not the time. Murphy's law, they had the devilry to show up when we were making love in the Indian corner. Maybe Alain subconsciously staged it like that as a statement to his ex. He'd told her about me the previous week when she'd phoned him to discuss sleeping arrangements. Seline had entered the house quietly while her colleagues waited outside. I don't know how much she saw but she did at least have the delicacy to *'coucou'* us from the portico of the kitchen without walking right up to where we were. With an 'oops', we quickly disengaged and dressed.

Seline was based in Paris but she had grown up in Provence where her mother still lived. She'd studied acting in the capital and this was to be her debut—the troupe's debut—in Avignon. She was pretty, with long chestnut hair and emerald eyes. Beneath a floral print dress that fell to just above her knees I saw the outlines of a thin, feline body. Gold Romanesque sandals showed off ochre-painted toenails. She sized me up with a calculating smile, and I knew that battle lines were being drawn. Before she'd even had a drink of anything she laid down the gauntlet, declaring that she wanted my top-floor study as her bedroom. I didn't refuse her request, but Alain did.

'I'm sorry but you can't sleep there. That's Ravinia's space and she needs it to work. You can stay downstairs with the rest of the group.'

Seline pulled a face and hauled her stuff up the two flights of stairs to my room. A mini tug of war ensued with some heated verbal exchanges.

'She's got to realise that she can't continue to pull these childish tantrums,' Alain fumed to me. I admit, I quite enjoyed the effect of those tantrums. In the end, Seline brought her things downstairs with diva-esque dramatics, maybe all part of the preparations for her play.

The performers—one other woman and three men—slept on mattresses in the long room, bought their own food and cooked their own meals. We thought we'd be able to arrange two sittings for lunch to allow us some breathing space, but in practice this was unworkable. Too many cooks in the kitchen, stepping on each other's toes. When they returned from their nightly performance in Avignon, we were normally asleep.

On the sixth night, I woke up in the small hours needing to use the toilet. I slipped on a robe and quietly opened the bedroom door. The top floor hall light was illuminated. Strange. We never left it on at night. Tiptoeing to the staircase I went up a few steps and stopped. The light in my study was on and the door was ajar. Curiosity got the better of fear and I continued up the stairs. Seline was sitting on the floor of my study amid a stack of photos, bent over an album that she'd removed from a shelf. Caught in the act, she didn't flinch.

'Did you find what you were looking for?'

'You mean photos of you and Alain? No.'

I joined her on the floor, my bladder unhappy.

'*Alors*, what do you want to know?'

'So where did you two meet? I mean it's rather sudden your relationship, isn't it?'

In her creamy pyjamas, her face looked pale, but her hair was magnificent.

'Actually no, we met more than three years ago. In Vietnam.'

Briefly, I related the story of our encounter, our reunion in Hong Kong and my holiday in Provence, taking pains to stress the strong bonds between us.

'Look. I'm sorry it didn't work out between you and Alain.'

A lie. I wasn't sorry at all.

'I can see you're still in love with him.'

She didn't bother to deny it. Her hard eyes glimmered but she didn't cry. She sat and stared at the photo album on her lap. I said nothing, feeling almost sorry for her. I could identify with feelings of rejection.

'Well, I don't have much faith in your chances with him. Be careful. He's not a one-woman man. He's probably stringing you along. Truthfully I'm doing you a favour by telling you this so you're not deluded.'

Pity devolved into anger. I grabbed the photo album from her and put it back on the shelf.

'Please leave my room. And stay out of it.'

As she walked out she shot me a look—of triumph.

I decided to keep this episode with Seline to myself, at least the next morning, wondering how she'd behave. No differently from before, as it transpired. But I never had to say a thing to Alain because that day it all came to a head. Alain was miserable with the arrangement, feeling cramped, constrained and awkward in his own home. He realised the situation would be unbearable for a month so he made a dozen calls and pulled a few strings with friends—promising god knows what. A day later Seline and the group decamped to another house in the vicinity and Alain heaved with relief. As she left I sprang her a 'you're the loser' victory smile. But her words nibbled at me.

Summer was no time for work. Although he didn't shutter the kitchen shop, Alain put pleasure before profit so we could indulge our whims. The heat finally arrived and it was all so damn glorious.

We lived outside, feasting under the plane trees on Mediterranean salads and fresh fruit. We idled in our new, hand-woven Mexican hammock that we attached to their sturdy trunks. We took long siestas and sipped chilled rosé wine as the sun disappeared behind the fields. Accompanied by Christophe and his friend, we drove to the market in Bedouin and other colourful villages that were reborn in the summer, when legions of locals and tourists piled in to capture a piece of their incandescence. We waded through neck-high water to reach a secluded spot on the banks of a river in Toulerenc where we picnicked on cold chicken and chunks of bread.

With green fingers, Alain tended to the garden and the cherry, apricot, fig, pear and olive trees that he had planted while I pottered around. We went over to friends' houses and entertained at home with lazy lunches and dinners. He whisked us to concerts and performances in Avignon (where we saw the theatre troupe in action) and to open-air restaurants with pretty tablecloths, comfortable chairs and carafes of ice-cool wine. At the end of July, Christophe and his friend left and there was silence, golden silence broken only by the chattering cicadas in the branches. I felt much more settled in the Vaucluse and a little savvier about things. And at last I was truly independent, comfortable driving my car beyond the confines of Carpentras.

August was devoted to sex and sculpture.

At home, with no one around, we could finally make love outside. We did so in the hammock and in the clumps of uncut grass bordering the garden. In an abandoned hut at the far rim of a nearby field, Alain fucked me from behind, both of us standing to avoid contact with the floor, he pumping into me, me pushing into him, my palms against the wooden struts of the walls, our groans let loose into the hot air. The sense of sultry pleasure continued with the feel of his sperm dribbling down my bare legs as we left that little hideaway. Yet rather than the physical sensations, it was the emotional thrill of being with Alain that I carried away.

We binged on sexual fantasy, driven by Alain's hunger for it and my hankering to explore it.

'*Mon amour*, I want to stack up some memories of you to see me through the weeks when you're in Asia,' was his preamble. As if he couldn't possibly do without.

Our staple was Aphrodite, the club *echangiste* on Rue de la Four inside Avignon's medieval ramparts. The mere thought of an outing there on a Friday or Saturday night was enough to send Alain heavenwards. His eyes gleamed with suggestive sparks and his lips thrust outwards, half a kiss, half a gesture of mischievous intent. He didn't seem to taste his dinner. He always chose my outfit, such as it was.

'This bra along with this top and these,' he'd proffer, holding up a pair of crotch-less tights or stay-up stockings. He himself wore a well-pressed, long-sleeved kurta-style shirt and black silk-linen trousers—casual but elegant. Jeans and t-shirts were frowned upon for men. Playtime started as soon as we entered the venue. He would bring me a glass of champagne from the bar and we would sip, surveying the scene.

'*Chérie*, let me see you dance,' Alain encouraged and I'd take to the floor under the strobe lights, eroticising my movements for him and sometimes a larger audience. In the darkened lounge, we would indulge in a carnal amuse bouche, the deep-seated sofas perfect invitations to heavy petting.

'Darling, let me feel your soaking, fuckable pussy,' Alain would whisper in my ear, wetting two fingers, sliding them into my panties, caressing and teasing, and slipping them into my mouth to suck. Alain normally wasn't one for talking while doing—only here, in this pleasure dome.

'You make my pussy so wet,' I would whisper at the feel of his erection through the fabric of his trousers. It was a truth that rolled off my tongue easily and naturally, given that my sex talk terminology in French wasn't expansive—certainly not something I practiced with my tutor. By the time we entered one of the specialised rooms upstairs, I felt so aroused that I was more than ready to embark on the main course—sex with strangers that now went all the way. That's right, with strangers. All the way. I'd crossed the line that I myself had drawn in the sand.

The first time I'd fucked another man, it wasn't at the behest of Alain. He'd dropped hints of his desire to see this happen, but the decision to proceed, the timing and the choice of target, were all mine. There were two things in particular that made me move my own goal posts: my fervent desire to please Alain and evolutionary thinking—the notion of fucking a stranger had become less strange.

I was astride Alain on a sofa, salivating for that first primal push onto him when a man moved in next to me. He looked to be in his mid-forties, clean-shaven with a slightly arched nose and a patrician bearing. I caught the scent of his musk. Pleasant. Making a split-second decision I whispered to Alain, 'Watch.' He smiled and shifted away to give us more space. I placed a hand on the man's thigh, the green light for him to respond. I wasn't aroused by this stranger per se but by the certainty of Alain's titillation in observing us.

Manoeuvring himself into position, the man began to suck my nipples. He had no need to remove my bra, worn for decor rather than support. I felt the familiar sensations of something staged yet at the same time uncharted. Now's the time. I turned to the rise in his trousers. The initial encounter with a new penis is always enlightening, if fraught with varying degrees of tension. Like a selected book, I like to take its measure, study its particularities and approach it with a laid-back deference. But this time I sought haste. Our union was a superficial construct and the sooner we came together the better. A few strokes and I disengaged to get a condom. Panties now off, I straddled the stranger and so began my debut in this new domain. As he clutched my buttocks, eyes closed, spurting breath, I peeked at Alain, spurred on by his open gape. Then the man spoke.

'Your knees on the floor.'

I moved off the sofa into doggy mode, he now in control, his thrusts short and jerky. When he came, my head was lodged uncomfortably against the sofa edge. He pulled out, holding the soggy condom, and I thought, how do we end this with dignity? Adroitly, Alain came to my rescue with an embrace that forestalled any awkward attempts at conversation. The man took his trousers from the sofa and retreated, I presumed, to the toilet.

'*Bravo ma chérie.*' And without another word, Alain proceeded to show me the extent of his appreciation.

Stranger fucking was easier on my psyche than the one-night stands I'd had in my teens and twenties. There was no need to worry about dialogue or figure out logistics, no bleeding feelings when the man bolted right after sex or wondering when someone would get dressed and leave when I wanted them gone. Most importantly, the man I loved was right there. At base, it was all a game, a charade enacted purely for the pleasure of increasing my partner's pleasure, and thereby heightening my own.

After that first experience, I was amazed at my ability to compartmentalise the coupling. We went to restaurants for varied cuisine, to the cinema and concerts for varied entertainment, and to the club for sexual spice—before having our own zesty reunions. Penetrative sex was my preferred option. I didn't mind a blow job, although I never allowed the nameless man to secrete into my mouth, mainly because I didn't want to have to swallow or spit the semen out. Most of the time the going down on wasn't reciprocated, which was just as well because with a strange tongue it was usually more miss than hit. But there were exceptions, such as the very handsome monsieur who had a most talented tongue.

'I wouldn't mind getting together with him again,' I'd teased Alain, after meting out a few superlatives about said talents.

Alain wasn't amused.

'No. I don't trust him. He came to the club on dishonest terms because he wasn't with his wife but a friend. That doesn't conform to the rules.'

Conform? Rules? Alain was jealous.

So was I the first time I saw him put on a condom and penetrate a woman. She was good looking—they were all good looking. But the jealousy fizzled sooner than I would have thought possible. He always kept me in sight, and there was minimal talking with the lady in question and no comparisons between her and me afterwards. Plus, it increased his desire for me. Alain was right. It really did seem safe.

The couples at the club came from all social classes, from banking to bar-tending. It didn't matter who you were as long as you formed a pair, passed muster with the heavy at the gate and paid the entrance fee; and once you were inside, adhered to its code of conduct and its creed: complicity between all partners. Male-only action was certainly not the spirit encouraged. In fact, women enjoyed the status of empresses in this particular setting and their exaltations exceeded those of the males who sometimes seemed mechanically engaged although the ambiance was always alluring.

I couldn't get over the attention I was attracting. In Hong Kong, men's eyes barely registered me. In Provence—and not just at the club but everywhere in public—they followed me with intensity and interest in their irises. On the male visibility scale, I'd gone from minus ten to one hundred and ten, which did wonders for my sense of womanhood.

Swingers' clubs, I soon learned, were as common as chateaux in France, where partner swapping was a popular mainstream hobby. Within a broad-based milieu, it is not a big exaggeration to say that an outing to a club *echangiste* was treated as casually as nipping out for a café-au-lait.

Our playgrounds expanded to include the nudist beach bordering the historic town of Saintes Maries de la Mer in the Camargue. It was a wild, unpopulated place of dunes and a long stretch of hard-packed sand. From the car park, it took about ten minutes to cross the dunes and reach the sea's edge, beach umbrella and food in hand. Alain chose our spot carefully, making sure we were in strategic view of unclad others. This was all a big game too, the looks that were exchanged, the skinny dips in the sea, and the embraces we intentionally fell into.

Alain, filled with hours of exhibitionist enchantment, could barely contain himself; as the sun sank he would enter me and we would thrust away, leaving only when the evening breezes arrived.

There was also the mixed sauna, housed in an innocuous building in a village near Avignon.

'Darling this is an adventure, relax and enjoy it,' Alain enthused on my first visit. Unlike at the club, single men were welcome and they hovered about us like hyenas over a carcass. I saw only one other woman there that first time, which perhaps explained the celebrity-like stalking.

As Alain guided me around, a towel covering my royal jewels, I noticed, with relief, how spotless the interior was. There was a sauna, steam room, swimming pool and a cosy living room featuring a bar, a stack of X-rated magazines and a television showing blue movies. Alain pointed to a closed door.

'Behind that door are individual cubicles with peepholes—for those who want privacy,' he explained, knowingly.

The sexual charge of this place was so great it could have lit up the building. There was not a taboo in sight. We began with a few minutes in the dry-heat sauna. After a refreshing cold shower, we went to the steam room where, as the sweat glistened, eyes bore down on me and hands reached out to touch the most erogenous zones of my body—which I didn't allow—and their own.

Everywhere I was pursued by naked men, some with their tongues almost hanging out, reminding me of a pack of thirsty dogs, and all with their penises on show. They drank in my every move, which didn't escape my lover's eyes. It was an immense turn on for him, but I felt intimidated by the unfettered display of flesh and the crude carnality all focused on me. If I gave them the nod, would they all try to fuck me or masturbate while touching my breasts, my pussy? How would that feel? I pictured my body drenched in semen from multiple ejaculations. While I rejected the reality of it, I warmed to the fantasy—maybe one for the times when Alain wasn't around.

'Are you okay?' Alain asked, as we showered again to cool off from the steamy heat.

'Are there usually so many men around and so few women? I mean, where are all the women?'

'It is a little one-sided today, I agree.'

The mention of 'today' brought home the inevitability of his previous visits to this place—almost certainly with Danielle.

'But the men,' he made a wide sweep of his arm in the spacious shower, 'the men appreciate a beautiful woman when they see one. You're causing quite a stir. You can't blame them for looking…and wanting.'

After the shower, we headed to the living room, sinking into the sofa opposite the large television. It was while watching acrobatic depictions on the screen that Alain whispered:

'*Ma chérie*, you can choose whoever you like. You just have to ask. So who do you want?'

Doubtfully, I studied the men on offer, trying not to make it too obvious. Maybe it was the penis overkill, the stark exhibition of so much desperate desire and pale flesh, but no one in the least appealed to me. Just as I was going to point blank refuse, into the lounge walked a man who bore himself with some dignity. I hadn't spotted him before and he was easily identified for being the only other man apart from Alain to wear a towel around his waist. He smiled at me and went to pour himself some water from a pitcher placed on the bar. He was youngish, with a mat of dark hair that fell over his face and a lean frame, not dissimilar to Jacques'.

'Him,' I whispered to Alain, indicating the man. Alain tactfully approached our target, who responded with a nod of the head. With his key, Alain unlocked the door and the three of us went into a curtained-off cubicle dominated by a large mattress covered in a clean, crisp white sheet. I noticed a packet of condoms on a narrow shelf. Alain watched hawk-like as the stranger began to caress me here, finger me there, his erection rubbing rabidly against my skin. The game 'me' had switched on but when the man put his lips to mine I turned my face away—kissing was reserved for Alain only—inviting him instead to 'lie down'.

I wouldn't kiss him but I did look at him as we fucked. His skin was smooth, he was attractive and agile, but I was glad he didn't take long to climax. All I wanted now was to feel Alain's penis inside me and his tongue in my mouth. We didn't even wait for the guy to leave (he parted with a polite '*merci*'). I was on the verge of coming when the fantasy, startling enough, came alive: a parade of erect penises in the steam room flashed before my eyes.

The journalist in me was fascinated by this world of public sex, so opposite to money-centred, puritan Hong Kong where nudity inspired giggling rather than ogling. The French seemed to approach making love with a single-minded maturity, an evolved sophistication, as if they carried a sexual savoir-faire chromosome that we Anglo-Saxons didn't, or at least that I didn't. I wanted some of that Gaelic sophistication to rub off on me. Anchored in relationships, the French had no qualms about having sex with strangers—not that I had carried out any sort of survey on the subject. Could it be that underneath the suave female surfaces I saw at the club there were miseries and jealousies galore?

Our adventures animated Alain, and, like he'd predicted, seemed to draw us closer in conspiratorial complicity. And I—I was cultivating my sexuality, discovering what tickled me and what tested me. And another thing. Outside the house I wasn't as haunted by the image of Danielle. So it all seemed positive except for…on some base level, in the burrows of my soul, I had disquieting questions. Why does he need the extra kicks? Why aren't I enough for him? How does all this fit in with what I really want, marriage and kids? From time to time this disquietude turned into a rumble, but I kept the lid on with a simple reasoning…we were still getting to know each other, it was early days. That ungainly word and what a cliché: I had to be patient.

Chapter 10

Unlike with sex, my role was confined to observer as Alain lost himself in his sculpture, which slowly filled the house. As an undergraduate student at New York University I had majored in History of Art. My coursework shone the light on the defining sculptural movements of the past from the Greco-Roman period through to the Renaissance right up to the modern era. But no one, not even my revered Rodin, made me salivate over sculpture like Alain. In my humble opinion, he had genius in his genes.

Of course, to compare was unfair. I was present to witness all stages of Alain's creative process, culminating in the painstaking physical labour, so a sculpture represented more than the shape that met the eye. Even if I didn't warm to every one of his pieces, I came to know them like my hands; yet they also remained enigmatic.

There was the pink marble cat in action that I called Bali Two after our real tabby that slept and foraged for food outside. There was the finely chiselled horse-in-gallop carved from multi-coloured Iranian marble. The Three Sisters, a marble bas-relief of three profiles merging into one another, reminded me of my own triangular sibling dynamic. Also made of marble was a speckled-grey oval pearl, bearing more than a resemblance to a woman's sex. The wooden bust of Shiva had taken Alain months to complete. Its sanctuary was a stand placed against the wall opposite our bed. Carved into the smooth mahogany surface, the eyes were closed in contemplation, the lips mellifluously proportioned, the head tiered with wooden orbs. The sculpture was invested with such innate spirituality that I often wondered what it thought of the lusty scenes played out before it day after day.

In the long room by the Indian corner was his very first marble sculpture, a spiral shell cleverly mounted on an invisible hook. It was the centrepiece of a water-filled basin, a fountain demarcated by chunks of rocks at the edge and pebbles in the interior. Alain had designed it himself and the effect was enthralling. He waxed delirious about marble from the famed Italian quarries of Carrara, a material that had transformed his vision.

'It is as hard as it is yielding, rebellious but submissive, when you know how to talk to it.'

His latest marble love was an angel. He spent hours whittling away her rough linear edges, her silky form emerging elegantly from its mass. The angel was dazzling, yet there was something icy about her. She stood outside on the gravel where she was being brought to life under a canopy that Alain had erected to provide shade. Often in the moonlight he would search her out, caressing her as he would a woman. It came as no great surprise that many of Alain's sculptures featured round, feminine curves or the imprint of a woman's sex. For I soon saw that what he was fond of in the flesh manifested continuously in his art.

I had never seen a sculptor at work before and had no inkling they wielded electric drills and discs, which produced reams of dust and sometimes broke down. When Alain sculpted, dressed in overalls with a protective mask and goggles over his face, he entered another dimension where nothing else existed. Once he'd finished for the day, he needed a cooling-off period when it was best to leave him alone. This man had been born with a chisel in his hand and ideas in his head. His dream was to give up selling kitchens altogether and devote his life entirely to his art, like any artist who eats, sleeps and breathes the next chef d'oeuvre.

Trance-like, he frequently conjured up before me the images crowding his brain that were begging to be born, of women, animals and statues for public places and private gardens.

'I sculpt to create forms of beauty, it is my way of contributing harmony to this world.'

At times, I wished I were a piece of marble to be moulded by his hands. How silly to be envious of inert material. But it was the silent third party in our relationship—other than Danielle, although she wasn't silent.

The day in August I turned thirty-three, Alain laid on a queenly feast, forbidding me to come downstairs until all the elements—candles, music, cuisine—were in place. His fastidiousness in creating exactly the right ambiance set against his distaste for conventional décor was a case study in human dichotomies. I did my part, dressing for the occasion in a new skirt that barely covered my rear. I felt quite the mollycoddled muse as he handed me a glass of champagne and sat me down at the flower-laden table in the long room.

The first course of caviar and toast bites was followed by grilled filet of sole accompanied by a glass of Grenache Blanc. A moment or two to digest then he whispered in my ear, 'and you, my darling, are the dessert'. He led me to the Indian corner and baring my royal jewels, proceeded with his own private tasting, followed by a delicious glide inside. By far my favourite course. Languorous from our lovemaking, we lolled back to the table for the post-dessert pudding, a dark chocolate mousse cake. Before I could take the first bite, he handed me a pillbox wrapped in tissue paper. Tearing it open I saw a gold band, regal in its simplicity. It was bothersome to have to control my emotions, whipped up by what this might portend.

'It's beautiful,' was all I trusted myself to say. I was just about to slide the ring onto the middle finger of my left hand when Alain swiftly intervened.

'No not there, put it on that finger,' he indicated my ring finger. Surely this was an engagement ring, a prelude to a proposal. I waited for the words, carried away by wedding dreams. What perfect timing, a birthday that would forever stand out among birthdays. I looked at his face expectantly.

'Glad you like it,' he beamed. But other than that—nothing. No further reference to the ring. Was this some kind of test or joke on his part? What did he think I thought? Is he expecting me to say something? But asking him if this was an engagement ring felt too risqué. It was up to him to make a move if that was his intent.

'I have a secret to tell you, it concerns you and me.'

The words he'd first tantalised me with at the home bash in April and a few times thereafter whooshed back. Of course, I interpreted them to mean marriage—but there they stayed, mysteries hanging in the air, without further elucidation. But perhaps the secret was this: An unspoken understanding that all this was leading to the registry office and a legal commitment. And the ring was part of that. So I kept silent and dipped into the dark chocolate mousse cake, my emotions in spin.

A few days later Benoit, a member of Alain's group, held a birthday party in the garden of his one-bedroom cottage near the village of Mormoiron. It started in the early evening under a light sky that burnished red as the sun sank. The garden was surrounded by fields and farmland on three sides. There were a few flowery shrubs in his plot but no trees, which gave it even more of an open feel. It was a clear, warm evening.

As usual all the gang were there: Benoit's girlfriend, Christine, a hat maker and designer who had recently moved in with him; Mathias, the electrician whose hand was behind all the electrical wiring in our house and his girlfriend, Vivienne, a petite brunette. There were Marc and Isabel, and Gregoire and Eliane, both parents of small children. Also present was Peppo, the handyman who'd crafted our wardrobes and kitchen shelves. And of course, Danielle and Jacques. But there was also an unfamiliar figure.

'Who is she?' I asked Alain, pointing to an exquisite creature chatting to Christine.

'Ah, that's Brigitte.'

So this was the woman Alain had lived with for four years in Aix-en-Province before his affair with Danielle. He had told me with characteristic frankness how thunderstruck he'd been when he first saw her, a decade ago now. It was a Saturday afternoon. Brigitte's sister had dragged her to a sale at an expensive furniture shop where Alain was then working.

'I took one look at her and was instantly besotted.'

'She is stunning.'

'You should have seen her then,' he mused. Alain had wanted marriage and babies with her, but at twenty-two, she wasn't ready for that and held him off. I stared at her, this Venus of almond-shaped eyes, sensuous lips and vermicelli hair.

Alain followed my gaze. 'Come, let me introduce you.'

Brigitte smiled welcomingly as Alain made the introductions, then left us to talk. My immediate impression was how unlike Danielle she was, being soft, languid, dreamy, ethereal, rather like a fairy in A Midsummer Night's Dream. I asked about her life and she told me she lived in Cannes with her boyfriend and their two-year old son. She visited the Vaucluse from time to time to see her friends, Danielle among them.

'Why did you break up with her?' I asked Alain later.

'We grew apart. She needed to find herself and I was hindering that. And I…I was restless.'

Restless. The word rankled.

Alain was immensely proud of the fact that he got on so well with his live-in exes—all apart from a musician girlfriend he'd lost contact with. They formed such a cosy little seraglio. But I struggled with it, feeling on the one hand that his attitude was admirable and healthy and on the other, irksomely incestuous. The haunting proximity of Danielle was the ubiquitous noose around my neck. One thing was for sure. I was the outsider.

Chapter 11

A week or so before my late August departure to Hong Kong Alain took me to one of my favourite restaurants. The Auberge de la Fontaine was in Venasque, a ridiculously beautiful village even by the standards of an area teeming with beautiful villages. Perched on a cliff, Venasque felt like a toy construct, its consummately crafted layout overlooking a heady topography of forested valley and plains, with Roman ruins thrown into the mix. The Auberge specialised in live classical performances—musical evenings where you would be served a concertina and haute-cuisine in one sitting.

'My beauty, I'm going to miss you. Are you going to be faithful to me?' The question, half way through our first course, was startling.

'Of course Alain.'

'Oh, but I know how things can happen when you're away, staying in hotels.'

'Work is going to take up all my time, besides I'm not interested in the slightest in being with anyone else. You know that. What about you Alain?'

'No, my darling, I have better things to do than to go chasing after women. I'm going to sculpt. I want to surprise you when…'

Alain's attention was diverted by the jack-in-the-box appearance of his friends Gregoire and Eliane.

'What's this? And I thought we had escaped you lot,' Alain joked. 'We're trying to have an intimate dinner before Ravinia flies to Hong Kong for work. What's your excuse?'

'We're with his parents, they're down from Paris for a week,' Eliane piped in, pointing to a table in the corner thankfully too far away for eavesdropping. Gregoire had a genial side but Eliane? She wasn't my favourite person, not just for being flighty and a reckless mother. Whenever they came over, she barely registered her five-year-old daughter who, not surprisingly, was an attention seeker landing in all kinds of trouble, her mother then screaming blue murder. Eliane, like Danielle, was a confirmed flirt, only higher strung, harder and sharper. Where Danielle mesmerised with her captivating gestures, Eliane used her sparky tongue and acerbic wit, and another tool in her arsenal: a mop of wavy red hair, which she coiled as if she were spinning a web. I saw her at work at parties and smaller gatherings, tartly weaving her way into the good graces of men she knew and those she didn't, never minding that her partner was in earshot. She smiled at me but there was something calculating in her look, her movements appearing contrived and choreographed. I didn't trust her for a second. She had never shown any curiosity about my professional past, but now she was full of questions about my trip to Hong Kong, all ingratiating, oily talk. Then she shifted gears.

'We're having some people over next weekend. We're counting on you to be there,' and she thrust Alain a look that said take advantage of her absence. Alain sighed.

'It'll be a break from the sculpting.'

I wasn't pleased. But I could no more tell him not to go than I could ask him to stop breathing.

I had expected to be put off by Hong Kong, its crowds, noise and rudeness after the perfections of Provence, but disconcertingly, the city had never seemed so ravishing. The skies were clear and you could see beyond the skyline of Tsim Sha Tsui to the rim of hills hugging the New Territories, quite a rare sight in the normally tempestuous month of August. Maybe it sparkled too because I was the old me again: an articulate adult, back in my stomping ground, able to indulge in humour. And happy to get to work. After a few days, Annie Leung and I boarded our Dragon Air flight to China. In Beijing and Shanghai, while she visited her contacts, I dashed to my interviews, thankful to find my journalistic skills still intact and my confidence gauge high. In the little time we spent together, sharing a hotel room, Annie, whose existence was defined by work, talked only of shipping, for which I was grateful (although I wasn't so appreciative of the six a.m. calls that came in for her).

This Cantonese firecracker had escaped the clutches of intense childhood poverty to become her family's success story. Her mother had raised her and five siblings alone because their father lived with another wife. Like millions of others in Hong Kong, they had shared one piddling room with a communal toilet and cooking facilities. Annie had been forced to leave school at twelve to work in a factory and help put rice on the table. But ambition had clawed its way through deprivation. At fourteen, she'd enrolled in night classes to complete her secondary education. For seven years, she'd slogged at the factory during the day and studied at night to get her diploma. The English and Mandarin she spoke? All self-taught.

At eighteen, she was hired by the company in whose offices I had worked. And so started her meteoric rise through the ranks. Her do-or-die doggedness, combined with a sharp intelligence, gave her the wherewithal to leave that firm at twenty-eight (three years previously) and start her own publishing venture with Chinese backing. She had no romantic life to speak of. A three-year relationship with a British man who jumped ship back to England with barely a goodbye had left its mark. At times, she talked wistfully about wanting to meet someone, but work was her true love.

In China, I couldn't stop gawping at the changes I saw. A decade ago on my first journey, Beijing heaved with bicycles and men in dark blue Mao suits. Cars were not common and you could only purchase little luxuries like ice cream and cosmetics in specially designated Friendship stores. My Mandarin was fairly good then, which was useful in arguing against the constant '*mei you*' (no, not, can't) I encountered from petty officials at every turn.

There was not much '*mei you*' this time around, although wearing a suit and not a backpack and staying in four-star hotels may have had something to do with it. In Shanghai, the pace of progress was even more dizzying. Next to the dynamism of East Asia, France seemed such a stuck-in-the-mud sclerotic. Part of the culture shock in moving continents had been to experience how slowly the wheels of bureaucracy ground. In France, a fax machine took a month to fix; a telephone line weeks to install; to get an official stamp for a document required ridiculous patience; banks were plodding turtles compared to Hong Kong's efficient ones and shops closed for three hours in the middle of the day, which is wonderful for a siesta and high blood pressure, but not if you've suddenly run out of bread and milk and have errands to do.

Back in Hong Kong, during the day I wrote my report at a friend's flat in Central and at night caught up with old mates at the Foreign Correspondents Club. It was pleasing to see the same bums on bar stools and to discuss weighty things like the future of Hong Kong under China. The only dampener was the absence of my Australian friend. She'd left Hong Kong for a reporting job in Jakarta. When acquaintances asked me about France and the man I'd jilted the television channel for, I had a ready riposte.

'He's everything I expected and more. You won't believe how much I'm learning.'

They thought I was referring only to the language.

One night at the Club a journalist chum of mine told me that the news agency I'd left (on good terms) was looking to hire a reporter for its newly established television arm.

'Are you interested? I know you wanted to get into financial TV and you missed your chance once. You could easily get an interview.'

I thought about it seriously for a moment. Here was another opportunity to get back on the career track, pursue my once cherished dream. Wouldn't I be rash to reject it? I'd found my professional feet again and I couldn't deny it felt good, being in a milieu I understood. And the fact that Alain didn't want children and I did—an issue that continued to wreak havoc with my emotions although I refused to concede defeat. A return to Hong Kong with a new job and a fresh start. Alluring. But who was I kidding? The head was no competition for the heart. I longed for Alain more each day with a pain that bordered on the physical. I missed his touch, like an electric current that produced in me instant erogenous secretions. I missed the look from his piercing blue eyes that invaded every pore of my body—a look that was never innocent when directed at me. Like the voluptuous views of nature, he had become an indispensable part of my existence. I dismissed this chance to rewrite my future, fanatically focused on the moment I would see Alain again.

Chapter 12

As the TGV braked to a stop in Avignon central station I experienced one of those déjà vu moments. There were the same heart-thumping, breathless, exhilarating sensations as six months before, and that same X-ray scan of the platform. Only this time Alain didn't appear. Instead, I saw Pierre, his brother, making his way towards me through the stream of passengers heading to the exit.

'I was afraid I'd be late,' he said by way of greeting, proffering an apology.

'Pierre, nice to see you, but where's Alain? Has something happened?'

'He's really sorry but he had a last-minute meeting with a client in Roussillon and couldn't make it in time. He called me an hour ago, asking me to pick you up. I apologise,' Pierre repeated.

'Please don't. It's very good of you to come, especially as you had to leave work early. Was that a problem?'

'Not at all.'

So much for the homecoming I'd imagined. I tried to hide my disappointment. It wasn't fair to take it out on Pierre, who insisted on wheeling my suitcase. With the adrenalin completely dissipated by Alain's no-show, exhaustion took hold. After more than twenty-four hours of travelling all I wanted—apart from seeing Alain—was a bed. But the thought of returning to an empty house was depressing. It was five o'clock, too early for dinner and I wasn't hungry, but nevertheless…

'Pierre, why don't we get something to eat? How about the Pizzeria in Mazan? By the time we've finished, Alain will be back.'

I'd been too revved up to doze in the TGV from Paris. But once in Pierre's Citroen, I slumped on the seat. I'm not sure how many times he called my name before I opened my eyes, realising we'd arrived at our destination in the Boulevard des Innocents. At this time of year, we could have sat on the terrace but I was chilled, partly from fatigue, mostly from the sudden temperature drop after Hong Kong's heat. A waiter seated us inside by the brick oven where the pizzas were cooked.

'Did you see Alain while I was away?' I asked out of politeness, expecting him to say no.

'Yes I did. He came to borrow the cauldrons again. For the fete this past weekend.'

'He had another party?'

Alain hadn't mentioned anything of the sort when I'd called him from Hong Kong.

'It seems so.'

'You didn't go of course.'

'No, as Alain told you I'm not one for big parties.'

He changed the subject.

'Tell me about your travels in China.'

'Well, there were lots of changes since the last time I was there. Beijing and Shanghai…developing so fast.'

Back to my faulty French. I missed the ease of speaking my mother tongue but I wasn't displeased to make the switch. I mentioned some of the modern touches that were transforming the urban landscape and Shanghai's growing likeness to skyscraper Hong Kong.

'What about you Pierre, have you travelled much?' I remembered his mother talking about the globe-trotting tendencies of his brothers.

'Unfortunately no. What exploration I've done has been in Europe although I did visit America some years ago.'

'The great Satan.'

'What?'

'It's what your brother calls America. You know, those dumb Anglo-Saxons.' I laughed.

'I rather liked what I saw in America. I wouldn't mind going back.'

He described his three weeks in New York, Arizona and San Francisco. He'd been charmed by it all and couldn't even complain about the food.

'Did you go on your own? With a friend?'

'I went with my wife—ex-wife now I should say. It was our honeymoon actually.'

'Oh.'

'It was her idea, and a good one. Better than going fishing in the Loire Valley.'

I couldn't tell if he was joking.

'I'd love to travel more, live abroad, as you've done. It's one of my dreams.'

'Well why don't you? I'm sure there are lots of opportunities as an engineer, in your niche.'

'Yes, there are. It's just difficult to make the initial move.'

'Maybe you need to follow a woman,' I couldn't resist adding.

'I'm quite happy for the moment to be on my own, *celibataire*,' he emphasised.

'How long ago was your divorce?'

'About eighteen months now.'

'Was it a difficult divorce? Sorry Pierre, I'm...' What was the word for prying?

'It's okay,' he said, but he had a glazed look that I interpreted to mean no more questions.

'You want to know why we divorced, don't you?' He broke through his haze, a hint of humour in his voice where there might have been annoyance.

'Not many of my friends even know.'

Including your own brother.

'I found out she was having an affair.'

He stared at his plate for so long I thought he wouldn't elaborate.

'Early on in our relationship she told me about her professor at the business polytechnic in Nice, where she'd studied. They fell madly in love. But he was married, and it was understood that he wouldn't leave his wife so she knew there was no future with him. When she left Nice after her degree she thought that was the end of it.'

'It was after we got married. He tracked her down, phoned her up. Asked if they could meet up. He'd separated from his wife. I don't think initially she meant to re-start things, even though I realised later that she'd never really gotten over him. I was her rebound man. Just as she was my rebound woman. The professor had moved to the Vaucluse so it wasn't hard for them to see each other and resume their affair. What she was doing became obvious. I think she wanted me to find out. After it was out in the open we talked, argued. What did she want? What did I want? In the end, she didn't want to give him up, and I had lost my trust. Voilà.'

'How awful for you.'

I was not going to grill him—tonight anyway—on what he meant by 'she was my rebound woman'.

We left the restaurant, returning to Pierre's car. When we turned into New Delhi Drive, it was like stepping into another world. Clocks, schedules and rat race strife were obliterated under the awning of Mont Ventoux and a purple sky. I was all excited again until I realised Alain's car wasn't in the drive. Damn him. Now I felt angry as well as upset…and spikes of doubt. The door was unlocked as usual, the hallway in semi-darkness. The first thing I checked was the answering machine, but there were no messages. Pierre carried my suitcase into the long room and I followed, unzipping it to extract my toiletries bag.

'Pierre, I'm going upstairs to have a shower and lie down for a bit.'

I was too shattered for any more talk.

'I'll wait here until Alain comes home.'

'You don't have to.'

'I will do anyway.'

'Thanks for staying. And for everything.'

I didn't want to be alone.

When I awoke it was still dark, the shutters drawn. For a second, I was confused about my whereabouts. Then I saw the outlines of his figure, his lips shaped in a faint smile, confident in his repose. He wasn't a night mover but remained as still as his sculptures. How much I wanted to rouse him, touch him, hug him. But I resisted the impulse and crept out as quietly as I could, wearing the robe I'd lain down in hours before, thinking I would only nap until Alain returned. A light sleeper, I normally would have heard the bedroom door squeak and felt Alain's weight on the mattress. That was jet lag for you. Downstairs in the kitchen it was freezing. I made myself a cup of vervain, which I drank at the table, the inky pre-dawn beyond the glass door like the void from which I'd just emerged. The silence—so complete after Hong Kong's rumble. I surveyed the kitchen, its haphazard order, the ashes in the fire, the slightly rutted floors.

His black-cover agenda lay on the kitchen counter. With a twinge of conscience I picked it up and leafed through, noting the entries during the period I'd been away. In his curlicue script, he'd jotted down a few client meetings, including the one for the previous afternoon. Fete was scribbled across the weekend just gone. Why didn't he tell me about it? I put the agenda back and sat with my arms around my bunched-up legs on the carved-out bench, ruminating, as slowly, light fluffed out the night and morning emerged. The unmentioned diary entry added to my insecurities. There I was, missing him madly, counting down the seconds, and he? In my mind his work wasn't a valid enough reason, even if that was being unreasonable. I washed my cup and went back to bed. I don't remember fading away. When I opened my eyes, the sun was streaming through the edges of the closed shutters and Alain was gone.

I leapt out of bed, running downstairs to the kitchen. He was listening to the radio, consuming a bowl of fruit.

'There she is, the beauty.'

He engulfed me in his arms.

'And you're the beast.'

Wriggling away, I berated him with my fists. I wouldn't let him off the hook so easily.

'You're angry about last night?'

I nodded, hands on hips for emphasis.

'Look, you could at least have left a message for me on the answering machine. You never have to work so much. You never see clients so urgently. Why yesterday?'

He raised both hands as if to signal a truce 'I profoundly apologise my darling. Of course I wanted to pick you up but I was caught up in something I just couldn't get out of. Not only was my meeting pushed back from the afternoon, but when I arrived in Roussillon, the client dragged me twenty kilometres to another house of his and he was so demanding that there wasn't time for even a quick call. But in the end it was worth it. I sold two kitchens. So we can afford to celebrate.'

'Seems like you did that at the party you had at the weekend, without mentioning it to me on the phone.'

'Come darling, I want to show you something. Then you'll understand why I organised some entertainment, very spur of the moment by the way.'

A glass of water in hand, I was hurried to the study. An airy space where you could easily wile away an afternoon, it contained a bookcase, the stereo system and a recently reactivated fireplace that Alain had broken startling new ground in adorning. There they stood in all their glory: the imposing flanks of a massive dog whose long and lean body branched into three heads and three paws, all in profile, mimicking the specimens of Egyptian art plucked out of a Pharaoh's tomb. The heads were twisted one hundred and eighty degrees in the direction of the rounded curves of the posterior. The sculpture was carved out of dirty pearl limestone from a nearby quarry.

'What do you think? I sculpted every moment I could to finish it before you came back. I launched it at the party. I didn't think you'd mind my having one since you're not a big fan of those things are you?'

How to describe its *je ne sais quoi* quality, the creativity that coursed through this canine? It was a one-of-a-kind masterpiece that would always elicit raves, even from individuals Scrooge-like with their compliments. That multi-legged, multi-headed creature was the undisputed showpiece of the study, which we henceforth called 'the three dogs' room.

That night Alain served my favourites—grilled lamb cutlets and champagne. Consuming the two together was a serious flouting of French etiquette. For the locals, champagne was an aperitif, never to be consumed with a meat dish *mon dieu*. It was only with his lamb chops though, Alain otherwise conforming to the custom of wine with a *grillade*.

We dined by the refurbished fireplace, whose filaments of flames cast shadows on the canine limbs. Alain was effusive with endearments, his repeated outpourings of 'I missed you' and 'I love you' sending my insecurities into a slumber. Afterwards, when the plates had been cleared, he led me back to his sculptural wonder for our own lusty celebration. Purposefully, I had removed the grate around the fire, moving the mattress close to the flames because I was cold. When a log disengaged and rolled to within an inch of my shoulders, Alain dexterously leaned over and shoved the wood away, saving my hair and a side of skin from a singeing. Not in the same league as the cockroaches but not so little either.

Chapter 13

Readjusting again to France, to the countryside, to the colder climate and the foibles of Alain's friends, I couldn't help but notice how nature was strutting its stuff. This was *vendange* time when the vines were at their most voluptuous, bursting with crimson fruit whose juices provided vitamins for hordes of insects. I had all the time I wanted to gaze at the tapestry of spectral autumn colours outside the windows, the plane tree leaves fluttering to the ground, the birds and bees gorging on the sun-drenched grapes that Alain didn't have a mind to harvest. And stare in mock meditation at Mont Ventoux. Come to think of it, this was a much more humane rhythm than Hong Kong's hectic pace, even if banks and repair shops took forever to render service. The cosmopolitan Asian city ran like clockwork, but the Cantonese were not exactly beacons of charm and courtesy. I realised I much preferred the slow-moving postal clerk in Mazan asking me how I was to a fast-reacting sales assistant barking at me for merely asking to try on a dress. Researching a book and working for Annie Leung were certainly less stressful than spending my days and evenings chasing stories for a news-hungry TV channel.

Once I'd completed my work for Annie I focused on the book. It was time to start the research so I jotted down the names of everyone I wanted to interview. Topping the list was Valérie, whose mother was best friends with Josephine. If there were any skeletons in the closet, she'd be the insider most likely to reveal them because she'd done quite a bit of her growing up in Alain's household.

From a curriculum vitae perspective her life breathed static. In all of Valérie's forty years, she'd never strayed much beyond Cavaillon. For two decades, she'd held the same secretarial post for a medical practice; for half that period she'd lived with her lover in the same one-bedroom flat. However, she was anything but dull. Valérie ventured to places far and wide in her extraordinarily fertile imagination that she let lose in her lapidary letters—these an expression of her passion for the French language, whose richness of nuance, cadence and poetic syntax she masterfully exploited on paper.

Every so often Alain would receive one of her long missives in which she described her feelings about art and literature, her thoughts liberally and lyrically articulated, without ever expecting a response. She was without doubt one of the most provocative thinkers I met in Provence and one of my favourite people. And she was a mine of information. What this petite, lively, voraciously literate woman depicted about Alain's elder brother was illuminating. Indeed about Alain himself. If the pair weren't quite the Brothers Karamazov, they were certainly a character study in opposites, in some ways bordering on caricature.

Both boys had been quiet as children for the Basque Italians, and in particular the paternal branch were, according to Valérie, a 'fiercely private, secretive, introverted and reserved lot'. Feelings were repressed not expressed. Proud to a fault, they were never ones to admit their weaknesses. They hid their pain and their wounds. Few words were spoken at home and silence was spread especially thick at meal times. Judging from the lunch I'd been invited to, it seemed Josephine had taken to Roland's jovial ways.

I was surprised to learn that Alain had been the more timid and delicate child, although he'd been caught not once but twice by Valérie in the act of kissing himself in the mirror. It was only in adolescence that, swooned over by girls, he morphed into an extrovert while Tristan passed through a 'dandy' stage then embraced simplicity and scorned the foppish ways of his younger brother. He let his hair grow, no longer cared about what he wore, turned away from the establishment and started smoking a lot of hash. Alain, a married, moustachioed insurance salesman, was meticulous about his clothes and appearance.

'So, has anyone told you about the brothers and the bets?' A shake of the head was Valérie's cue.

'Alain would sometimes stop on the road to give a lift to his brother, who used to hitchhike everywhere. Can you picture it? Alain in his BMW, dressed in a suit and tie, and Tristan, *un baba-cool*, totally dishevelled-looking. Now, if another passenger happened to be in the car with them—someone who didn't know the family—Alain would say, "that's my brother". The usual response was "no way, you're joking, I don't believe it". So they would place bets. Lo and behold, when the brothers whipped out their identity cards the person would be amazed.'

As twenty-something siblings Tristan stood out as the non-conformist, slipping into an alternative lifestyle where money was important only insofar as it provided largesse to his friends and something to smoke. He spent his salary on feeding and entertaining the regular comers who streamed into his ramshackle cabana in Salon-de-Provence, where dishes would pile up in the sink until necessity forced a clean-up.

'There was something of the natural leader about Tristan but not in a boisterous way. I know this sounds ridiculous but he really did radiate an inner force, through the haze of his hash smoke,' she smiled. 'He was an altruist, always ready to help others.'

Tristan paid no attention to women—as anything other than friends that is. Hard as I tried to prise out a love interest in his life I couldn't. Valérie recalled that when he was around fifteen he'd had a girlfriend for a few years. When I tracked her down, she told me they'd never been lovers. Thereafter he was rarely seen alone with a woman.

'No, he wasn't gay,' his nearest and dearest insisted; indeed his sexuality was a great mystery. Given his later embrace of asceticism I was inclined to believe that he was, for want of a better word, asexual. Simply not interested in pleasures of the flesh while his brother, from that first testosterone rush, could focus on nothing but sex. 'As a toddler I was already flirtatious,' he told me rather proudly.

Actually, there was one thing the brothers did have in common: their artistic gifts. Tristan's talent as a draughtsman was evident to the architect who had hired him straight from an apprenticeship in masonry. His boss venerated him, and for that reason excused his protégé's lateness, his unkempt appearance and his idiosyncrasies. For his part, Alain was sculpting out of wood as a boy meandering through the Givronex forest. There was one other trait they shared—extremism. But perhaps that is just another way of describing their artistry and tenacity.

I assumed I would have to tread delicately in questioning Josephine about her son. The impact of his death was still raw. It wasn't that long ago that on a backpacking trip to India her grandson Jean-Marc (Sylvie's son) had turned up at the ashram where Tristan had died and was told the tragic news, which he relayed back to Provence. This was one and a half years after his death. No one in India had contacted Tristan's family because they apparently didn't have any addresses or phone numbers. So I was pleasantly surprised when Josephine opened up to me quite readily during an afternoon visit to the house, not even attempting to hide the tears that rolled down her cheeks as she recounted memories of her eldest son.

'Tristan had been in India oh, about nineteen months, when I received a photo of him that some French people had taken in the Himalayas. This French couple had met him somewhere there and he'd asked them to send me a photo. In that photo he looked terrible, absolutely terrible. He was completely white, all skin and bones, like a skeleton. After I got that photo I had nightmares, I couldn't sleep. I was haunted by that horrible image of him. My suffering went on and on. Then one morning, I heard somebody in the hallway. I got out of bed and went into the corridor to see who it was. I looked. It was him. Tristan was standing there. He hugged me and he said to me, "Mother, you must stop worrying about me, I'm fine, I'm in good hands." He repeated this over and over again. Then he was gone. After that I was calm and stopped worrying and the nightmares went away.'

I thought this was fascinating because Josephine was no psychic, spiritual medium or believer in magical realism. Her feet were as firmly planted on the ground as Provençal potatoes but she swore to Tristan's presence as if it was the most natural thing in the world.

Her grandson Jean-Marc had brought back from the ashram the journal Tristan had kept during his first year or two in India. It was a keepsake as precious as gold to Josephine so I was grateful that she allowed me to make a copy. It was full of intricate ink drawings. One of them caught my eye. I stared hard at it, and then rushed to show Alain.

'Alain, look at this. He sketched the house.'

Tristan had drawn an almost exact replica of Alain's abode with the two plane trees outside, the windows, shutters, doors and garden all but identical to the actual layout. Alain studied the drawing with interest:

'This doesn't surprise me. My brother did have a weird sort of sixth sense.'

Nothing seemed to be beyond his prophetic powers. The written entries revealed little about Tristan's feelings, but quite a lot about daily life at the temple in Maksar where he'd initially lived, the monsoonal downpours, the mosquitoes, the heat, his impatience for news from France and the contents of the food parcels that his mother and sister had sent him from time to time. He was quite a gourmand then.

Sylvie titillated me with, 'Oh, I could tell you so many stories about my brother before he left.'

But she never did. She was as closeted as Josephine was open, perhaps thinking it would be disloyal to the memory of her dead sibling. Yet I detected anger and bitterness in her at Tristan's departure and the fact that he had never come back to visit his family. Utterly understandable emotions. Maybe she had regrets about not journeying to India, as Alain had done. She, Pierre and their mother knew nothing about the suspicions of foul play behind his death.

'Why say anything about this when there's no proof. It would only be cruel,' Alain said.

I wholeheartedly agreed. There would be no mention of any such thing in my book, although I liked to think that one day—on the ground in India—I'd be able to do some poking around to sate my own curiosity.

From the few occasions we'd met, I felt that Sylvie mistrusted me although to my face she was always personable. Once she even invited me over to stay for a night while Alain was away at a trade fair in Marseille. Her husband, Henri, like herself, was a heavy smoker, which he somehow got away with as a professional French horn player. Henri was a clown famed throughout the Lubéron for his wry wit and anecdotes, a role his physique definitely embellished, what with his exaggerated moustache, moon-shaped smile and spry shortness. I laughed not at his jokes, which I didn't get the full gist of, but at the comical contortions his face made while he told them.

His wife was a big fan, egging him on in his mode as raconteur. She, un-clownish and on the skinny side, was a performer of a different kind. By day she worked as a secretary in a dental practice and in her spare time took acting classes. They lived in an unpretentious house on the outskirts of unpretentious Cavaillon. The town didn't have the historical gravitas of Avignon but not the tourist hordes either. The first thing I noticed when I walked into their home was the mantelpiece above the fireplace. On it stood a wooden bust of a woman. Her lips were full and her breasts so perfect they begged to be touched. It was vintage Alain.

'That's not a sculpture of you is it?' I couldn't help asking Sylvie, pointing to the bust.

'I'll take that as a compliment, but no…absolutely not. I don't remember how it found its way here. I think Alain left it somewhere he used to live and it was dropped off here, waiting for collection. He never asked for it back though and it's found its niche. He must have been in his early twenties when he sculpted it.'

Pierre joined us for dinner that night and it was interesting to observe the sibling dynamics. Brother and sister had a close connection, certainly, and each their own prescribed roles, as is standard in families. Twelve years his senior, Sylvie babied him. But it was really Pierre who humoured her and her need to be important in his life, perhaps because she'd lost one brother and the other was too independent a cannon to count on. In his measured moderation, Pierre stood out. I wondered if he cultivated this as an identity. If you can't beat them, don't attempt to join them. Go the other way—admittedly the essence of how I'd sometimes felt with my siblings, especially Lilly. But it was wrong to pigeonhole him. I'd witnessed a side to Pierre that was candid and quite emotional. I was still digesting his avowals about his divorce. He seemed to pine for adventure—an armchair traveller who wanted out of the chair.

Sylvie had an array of framed family photos displayed on mantelpieces and side tables. It was only when I saw these that I was struck by the total absence of photos on show in Alain's house. It certainly wasn't for lack of material. Photos of the family—particularly of Tristan and Christophe—and former girlfriends were crammed into boxes stacked on shelves in the three dogs room. At Sylvie's, there were several photos of her and Tristan standing together, revealing a young man with unkempt hair and a face of sharp edges and wild good looks. There was one of her and a pensive, twenty-something Alain taken in someone's garden. In the photos, Sylvie's astringent eyes seemed to follow me no matter the vantage point, just as they did in reality. It was unnerving.

'So, how's the book coming along?' she asked as we tucked into her warming chicken and potato stew. It was a fair enough question, albeit raising my guard.

'I've just started the research, you know, talking to a few people. Getting some information and opinions.'

'Oh, who have you spoken with?'

Something told me not to mention Valérie.

'Your mother actually. She told me some interesting things, nothing you don't already know of course.'

'Hmm.'

She didn't enquire as to what those 'interesting things' were and her expression remained inscrutable, perhaps a testament to her good acting skills. I wondered whether she was having an internal debate—and if I'd been insensitive. After a few moments she broke the silence with, 'Will your book be an accurate portrayal of his life or a fictionalised account?'

'Well, as accurate as possible. It depends on how much information I can get. And I'll need to go to India of course. That will be crucial.'

She studied her fork, idle on her plate, for a good ten seconds before she replied.

'In my opinion, it would be better to fictionalise it. It's far too easy to make mistakes and misrepresent a life.'

How to respond? According to Alain, Sylvie had made no objections when he'd asked her if she minded my taking on this project. Maybe she believed I wouldn't do it. Now it seemed she did object, which was a concern because I had no wish to antagonise her. How come she hadn't been frank with Alain?

'Yes, it's easy to make mistakes, that's true,' I echoed. 'But I promise to be faithful to the truth.'

'What do you think about the book Pierre?' She turned to her brother.

Pierre raised his eyebrows and shook his head, indicating he preferred not to participate in this particular conversation. When I'd told him my intentions that afternoon at his mother's place, he had wished me luck without a hint of fractiousness or fear that I would despoil the memory of his brother.

'Pierre, I asked you a question,' Sylvie insisted.

Cornered, he faced her. 'You might learn things you never knew about. Things that would help you to process his loss.'

Sylvie turned ashen. It wasn't what she wanted to hear. I wondered what things Pierre was alluding to. Concrete instances describing Tristan's selflessness? Examples of how, as a sadhu and guru, he'd been of service to so many people, to whole communities? Later, when Pierre and I were in the living room, Sylvie having shooed us away from helping her in the kitchen, I questioned him.

'The purpose of the book is to trace the trajectory of his journey in India, right? His own spiritual path and the spiritual sustenance he gave to communities around the ashram?'

'Yes, to describe his life, the uniqueness of what he did, what his disciples felt about him.'

'And that's what I think will help Sylvie. To know that he followed a path where he was true to himself—which involved doing many good deeds for others as a holy man. And I'm assuming he did many. At least that's how I feel. She feels betrayed because he never came back to see us. But he couldn't have done. Sadhus have to sever all ties with their blood family, as I'm sure you know. It's one of their three cardinal vows, along with poverty and chastity.'

'You seem to know a lot about sadhus. Have you done some reading?'

'A little, yes. I had no idea, all the time that Tristan was in India, what a sadhu was really about. When my nephew told us about Tristan's death, I made it a point to learn.'

Reading up on sadhus was a vital part of my research. I'd had some books on the subject sent over from England.

'Did Alain ever speak to you about his trips to India, seeing Tristan? He's got lots of photos.'

He furrowed his brow—the mention of Alain.

'A little bit,' he said vaguely. 'I've seen some of the photos. My brother didn't look like the brother I'd known. He resembled…'

'Jesus…'

'Yes, with his long hair, the long beard, white skin covered with ash, skin-and-bone body…'

I wanted to know if he'd told Sylvie that Tristan had taken an oath to cut ties with his family in France. But before I could ask Pierre, Sylvie came back into the room and he changed the subject.

Back at home the following day I sat down at the piano to tackle some scales. I had in mind a little music, a little exercise before preparing dinner for two. Alain was returning that evening. I began to shiver despite the two jumpers I was wearing and the mild headache that had started in the morning turned into an unbearable throb. I seemed to have the makings of a migraine, quite unprecedented for me. I closed the piano lid and went to hunt for some paracetamol, only to discover that we had none. I couldn't brave driving to Mazan, and besides, the pharmacy was closed at this hour. What to do? Just then I heard a car roll into the driveway and shortly after Danielle's voice echo from the kitchen.

'*Coucou, tu es la* Ravinia?'

'Upstairs.'

My head hammered even more with the effort of shouting. She waltzed into the bedroom, a bounce in her legs and a jangle of her arms, arms that had embraced, encircled, gripped…

'I thought you could do with some company.'

Never had I been so glad to see her.

'What's wrong, you look as pale as a ghost sitting on the bed like that?'

As soon as I told her, she flew into action.

'Right, I'll get some stuff from home. You lie down. I won't be long.'

She must have exceeded all speed limits. Before I knew it she was back, handing me a glass of water and two tablets.

'Take these and rest. I'll stay in case you need anything.'

Rest I did. I even managed to sleep. When I emerged several hours later, she was in the kitchen reading a magazine. A pot of soup was simmering on the stove.

'Thanks for your help. My head feels much better.'

'Great. Come on, have something to eat. I went home again and brought the remainder of last night's dinner for you.'

She had also gifted us extras—some figs and apples. As she dished out the soup, I thought what a mother hen she could be—albeit a seductive one.

'Bad headaches. I only get them when I'm hung over, which is often enough,' she giggled.

'This is the first time for me, so intense like that. I have no idea what caused it. I only had one glass of wine last night.'

'Hmm. Maybe it's because of stress. How are things going with Alain?'

The odd thing about Danielle was that, as much as she was a chatterer, she could also be a good listener, which didn't fit the self-obsessed profile. Worse, she could be disarming, drawing out confidences that were meant to stay underground.

'With Alain? Things are good.'

'No stress, no complaining? That's reassuring. Because well, stress in a relationship can be a killer.' And she used this as a springboard to launch into an abridged history of her relationship with Alain, which I listened to with equal amounts of fear and fascination.

'I was the happiest woman alive when I started living with him. He was my dream come true. I thought I had the ideal life, everything I always wanted. A man with charm, looks, brains, who was crazy about me. But as time went on there were things that bothered me. For one thing, Alain tried to change me. And he always had to be right about everything. I started seeing Jacques just as a friend and we drew closer and closer together. He was a great person to talk to and so I confided in him about Alain. Inevitably we formed an attraction. We talked about having sex, we agonised over it and in the end, we gave into it.'

Change? Being right? Was she saying all this because she had to find fault with Alain to explain her betrayal? To peg the blame on him when it was her own destructiveness that had led her astray? I wanted to un-hear what she'd told me, because it was a spoiler. The rest of the afternoon had been fine. In fact she'd been a wonderful nurse, which only made my suspicions of her lingering lust for Alain all the more horrible and confusing.

Chapter 14

'We're here and we can't wait to see you,' my father greeted over the phone. His was the call I'd been waiting for and it arrived at eleven in the morning the day after my piercing headache. He and my stepmother were at a hotel not ten minutes away. They had flown in the previous night from London after a week of family time with Lilly, Nick and grandchildren. They were impatient to meet the man who had cleaved me away from a career in television and I was eager to reassure my father, still troubled about my trading one for the other which, in his estimation, left me one very vulnerable woman. I picked them up, brought them to the house, led them to the three dogs room and plumped them on the sofa—purchased as a concession to me—whose cotton covering had vivid Picasso-like motifs.

'You sculpted this?'

My father, analysing the statuesque canines, addressed the question in French to Alain, who had welcomed my parents with Mediterranean warmth, proffering hugs instead of kisses.

'And these others,' I chimed in, pointing out the new additions within spitting distance of the fireplace. They were all carved out of stone, a material that had momentarily replaced Carrara marble as flavour of the month. There was Diva, the earthen-red pregnant goddess whose head tilted heavenward in ecstasy and whose breasts spilled heaviness; and Cleopatra, half woman, half winged bird in flight. Both were portrayed in the throes of orgasm, not a trait to mention to guests, especially parents.

'And this,' Alain touched the sculpture, 'is the Marquis de Sade. I carved his face in two days.'

Haughty and smirking, he had a Roman emperor's hooked nose and a bouffant hairdo, as befit an eighteenth-century Marquis. He seemed to be the odd one out among the new crop, although perhaps not. He was the master, sneering at the females with the disdain so common among those who use sex and sadism as weapons of subjugation.

When we showed them our bedroom my stepmother honed in on Shiva, the omniscient god who, I liked to think, maintained household harmony and kept love blooming.

'The detail worked into the wood is astounding,' she marvelled. She herself was a painter with a keen eye for intricacy, so her comment carried heft. I was her interpreter for, unlike my father, she couldn't speak a word of French. My father had learned the language while studying for a Master's degree in cinematography in Paris in the early post-war years. In France, he'd been introduced to Picasso and had mingled with renowned writers, cineastes and communists. This was but one chapter of his richly unconventional life.

Alain was a gracious host and effusive with his guests but it was not in his nature never to provoke. He chose his moment on the third night of their visit, during a dinner of salmon grilled over the embers.

'In France, we have a very frank approach to sexual expression,' he uttered with the didacticism of a Sorbonne professor, not how he normally spoke. He'd steered a discussion of distinguished French writers and French cultural exclusion onto the subject of sex, using some of the famed cinematographers, sculptors and photographers to back up his assertions of how France was in the vanguard of breaking taboos and bringing a private matter into the public domain 'for the good of society'.

'*Bref*, monogamy in the strict sexual sense is seen as narrow-minded and we think that sexual exploration for pleasure is normal and an important part of self-expression.'

No doubt he thought the subject tantalising for my father, who was a sexologist, a calling that came when he was sixty-five years old. He had read voluminously on the subject of human sexual relations but intent on more formal education, had enrolled in a PHD program in sexology.

As Alain pursued his theme at dinner, I thought how my dad almost certainly shared his views and savoured exchanges like this although probably not with his children around. My dad might be Mr Liberal to the world, but I don't think he wanted to know—and I certainly didn't want him knowing—the sexual ethics of his daughter's partner, especially as they hinted at non-conformity in the bedroom—non-conformity, that is, in the Anglo-Saxon context. I cringed as Alain spoke about sexual exploration and bore down on my stepmother, who thankfully couldn't follow the drift of the men's talk. Diana was ten years younger than my father and had a youthful bearing and glow. She had great talent as a painter, her canvasses of oils and watercolours garnishing the walls of their house. Although she couldn't decipher Alain's speech, she wasn't immune to his charms and at one point whispered in my ear:

'He's very good looking. And I bet he's great in bed. Don't worry, you don't have to say anything.'

Inwardly I cackled.

Alain accompanied us on just one of our diurnal excursions, to Aix-en-Provence. They were a sideshow to watch, he and my father, both using precise arm gestures like Petanque players to make a point during their spirited talks. Shortly before we said our goodbyes, after four days of balmy weather and bouts of parental nostalgia, my father took me aside. Alain had left for a work rendezvous.

'You seem to be happy here with Alain. Are you?'

'No, not happy. In heaven. He is, well, larger than life as you've seen and I adore him, but it's not just because of him. I love the surroundings, the way of life and…the chance this is giving me to do something creative.'

'I'm glad to hear that. Certainly Alain is charming, intelligent and a talented sculptor. He seems to care for you. My assumptions about him appear to be wrong. You know that all I want is for you to be happy. I would hate to see you get hurt. Just make sure he's serious about his intentions and treats you well. You took a huge risk in leaving Hong Kong and a stable job for him. He didn't sacrifice anything. Don't forget that.'

Had he forgotten he was a role model for risk-taking? When I was three years old, he and my mother had moved us from Los Angeles, where he was earning large sums of money as a television producer, to Europe, where he had no job, no contacts nor even the right of abode. My parents couldn't stand the smog in Los Angeles or its hedonistic mentality. Primordially, though, they'd wanted to educate their children in Europe. It was either the stupidest thing to have done—to pick up and leave with three little children and no work—or the shrewdest. Personally I think it was the latter because it meant my sisters and I got to grow up in London with British accents.

My father's gamble had paid off, and I don't mean financially. With a tremendous amount of persistence, a loan and a little luck, he'd set up an independent publishing house specialising in history, science, healing, ecology, nutrition and psychology. His clients eventually included a potpourri of award-winning writers in their fields. Before my birth, he'd written for radio and produced headline-grabbing television programs. I was born in Argentina during a year-long writing sabbatical my mother had encouraged him to take. He was also a veteran of World War II. It wasn't the vicissitudes of the trenches on the Pacific Island of Guadalcanal that made him seem invincible to me but surviving the treacherous Pacific Ocean undertow after he'd been swept out to sea; and pulling through a long bout of cerebral malaria. The stories of his escape from death were often recounted to me as a child. They were part of family lore.

Yet here he was, very much alive and with a vigour and physique that did not match his seventy-three years. He was devoid of wrinkles and furrow marks on his brow, his warm, kind eyes expressing pathos and curiosity. He still had all his hair—albeit the white tinted brown—and a predilection for weighty issues, shunning small talk. He had salt-of-the-earth genetics. But he also swallowed mountains of supplements, exercised rigorously, ate virtuously and had tried every organic, immune-boosting concoction on the market.

He and my stepmother had recently left Manhattan for the quieter pastures of New England. Retirement was never a word that crossed his lips although his pace had inevitably slowed from the heady days when he ran an international publishing house in London. I adored my dad. I had always been a daddy's girl, always clamouring to sit on his lap when I was small, feeling safe and loved in the enclosure of his arms and never wanting to leave.

It was a week after the parental visit. The breakfast plates cleared, Alain and I were gazing through the kitchen's glass door at the garden, bathed in autumn colours, the plane trees shedding their crinkly leaves. The birds chirruped and the radio disgorged news, the only intimations of a world out there that was frantic and chaotic. Alain wiped away some crumbs that had fallen onto my skirt. I stole a glance at him—stole because I didn't like him to catch me in the act of staring. His face, as usual, was a blend of intent, action and illumination. It was unable to mask pleasure, or for that matter irritation and impatience, although as a salesman he could easily fake a smile.

'When I asked you what your father and step-mother thought of me, you answered me vaguely,' he broke the silence.

'Not vaguely. I said they liked you.'

'You said they liked my sculptures.'

'And the man who made them. They did like you.'

'You've been distant with me since they left.'

'What do you mean?'

The truth is that my father's veiled misgivings about Alain were ricocheting around my brain and I had been unusually cool towards him. I was trying to sort things out. First, my status in France and how I could legalise it since a tourist visa wasn't a long-term solution. But really, it was the issue of commitment that grated. Alain loved me but I wanted something more, something as durable as Carrara marble. His now-and-again dangling of a 'secret' was a giant tease. It was also extremely confusing, if not outright baffling, because he'd made it clear that ideologically he was opposed to marriage. His mind change must have happened after Brigitte, because with her he'd wanted matrimony. Facts and feelings wrestled in my head. It was only eight months since my move, too early for talk of nuptials, but then again some partners proposed after just weeks of knowing each other. And if marriage for him was only a chimera, then what? Was I expecting too much, too quickly?

'I mean,' Alain gently tapped me on the right side of my face just above my ear, 'that there's a lot going on in your mind that you're not telling me about.'

'You're right. I do have a lot on my mind Alain. Bureaucratic things for a start. I have no legality here, no security, no official way to work if I need or want to. I feel sort of…vulnerable.'

I looked away, glad I'd unloaded a little but worried I'd said too much.

'Look at me.'

'What?'

'I propose,' he strung the verb out, 'that we get married.'

I shut my eyes and opened them, ready to see a jokester, but this was no charade.

'Did you say get married?'

'I did.'

'You don't have to do this so I can stay here legally, or out of obligation you know. Because if those are the reasons I refuse. Besides, I know you don't really believe in marriage, having been married before and all that.'

'I rarely do things out of obligation. You're right that I don't believe in marriage—as a general rule. But this isn't general. This is very specific. I want to marry you. Ravinia.'

'And what about…what about…a child, children?'

'It's a negotiable subject. Meaning I am very likely to be persuaded.'

'Is that a yes?'

He nodded, smiling. There was justice after all.

'Come on,' he enveloped my hands in his—his hands were never cold. 'You haven't answered me.'

'*Oui*. If you really insist.'

Once it was decided, Alain wasn't keen on lingering. But when we went to the town hall in Mazan to make enquiries, we realised that marriage was far from a simple affair. There was a mountain of paperwork to process. Not only did I need the originals of half a dozen different documents that I didn't have, but they all had to be translated into French. And of course, there was the requisite publication of Banns at the town hall. The earliest we could do the deed, we were told, was March.

I didn't mind. I preferred a drawn-out erstwhile engagement. I wanted to savour the anticipation of a wedding rather than have it over in a heartbeat. And savour it I did. It followed me, a default setting in my mind, and sometimes I couldn't tell the dream from the reality because in this life I was leading they were one and the same. I'd shrugged off a promising career in television but I didn't miss any of it. Not for me the work-week rat race in Hong Kong or anywhere else.

I was a goner for the mornings when, before breakfast, we would lounge in our big bed and shower in the bathtub with full frontal views of Mont Ventoux.

'Bad girl bad girl,' Alain would scold in English, spanking me with feigned fervour if I ever so much as mentioned another man in passing, even the handsome local butcher who sold us the choicest cuts of meat.

'You'll never find anyone else who makes lamb cutlets like I do, and for that reason you'll never be able to leave me.'

Oh his lamb chops, juicy tender slabs of meat marinated in olive oil, thyme and rosemary, ember-grilled to heavenly perfection.

'You'll never find anyone else who can speak Mandarin and loves your lamb cutlets as much as me,' I joked back.

'*Je t'aime*, Ravinia…'

Ravinia. It was funny how I much preferred to be called my given name in French. Ravinia sounded melodious not onerous or perhaps it was just that Rai sounded guttural and aggressive, like an imperative. So I was Ravinia in France but Rai in England, where years ago I'd banned the use of my long name. I'd hated it from the moment I was mocked in primary school—'hello miss vagina' being the tag line. In secondary school, Ravinia was savaged for sounding like a snooty nineteenth-century nom de plume. It was hardly what my mother imagined when she'd chosen it, a final flight of fancy for her third and last child. The idea had emanated from Italian neighbours in Buenos Aires, where I was born. As a child I'd felt it unjust. Why couldn't I have been given a two or three syllable name like my sisters? Why a four-syllable behemoth? I knew my mother had been hurt by my refusal to answer to a name she considered exotic. Today, if she were alive, I would have given her free reign to call me anything at all.

Alain and I continued to frequent the club in Avignon, up the siren steps where men and women acted out their fantasies on the sofas and other surfaces. Even when we were inseparable, his eyes drank in the exuberant X-rated activity unfolding around us and as a matter of fact so did mine. Translated into sculpture we would have been two torsos melded together, only perhaps with the faces tilted away and the eyes peeking to the sides. The club was part of our collusion, our shared complicity, just as Alain had promised it would be. Naturally our sexual sorties were not for public consumption, Alain guarding them as close to his chest as a cultist his sect membership. I appreciated the fact that under this roof, job, profession and socio-economic status were superseded by a common desire to share fleshy delights. No one ever asked, 'excuse me and what do you do for a living?' before reaching out in exploratory excitement.

I was never worried about bumping into anyone we knew at the club, feeling sure that Alain wouldn't have chosen this particular venue if there was a chance of that, although the thought of crossing paths with Danielle flashed into my mind from time to time. However, reality did intrude once when I went into an office supplies shop in Carpentras. Wandering around the aisles in search of some fax paper I saw that one particular sales assistant was staring at me in a rather curious way. He looked familiar but I had trouble placing his face. And then it hit. He was a man I'd been with, had given a blow job to for Christ's sake, at the club. I nodded to him in recognition, counted to fifteen then dove for the door, embarrassed to the tips of my toes.

Chapter 15

Julia was the first of my siblings to pay us a visit. Alain was more than happy to have her stay with us for two weeks so he could put a face and assign characteristics to a voice he heard frequently on the telephone. On a summery October afternoon, I picked her up at Marseille airport. She'd flown over from London after a week with Lilly, a needed break from her physically demanding job as a massage therapist.

We hugged each other tightly but the truth was we hadn't always been close. In fact, I'd hated her—piano playing apart. Rivalry had asserted itself early on with numerous petty jealousies. I had, for instance, been the reluctant recipient of her hand-me-downs and I resented the freedoms she was allowed and I wasn't. But by far the worst, she'd had the audacity to fawn over Lilly and not pay me any attention. Our births were only twenty months apart, but from an early age she'd thrown her lot in with Lilly and who could blame her? They were a complementary fit: Lilly, extrovert, exciting, outshining us all since the day we were born and Julia, a bookworm and pianist with a crowning intelligence who sought to be more like Lilly—as did I. As young adults, their paths had sometimes deviated sharply and at times I'd been convinced—indeed hoped—that their polar opposite-ness would prise them apart. Julia, for instance, was a teetotaller against Lilly's penchant for snorting cocaine. But after the binges and Lilly's 'out of order' disappearance for days at a time, they'd always reunited, tuned in to each other like radio and receiver.

Being the third daughter and the youngest felt like a kind of punishment. When I was little, I'd fantasised about having a kid brother who would dote on me and share my hobby of riding on red double-decker buses. At seven years old, I did find a partner in crime, a girl who lived down the road. Our parents allowed us to go on outings to explore the wilderness—which was anything beyond Highgate Village. We would sit for hours on the upper deck of the first bus that came along, thrilling at the sights as the bus rumbled to its terminus.

I lost contact with the neighbour but in my late twenties found friendship with my sisters. I don't remember who started the long breakthrough conversation, who said sorry first, who was the first to cry. I know it happened in Hong Kong when the two of them came to visit me. I was surely the first to dish out blame:

'I felt completely rejected and excluded by you. Do you know how it feels to be a fly on the wall, to feel like you don't exist, that you don't count, that you're invisible? All I wanted was to be noticed by you, included, given some attention,' and so on. They blamed in turn:

'You hurt us too with your hostility and anger, shutting us out.'

'It was my way of paying you back for ignoring me.'

'You know, don't you, that we got into big trouble with Mum and Dad for leaving you out. But there's something you've got to understand. Our excluding you was never ever intentional, never ever done on purpose.'

Yeah, I got that. It's just how things were with symbiotic, soul-mate sisters.

It was a turning point in my life, being able to express a backlog of repressed emotions, letting them loose, having my pain acknowledged. But life is messy. The three-way dynamic—the duo plus one—didn't entirely disappear even as our one-on-one rapports grew roots that were strong and unshakeable.

Julia and I were much more alike in personality, sharing many particularities. Both of us were forever seeking a spiritual sense to our existence, maybe because, as introverts, we were more prone to self-doubt, a lack of self-confidence and internal angst. The intense connection we had formed in recent years was founded as much on our spiritual quests—through books, meditation, and enlightened masters—as a desire to mend fences.

Julia had the same reaction when she first saw the house as did most every newcomer: absolute bedazzlement followed by puzzlement over Alain's idiosyncrasies, such as no keys to any of the door locks and sculptures used as toilet-paper holders. Julia had breezed through her French A-level but she was reluctant to speak; her vocabulary was rusty and she didn't want to feel like a fool, which I well understood. So she listened a lot as Alain philosophised about sculpture, Carrara, Provence, books, history and cuisine. A slide show of emotions registered on her face, from fascination to scepticism and I knew she was mentally taking notes, observing all the while his ardour for me: the constant caresses and steamy glances.

'He's potty about her,' she told Lilly over the phone. 'Honestly, those two lovebirds can't keep their hands off each other.'

Even so, she grew a little jittery when she saw that Alain had his own very particular way of doing things.

'He's a little intimidating to be honest. I'm not sure I dare cut the cheese or bread since I might not get it right.' This was said with a laugh, although I could tell she was quite serious.

It's true that Alain was exacting—a perfectionist. There was an Alain way of doing things, which he considered the right way of doing things. But far from being a weakness, I considered this an assertion of his confidence, his belief in himself, his tenaciousness whose results were visible in the art and aesthetics around us. I'd strived at times for perfectionism in my work, but it wasn't my usual modus operandi. Nevertheless I had become more mindful in my movements, whether it was kindling a respectable fire or choosing delicacies from shop shelves.

Julia, a studious non-drinker, did dare, however, to sample a drop of Alain's high-potency snake brew, brought back from Ho Chi Minh City. It was kept in a glass container in the three dogs room and brought out for special occasions. I still had not mustered the courage to taste what was a guaranteed short cut to intoxication.

That October we were graced with the mother of all Indian summers. Enjoying the sunshine, we strolled along the cobble-stoned streets of Les Baux, lingered in the shady squares of Roussillon, and ambled around ever-engaging Avignon.

'This is where I play squash with Jacques and Danielle,' I said, pointing to the public facility outside the city gates as we drove past. I took Julia to meet Fred, the dashing young butcher in Mormoiron, whose lamb chops enriched our lives. I brought her to a yoga class in Carpentras and to see Alain's kitchen shop—I'd suspended my French lessons during her visit. We spent an afternoon horse riding through woodlands, the steeds from a stable twenty minutes away.

One morning we left for the Bouche du Rhône countryside, where a brother of one of Julia's massage therapy clients lived. We had a pleasant lunch with the brother and headed off just as a downpour got underway. We were passing through Orange when steam started streaming from the bonnet. I pulled over at the nearest shop and dashed inside to use the phone.

'Alain, we're in Orange. There's a problem with the car.'

'What is it?'

'Something to do with the engine. Smoke is coming out.'

'Okay stay right there. I'll come as fast as I can.'

When he arrived, he took one look at the car and threw up his arms in a gesture that didn't bode well.

'Ravinia and Julia, you should be ashamed of yourselves. This is what happens when it rains. It's only the steam escaping because of the contact of water with heat. There's nothing wrong with the car.'

We looked at each other, our embarrassment producing goofy grins. Our gaffe greatly amused Christophe, who was spending the weekend with us. Christophe was a keen spectator of the intellectual tugs of war between his father and I, with Alain vaunting the virtues of France and I the assets of Asia. Now Julia joined in, giggling along with Christophe as Alain took pot shots against the Anglo-Saxons, whom he liked to brand as an inferior breed just to rile me.

'Ah my son, never fall for an English woman, what a catastrophe they are.'

Alain had never stepped foot in England or America, but that didn't stop him from railing against them as a 'provincial pair' responsible for all the ills of the world, specialising in 'polluting the minds of young people with their crass culture and hamburger junk'.

France, naturally, was the repository of all that was tasteful in the West, although he denied to the depths of his being that he was in any way jingoistic, flaunting his irreverence towards politicians, priests, the army, big corporates, and any and all officialdom.

Hollywood stank but if a new James Bond film came out he would rush to see it, failing to see any irony whatsoever in this fact. He had great admiration for that indestructible secret service spy, but Britain?

'That washed up little island has never produced any noteworthy artistic genius ever.'

'Um, what about Shakespeare?' I countered. I'd been a diehard Shakespeare fan ever since seeing Much Ado About Nothing in Regent's Park at the age of eight. I'd grown up with him, studying his plays with devotional fervour in my English literature classes at grammar school. One of my parents' friends had given me a book packed with his quotes, which I'd kept on my bedside table. I hadn't been shy about sprinkling them into conversations and arguments, shutting up only when people told me how annoying and pretentious this was. After that, I'd kept the quotes to myself. (Sadly the book was lost along with some other possessions during my move to Hong Kong.) Alain knew I had a thing for the playwright.

'What, so you think Shakespeare was British? Nothing of the sort. He was a native of Brittany. His mother was in labour with him for ages and ages and it was agony, but amazingly his father was able to calm his wife, telling her to repeat the words, *j'expire, j'expire, j'expire*. Sure enough, it became her mantra, and so often and fast did she say it that it turned into JAKE SPEER. When her son emerged and she saw his perfectly formed face, she knew what to call her baby, the future bard.'

And what's more: 'You think the English were strong and were the first to defeat the Chinese? Pah. Way before the British stepped foot in China, 500 Frenchmen sailed to the mainland and defeated an army of one million Chinese. Their weapon? six-month-old Camembert. The odour made the enemy flee.'

Alain threw a number of dinner parties for Julia, never missed by Jacques and Danielle. My sister had plenty of opportunities to study this woman who wiggled her hips and torso incessantly, as if keeping her clothes on was the hardest thing in the world. I told Julia about her and Alain, their steamy relationship, their stormy ending and my suspicions of her lingering lust.

'I don't know how you can be so accepting of Danielle. I could never be like that if I were in your shoes.'

'Maybe it's healthy that they've overcome their past and remained such good friends.'

Hardly convincing but I lacked the courage to explain that she was my sometimes confidante as well as my always nemesis.

'How did she react when she found out about your marriage?'

'Not how I expected.'

'What do you mean?'

Shortly after Alain proposed to me in the kitchen, I'd volunteered to break the news to Danielle and Jacques, feeling a little guilty at how much I looked forward to the moment.

'Why so eager?' Alain had chided.

But he'd been eager, inviting them over for dinner two days later. Barely had the pair put their coats on a chair when, eyes pinned on Danielle, he'd made the announcement. I'd expected a frown, a facial freeze, teary eyes. Instead she'd given one of her pouty, plucky, vixen-ish guffaws.

'Getting married! You mean it's still done these days?'

She'd seemed unfathomably pleased.

'Getting married!' she'd repeated. 'Well, we've got to give you the party of all parties. What are you planning for a celebration?'

Was this expert acting? The focus on the fete the only way she could handle what I hoped was a clear and forever message? Alain had laughed, yet there was something in his expression that hinted at what, disappointment? Puzzlement? But it was only for a second.

'So, how much time do we have to prepare?' I'd noted her use of the word 'we'. I'd surveyed her like a hawk that evening, thinking that maybe she'd have a delayed reaction and would let something slip, especially with all the alcohol she'd consumed. But if anything, she'd seemed more spirited than usual.

'I don't understand,' I told Julia. 'She was pretty gleeful about it. Perhaps she doesn't have designs on him after all.'

'It does sound puzzling. One thing that I don't understand is how Alain doesn't see that it's inappropriate that she's around so much, let alone that she continues to flirt with him.'

'He gets it but it's complicated. They were good friends before they were…before they became lovers. And of course she works for him. And he's always saying that she flirts with everyone, not just him—and he does have a point there. She needs to be a magnet for men in general and her flirting does tend to lack discretion. Still, I don't think he gets how insecure I feel around her and how much her behaviour galls me. As the newcomer around here I lack balls. But slowly that will change. Especially after the wedding, at least I hope it will.'

'Well, here's to growing balls,' said Julia, clinking her mug of vervain with mine.

One night when half a dozen people were over, Alain asked Julia if she would play something on the piano. I looked at her thinking nah, she'll never accept. But to my amazement she got up, sat down on the stool and began to play. Her genius was the stuff of legend. Even as a ten-year-old the Mozart, Beethoven and Debussy she memorised resounded with technical perfection and emotion, winning her medal after medal at recitals and the gift of a Steinway piano from an unknown benefactor. She was good enough for the professional stage. But being a child prodigy came with baggage. At eighteen she quit playing, which was a great family tragedy.

'Why?' I asked my sister a decade later.

‘Because it was the only thing I felt Mum and Dad loved me for,’ she confessed. It didn’t matter that it wasn’t true. It was how she felt. She must have tinkered on her Steinway from time to time because her classical performance in front of us was flawless enough to halt conversation and wine glasses in mid-air. As she played, that sound, her sound…transported me back to our Highgate house, the magic of the music seeping through the living room door as my mother cooked dinner and I did my homework.

Alain took warmly to Julia and I was glad he made it a point to complement her. She never felt she was attractive, but oh, there were times when she was ravishing, when her skin was clear and smooth because Julia’s pores betrayed her emotions. Rash-like blemishes on her face were a proxy for anger, sadness and unhappiness, just as the lack of them signalled harmony. She wasn’t small-boned or long-legged; rather, her body was a mass of muscle, toned from massaging and regular gym workouts.

‘Maybe we should move to Provence, lead a less hectic lifestyle. Maybe it would bring on a baby.’

Usually she kept silent about trying to conceive. It had been hopes up, hopes dashed for more than three years now. They had done all the tests, had repaired some of the glitches, so now there were no mechanical issues, just angst. The fact that Lilly was so fertile must have grated on her but she never complained about it and what’s more, was a devoted auntie to Lilly’s kids—I had many more jealous bones in my body than she did.

Doug, her husband, was a professional food stylist and photographer from Colorado. He played the bass and had a passion for windsurfing. He and Julia had met seven years previously in Hawaii, which was coincidental as both were then living in Manhattan. Julia had attended a spiritual retreat near Hilo and Doug had been in the area to practice his favourite sport. They’d met at the house of a mutual friend, falling for each other against a backdrop of black volcanic ash and crashing waves. Julia and Doug gave each other a lot of space, the freedom to stretch their wings, but they couldn’t tolerate separation for long.

‘Come on, you love Manhattan and your work. You’d be chafing at the bit here.’

She was one of the most sought-after massage therapists in the city, her powerful pianist fingers relaxing muscles and seeping away stress like snow ploughs clearing roads. Over the past year, anxious that too much exertion might foil conception, she’d cut down, now doing at most two massages a day.

‘So, are babies part of the plan for you two, post-marriage?’

She said it lightly but I wondered if it hurt to ask. I told her about Alain’s initial refusal, which, from shame and pain, I’d kept to myself. But that was in the past. I described my elation at his change of heart.

‘What he has made clear is that babies are not for tomorrow. He wants to give it at least a year. And I’m okay with that.’

‘You’re lucky. Normally men who are reluctant about fatherhood—well in his case additional fatherhood—are not so easily swayed.’

‘He knew it was part of the deal I suppose.’

‘Do you think you’d marry him anyway even if he’d said no to kids?’

‘The decision would have undone me. I really don’t know. But he’d better not change his mind about children.’

I was sad to see Julia go. Provence was the first dedicated time we’d spent together in a long time, perhaps ever, and it was special in a way that I thought might never be recaptured. The recompense was her promise to return for the wedding, however no-frills it might be. Enjoying a pre-departure drink at a café in Avignon station, I gave her the parting gifts I’d wrapped that morning.

‘You don’t have to open them now.’

‘Just a peek.’ She tore the paper.

Inside the first box was an antique silver candleholder that I’d found in a shop in Avignon. The exterior of the base was etched with green filigree frogs.

‘A fertility candlestick. Frogs lay lots of eggs.’

From the other box she extracted a necklace with jagged shapes of moonstone and quartz.

‘Fertility crystals. Even if you have some, it can’t hurt to have more.’

She put the necklace on, blinking back tears.

Drinks finished, we said our goodbyes on the platform.

‘Alain’s a charmer and you’ve got a good life here,’ she finished on a high note. ‘Just stand up to Danielle and don’t forget those balls.’

Chapter 16

I suppressed yet another yawn and surreptitiously looked at my watch. Ten past eleven. It would be another two hours at least before any of our eight guests scrambled to their cars, their alcohol intake many times over the official limit, not that anyone ever paid this the slightest bit of attention.

Another dinner that was testing my patience to the limits.

They always began well, with some one-on-one dialogue where I could now confidently hold my own. But then the group dynamics took over, ending the tête-à-tête with the person next to me and creating a kind of sink hole. The swift volleys of argot that pinged from mouths elicited at times rollicking laughter or vociferous hoots. By the time I'd framed a response or a question to some point or other, the talk had moved on. I sat there, trying to look animated in my boredom, too sober for my own damn good as glasses of wine and then whisky were replenished before they were again emptied and joints did the rounds. Inebriation would have been a panacea for these prolonged evenings but my tendency to vomit before getting hammered put paid to that. What did provide stabs of adrenalin were Alain's caresses. Every so often he would leave his seat, come over to mine, plant kisses on my neck and whisper in my ear, 'I'll fuck you later.'

Alain had concocted a winner as usual. Chicken fricassee with olives, artichoke and asparagus tips. But his skills were half the problem. Delicious dishes tended to be dissected ad nauseam, part of the larger context of vacuous conversations about food, wine and fetes that dominated every gathering, seasoned with mounds of gossip.

'Ah, you've hit the nail on the head with this Gigondas. It has just the right tone, not too heavy, not too musky,' Benoit congratulated Alain after a first bottle was opened. 'It brings out the flavour of the chicken like the hen was reared on it.'

Every other person around the table (bar myself and Christophe) then pitched in with their reviews, bringing to bear their considerable expertise on the matter in terms of good vendange years and climatic conditions for the Gigondas, which then led to further discussion and further feedback, etcetera.

I loved to eat, but to discuss the entrails of every morsel I swallowed and the merits of this or that recipe? It was the same with vintages and grape varieties. A comment or two on the contents of a glass was fine, but an extended debate over this Côtes du Rhône appellation or that Bordeaux label sent me to sleep. Perhaps it was an Anglo-Saxon small-mindedness, and a certain maladroitness in the science of cuisine that fed my impatience over detailed discussions of delights prized not just for their gastronomic importance but also for their cultural significance. I wouldn't have minded so much if the conversational menu had been more varied. But what I considered meaty topics were off the table.

No one in this milieu seemed to give a toss about life outside Provence, let alone France. The rest of the world was irrelevant from the vantage point of the Vaucluse, intellectual curiosity a very rare commodity indeed. To me, the whole setup smacked of the very banality that Alain so despised. I often wondered how he, so widely travelled, so hard on the humdrum, put up with it.

'I do get bored at times but my friends keep me grounded,' he responded when I challenged him on it. To be fair, he moved in wider circles. In fact, Alain knew quite a cross section of people, including other artists, a smattering of intellectuals and even a scientist, but they were not local so we hardly ever saw them. Alain knew that I was restless, but I didn't want him intervening or altering the conversational flow for my sake.

Displaced by an elbow my napkin fell on the floor. I reached down to pick it up and for some reason looked under the table. Well, lo and behold. Eliane's fingers were stroking a protuberance in Antoine's trousers. I stared for a few seconds to be certain this was no illusion, then drew back up as discreetly as I could. Gregoire, Eliane's partner, was three chairs down from her, sitting next to Alain. From where he sat, Eliane's limbs were not visible, thanks also to a tablecloth that fell to the midriff. Antoine's live-in lover Amélie sat two places down from me, across from him to the left. I 'accidentally' dropped my napkin again to get another look. This time I worried I'd been too obvious but Eliane and Antoine—and all the other diners—were oblivious. Eliane's face was flushed but that could have been down to the wine. Feigning interest in her conversation I studied her, this hard-headed flirt, forever needing to prove something, a sign of what, childhood deprivations? Parental love denied or given short shrift? She was talking across the table to Alain—not a glance did she steal sideways, not an eyelid did she bat, but that hand must have stayed in place because she didn't raise it.

'It's outrageous.'

Something about some shelves she'd bought having a nick in them and the shop offering only an exchange of goods, not a cash refund. Outrageous? That's a bit rich. The target of her touch, meanwhile, wore a grin, which was perhaps habitual—I couldn't say as I didn't know him well. He worked for the French oil company Total as a deep-sea diver. He'd disappear for a month on an oil rig, then resurface for a month's leave at home. Broad shouldered, big-nosed and big-handed, he was good looking in the manner of a young Gérard Depardieu, with the same swishy cloak of hair. He and Amélie were parents of two kids, six and four. Amélie had a great smile revealing toothpaste-advert teeth and strength in her voice. She was someone whose ire you wouldn't want to ignite. Were the two poker-faced dinner invitees having an affair? Or was Eliane's sleight of hand the prelude to one? Eliane must have known she was playing with fire but did she care?

Really, I shouldn't have been surprised. After all, this was just another sexual subplot being played out at another social gathering, more of the same overcharged hormonal interactions. The air of sexual intrigue that suffused get-togethers, especially parties, was as thick as the conversational depth was thin. It was hard to ignore: the covert and not-so-covert looks, the innuendos, the sexual ribbing and the hands that touched body parts they had no business touching for a brief second in full view of everyone—and now the public 'hidden' gestures like the one I had just witnessed.

There was an element of Machiavellian *liaisons dangereuses* in the sexual machinations that went on socially, perpetuated especially, but not uniquely, by Danielle and Eliane. The men were hardly blameless. There was a rampant strain of male chauvinism and something else pertaining to the gang: an incestuous underbelly. I began to wonder if there was something in the water or the wine that fed it. All I knew is that members of the clique tended to date and mate with each other. For example, before Danielle, Jacques had spent ten years with Isabelle, who was currently living with Marc. Matthias the electrician had previously been lovers with Eliane. And Isabelle's father had spent a decade with

Danielle's best friend Yvette, who lived in Paris. Incidentally, Yvette was the sister of Danielle's former boyfriend (before Alain), a junkie who had died of AIDS. Not forgetting that Danielle used to be very chummy with Alain's former lover Brigitte.

Not all group members were implicated. Christine most certainly did not fit the hussy mould and her partner Benoit was no macho. Thus, I felt infuriated when a few weeks previously I had seen a woman—an acquaintance of Benoit it seems—come onto him at a fashion show staged by Christine in the gymnasium of a school. Alain and I were standing nearby, watching models parade hats and outfits along a runway erected for the occasion. Our attention was diverted by this woman, who disgracefully placed herself in front of Benoit, blocking his view. We caught Benoit's deft disengagement from the hands suggestively placed on his shoulders. She had chosen her moment, when Christine was fully occupied with her models.

Christine, who I liked a lot, had a big heart and a serious smoker's barrel-chested laugh and cough. Two years before she'd emerged from a long-term heroin habit and at thirty-six, suffered a raft of health problems, including arthritis. She was on medication for her maladies that caused her chronic pain. Of broad build, she was a little wide in the waist with proportionate thighs but so what. Yet in this milieu it mattered. There were no anorexics in the group but the female standard around here was trim and slim. Being overweight, even slightly, was dissed. The fact that she was at least a size larger than anyone else in the circle, including myself, was snidely commented on. I once overheard Yvette smear Christine as a 'cow with a lot of extra padding'. Her weight seemed to make some bad minds think they had carte blanche to her boyfriend—the intimation being, what was he doing with her when he could find someone with a better figure.

Christine had a cheerful disposition but it must have been brutal for her, this thin-consciousness stuff. It was challenging enough for me, and I had a lean frame, though I was certainly no twiggy. In Hong Kong, I'd dieted to fit into smaller-sized jeans, often feeling ungainly next to swan-limbed Chinese lasses. Even now, I'd assiduously cut out the carbs after consecutive days of mini overindulgence, egged on by Alain who was conventional French to a fault when it came to body weight and shape.

How the women in Alain's circle maintained their figures was a bit of a mystery. From what I saw at lunches, dinners and drinks they didn't deprive themselves of bread, cheese or pudding and there was no stinting on the booze. Tonight's menu, for example, translated into high-carb counts: toast bites, rice served with the chicken, bread to soak up the sauce, tiramisu and chocolate mints to finish. Plus all the alcohol. True, the women had smaller portions than the men and snacking in between meals was frowned upon. Maybe they didn't have breakfast and allowed themselves just one meal a day, surviving otherwise on caffeine and cigarettes. Maybe they endured stints of living only on asparagus. I assumed they weren't all that big on exercise because I never heard it discussed but that impression might have been totally wrong. After all, I did regular home workouts with weights, went for long walks and on occasion played squash with Danielle and Jacques.

Christine had confided to me that the devastation of finding out she couldn't have children had led her to drugs. Benoit was happy to have her above kids or anything else and they seemed a solid match. She'd found purpose in her craft, designing bespoke 'hats for every head'. She was bending over backwards to breathe life into her fledgling hat association, inventing ways like that soirée at the school to publicise her hand-made wares.

I hoped that Christophe, decent as he was, wouldn't be overly influenced by the sexual skulduggery that thrived around him. His father's input, I had to admit, didn't set the best example.

'Don't you have a girlfriend yet?' Alain had quizzed him this very afternoon at lunch. 'At your age I wasn't dilly-dallying but out there pulling *les gonzesses* (chicks). Ah, *les gonzesses*. Get busy *mon fils*, what are you waiting for? Do your father proud.'

Poor Christophe. His face reddened as Alain hectored him for still being a virgin. And then looked aghast when his dad offered to initiate him through the good offices of a prostitute. '*Arrête papa arrête, tu me gonfles,*' stop dad, you're really getting on my nerves, he attempted to shut him up. To his credit Christophe showed some sangfroid when Alain began to lecture him about how awful his taste in music was and how it was a sacrilege to eat at McDonald's.

'It's my life not yours. If you're not happy about my choices that's your problem,' he retorted. Alain, for once, actually looked stricken.

'Bravo,' I cheered Christophe, and to Alain, 'You know, you can learn a thing or two from your son.'

But in ways that were hard to fathom Christophe was obedient and had the patience of a birdwatcher. There he sat, next to his father, sipping a glass of strawberry Grenadine and stifling a yawn or two, but staying firmly put. On the weekends reserved for his dad, he would always accompany us to friends' houses for drawn-out dinners. He was almost always the only adolescent at the table and must have battled a great deal of ennui, but never once did he pressure his father to go home.

After the guests had finally left and Alain and I were alone, I told him what I'd seen under the table. He chuckled.

'Amélie told me tonight that she and Antoine were trying for another child.'

'Bastard,' I said, referring to Antoine.

'Why do you say that?'

'Why?' I was incredulous.

'Look, it was probably just a one-off. Doesn't prove anything.'

To me it proved plenty.

Chapter 17

One morning after he'd thrown open the shutters and returned to bed, Alain asked in that casual cum rhetorical way of his: 'Darling, what do you think about having a threesome at the house?'

'With a woman?'

'To start with.'

'Do you already have someone in mind?'

He raised his eyebrows, his face as always unrumpled by sleep.

'No but I like challenges. And in particular this challenge.' He encircled me from behind.

'What kind of…scene…are you thinking about?'

'Oh, a varied menu and full participation by all parties.'

His hand moved slowly southwards from my stomach.

'I authorise you then with a very important mission. Finding the right candidate.'

And my Pavlovian reaction to his touch brought that conversation to an end.

A few days later—on the first of December to be exact—Alain came bounding into the house all excited.

'*Chérie* I've found the perfect person for a ménage à trois.'

His blue eyes were agog, hands almost clapping. You'd have thought he'd just sold ten kitchens.

'You have? That was quick. Who is she?'

'Well, you'll never believe this but I bumped into a woman at Leclerc who I hadn't seen for a long time, about fifteen years in fact. Monique's her name. She and I had a brief fling once—that was when I lived near Aix.'

They'd spent ten minutes catching up on the decade and then he cut to the chase with a proposition.

'She agreed right away,' he said, limbs fairly twitching. 'She's charming and discreet. And just to reassure you, she's happily married with kids.'

I quickly did the maths. Fifteen years ago. She must be quite a bit older than me.

'And in very good shape for almost forty,' he added, as if reading my mind.

I marvelled at how easy it all was. Bump into a woman at the supermarket who you've already screwed, broach the subject of a threesome. She agrees and it's settled. I was fine with the fact that he'd chosen her, crediting him with good taste and finesse in such matters. The only minor consideration was the precariousness of the timing because the very same day that Alain had arranged our session we were staging one of his colossal parties, which meant hours of preparation and three days of rabblerousing, little sleep, people everywhere and alcoholic oblivion. But that probably just tripled his excitement. Alain was a softy for a *coup de folie*.

Waiting for our guest to arrive at noon on the prescribed Saturday, Alain fussed over my hair and the ensemble that had become my stock in trade for our sexual sport—crotchless tights, short skirt and revealing top. He was casually dressed in jeans and a kurta shirt, showered, scrubbed and scented with Armani musk, something he made sure never to run out of.

Look at me. I felt unrecognisable, sexually speaking, from the woman who had left Hong Kong. Not that I'd been an innocent then. But now, I wanted to indulge the whims, to cram in what I'd missed, to experience what could so easily be had. Yet there was something darker that propelled me. I was in silent competition with Danielle for desirability. If I became the exhibitionist I imagined she surely was, expanding the boundaries, open to everything, then I could hush the ugly doubting voice that taunted, 'It was only about sex.'

Wasn't there some hypocrisy and self-righteousness in all of this? Or was it merely confusion or illusion? There I was, damning the constant sexual shenanigans of the group, while partner swapping with Alain. No, I argued with myself. These worlds were far apart, yes indeed they were. The one was craven, malicious and destructive, feeding on insecurities and incestuous ness, while the other I considered healthy exploration that caused no harm to any of the participants. What Alain and I did was based on mutual desire, mutual respect, *entre nous*. Openly flirting with a friend's partner, treating crude sexual innuendos as harmless jokes, striving constantly for sexual one-upmanship, this disgusted me. The worry was that Alain didn't see the sexual chicanery around him as anything more than a bit of amusement.

Finally, we heard the approach of Monique's car and seconds later her steps on the gravelled drive. Alain greeted her at the door, brought her into the three dogs room and made the introductions.

'*Enchantée*,' she kissed me. She smelled good.

I'd been curious about her looks and demeanour, wondering if she was a Danielle-type personality (I hoped not) or very different, since all Alain would reveal was that she was blond, small and very appealing. Thankfully Monique was in the 'very different' category. She came across as soft spoken and demure, even though she too was dressed to entice: skimpy skirt, stockings and pumps. I wondered if she'd been in a threesome before. Maybe she was bisexual. Even though I was firmly in the hetero camp I couldn't say I wasn't attracted to women, certain women that is. And now that I saw her in the flesh, that included Monique.

We sipped champagne, put titbits of smoked salmon and pâté in our mouths and made small talk that had nothing to do with sex. *When's he going to get things going?* A moment later, Alain slid towards her, put his hand on her knee, and moved it ever so slowly along her thigh and up her skirt where he let it linger, to a warm reception I noted. Alain's adroitness in the execution of his role and the look of complicity he shot me were as seductive as anything in Carpentras' best confectionery shop. In the next heartbeat, he got up and we followed him upstairs to our bedroom.

There was a moment of awkwardness as we sat on the bed while he undressed—but then the maestro began choreographing so we didn't need to think too much about who should do what to whom. He took his time removing our attire, savouring the exposure of breasts and pussies. Monique wore a nothing-to-hide bra, the kind that barely covers your nipples; the kind that Alain had bought me with such urgency in various cuts and colours in the Cavaillon lingerie shop. She also had the same sculpted royal jewels look. In fact it was all over Provence, judging from the vulvas I'd seen. A pubic bush now seemed so fuddy-duddy. My god, I'd often thought, what must Alain have thought of me pre-shave.

He began caressing us in turn, feverishly aroused, which aroused Monique and I, bringing us together. We were a little timid with each other at first, becoming increasingly bolder as Alain helped himself to the parts of our bodies that were not being licked, sucked or touched with tongues or fingers.

From time to time I peeked at the mirrored wall, reflecting back our sexual asanas, and wondered which of us he was going to come with. I was pleased to discover that Monique was not a high-pitch moaner or an exaggerated thrasher; she expressed her pleasure more subtly, which I found appealing. She must have had done what we were doing before because her fingers and tongue knew what to do, how much pressure to apply and when to speed up and slow down. Alain penetrated her more—wearing a condom—but I was secretly pleased that he poured himself into me. After about an hour, she said she had to leave. We dressed and said our goodbyes.

'How did you like her darling?' Alain asked as she drove away.

'I would have preferred a little less makeup.' I wanted to muffle the praise. 'But you picked well.'

Our tryst was genuinely enjoyable. The same could not be said of the party. There were bad omens from the start, including my attitude. I was in no mood for a drawn-out, drunken, full-on fete. A little fete would have been fine—a blow-out night with a curfew, say, of mid-morning. It was the two days of carousing afterwards that I had an issue with. This time round I didn't feel like giving myself a pep talk. I didn't feel like being easy-going, flexible and go-with-the-flow. I felt belligerent and had tried stalling.

'Alain why don't we do this one after the New Year, in January when people need something to look forward to?'

'It's been about three months since the last fete. I usually hold four a year. Time to get going. A nice little send-away before some people go on holiday.'

Bite your tongue and pull yourself together. I resigned myself to the inevitable.

As soon as Monique left, Alain placed the chilli-filled cauldrons (borrowed from Pierre) on the cylindrical gas hobs. An hour later one mysteriously fell off the hob, spilling its entire contents on the floor. It was the first time this had ever happened. Alain had a fit at first and then shrugged it off. 'Half the amount of chilli means people will just have to eat more bread and cheese.'

At around five, Vicenzo's car pulled into the driveway. Yet again he'd motored over from Italy purely for the party. The first time I'd met him, when Alain had taken me to Genoa, he'd seemed humble and approachable, an amiable artist. But he'd been on his own turf then, arm in arm with his inimitably delightful girlfriend who, unfortunately, never accompanied him on his forays to

France. Now I considered Vicenzo nothing but a cavalier curmudgeon even if he was a talented sculptor and Alain's mentor.

The sheen fell off him in slivers, but particularly when Alain told me how his girlfriend worked to support him financially so he could sculpt, yet he would never dream of marrying her because he valued his freedom. Certainly, his unfriendly attitude towards me won him no plaudits. Every time he called the house and I picked up the phone he barked, 'Is Alain there?' never once asking how I was. In person he wasn't much different, barely tossing a word or a look in my direction, if not to ask for more food or wine. He was the only one who hadn't said a word to me about the nuptials, not even cracking a bad joke. I had no time for him.

The dress motif that night was the musical 1950s. Figures with wide-swing poodle skirts, Elvis shades and other retro effects poured into the house. Costumes were a code for anything goes, including the come-ons and coquetry and the harder core stuff. Around two in the morning I went up to the top floor to relieve myself, finding the downstairs toilet perennially occupied, probably only half the time for its designated purpose. My needs taken care of, I was just about to go back down when I noticed that the door to Christophe's room was firmly closed. That's funny. There was a problem with the door jamb that Alain hadn't gotten around to fixing, which meant the door couldn't stay shut. Christophe himself was in Miramas.

Something's wedged against the door from the inside. I tiptoed over and listened. Was it the figment of my fantasy or could I hear noises? I should have gone downstairs, rejoined the crowd, but the devil was in me. I pushed open the door, which gave way easily—a single book being the barricade. The bedside lamp was on, illuminating two semi-naked bodies on the bed, the woman astride, her breasts billowing out of a chemise. I recognised the beard: Vicenzo's. I stood riveted, shifting my eyes from the bodies to Christophe's Olympique Marseilles football t-shirt lying crumpled at the foot of the bed. The woman, who hadn't budged, turned her head to glare at me. She was vaguely familiar, a face I'd seen at parties. Vicenzo's succinct sarcasm cauterised my stare.

'I think you can see we're busy.'

Without mouthing an apology I left, wondering if they'd put the book back in place. I'd really made an enemy of him now. I mulled over whether to snitch to Alain but thought better of it. He might chastise me for intruding. Maybe he wouldn't consider what Vicenzo was doing was cheating because maybe in

Vicenzo's eyes it wasn't. His girlfriend might know about his infidelities—I assumed this was not a one-off—and tolerate them.

Later that morning, when the sleepover set had risen, there was Vicenzo, sipping his coffee in the kitchen, laughing and joking with Alain as if nothing had happened—which in his mind it hadn't. I only hoped that Vicenzo's influence on Alain didn't extend beyond the boundaries of art.

Chapter 18

For Alain, a voyage over Christmas was de rigueur. His previous trips were a mixture of wanderlust and, as he frankly admitted, plain lust. This winter we'd decided to break with tradition and stay put. French discontent was boiling over. Everyone was on strike, or threatening to go on strike, including air traffic controllers and train drivers, putting transport in and out of the country in jeopardy. To hell with that, we thought. Our honeymoon was only a few months away.

The Sunday afternoon that Alain brought out the projector and the rollup screen, snowflakes were pounding down, coating the bare branches of the plane trees and the leafless vines. How barren the landscape looked in the dead of winter, an endless palette of browns and greys, not a vivid colour in sight. Propped against sequined cushions in the Indian corner, I watched slides of Alain's Brazilian flight of fancy six years previously, to a running commentary and conflicting feelings.

'That's Joao, the legendary master who taught me capoeira in Salvador de Bahia.'

Judging from his protégé's skills, the maestro deserved Alain's accolades.

Slides of cities, pampa, jungle and beach came alive on the screen, backdrops for the cast of incomparable characters he had met. And then a woman like no other.

'Who's she, a conquest?'

A cacao-skinned beauty sat sidewise on a low wall, beyond which was a sandy enclave. Her face was turned to the camera, her expression a mix of Lolita and Gina Lollobrigida.

'That's Zuara and the truth is, she seduced me. We met in Recife, at a café where she worked. She asked if I wanted to meet for a drink when her shift was over. I couldn't very well refuse.'

‘Poor you, what a sacrifice. She looks very young though,’ I tut-tutted, her youth making me feel middle-aged.

‘She told me she was twenty-one but who knows? Brazilian girls grow up quickly.’

Next was magical Madagascar, a ‘trip of a lifetime’ shared with Vicenzo. I felt like I’d been to the Ile aux Nattes, so much did he rave about it. On this Indian Ocean speck, he’d lived in a bamboo hut on the beach, ate the fish caught by his fishermen friends, sang under the stars at night and made love to the Malagache mulatto he’d brought with him. The song that he’d composed about the island, the song he’d first sung to me in Vietnam, was my singular golden oldie.

Alain described his holiday with Danielle, their month zigzagging across Cuba and I thanked my stars he had no slides. When he said they had been constantly, if indiscreetly, approached—on the streets, in restaurants, even at bus stations—by men and women, Alain made it seem as if sex was the favoured sport of these islanders, even more so than for the French. No way was I going to ask if they had accepted any of the invites.

Several months after their split Alain had gone to India at the behest of Arjun, the most fervent of Tristan’s followers. The same Arjun that Alain had mentioned to me in Paris. Alain had attended the festival of prayer and celebration organised by Arjun on the second anniversary of Tristan’s death. The festival took place near the village where Arjun lived, in the foothills of the Himalayas bordering the jungle. With Alain’s camera, someone had taken snaps of this ceremony. In one slide, Alain was captured sitting alone, with a faraway Heathcliff gaze. He looked so darkly appetising it was unjust.

‘Alain, why do you look so sad here? Was it because of your brother?’

‘That was a bad period for me. I was still traumatised by the break-up with Danielle.’

I was sorry I’d asked.

There were snippets from that India trip, however, that were humorous. Alain had accompanied a young sadhu called Shiva Shankar to the place in the jungle proper where Tristan had lived on and off for four years, among wild animals in hellish heat and bone-chilling cold. The two of them had set up camp in the exact spot where Tristan had slept, which was a veritable shelf raised above the riverbed, framed on one side by a huge banyan tree whose canopy formed a natural roof. The sadhu had told Alain that in the cooler night air the big animals liked to come out to play…and feed.

'We were lying in our sleeping bags when all of a sudden I heard ferocious growling. It seemed that two tigers were fighting nearby, down below on the banks of the river. Their rumblings grew louder and fiercer. It was a moonless night, pitch black except for the flames of our fire. All of a sudden Shiva Shankar moved closer to me and said wickedly in English, "Tiger coming to eat French meat."'

Alain shook with laughter in the telling of it, and so did I.

India. I had tasted it: the impossible chaos, crowds and colour of a land, actually many lands, which remained a riddle of poverty and beauty. And like no other place on earth. The initial encounter with India is a bit like getting your first period, profoundly transformative. I was fourteen when my father, through his work, procured four free tickets to Bombay. 'Take your daughters,' he told my mother.

I will never forget the bumpy ride into Bombay from the airport. The site of a never-ending sea of filthy plastic and cardboard shacks where people slept, ate and shat was both brutalising and mesmerising as a first experience of Third World poverty. No slides or photo albums could ever attempt to sum up the momentousness of that voyage, from which sprang my passion for travel.

Whatever I could save from a medley of part-time jobs, starting at age sixteen with my undergraduate studies, I spent on overseas travel. I funded all of my trips, each one feeding my zeal for the next. I had passports so thick with inserts they stretched into accordions. During the year I spent in Taiwan, I earned the cash to travel by teaching English alongside my Mandarin studies.

That snowy Sunday after Alain rolled up the screen I fetched some of my photos—some neatly organised in albums, others in no particular order. Alain began riffling through the snaps I had taken with my dinky instamatic camera and honed in on the visuals from Tibet.

'Tibet. One place I'd love to go.'

I was twenty-three at the time, travelling on my own, and afraid of very little. Getting to Tibet had been half the fun. In that era, the only overland access point into the country was from godforsaken Golmud in Western China. From that remote Qinghai town it was a heart-racing, two-day bus ride over mountain passes that I thought the wheels would never be able to negotiate. That feisty old bus pulled into Lhasa at nine in the morning on a sunlit day, the altitude proving even more dizzying than the vertiginous ascent. After a week in Lhasa, I'd decided to trek overland to Nepal.

'I was told there was very little food outside of Lhasa so I bought what I could find in the city markets, instant coffee, powdered milk, bread and honey. And it was true. There was hardly any food, although there was plenty of yak butter tea. Horrible,' I grimaced. I didn't know the French word for rancid.

'This photo. It was taken near Gyantze, the third largest town in Tibet,' really just a clump of mud-brick dwellings and muddy lanes. 'This is the rocky hill—a mini mountain—I climbed.'

When I'd reached the summit, it seemed to me like I had the world to myself. I'd looked way up and way down over a stunning mountain and valley landscape devoid of humans. For countless minutes I'd sat on the brown, barefaced rock and stared, trying to imprint the intensity of it.

'After Gyantze I met an Australian, that's him in the photo.' You couldn't tell from the image how nimble and resourceful this pink-cheeked, stocky lad was.

'Lucky for me, he was also going to Kathmandu so we joined up. To cross Tibet, we had to take any transport we could find, buses, tractors, trucks, donkey carts but a lot of the time we just walked.'

And walked and walked, making the dizzying descent from the barren Tibetan plateau across the Zhangmu border point into the semi-tropical valleys of Nepal—all on foot—shedding clothes as we went. Down, down, down, from the ear-biting cold to the pungent humidity.

'At one point, we had to cross a stream up to our waist, holding our bags up above our head. Along the way there were, I don't you how you call them. These things that stick to you and drink your blood and that you have to pull off. Leeches in English.'

'*Sangsues*.'

'*Sangsues*,' I repeated. 'Every five minutes we had to stop and burn them off. We tried to cover our skin. But still they stuck to us.'

'You're a warrior, you know that?'

'In Tibet we slept on floors, mostly in people's homes. Inside they lit fires. The smoke burned our eyes. There was no water, so we couldn't wash, not even our hands. And the toilets…they were holes in the floor on the roof, in the open air. You had to climb ladders to get to the roof. It was very difficult at night. My food ran out. We had to drink a lot of yak butter tea.'

‘When we finally reached Kathmandu, we looked like…’ I scrunched up my face. We’d been dirty, bedraggled and beyond exhausted, but exhilarated. That visceral high of having a shower after three weeks, the sensation of hot water on the body, of a bed, of being able to eat croissants and veggie burgers and drink sweet lassies had been a Shangri La. Our survival no longer an issue, and with some precious privacy, the Australian and I had at last been able to sleep with each other, the romance ending when he split for India.

‘My little adventurer.’ Alain cradled my face. ‘I think I’ve met my match. We both like to stretch the boundaries. We are both made of the same mettle, *non*? Someday I’ll take you back to Tibet, and you can show me your mini mountain.’

Sometimes in life you know when you’ve reached the top. You know that the moment is unparalleled. At other times, you realise only afterwards that you’d scaled the pinnacle and there could be no climbing back.

Chapter 19

'There she is everyone, look!'

From the dining table in the long room, I pointed to the cropped glass window. The stubborn metallic clouds had dispersed, revealing the smooth upper lines of Mont Ventoux. My talisman had been under cover for a good part of the winter and even early spring, but on this blustery March morning the clouds had answered my silent request. We were a smorgasbord of food and faces, which swivelled as I made my excited pitch.

'Very spiritual,' Julia nudged Lilly, referring to the mountain.

'A good omen for tomorrow,' assured Lilly, staring out the window.

'Never mind the wedding. It would have been a sacrilege for you to come here and not see Mont Ventoux.' The thought had depressed me.

'It's a beautiful day,' Alain interjected. 'Why don't you take a walk to Mazan this morning?'

'Us? Won't you be coming?'

'I thought I would sculpt today. Get back to my Buddha.'

He was fashioning him out of white marble, a material once again elevated to favourite, stone having been discarded. My family's here for just a few days, surely you can wait till everyone leaves to sculpt, I felt like saying, but held my tongue. I could see that Alain was elsewhere, his silence and distant gaze giveaways. He needed to be alone, an antidote to the stresses—happy though they were—of the past few days and the build-up to tomorrow's climax. He'd had less time to sculpt of late, the administrative demands of La Belle Cuisine consuming more hours, much to his frustration. To this I ascribed his recent heightened moodiness and testiness with me, not linking it to nervousness about the nuptials.

He'd done his share of the legwork for our visitors, ferrying them from Marseille airport to the house in a friend's Peugeot station wagon. Unfortunately the contingent flying in didn't include Julia's husband, who'd been unable to wriggle out of a work commitment in New York. Also absent were my father and stepmother. I hadn't asked them to come because they'd only recently made the pilgrimage to Provence and I sensed they'd be relieved to be off the guest list, but they sent hearty congratulations from afar.

The previous afternoon we had taken everyone into Carpentras, stopping at shops and a distillery for a *dégustation* of a local vintage or two. We'd also shown them La Belle Cuisine. Lilly, predictably wowed, had sucked in lips as she ran a hand over the pink Provençal surfaces.

'I'd love one of these kitchens.'

'Reckon you could ship one of these to London?' Nick had asked.

I hadn't seen the kitchens in a while because my French lessons had stopped in mid-January. My tutor had found full-time work and I wasn't up for a replacement. I'd given him a glowing reference, my spoken French now pretty decent—unlike my bank balance.

'You've got to come to London,' Nick had told Alain. 'We'll have ourselves a couple of nights out on the town. I'll take you to one of my tattoo parties. You've never seen anything like it.'

Nick's removable tattoo business was paying the mortgage on their house in Muswell Hill and then some.

'Tattoo parteez?' Alain had echoed, probably imagining women in various stages of undress parading their patterns. '*Chérie*, we go to London.'

That evening Alain had prepared his trademark ember-grilled lamb chops and salmon, washed down with bottles of red and white Burgundy. He'd been on form, captivating my family with a rousing history of the house and his sculptures—in English.

'This one you see? This my first marble sculpture.'

He'd pointed to the long spiralled shell surging from the fountain.

'This, the cat (the beautiful Bali Two) and this, my Iran horse. I make this stone sculpture of dogs,' he'd continued, standing in front of the three dogs fireplace.

'Aaaah, here is Diva.'

The pregnant goddess stared heavenward in ecstasy.

Gravel, grass and sand dust crunched under our feet as we walked in two formations, Julia and I in front, Lilly and Nick behind. We followed the path that bisected bucolic pasturage, passing family-owned farms and fields sprouting skeins of colour, erasing the drab of winter. It was like a scene from Louis Bunuel's film The Discreet Charm of the Bourgeoisie—the friends walking along country roads, walking and sweating, walking and sweating—only we weren't dressed in elegant suits but jaded jeans, and we weren't bourgeois. Nick yearned to be, but his cockney accent gave him away, and he couldn't have cared less about table etiquette, or any etiquette, but he did earn more money than any of us and we all assumed he'd be wealthy one day. We combed the cobble-stone lanes of Mazan up to the remnants of the wall that encircled its medieval quarter and down to the two pre-Roman stone gates, still standing. On our way back, we passed the town hall where our vows would take place. It would be a simple civil ceremony followed by a celebration with family and friends at the house. Even this was a concession from Alain, who had wanted only two witnesses and no fanfare at all.

'I still can't get over the massive change you've made.'

That was a Lilly statement of approval.

'Which would make a good book by the way. From crazy urban Hong Kong to rustic Provence.'

More like sex-fuelled Provence I thought, suppressing the urge to blurt out the details of the demi-monde I'd joined. During Julia's previous visit, there were moments when I'd come close to revealing the craven sexual script that went together with the pastis and parties and my disgust over it. The script enacted by Danielle and others over and over again. The feeling that I was being sized up for my abilities to sexually captivate Alain as much as she had because everyone was constantly reminded of her seductive charms. The feeling that it was fine to fuck your friend's lover behind their back.

But I had always held back. I couldn't tell Julia half the story and keep silent about the club, sauna and beach. Not with a clear conscience anyway. What if my new sexual normal was taken to be abnormal? That was unlikely though. Julia was open-minded and shocked by very little. And Lilly? What hadn't she done?

'You've all heard of the Marquis de Sade of course,' I said as we approached the Place Napoléon. 'Well, you'll see the family's chateau in a minute. It's now a retirement home. The Marquis' father and uncle were born in Mazan and the man himself spent quite some time here, entertaining his friends and putting on theatrical performances.'

‘I’ll bet he threw some wild parties,’ guffawed Nick. ‘Must be fun to have a sadist around to jazz things up.’

‘I wonder if the women in his circle would have agreed with that,’ Julia retorted.

‘Well, he seems to have been a night owl. Legend has it that while the Marquis was shacked up in his chateau, lamps stayed lit all night, shadows of bodies visible from the windows, the moans and thwacks keeping the guards well amused.’

I was only repeating what Alain had told me. We idled on the pavement in front of the property, ringed off from the road by a beefy wall higher than our heads.

‘Let’s take a look inside,’ ventured Nick, always up for vaudeville. We went through a gate, beyond which lay an unkempt garden, brambles, bushes and trees forming a cover of darkness. A path leading up to the entrance cut through overgrown thicket. The chateau walls were stained a clottish brown, and were crumbling in places, birds’ nests poking out from some of the upper ledges. The setting wreaked neglect and I wondered about the men and women living out their last years in this once-proud family estate. Looking up at one of the creviced windows, I froze. A pair of eyes were staring back at me through the dirty glass. Eyes that weren’t welcoming. It was a woman’s face. Or was it a ghost?

I looked away.

‘Come on, let’s go back. It doesn’t feel right to be gawping,’ I gathered the herd. ‘We’re trespassing.’

‘Hey, I want to check it out. It might be the perfect place for my mum in a few years’ time. More of an excuse for us to visit.’

‘Honestly Nick,’ Lilly was exasperated. ‘We’re leaving.’ I was surprised by her reaction. Normally she had no such inhibitions. Perhaps she’d seen those eyes too. Nick held his ground as everyone headed to the road. ‘Bye’ hooted Lilly. Reluctantly, he followed us down the path to the gate.

Flinging open the shutters, Alain leaned forward into the air.

‘*Un temps magnifique*. It’s a little windy but at least we won’t be needing umbrellas.’

I clocked his good mood. *Dieu Merci*.

‘You mean for the something special happening today?’

‘What something special?’

'Come here and I'll remind you.'

Alain played at resisting.

'Isn't it bad luck to do it before we exchange vows?'

'I thought you weren't superstitious.'

'I'm not, but I'm covering my bets.'

Instinctively I instigated sex but my focus was elsewhere, on the drama in my head. Married. In just a few hours. Everything in my life suddenly seemed conspired towards this day. The weight of it all. The weight I assigned to it. Really, I was just another over-excited and over-dramatic woman on her wedding day, blissfully hopeful about the future. The future…him and I…waking up together for always…a couple of tots, two would be good. What a paradise for them, the pure air, nature, the space to play, ride bikes and run around. What an imaginative, creative father they'll have, exposing them to the wonders of sculpture, capoeira, music, speaking to them in French so they'll be bilingual. Big brother Christophe, he'll be a good role model, we'll travel around the world together. I'll write from home while Alain sculpts, maybe continue working for Annie-Leung. He'll outgrow the sexual escapades, be a responsible father because he knows what's involved…

Our lovemaking over, I came back down to earth although the reverie didn't completely fade. Gazing out from the bath, I half expected to see fairy lights strung around Mont Ventoux and a sign across the summit saying: 'Congratulations to the bride and groom.'

Breakfast was a boisterous affair. Normally Lilly would have been slicing bread, breaking eggs into a bowl and brewing tea or coffee while we were still rubbing sleep from our eyes, but we managed to subdue her, relegating her tasks to relaxing in the long room while we prepared the food. Barely had we finished when the groom's 'first man' arrived. Franco was accompanied by his girlfriend. The fact that Franco had a girlfriend was a *cause célèbre*. After two forlorn years, he had fallen in love with two females who both wanted him—full time. He double-dated for a good six months, incapable of choosing between them. Alain joked at his predicament.

'He's gone from famine to feast, let him enjoy it although it's a good thing that he has no job because two women are work!'

Finally he had dropped the much younger university student in favour of a dynamic mother of three children by two different fathers. She was a virtuoso at the piano, which she taught for a living, and was passionate about art, culture and travel. For these factors alone, I could see why Franco had opted for her. Plus she was pretty and small, which was good for short and stocky Franco.

Franco had moved in with her because he no longer had his house. The municipality had pulled it down, much to his chagrin. In their topsy-turvy household on the fringes of Marseille there was kids' clutter everywhere. It reminded me of the nursery rhyme 'the old woman who lived in a shoe, she had so many children she didn't know what to do,' only his girlfriend wasn't old but thirty.

Olive-skinned, shaggy-haired Franco was warm and engaging, the opposite of Vicenzo. A smile always creased his face and a joke tottered off his tongue. He could be a bit of a macho brat but I gave him enormous credit for taking on a brood of children that he seemed a genuinely good father to. I don't know what he thought of the wedding, but I knew he was happy about the trip that Alain and I were planning afterwards. He'd volunteered to look after the house while we were away, ravenous for some alone time with his drums.

The ambiance at the house was suitably festive. We were the jolly adults in Renoir's Luncheon of the Boating Party. Joints were rolled and passed around, Julia and I the only abstainers. While the women wagged their tongues—my sisters talked the tempo of a fast-forwarded tape—Nick fiddled with his video camera. Danielle made a splashy entrance, her black Marilyn Monroe ensemble maximising the contours of her Madagascar tan.

'*Coucou*,' she crooned, and made the rounds of kisses, jangling her bracelets as she bent her face down or lifted it up, finishing with a '*ca va*'? before targeting the next cheek, reserving a particularly bright smile for Alain. She was still on a high from a month-long holiday with Jacques to Madagascar, photos of which she had practically tugged at my sleeve like a toddler to show me. Much as I didn't relish her presence, it would have been unthinkable not to invite her.

At the penultimate moment, I went upstairs to put on my dress, a mesh of aquamarine, purple and green Thai silk. It had a wide V-shaped neckline, was puckered in tight at the waist and fell to just below the knees. The dress was the pricey custom-tailored castaway of a Thai girlfriend of mine who had given it to me years before. I don't think she'd ever worn it, deciding it wasn't her style. But it was mine. Alain had never set eyes on it because I was saving it for a special occasion. My only accessory was a wide-brimmed, violet velvet hat made by Christine.

Entering the kitchen I expected a 'wow'. Instead, Alain did a double take, eyes almost popping out of his head.

'What's this? I'd prefer you to wear jeans than this…this horror. It's awful.' His mocking remarks were audible to everyone.

'You don't like it?'

My astonishment quickly devolved into a crushing feeling of failure. I looked down at my dress as if seeing it for the first time. Were the cut and the colours ugly? The style inappropriate? The length unbecoming? What was wrong with it? But I couldn't find fault. Nor had my sisters when I'd shown it to them the previous day. They'd heaped on the praise. All three of us couldn't have bad taste surely.

Everyone was silent. It was bad enough that he'd vetoed the dress I'd chosen, but doing it in front of our guests? All eyes apart from one pair shifted uneasily to the ground. Only Lilly stared, defiantly and blisteringly, at Alain, her look expressing what her mouth was fighting, I knew, to keep in check. Oh god. I can't believe this.

'It's more appropriate than wearing white.'

Nick's little lob sliced through the silence and earned my gratitude. Alain's frown fizzled and he broke into a laugh as if the insult was really just a joke.

'I guess it's not that bad,' Alain pointed to the dress.

I fisted him a weak punch on the arm and the tension dissipated but I still felt unstitched. Nick was the only member of the family who had no grasp of French, although he had picked up the gist of Alain's comment. Faking a calm I didn't feel, I explained the origins of the dress for the sake of the men, who hadn't had a sneak preview.

'So you thought it through,' Nick summarised. 'Something old, something new, something borrowed, something blue.'

It hadn't occurred to me. Obviously I was superstitious.

There wasn't time to cry, or to change into anything else for that matter, as we had an appointment to keep. Dividing up, we bundled into three cars for the two-minute drive to Mazan, my sisters now proffering hugs and clucking around me like ladies-in-waiting. Displaying tact, they said nothing about Alain's comment, but I felt their solidarity. Franco tailed Alain, who was outfitted in a white Caftan shirt, black bolero and chino trousers—everyday attire. Arriving at the town hall, we were told to wait outside in the gravelled parking area as they were not yet ready to receive us. Nick ran around filming with his video camera as members of our motley group stamped their feet and swung their arms to protect against the mistral that had whipped up overnight. There were eleven of us, including Christophe and Pierre. He was the most formally dressed for the occasion, his burgundy gabardine suit and crisply ironed shirt setting him apart from the others, to his credit I thought.

'You look beautiful,' Pierre had greeted.

'Thanks. Your brother doesn't think so.' Sourness had crept into my voice. Sensing Pierre's embarrassment I immediately rued my words.

'All ready?' he asked, and I wondered if he was referring to the civil ceremony or the celebration planned for afterwards. Up until I saw him I wasn't entirely sure he would show up. Not that he was opposed to the marriage, which Josephine had told him about. On the contrary, he'd been quick to congratulate me when I'd popped over to collect his cauldrons for our most recent fete in December.

'So, I hear you two are getting married. Wonderful news. It's happening at the town hall in Mazan right?'

'That's right and I have a request.'

'Which is?'

'That you come. Christophe will be there.'

'Thanks for the invite but I really don't think…I'm not one to…'

The smile was erased.

'Come on Pierre. Do it for Christophe. Your mother and sister won't be there. So you and Christophe have to represent the family. Otherwise, well, it won't be at all even.'

Lopsided is what I meant.

Unfairly or not I'd backed Pierre into a corner. It's true that I wanted Christophe to have his uncle around, but I also wanted my family to meet him and there was no more fitting occasion. In the end Pierre gave in to my request, not that this helped demystify the frozen formality between the brothers. The two lived just fourteen kilometres apart, but it might as well have been an ocean apart for all they saw of each other. Alain stonewalled on the subject when I asked.

'Just because we're brothers doesn't mean we have to be close. We're very different people that's all.'

'But you're family! It doesn't matter if you're different.'

'Maybe not but we don't have much in common.'

'But that doesn't matter either. Besides, you do have things in common. More than you think. I mean, you're both intelligent, curious. You like books and…'

'Look, you can't force chemistry between people.'

A bizarre statement about a brother, a strong statement, which had the desired effect of shutting me up. Pierre was equally evasive when I'd asked him why he hardly saw Alain.

'Oh, a younger brother is just a pest and we're very different people.'

Always this reference to being different. I didn't buy it. There was obviously something more at work—maybe to do with Josephine or the father that I wasn't supposed to know about. Inwardly I threw up my hands, resigned to accepting their explanations at face value. Oddly enough though, Alain hadn't objected when I told him I'd invited Pierre to the town hall. Maybe he felt he'd gone far enough, banning his mother and sister from attending the venue, much to my annoyance.

'My mother and sister don't need to be there. I'll take responsibility for that,' he countered when I pressed him on the issue. 'It's nothing to be upset about, they won't take it badly. What's important is you and me. Besides, your family will be there, which is what you want and that's fine.'

Fine for him, a shame for me. I'd pictured Josephine as the grand dame at the town hall, dressed in an ankle-length skirt, a bosomy blouse and woollen shawl, arm in arm with Roland, making a nice foursome with Sylvie and her husband.

I knew that Alain was loathe to have the slightest reminder of the pomp and ceremony displayed at the venerable Monastère Notre-Dame de Givronex, when he'd been a dandy in his early twenties tying the knot before the entire clan and community. I understood why he wasn't keen on the presence of his mother—putting it down to his dyspeptic relationship with her, but why bar Sylvie? Then I found out that Alain's explanation was all just bluster because Valérie the valiant letter-writer told me Sylvie was against our getting married and wouldn't have come even at the barrel of a gun. In Sylvie's judgement, I just wasn't right for Alain. Valérie indicated that the book I planned to write about her brother had turned her against me. She was incensed that I was poking my nose into private matters that didn't concern me. So that was it. Confirmation of what she'd hinted at that night at her house.

'What do you suggest I do about Sylvie? Should I just drop the project, or maybe write the book as fiction?' I'd asked Valérie. I didn't want to incur Sylvie's wrath or cause a ruckus in the family.

'Talk it over with Alain. See what he thinks.'

'You know, out of everyone, I would have thought Josephine would be against the book. In that case I wouldn't have even started the research. I know I'm an outsider. I know it's an interference.'

'Sylvie has her internal struggles like we all do.'

Families: complicated things, especially in a foreign language. I decided to put the matter on hold till after our *voyage de noçe.*

I thanked the heavens for the fifteen-minute wait outside the town hall because that's when Alain largely redeemed himself. It's amazing what a palliative some tight hand-holding can be. And his whisper that in fact I did look pretty. But these didn't erase all the hurt. He never apologised for slamming my dress out loud. He could have done it in private, or not at all. So I wasn't as happy as I thought a bride should be on her big day, my stream of consciousness wandering to some dark places. However, just as we were summoned inside, the penny dropped. Maybe Alain was acting out his own anxiety. He'd had the jitters, not uncommon for a husband-to-be, which he'd simply taken out on me. This thought made me feel better.

We were led up two flights of stairs into a Chateau de Versailles-sized room where about thirty chairs were arranged in rows, taking up perhaps a third of the space. There was nothing much to look at apart from thick-trunked tree tops and the mistral-whipped sky visible through a series of windows. Several chairs shifted as we sat down. There was hushed giggling from the groom's entourage. They were greatly amused. Marriage, after all, was a highly unusual, maybe even freakish occurrence in these parts. There were only two married couples amongst Alain's very broad circle of friends, and one of them was a Scottish pair so they didn't count.

Where I was, getting married was as passé as the Peugeot 104. The Provençaux just didn't do it. Not even for the sake of their offspring; especially not for their offspring because as single mothers cohabiting with their partners they could claim more generous child benefits. Marriage was as obsolete for financial security as it was for romantic notions. It was bourgeois claptrap. Some of Alain's friends talked about slavery in sweeter terms than becoming a spouse.

We were told that our marriage was the first to be held in Mazan that year. Maybe I was mistaken but the trusted civil servant, a Monsieur Rombaud, seemed a little rusty around the edges. He paused frequently during the proceedings as if he couldn't quite remember what to do or say next. He read out reams of lugubrious texts (were all those words necessary?), which I was much too fidgety to absorb, distracted by the whispering and barely suppressed sniggers from the back benches. Finally the moment arrived to say '*oui*' and a gold wedding band appeared on a red velvet cushion—the best part of this whole procedure. I now wore two gold rings (including the birthday ring). Alain and I kissed to raucous applause.

Tunnel-visioned, I failed to notice a photographer in our midst discretely doing his job. We found out several days later that our nuptials had made the front page of the Mazan Gazette. Alain was the first to discover his celebrity status when he entered the *magasin de tabac* and was given a hero's handshake and wishes for a happy married life. He brought home a copy. Franco-American marriage, blazed the headline. Our match had been captured in a visual: Alain in bohemian-style black and me in my sophisticated Thai silk dress and Ascot-worthy hat.

I'd asked my sisters to select between themselves whose signature would grace the marriage document, unwilling to make that decision. Maybe they tossed a coin. In any event, Julia copped the pen. Alain and I emerged from the town hall into a shower of confetti, trailing us to his Fiat.

When we pulled up at the house a good half hour later, Valérie the letter-writer had already arrived and soon after, the full gang assembled. Glasses of champagne were raised in toasts to the two of us. Poor Christophe was the butt of many a joke about how his wicked stepmother would now make life miserable for him, ruling the roost with an iron fist. I was teased about my new official status as 'Madame Calvignac' (Alain's last name), even though I intended to keep my own surname. And then came the *voyage de noçe* jabs. 'Ecuador? Why Ecuador?' This, even though his friends were used to Alain's globe-trotting ways.

Well after dark a van arrived with paella, piping hot mounds of golden saffron rice laden with chunks of chicken and seafood. I was relieved that the food passed muster with Alain, who wasn't keen on catering. Catastrophe was narrowly averted when someone almost ran into the chocolate mousse cake I was carrying to the table—the ersatz wedding cake because Alain had vetoed a traditional one. That didn't stop Christine turning up with a two-tiered, white-frosted whopper made, she said, 'just in case' I had overlooked the dessert. I felt bad for her because, tasty though it was, it was hardly touched.

The runaway hit of the evening was Julia's Hawaiian love dance.

'Can everyone please sit down,' Lilly requested in French as soon as stomachs were sated. People grabbed chairs, the lights were turned off and candles quickly lit in strategic spots in the long room. Music was switched on and Julia swept into the room. Wearing a brightly coloured sarong, she looked like a piece of Hawaiian art, a flower behind one ear, a garland around the neck, her henna-tinged hair thick like palm bark.

To the melody of Hawaiian hula she moved in graceful sweeps, gesticulating her hips, undulating towards Alain and I with arms outstretched and then receding, pouring love into her dance and onto us. The emotion it stirred was intense. I glanced at Alain. He seemed enthralled.

'Where did she learn to dance like that?' he whispered.

'Hawaii.' Now was not the moment to explain how she'd mastered the technique at spiritual retreats in Kauai and the Big Island, paid for by her back-bending massages.

For the rest of the evening there was not much English-French mingling, not from any show of unfriendliness but out of a natural inclination to converse in mother tongues. Every now and again Alain would shoot over to where I nested with my family and plant a kiss on my lips before decamping to his friends—the objects of much grilling by Lilly and Nick.

'The small, dark-haired woman over there? That's Vivienne. She lives with the electrician Mathias—that's him over there. He's originally from Sicily. They have a daughter together and she has an older son from another man. Vivienne used to work part-time in Alain's kitchen shop along with Danielle.'

They all knew who *she* was and what *she'd* done and no doubt they were uncomfortable for me, but Danielle was charming with them, providing some insight into the dilemma I faced. They could see her carousing in a corner with Jacques, Alain, Franco and several others, her ring-encrusted fingers touching the men, a shoulder here, an arm and knee there, the groom's included.

'Who's he?'

'That's Peppo. He did most of the handiwork around the house. He makes the best *tarte tatin*—apple tart that is—in the Vaucluse.'

'I must say Alain's younger brother—Pierre isn't it?—is very nicely put together.' Lilly was looking at him. 'He seems a bit serious though. I noticed when we were waiting outside the town hall and during the ceremony he sort of stood apart, separate from the others. What's he like?'

'Pierre?' He was deep in conversation with Valérie and her partner Antonio, who was a civil rights lawyer.

'He's quite reserved, so unlike Alain in that respect—their personalities are very diff…distinctive—but he's a kind soul. Earnest and down-to-earth. He's an engineer.'

I lunged into some family history, recounting the father's financial ruin and heart attack, Josephine's pounding the pavements to support Pierre, the flat in Arles, the dead brother in India and the unexplained schism between the two younger siblings.

'There's something melancholic about Pierre,' I said. 'I think it's to do with his divorce eighteen months ago. I guess it's taken a toll on him.'

All faces fixed on Pierre, taking his measure. He was holding a glass of wine, frowning slightly as he listened to Antonio, expressing agreement with nods of the head. Contemplative yet focused, Pierre seemed a misfit in this milieu, dressed in his tailored burgundy suit, his lush hair combed to the side, tall and straight-backed. Knowing his discomfort and reluctance to be among us, I felt a pang of guilt.

'I'd like to find him a good woman,' I caught myself saying.

That raised eyebrows.

'He could easily meet someone if he wanted to, surely?' remarked Lilly.

'I suppose so. He says he's happy being on his own, but he's just nursing wounds.'

'Of course he is. A year and a half after a divorce is not very long…for some men, that is. I guess he's just not ready for a relationship.'

Julia was on the verge of offering him therapy.

All this emotional verbiage was too much for Nick.

'Well, if your marriage goes belly up and Alain splits then you can always team up with the brother.'

'Nick, really,' mock-scolded Lily, who then burst out laughing along with Julia and I, finding his outrageous words funny.

Catching her breath, Lilly then said to me, 'I suppose you'll be spending lots of time with Alain in Carrara.'

I'd mentioned to Lilly that Alain yearned for more than fleeting visits to the Italian region that boasted the world-famous marble quarries where Michelangelo had made his mark.

'Yes, I hope so. It's on the cards.'

Lilly crooned over Alain's sculptures, all that Carrara marble perhaps sparking some wistfulness for she was a culture monger at heart.

At around midnight, someone turned up the stereo full blast, the hard liquor appeared and Mathias and a few others began to drink themselves into a stupor. Danielle was knocking back shots of something. So was Gregoire. He was barely twenty-nine but had already perforated a lung from excessive smoking and drinking, a condition that had only recently put him in hospital for several weeks. Apparently, he hadn't learned his lesson. Refusing to let this devolve into a drunken rave, I lowered the volume a notch so we could hear ourselves talk—to the consternation of Gregoire, Matthias and Danielle. But I didn't care. This was my party. For once, I would do what I liked.

Like a cow regurgitating, I chewed over the events of the day, wanting to remember…and forget. Alain had succumbed to sleep around three-thirty, but an hour later I was still awake, tossing and turning. The house was somnolent, offering nothing to distract my thoughts, Shiva shrouded in darkness. I reheard Alain's 'horror' slur of my dress, his vigorous '*oui*' to the civil servant at the town hall. I thought about our hurried lovemaking in the car on the way back to the house. We'd pulled off the road onto a green verge and before the engine was idled I'd removed my lace-edged panties and carefully hiked my dress up above my crotch—I was wearing stockings. Alain manoeuvred himself into the front passenger seat. As I wiggled to make room for him I heard a rip as a morsel of material caught on the sharp handle of the storage drawer.

'Oh, what a shame.' Alain tried to sound sincere, but he couldn't pull it off, the words catching in his throat. I decided to laugh rather than berate. He probably felt like ripping the whole thing to shreds. At least, I thought, the spoiling of my dress would remind me of our first coupling as husband and wife.

And then came the worst. I played back that awful scene, the cluster of people at the door, dawdling in their coats before a reluctant exit into the cold night air to their cars. My family had gone up to bed. I was just about to give Christine the bag she thought she'd lost when I caught sight of Danielle sidling up to Alain. She whispered in his ear for several long seconds and when she finished she put her finger to her lips, as you do to connote a secret. Alain said nothing. His face was in profile so I couldn't see his expression. After that, she tugged Jacques and they left. When finally we were alone, I wanted to grill Alain. But I couldn't bring myself to ask him about those whispered words. She was just drunk, I tried to reassure myself. Miserably, foul-mouthed drunk.

Chapter 20

A sunset sky reflected bronze and silvery tints onto the silky mass of the lagoon stretched out in front of us. We had just emerged from bathing in its warm waters, dissolving the grit from a day spent hiking a trail through the rain forest under trees as tall as giants' limbs. Every now and then we had stopped on the prompting of our guide, whose keenness to reveal the secrets of the flora and fauna impressed us as much as the actual information he imparted on what could kill you or heal you.

It was heaven, this spot in virgin-forested Cuyabeno National Park in the Ecuadorian Amazon. I relished the serenity, for once not somewhere in the past or future, happy, simply, to be with the man I'd married. But not Alain. Here in this wilderness, his mind was anchored in Provence. As we lay in hammocks strung up on a raised wooden platform staring out at the darkening mysteries beyond, he suddenly burst out, with such force it sounded like one of the Ten Commandments:

'I'm going to get rid of La Belle Cuisine. It's become an albatross around my neck. Too draining. And it's taking time away from my sculpting.'

'Alain, that's a huge decision. Are you sure?'

'About closing it? Absolutely. With distance I can see things more clearly. The solution is obvious.'

When Alain had first broached the idea to his friends of setting up a kitchen shop in Carpentras, they'd told him he was nuts. A venture like that will never survive, you're throwing money down the drain, they'd argued. Alain had ignored the pessimists, pumped every last centime he had into the project, leaving himself with just enough to live on for one month. Within the first four weeks of opening he had sold seven kitchens, and the money started to roll in. That was four years ago. Now, he felt a victim of his own success. More business meant more effort and more paperwork, and less time for his hobby, even if his schedule would be the envy of most of the world's workforce.

‘I’m tired of the hassles and responsibilities of shop owning. And why should I continue? We can live comfortably on the commissions I make from selling kitchens for other retailers.’

‘It sounds like a fait accompli. Will you close it right away?’

‘No, unfortunately I can’t do that because of Danielle. If I lay her off now, she won’t be able to claim unemployment benefits. I need to put her on the books for a few months first.’

Danielle, intruding even on our honeymoon in this armpit of the Amazon. And yet…if he did close the shop, she would be less of a factor in our lives, one more step removed. I wondered how she’d take this news. Being jobless wouldn’t be funny, unemployment benefits or not, and those benefits wouldn’t last long if her earnings were declared for only a few months. Alain’s off-the-books approach had turned out to be not so clever after all.

I thought of the outlet, all the hard work that had gone into it, the hopes it encompassed, the kitchens meticulously crafted. A shutdown was sad. But to Alain the business wasn’t a challenge anymore. And he thrived on challenges.

‘You know what? It will mean more freedom. Freedom for me—us—to go to Carrara. Let’s plan a trip there soon after we get back.’

His eyes bore into the expanding half-moon shadows, as intense and illuminating as the jungle fireflies. Carrara, city of marble. It was almost as exotic to me as the Amazon.

The ten of us pitched up in this camp were called to dinner at a long table I assumed had been carved from the wood of jungle trees. We devoured river fish, vegetables and rice to the squawk and chatter of night animals whose voices never revealed their whereabouts.

Later, Alain and I lay on our mattress inside the translucent mosquito netting that separated us from some very beefy-looking insects, and the other travellers—all of us sleeping on a second platform raised several inches from the ground. Our ‘tent’ was next to that of a Spanish couple. For the past three nights they had waited until it was respectably late to make love, and we had followed suit.

Tonight, again, I heard the young man’s heavy breathing, the quickening pace of his thrusts and the woman’s stifled groans. Imagining what you can hear but can’t see is a powerful aphrodisiac. Alain put on a condom—useful in a jungle where we had no access to a shower—and we began to make love. The thought that the Spanish couple could hear us was a further turn on. After he pulled out, I put my hand between my legs for that final run. When I'd finished, Alain whispered: 'Why don't you come when I'm inside you?'

The question was baffling.

'But I do Alain, all the time. I don't understand.'

'Yes, but you always use this.'

He squeezed my hand.

'You mean…? But Alain, so what?' I stuttered.

'Why do you need your hand? I should be enough for you.'

It was astonishing, this fuss over a little masturbation and also deeply disturbing. Alain, after all, was not some inexperienced youngster but a connoisseur par excellence of women. He should know the nuts and bolts of our bodies. Not every woman could come from penetration alone. I should be enough for you? He'd never said a word about this before. How long had the question been festering?

As he drifted off, I wrapped a sarong around my t-shirt and with my torch, crept out of the net. I found my Reeboks on the floor, carefully picked them up, shook them for a good fifteen seconds to root out any insects, and put them on. A few steps beyond the platform I raised the sarong while holding the flashlight and squatted, feeling the release of urine.

Enough surprises for one day.

Franco picked us up at Marseille Airport, looking more relaxed than he had three weeks before, his holiday from kids and clutter in Mazan obviously restorative. He was due to return home the next day.

'So, honeymooners, how was Ecuador?'

The way he crooned 'honeymooners' annoyed Alain.

'I do apologise. So, how was your Amazonian holiday?'

Coursing along the motorway under the late March sun, we ran through our itinerary. The arrival in Quito, our overland journey to beaches and villages dotting the Pacific coast followed by an expedition to cool mountain valleys. We recounted our jungle adventure, replete with dugout canoe rides along still black waters and the lore of age-old shamans. The trip had been wonderful, the only spoiler Alain's finger zinger two days before our return to France.

'So, the drums have had a good workout I assume,' Alain said to his friend.

'Yeah, they've never sounded better. But I have some bad news for you two.'

I braced myself for disaster.

‘The two hens that Danielle and Jacques gave you as a wedding present? Well, they died. I think they were killed by foxes.’

The pair had brought them over in a straw-filled crate, a unique gift to say the least.

‘They should start laying eggs soon,’ Danielle had reassured us. Not knowing what to do with them we’d released the chickens into a shed where we kept the kindling. It seemed the only viable option.

Expecting Franco to announce that the house had been burgled or half burned down I breathed out relief. But then, I couldn’t help wondering…was their death some kind of an omen?

Less than a week after our return Josephine and Roland came over for lunch. We hadn’t seen them since November. I felt guilty as I kissed them, hoping they weren’t offended at not being invited to the town hall. But Josephine didn’t give it a mention. Ensconced on the sofa, a tisane in hand, a fire spreading its warmth through the copse of canine limbs, she did, however, enquire about Ecuador. Roland busied himself with a book he picked off the shelf. Alain was in the kitchen, from where wafted the aroma of the coriander and thyme fish soup he was preparing.

The preliminaries out of the way, his mother got down to business, chafing to ask but one question.

‘*Alors*, what has your research uncovered about Tristan?’ She looked at me as if I could solve the mystery of the Holy Grail.

‘I don’t have much to tell you, to be honest. Because of getting married and our travels, I haven’t had time to interview more people.’

I couldn’t bring myself to talk about Sylvie’s misgivings, which I’d shared with Alain. As I suspected he would, he’d encouraged me to continue with the project, saying he’d find a way to placate Sylvie, whatever that meant. Josephine, in contrast, was galvanised by my research, on tenterhooks to find out the least little nugget.

‘I’ve been re-reading his letters though, including the ones he wrote to Alain. It’s incredible, isn’t it, how he walked to the Himalayas and back on foot.’

At this, Josephine’s hand shook, spilling a few drops of tea.

‘He walked to the Himalayas? What do you mean?’

‘Yes, you know, his trek to the mountains on the orders of his guru.’

Her world seemed to stop. Her mouth hung open.

'You mean you don't know?'

'No.' The creases under her eyes appeared to double, and her firm chin wobbled. Roland took her cup.

'Well…the best thing is to show you the letter where it's described. I'll be back in a minute.'

I dashed up to my study. The first page of Tristan's letter to Alain was written in large script, reduced to a tiny scrawl by the fourth and final page. In it, Tristan described how his guru had set him this challenge to demonstrate his devotion and faith. He wanted to become a sadhu? Well then, he had to walk barefoot to the hallowed Hindu pilgrimage centres of Badrinath, Kedarnath and Gaumukh, the source of the River Ganges. Barefoot, every step of the five hundred kilometres there—and back—through dusty planes and forests, across gorges, up high Himalayan passes and across glaciers.

It seemed to require the feet, literally, of a god.

Tristan's clothes—mere cloths covering a portion of his body—were fine for the heat of the flatlands but not for the freezing mornings and nights of the passes. Setting off with just a few hundred rupees in a string bag there was not much he could buy along the way. For food and a place to sleep there were ashrams and temples, but outside of these he was on his own. Tristan had fallen gravely ill on that mandated mission and was apparently nursed back to health by some kind-hearted sadhu who took him under his wing. The amazing thing was he did it. He returned to his guru more than one thousand kilometres and six months later.

Josephine was ready with her reading glasses when I returned. I handed her the envelope and retreated to the kitchen to give her some privacy and to prise out some answers from Alain, who was slicing tomatoes on the counter by the sink.

'How come you never mentioned Tristan's pilgrimage to your mother, or gave her his letter to read?' I kept my voice low.

'I'm sure I did.' He put the tomato slices on a serving plate and sprinkled them with salt and olive oil. 'Why would I not? But I can't precisely recall. It was a long time ago.'

'But Alain, this is something quite enormous for her.'

It was hard not to sound reproachful.

'Maybe she forgot?' He washed his hands.

'Not possible. You know that.'

He dried his hands, his mouth pinched inwards in exasperation.

When Alain and I walked into the three dogs room, Josephine's eyes were still on the letter, clutched firmly in her lap, her cheeks wet. Roland, no longer reading, had a protective arm around her, his expression glum.

'The photo. That photo. Now I understand. It was taken on his journey, in Kedarnath. On his pilgrimage. Now I understand why he looked so skeletal.'

In the letter, Tristan had mentioned running into a French couple in Kedarnath. He had asked them to take some photos of himself to send to his family in France. Why had I never made the connection?

Josephine removed her glasses and wiped her eyes with a tissue unearthed from her bag.

'Mother, I could have sworn I told you about Tristan's journey, showed you the letter.'

Alain was standing by the door, uncertain of what to do. Why didn't he approach her, comfort her? He sat down beside me, shaking his head. The tension was palpable.

'I'm truly sorry,' Alain finally conceded. 'My memory is not reliable. When I saw him in India, he talked about his pilgrimage, but not much. And I regret that I didn't ask him many more questions. There's a lot I would love to know.'

Josephine nodded, too choked-up to reply. When she could speak, it was to forgive.

'I don't blame you. I'm just struggling to absorb it. What he did is overwhelming.'

'Yes it is,' Alain echoed.

The men did most of the talking at lunch. Josephine was dry-faced but subdued, lost in thought about her son's exploits. His mission must have seemed nothing short of mythical to her. And yet this test he'd been set was nothing particularly unusual. From what I understood, it was a rite of passage for those aspiring to be mystics. But for a mother who had to have felt abandoned by her eldest son, the feelings it provoked were painful.

After lunch, Alain took Roland into the garden to show him his latest work-in-progress. His Buddha was emerging from a slab of white marble, the head and upper torso curved like the contours of his angel. Alain hadn't yet started on the legs. No doubt the men were also keen to take advantage of the balmy April weather. Spring had gone to work with alacrity. Buds had popped open and the plane trees were in renewal, more leaves appearing on their limbs every time I took the car out. The grass was a vivid springy green and the vines had shed their forlorn look. All the elements exuded expectancy, like a shop awaiting delivery of inventory.

Josephine and I returned to the sofa in the three dogs room. She began to talk about Tristan again, his motivations, his determination, his resilience. Her distress had relaxed into détente, and she even smiled when I said that Tristan had proved to be braver than Asterix. She asked to see the photos that Alain had taken on his trips to India, photos of her son that she'd already seen, and I was happy to oblige. Don't you think he resembles the iconic images of Jesus Christ? I was tempted to say, thinking she'd take it as a compliment. But perhaps it would only upset her. After the photos were put back, I took my chances.

'I wanted to apologise to you about our wedding at the town hall, the fact that you weren't invited. I felt terrible you weren't there.'

'Oh, don't feel bad about that. I completely understand. You don't have to be sorry at all.'

She answered in such a way as to infer I wouldn't have expected anything else from my strong-willed, brilliant son.

'How has he been since you got married by the way?'

'He's been good, fine. Why?'

'Well, you know, I just wanted to reassure you.'

Her manner was maternal, verging on the conspiratorial, the way she drew near to me and lowered her voice a notch.

'*Alors*, don't be surprised if he does some strange things. It would be typical of him.'

She gave a knowing shrug.

'Whenever he feels forced to do something he rebels, like when he had to serve in the army. He goes crazy for a while but then it blows over. Nothing to worry about, he'll get over it.'

Forced, forced. That word was anomalous.

'What do you mean? He wasn't forced into marriage. He was the one who proposed to me.'

Josephine realised her blunder.

'Really? Well, maybe he just said that to me to…to…because he thought I wouldn't approve, or because he thought that's what I wanted to hear. After his divorce, he said he would never remarry. But he's allowed to change his mind of course. I'm no one to judge. As long as he's happy.'

No wonder she hadn't made a fuss about not being invited.

'May I ask what he said to you? About getting married?'

I'm sure she didn't want to step into a minefield but lying didn't seem to be her strength. She sighed.

'He just told me that he needed to marry you so that you could stay in France legally. That he owed you that. As I said, it was probably because it seemed the easiest way to approach the subject with me. He's a very private person as you know. In any case,' she brought the matter to a head, 'remember, if he does start acting, eh, a little crazy, he will snap out of it. So please don't worry.'

Once she was gone and I had time to reflect, I decided that what Alain had told his mother wasn't out of character at all. While she seemed to worship him, Alain kept her at arm's length with a tempered hostility, the reasons for which I couldn't begin to fathom. The way he hardened in her presence, his splintery tone. I could well imagine Alain feeding her untruths, if only to keep explanations to a minimum, even to preserve his honour that 'I'll never marry again.'

Well then, I had nothing to worry about.

Chapter 21

Occasionally Alain had clients over for dinner, mainly to celebrate a sale or an installation. The couple that came over that Friday night had recently moved to the Vaucluse, bought a house in Bedoin and a kitchen from La Belle Cuisine. Alain had warmed to the pair and looked forward to a witty evening. They were indeed entertaining, regaling us with stories about some misanthropic mayor who had made life hell in the town they'd upped sticks from in the Dordogne. We were six at the table, including Danielle and Jacques. The food as usual was full of flavour and the alcohol flowed. It was past two in the morning when the clients left. At which point Alain, sozzled by his Vietnamese snake brew, decided he wanted some hash and invited himself over to Danielle and Jacques' place, where there was always a stash.

'You're my wife, you have to do what I tell you. Drive me over.'

His attempt at humour wasn't funny. I was furious—at him and Danielle. I shot her imploring looks, willing her to say she was tired, but of course she didn't. On the contrary, I detected a certain schadenfreude in her manner. I refused to chauffeur Alain, who grabbed his jacket and car keys and left, but then was hit by the mother of all regrets. What if he crashed? I didn't sleep a wink until he crawled into bed at dawn.

'What were you thinking of last night?' I railed at him when he appeared in the kitchen at noon. 'You know you could have died in the state you were in. I was so worried.'

Left unspoken was my jealousy. Was the hash genuinely the draw or Danielle? I expected Alain to apologise. Instead, he looked at me as if I were a viper, hands on hips.

'You were worried, really? Then why didn't you drive me?'

'But Alain, why did you need to go?'

'Why not? Are you trying to control me now? Why shouldn't I have gone? You're the one at fault for not taking me.'

'It's not about control. It's about concern. But yes, I was upset that you hurried out like that to get stoned…when it was so late,' I faltered.

Cold eyes, pursed lips, an acerbic tone I'd never heard before. My own shaky voice. Our first row. I was hurt and perplexed, failing to understand the aggression of his response, which seemed disproportionate to my critique, or was it? I thought we could talk it out. He obviously felt attacked, so he attacked, and I tried to defend myself, sounding lame and limp. Arguing in French—not my forte. In fact, arguing at all.

'Don't force me to change. You'll regret it.'

'I'm not forcing you to do anything.'

I thought of what Josephine had told me.

'And I didn't force you into marriage, as your mother told me you'd said.'

The words spilled out and I watched their effect on Alain. First surprise, his mouth opening for a second then clamping shut. Then fury, his lips bunching together, head turning slowly from side to side, eyes narrowing. He pointed an index finger at me, portending, I thought, a flood of angry words. But he said nothing. He stormed out of the kitchen.

For three endless weeks after our altercation, the Alain I knew and adored disappeared. He who used to scoop me up with his eyes now barely registered me. When I woke in the morning, he was already downstairs. When I joined him in the kitchen, he would quickly finish eating, put his plate in the dishwater and mumble something about a client and scoot off. He was frequently out for lunches and dinners, disappearing with friends. He was hostile not just to my words but to my touch, withdrawing to an unreachable place. At night in bed, he kept his distance, an invisible barrier dividing the mattress. His opprobrium filled the house.

For the first week what little food I could manage caused stomach cramps and diarrhoea. I knew this end-of-the-world feeling, the knotted gut and the other organs that felt constricted. I confronted him, but all my questions—what's going on, why won't you talk to me, what have I done—were left hanging.

'Is it what I said about your mother, telling me you felt forced to marry me?'

'You need to ask?' was his four-word summation.

After a few days, I stopped asking. Instead, I cloistered myself in my study, sat at my desk and stared for hours out of the window, trying to decipher what had happened to my husband. Had he really felt forced into marriage? Was he more peeved at me because of the argument we'd had, feeling I was being controlling, or because the truth had been unmasked?

Forced into marriage. I hadn't forced him. But what if he felt that way and was now rebelling. It all seemed to be leaking, his fear of being puppet-pulled, of losing his independence, of being 'bourgeoisied', even though in the crowd we ran with, it was more unique to be married than not. If what he'd told Josephine was true…the ramifications didn't bear thinking about.

There were times when I itched to call his mother, to hear her say don't worry, it's just a phase, he'll soon snap out of it. I came within an inch of picking up the phone. But if I couldn't actually do it I used her words as a mantra, and gradually drew myself together. I made a stab at starting the book. I resumed yoga classes in Carpentras. I played the piano when he wasn't around. I filled the house with flowers, bought him champagne and gifts and placed bits of paper with quotes from Khalil Gibran in a trouser pocket and by his shaving cream. Nothing shifted but I felt less brittle.

One morning, fourteen days after his U-turn, he suddenly announced he was going to visit one of his outer-circle friends in the Carpentras clinic where she'd just given birth to a baby girl.

'You should come with me, to congratulate her.'

There was no enthusiasm in his voice, but at least he looked me in the face. I accepted, knowing my presence was merely protocol, yet hoping it would lead to a thaw. Lillian and her husband Glen were young, earnest, hard-working Scots, the married couple I mentioned. They lived in a statuesque house on their family-owned *vignoble* not far from us. Glen, hailing from a long line of agriculturalists, cultivated grapes for wine and they also grew most of their own vegetables; they were a productive, two-person, French-speaking enterprise.

In her semi-private room Lillian was sitting up in bed, baby in arms, hair the colour and length of straw, tired but content. The bouquet of chrysanthemums we had brought was placed on a side table featuring other floral displays.

'Do you want to hold her?'

I lifted her wee daughter, swaddled in a blanket, and laid her in the crook of my arm. The act of cradling invoked tremulous emotions. If Alain felt cornered into marriage, what about my chances of motherhood? Must not dwell on that. Alain faked an air of blitheness around the new parents, acting the part of a newly-wed. He certainly didn't want any dirty laundry hanging out for this industrious duo to see, not that our marital woes would have been of much interest to them at this particular juncture in their lives. The thirty minutes of pretence, however, must have been draining.

'I feel like going to the sauna. What about it?'

Alain shot the words out the second we left the clinic. I could have refused I suppose and insisted we go home, some tit-for-tat treatment. Instead I nodded, electrified. This means touching. Sex. Used to dollops of it every day, the lack of physical contact felt like a fatwa. Alain didn't say a word in the car.

Once at the sauna, we followed our usual trail through the steam room, dry heat sauna, showers and the softly lit lounge. There, spread-eagled on the sofa, lay a dark-haired beauty with a heavy-set man fingering her in foreplay. A scrum of salivating singles hung around, stroking themselves. So this was where all the action was; I was wondering why the place had seemed so empty. She clearly relished being the centre of attention, a masturbatory Madonna for her audience.

'That's how I'd like you to be,' Alain said tersely, watching her intently. Hadn't I shown enough exhibitionist élan at the club and on the beach? Was this poke in the ribs an illusion to Danielle? Or act X of his rebellion? A few minutes later the woman and her partner got up, unlocked the door that led to the private cubicles and disappeared, leaving behind a flock of frustrated fans (singles could enter only if invited). We followed them in, using our key. It wasn't hard to locate their cubbyhole. Alain stuck his head in to ask if we could join them. They ushered us in.

It turned out to be a perfect case of 'you can't tell a book by its cover'. Her lover lavished her long and curvaceous torso as Alain, erection bared, joined in, caressing and licking where he could. I sat on the sidelines, unsure of whether to be a spectator or player. The minutes ticked by, the air a mix of musk and sweat. And yet…Instead of writhing in ecstasy, instead of bucking like a whinny, instead of screaming *oui oui oui*, instead of having a visibly volcanic orgasm or three, the woman had the effrontery to barely budge, minimally expressing the pleasure I assumed she was feeling. Hardly the femme fatale of Alain's fantasy! Disenchanted, Alain pulled me out of the cubicle. I secretly gloated over his deflation, hoping it signalled some intimacy with me. But this was not to be.

'Let's go,' he ordered.

'Why? Come on, let's stay for a bit. We've only just arrived.'

'I'm no longer in the mood.'

Defeated, I followed him out.

A week later, the tide turned. There was no warning, no particular event to mark his swivel. I was in the kitchen when he came up and threw his arms around me with three-hundred-and-sixty-degree passion.

'*Ma beauté*, I'm feeling much better in my head, much better,' he incanted. Without further explanation he led me to the long room and with Mont Ventoux in the background, the fountain gurgling and his sculptures staring into the ether, he enacted his fervour. '*Je t'aime*,' he breathed. I felt as if I had woken from a drowning. Later, at a bistro in Carpentras, I stuck my neck out to ask what had happened. For a minute, seeing him grimace, I thought he would dodge the bullet.

'Post-traumatic stress disorder,' he finally said.

My face slid.

'That's a joke. Come on, smile,' he touched my lips. 'I was scared.'

'Of what?'

He downed a glass of Perrier.

'Of being on a leash. I need to feel free,' he put the glass down. 'It's part of being an artist, part of my make-up. What I need to be able to create. If I don't, I will escape.'

'You're as free as you were before. I won't stop you. Marriage doesn't have to change a thing. It's just how you choose to view it.'

'I know. It's not you. It's me.'

Easy to say.

'This wild thing inside me,' he tapped his head, 'is its own master. It doesn't like to take orders from anyone.'

'Why didn't you tell me any of this, talk about your fears, before we got married?'

'It might have put you off.'

He can't be serious.

'That might not have been a bad thing.'

'I'm sorry,' he sounded earnest. 'I want it to work out.'

'So, what you told your mother, was it the truth, or not? Did you feel forced to marry me out of obligation, although it was you who proposed, remember?'

'That was outright wrong of her to say anything to you. I told her that only because of Sylvie, who is not the most open of people, and a little distrustful of foreigners. I knew my mother would tell Sylvie what I'd said word for word.'

‘But why lie to Sylvie? Why not tell her the truth? Why take her side against me—making me look like the bad person in all this?’

‘I apologise. It was just easier that way, but I admit, it wasn’t right.’

Easier? That wasn’t a satisfying answer. And there was no answer to the scariest question of all: Can a rebellious spirit be quelled, or is it like a Pandora’s box, once let loose, always a threat?

Later, I phoned up Julia and told her of Alain’s ‘return’.

‘I hope the good guy is back to stay.’

She didn’t hide her concern.

‘Yes, let’s hope.’

She alone of my clan knew what had happened for I’d had to confide in someone. The shame of it.

That very evening we went to Peppo’s forty-fifth birthday party, thrown by none other than Peppo himself. A roll-up forever dangling from his lips, Peppo had laid out a hearty spread: skewers of chicken, red peppers, aubergine and mushrooms, an assortment of pâtés, cheeses and slices of sauçisson, bagpipe-sized baguettes, sun-ripened tomatoes, devilled eggs and salads of beetroot, carrot and endive. But his bottom-crusted *tarte tatin* was the knockout. All three pies disappeared from his dining room table quicker than the bottles of champagne.

Danielle was there of course. She hadn’t been round to the house during Alain’s sulk but I knew he’d seen her and Jacques. She greeted me brightly with a look that said she was *au courant*. Brigitte, her predecessor in Alain’s bed, was also present. Alain kept me close, a stun gun to my anxiety. Just once did he leave my side, to dance with his two former girlfriends, a sign of supposed maturity and part of the *bonhomie* he was so proud of. As I leaned against a wooden bookshelf in Peppo’s living room, watching them move with unspoken familiarity, my imagination ran riot. I understood why women drooled over him, the way he captivated with every damn bit of his body, from the witticisms that rolled off his tongue, the laugh that made you laugh, the bluest eyes, the confidence, the seduction—the disgustingly irresistible charisma powered by talented manipulation.

Oh god, what an intimate trio they make. Gripped by a morbid fascination, I had scoured through stacks of photos of Brigitte that Alain kept in a box in the three dogs room, searching for I’m not sure what, the key to their relationship? I don’t think with her it had been ‘only’ about sex. He had sought something more conventional. Even so I wondered, not for the first time, if she and Alain had partner swapped.

Unlike with Danielle, my feelings about Brigitte weren't messy. All of me liked all of her. At first, I found it hard to see past her beauty and how blessed I thought she was because of it. It put her on a pedestal with men but she was no flirt; she had no need to be the queen bee of any gathering. The more we talked, the more her other qualities stood out—patience and forbearance among them—as well as the imperfections of her life. That night at Peppo's she revealed how she had been suffering from a mysterious back pain that no therapies had succeeded in easing, causing her much anguish. She needed to find a job but lacked direction and felt extremely insecure because of it.

'What about you, do you have any plans for work?'

I told her about the trip to Hong Kong for Annie Leung and similar ventures to come as well as the book I'd begun.

'Alain always talked about how he wanted to live with a woman who had her own creative projects. And now with you, he has that.'

Yes, but it felt irrelevant. I was desperate for reassurance. I wanted to reveal Alain's about-face to her. How would she interpret it? But there was no chance that evening to find out.

Chapter 22

'You'll be fine on your own,' Alain soothed, kissing me goodbye at Avignon train station. 'The house is totally safe,' he repeated, reminding me again that he'd never had a problem with break-ins and that locks were in any case no hindrance to robbers, not that there would be any.

'If you need anything just call Peppo or Jacques, Benoit, Valérie, Pierre…'

It was a Sunday morning and he was leaving for Paris. After swearing he was through with the home furnishings fair and Marc, he had changed his mind at the last minute.

'The money is too good to pass up,' he argued, although I had said nothing in opposition. Despite my fears about sleeping alone in the house, I agreed with Alain that I should stay in Provence. I had my own work and besides, I had no wish to be a punching bag for an exhausted husband and his aggressive boss.

It felt uncanny to be the one waving him off.

'Good luck with Marc. And sell lots of kitchens.'

'And then we'll go to Carrara. I promise.'

And he was gone.

I drove straight to Cavaillon where I spent much of the day with Valérie, picking her brains again about Tristan. She picked my mine too, dumbfounded to learn about his hike to the Himalayas. Alain hadn't mentioned it to her either, which she put down to a memory lapse.

'With his mother I doubt it was a deliberate omission. He had nothing to gain by that. Tristan is a sensitive subject and free and easy communication within the family is not their strong point, at least between older and younger generations. And maybe particularly between Alain and his mother.'

'Josephine talked to me very openly about Tristan. Maybe it's easier because I'm an outsider. I've noticed that Alain changes when he's with his mother. He becomes hostile and shuts down. What's that about?'

'He was always very close to his father. I think he idolised him. It's possible he holds a grudge, blames Josephine for his father's death—on an unconscious level of course. Or he sees parts of himself that he doesn't like reflected in her.'

A memory surfaced. The only time I'd ever seen Alain cry was once when he reminisced about a boyhood fishing trip with his father on the Durance River. Realising it, he quickly dried his eyes and changed the subject.

'Just remember, they may hold each other at arm's length. But whatever rivalries there might be, their blood runs thick. The family sticks together against any exterior threat.'

Threat. I was living with one—the one inside Alain's head. I could have confided in Valérie about those three terrible weeks, but pride, and prejudice against hearing myself describe his awfulness, held me back.

That evening I considered sleeping in a tent in the garden where I thought I'd feel safer but the inconvenience of this outweighed the pros. Lights, lights, that's what I need. I kept the lights on in the hallways, the study and the kitchen. But that didn't stop the habitual creaks in the wooden ceiling beams and in other places that I could never identify; the kind of creaks that now sounded like footsteps. How inconvenient to be afraid in my own house. Not even Shiva, guardian of the bedroom, could erase my shivers. I was unable to fall asleep until dawn, waking up to the sound of the phone ringing. I darted downstairs to the kitchen as quickly as I could.

'Darling, is everything okay?' It was Alain in Paris. 'You took a long time to answer.'

'Everything is fine.'

'You sound breathless. Have you been running?'

'No no. I was just taking a nap and rushed down the stairs.'

'At eleven in the morning?'

'How is Paris?' I diverted.

'It's raining here. I'm at the stand now. Marc is the usual pest. What are you up to today?'

We spoke for a few more minutes before he rang off with, 'I love you. I'll call again soon.'

The next night was a repeat performance of fearful imaginings and insomnia. After a third night of Calvary, I'd had enough. I needed company. But who? I considered the usual list of suspects. I knew all of them would invite me to stay over. It was tempting, yet I was reluctant to leave the house. What about Pierre?

He'd stayed overnight once, when Alain was at a trade fair in Lyon. He'd come at Alain's behest, bizarre as that had seemed given their un-brotherly bearing towards each other. I sought the list of contact numbers Alain had jotted down. It was after seven when I called. After endless rings, I was just about to put the receiver down when he picked up.

'Pierre, hi, it's Ravinia.'

'Good timing. I just got back from work.'

'I thought I'd say hello. Alain's away at the home furnishings fair in Paris. He's not back for more than a week. I hope I'm not bothering you.'

'The fair? Of course. So you didn't go with him then?'

'No, we decided I'd stay here.'

'So it's you and the ghosts.'

I laughed.

'Lots of those. With no locks on the doors they're free to come and go as they want.'

'Do you want me to come over? Sleep in Christophe's room?'

A long pause. How did he know?

'*Alors*…eh…ah…'

'Yes or no?'

'Yes. Please.'

He walked in the door half an hour later with a leather-strapped sports bag and a grey suit over his arm.

'The least I can do is offer you dinner, assuming you've not eaten.'

'I haven't and that would be lovely.'

Lovely also not to have to eat alone. We tucked into the cold chicken, Tomme de Savoie, salad and bread I'd laid out. I was just about to pour us glasses of a Les Beaux de Provence red when Pierre held up a hand.

'Not for me please. I'm not drinking.'

'Oh really? How come?'

'I've started running. And cutting out some un-virtuous items, like wine and desserts to get in shape. I've decided to train for the Paris marathon.'

'When is that?'

'In April.'

'But that's practically a whole year away.'

'It takes time to build up endurance, especially when you've been sedentary and piled on the kilos.'

What kilos? Though sturdy, he didn't appear to carry an ounce of extra weight. When I made a comment to that effect, he clarified that, 'it's more that I used to be very sporty and I want to get back to that'.

I filled our glasses with water.

'Here's to virtue then.'

Building up stamina and becoming fit was all well and good but I noticed the lines under his eyes.

'Pierre, you look exhausted, like you haven't been sleeping well either.'

'Just not as much as usual. I've been waking up early to go jogging and working long days on a new project in the office, quite a bit of stress and not much sunlight. And you? Scared of the creaks?'

'At night, all alone, the creaks sound human. I know it's safe here but without locks and no neighbours nearby…Maybe it's because I've lived too long in apartments with people crammed close together. I don't know.'

When my yawns became more numerous than my sentences, Pierre shooed me off to bed.

'Go upstairs. I'll turn off the lights.'

'Not all of them Pierre. Leave the one in the kitchen on.'

'I probably won't see you in the morning as I'm up at six. If you want I can return tomorrow night.'

'Pierre, it's a lot to ask. You have your work and your life.'

'Yes or no?'

'Yes, if you're sure.'

I slept that night as if for a season. It was past nine when I awoke, with the energy to climb Everest. Thanks to Pierre, there were no more scary nights, now only worried nights. I hadn't heard anything more from Alain since that first phone call from Paris. I deliberately hadn't phoned him at the exhibition hall or his hotel to give him some cherished breathing space. But it was killing me, this waiting game. It wasn't supposed to be like this when you were married. Nevertheless I stuck to the logic. Surely, if I gave him a wide berth, room to disappear a little, he'd appreciate that.

'You look upset. Is anything wrong?'

Pierre and I were at the pizzeria in Mazan on night number five of his babysit. I was fidgety, shorn of my normally robust appetite.

'I haven't heard from Alain in a week.'

'Why don't you call him?'

'I could but…it's better if he calls me. He might be with a client or something and I don't want to interrupt.'

Feeble excuses.

'There's a reason he hasn't I'm sure.'

'Yes, but perhaps not the one I want to hear.'

He didn't attempt to cheer me up with possible explanations, fibbing or filtering. In silence, we sipped our water.

'Last time we were here, you talked about your ex-wife. You said she was your rebound woman. I'm being nosy again but what did you mean?'

'You remember that? It was a slip of the tongue.'

He cradled his glass, his shoulders hunched, suddenly all serious.

'I apologise. Please ignore the question.'

Our food arrived, served by one of the two waiters in the family-run place. He was the moustachioed father, who took orders and set down the plates with few words but a genuine smile. The restaurant was crowded, children and elders congregating at Mazan's prime pizzeria. Pierre took a few bites of his medium-rare steak, chewing as he ruminated. The lines under his eyes were still there.

Once he began to talk he didn't stop.

'I met Flore during my last year at university. I was studying civil and structural engineering. She was in the faculty for Sports Science—a northerner from Lille. She chose Marseille because she wanted to be in the south, by the sea. She was smart, intense…very driven, but a little wounded too. Her parents' divorce when she was a child had left its scars. She had a gap between her two front teeth and played tennis and badminton with a ferocious hand. She was tall, with short hair. As a child she'd had a lazy left eye. She wore glasses for it and still had a bit of a squint in that eye. She spoke her mind, she wasn't shy. The first few times we saw each other it was in a big group. She was a friend of one of my friends. We started talking and I invited her to dinner. I took her to a Greek restaurant because she'd mentioned something about liking Greek food. That night there happened to be a birthday celebration, so there was music, dancing, plate-smashing. It was hellishly noisy, we had to sit close to each other to be heard…maybe that's why we shared some deep confidences. All I know is, that night was it for me. She said she fell in love with me twenty-four hours later, when we saw each other again for a drink at the university. After that, we were never apart. I got my degree and was hired by an engineering company, which paid enough so I could rent my own flat in Marseille. As soon as she could she moved in with me. I was twenty-three, she was twenty-two. She was my world. I never would have sought more. I was…so happy. We got engaged, were planning to get married…children, everything. It was a case of perfect alignment. We lived together for over four years before the juggernaut.'

He crashed his palms together.

'She was swept off her feet by another man. Someone I knew. She told me before I found out about the affair, which was brave of her I suppose. Virtually overnight, she packed up and moved out. I didn't hear from her for many months and then one day I got a call. She told me she was pregnant by this man and that he'd ended the relationship because of it. I asked if she wanted to see me but the next time she called it was to tell me she was returning to Lille. I don't know what happened because I never heard from her again.'

Pierre sat back in his chair, head lowered, hands clasped in his lap. He seemed to be weeping but without the tears. Maybe he'd shed too many. I had to restrain myself from asking who she'd run off with even though I was dying to know. When he looked back up, his eyes were opaque.

'When I met my ex-wife, I was still aching for Flore, in need of an anaesthetic. And she was it. Deep down I knew it wouldn't last, I wasn't in love with her, I don't know if I loved her at all, and I think she felt that. That's why I didn't fall apart when I found out she was having an affair.'

I shook my head. I had to wait to respond, the lump in my throat strangling sound.

'You've been unlucky in love, very unlucky. It's hard to understand.'

But I understood better now the patina of sadness behind his smile.

I saw the answering machine light blinking as soon as we walked into the kitchen and almost tripped in my rush to press the button. There was a message from Annie Leung in Hong Kong offering more work, a trip to Hamburg for a shipping report. Very good. A click, and then Alain's voice.

'*Ma chérie*, I'll be back Sunday afternoon. Not sure what TGV I'll get so I'll take a taxi from the station. Paris has been even crazier this year and there were *quelques crises* avec Marc. He's impossible. I hope you're being good. *Je t'embrasse fort*.'

Pierre was smiling at me. He seemed to be as relieved as I was.

The following afternoon Danielle stopped by. It was the usual *coucou* call for a cup of something and a chat. I'd spent the day alone so I didn't mind the company although I promised myself I wouldn't mention anything about men, or at least my man. I brought our drinks outside so we could take advantage of the hot May weather, a boon for the region's viniculture. Seated at the table under the plane trees, Danielle lost no time in asking how things were with Alain.

'We're fine, just fine.'

'That's good to hear. I know you went through a rough patch.'

What had Alain told her?

'Well, it's all good now.'

She ignored my laconic replies.

'I know he can be difficult, so I wanted to tell you that if you ever need to talk about him, I'm here and can help.'

Which statement she took as a cue to embellish on her past hot-blooded relationship with my husband. Only this time, her version of what had happened between them was quite different to the one she had presented in September, and all the more incredible for the helping hand she had just proffered to me.

'Alain and I were really happy together,' was the gist of it. 'If it wasn't for the stupidity I committed with Jacques we'd still be together. And the sex with him, *c'était le top, le top*, the best I've ever had.'

Why was she telling me this? Was it torture, tactlessness or stupidity? Was she aware of her script rewrite?

'I hope he's sold lots of kitchens and can spend more time in Carrara.' She said this with genuine concern before driving off, leaving me speechless.

Nevertheless, I tried to feel some compassion for Danielle, the fact that she'd not had an easy time of it. Her father had walked out of their flat in Port-de-Bouc when she was just a baby. She'd never known him. Her mother had struggled to raise her and her brother, a succession of men in and out of her bed. Danielle's suffering over this primal abandonment had, not surprisingly, stalked her into adulthood, giving rise to her relentless need for male attention. Her brother was in the process of destroying himself with hard drugs. In a month or two, she would be unemployed and she was as confused as ever about what she wanted to do, although she definitely didn't want to be a secretary anymore. She yearned to find a niche where her flamboyant nature would be an asset. But apart from her Bac, she had no qualifications and not much official work experience. Below the seductive, insouciant surface she was a tangle of insecurities and melancholy.

Maybe an hour after she'd left, the phone rang.

'Hello,' I greeted.

'Hi, is this Danielle?' a male voice asked, surely realising it wasn't.

'No it's not. I'm Ravinia. Who is this?'

'My name is Jean George. I'm looking for Alain.'

The name rang a bell. Ah yes, he was the young, black, handsome stud based near Nice, who Alain had spoken tantalisingly about as the perfect partner for a threesome. 'You'll like him, I promise,' Alain had assured.

'He's in Paris at the moment, he'll be back…in a few days.'

'Alain phoned me up some time ago. He wanted to arrange a meeting, do you understand what I mean?'

'Yes I do.'

'So, what happened to Danielle?'

'They're no longer together. I live…I'm married…to Alain.'

'Ah really? I'm in Orange for the weekend. We could get together for a drink. For a little introduction.'

'I think it's better to wait till Alain comes back.'

'Are you sure? Some preliminaries won't do any harm.'

'I'm sure.'

That's how I knew that Danielle had done it all: The club, the sauna, the beach, the threesomes and god knows what else. And that she'd fucked Jean George with Alain right beside her—if not inside her.

That evening, when Pierre and I had finished dinner and were relaxing over mugs of tisane in the kitchen, I decided to let down my guard.

'Danielle came over again today.' I paused for emphasis. 'She has this way of telling me things I don't want to know about her past relationship with Alain. Very personal things. And it's really upsetting.'

Silence.

'You know something? I believe she still desires him and regrets her "stupidity", as she calls it, with Jacques.'

Again no reaction, which really irritated me. I persisted.

'How well do you know Danielle?'

Pierre must have realised I wouldn't let it go.

'Inasmuch as I've been in her presence, only superficially, which is enough. Truthfully, I've done my best to keep well away so I'm afraid I can't be of much help to you in deciphering her motives and actions. I can understand, though, that it must be very difficult for you that she still works for Alain and comes to the house. And I'm sorry she upset you today.'

He looked at me as if analysing a technical drawing, but when he spoke again it was with unexpected emotion.

'One thing I do believe. She cannot pose a threat to you and your marriage. You are a woman of integrity.'

Was I? And anyway, what was integrity compared to sexual nirvana. But then, Pierre was far removed from the destructive sexual cinema that thrived around here. Maybe that's one reason I enjoyed his presence so much. Not from him any smutty innuendos, double-entendres or drama. That, and the fact he was curious about the world, a thinker and reader, just like his brother. During a lengthy discussion about literature Pierre said he had a preference for historical biographies and science fiction. He spoke about his favourite authors—classical and modern. And I spoke about mine, revealing my lifelong love of Shakespeare and my book of quotes.

'Have you read any of his works?'

'A few. Some of the better-known plays, Macbeth, Hamlet, but only in French.'

'Ah but you see, Shakespeare was actually French, according to your brother.'

I repeated Alain's *petite histoire* (*j'expire…j'expire*), which extracted a wry smile from him.

Pierre's stay at the house while the owner was away had become an unspoken ritual, wonderfully reassuring for me. Not only was he easy to be around and interesting talk to, he also raised my level of gratitude—for one thing that I didn't share his routine, anchored in the real world of a daily office job and a commute. In the mornings, he was usually gone before I awoke. In the evenings, entering through the kitchen, he took off jacket and tie and draped them carefully over the back of a chair. I wasn't used to seeing suits or ties in the house. The ironing board had come out—it rarely did—put to use each night as Pierre ironed a shirt. He'd brought over enough shirts for the week so he didn't have to make daily trips home. He took care to smooth out the wrinkles, paying particular attention to the cuffs, the collar and the awkward shoulder seams, wielding the iron with patience, unlike me, producing sloppy results because I hated to iron and it showed. Meticulousness, a methodical approach, an eye to detail and an ability to be in the present while undertaking the task at hand no matter how tedious it was, these were other character traits that the brothers shared.

Not that their 'otherness' wasn't apparent in the littlest things. Where Alain had a bullfighter's confidence in the way he moved, listened and spoke, Pierre was of a quieter disposition and displayed more economy of movement, all part of his more measured cadence and everything-in-moderation philosophy. Not that he'd voiced this philosophy to me but it was how I interpreted his actions and the way in which he approached and lived his life. He certainly seemed to have more modest appetites than his brother and very different expectations, nothing at all wrong with that—indeed maybe it made for an easier, more fulfilling existence. Alain frequently laughed and laughed out loud, whereas Pierre was more likely to break into a smile that took a few seconds to reach his eyes but when it did they lit up. It was silly to compare their quirks and mannerisms but it was engrained in me. When I was growing up, people were always commenting on how different or similar I was to my sisters, which variously irked or delighted me.

One thing though: I couldn't help wondering, every time I saw Pierre pull into the drive, why he was doing this for me. Staying over at his brother's house, where he never randomly ventured, was a sacrifice no matter how you cut it. I supposed it was because of his innate altruism—more in the cast of Tristan. Yet he seemed to enjoy the company along with the home-cooked meals. At times, I caught him looking at me pensively, a look that seemed to hark back to some memory. Maybe it was a reflection about Flore or his ex-wife. Maybe his staying over reminded him of life as a couple and happier times. Perhaps it had nothing to do with echoes of the past but that he felt sorry for me—a foreigner still finding her way among some wily locals like Danielle. The thought never occurred to me that other motivations might be in the mix.

Chapter 23

Alain returned on Sunday at four in the afternoon with a suitcase full of pricey lingerie for me and horror stories about Paris. Pierre had left that morning, the ironing board put back in the bedroom opposite ours. I could wait to hear Alain's stories, but not to satiate the craving.

'Come with me,' he motioned as he went up to shower.

'You go first. I'll be up in a minute.'

I scrutinised his purchases, choosing a black lace bra with matching panties, garters and stockings. Not bad for size. He was waiting for me, lying naked and erect on the bed. He appraised his selections as I cat walked around the room, the sidelong mirror throwing back an image of breasts nudging out of their holders like cupcakes and legs and buttocks more toned than they had ever been thanks to the daily exercise with weights. I went to the bed, kicked off my shoes and straddled him. A long, greedy kiss, the two of us writhing on the mattress, the jolts of pleasure not just in the obvious zones but along my spine and at the crook of my neck. I pressed against his shoulder blade muscles, the staunch mass of his back, his firm buttocks. When he pushed inside from behind I almost fell onto my face, my arms unsteady. But how exquisite it was. My body was a sparkler that refused to extinguish. Afterwards, catching my breath, I told him that Jean George had called, not mentioning he'd first thought I was Danielle.

'Jean George told me you'd spoken to him about a threesome.'

'It's true. He said he'd get in touch when he was in the area.'

'How did you meet him?'

'Believe it or not, through a client. He was the client's nephew. He came along to one of the lunches we had where I clinched a deal for a very expensive kitchen. He invited us over to his house for dinner one night and things just progressed. With the understanding of course that nothing was to reach the ears of his uncle.'

'Well?'

'I can see that you don't need much persuading.'

'You've made him sound alluring.'

'I'll phone him. We'll make a day of it in Nice, shall we?'

Just as much as the sex, Alain was rabid for some home cooking.

'I think I had one decent meal in Paris. Those Parisian bistros, I don't believe it when they say they use fresh produce. And the meat. What a sacrilege. You can smell the stench of fear in the lamb and beef. And the bread is mouldy.'

'Well then, you ate in the wrong places.'

He burrowed into the fridge, removing a wedge of cheese, some lettuce and a handful of olives. In the pantry he grabbed a ripe tomato and a cucumber. With a look of rapture, he devoured all these various edibles along with a slice of grainy country bread, licking his lips at the last swallow. Only then did he start the cooking.

Over a dinner of grilled fish and braised endive he explained the drama.

'One of Marc's sales staff, a new recruit, gay and outgoing, got himself into trouble in a bar. Must have been the third night we were there. He was beaten up by some drunk in a brawl. Maybe it involved drugs, who knows. Marc got a call from the hospital the next morning. The man had a couple of broken ribs and a smashed jaw. So he was out of commission, which meant much more pressure on me and Sylvester—another new recruit. The foul-mouthed Marc refused to pay the extra charges on his hospital bill. Several times I came this close to quitting.' He demonstrated with a thumb-finger gesture.

'And the evenings. You ate with Marc?'

'Only twice. For the most part, I ate alone. I spent one evening at the Musée d'Orsay. Mostly I walked around, just to get some air. You know how much I love being cooped up. Thank god you didn't come.' He meant it nicely.

'Was it busy? Did you sell a lot?'

'I broke all records.'

'Congratulations.'

As blithely as I could I told him about Pierre staying over in Christophe's room.

'You mean he stayed here for a whole week? And you didn't tell me?'

'I wanted to, but you didn't phone.'

'But you could have phoned me, left a message at the hotel.'

'I wanted to give you some space so I purposefully didn't call. I honestly thought you wouldn't mind. He stayed over once when you went to Lyon for a night, remember? It was you who asked him to. The truth is, I was exhausted, scared to sleep alone in the house. He did me a favour. Don't even think for a second…'

'He needs to get a life.'

'What does that mean? He has a life, a very full life. He's taken up jogging now, to get fit. Wants to run the Paris Marathon. I know you two are not close. It's a real shame—I know, it's not my business. He's been through some really tough times in his life, things I don't think he's recovered from yet. I mean, how terrible to have the woman you love go off with someone you know. That seems to have done him…'

Abruptly I stopped. Alain's expression, it was eerie.

'I see he's divulged the saga of his love life to you.'

'He just told me about losing the woman he was engaged to. It was because I asked him about his marriage, or rather his divorce. I was curious.'

'You were curious? That was prying and it wasn't appropriate.'

A mean-ness was mapped on his face.

'Alain I'm sorry.'

I wondered why I was apologising. Why such anger? I thought about Tristan and my digging in to his life. Alain didn't mind that.

His first night back, ending in a bust.

The critique started the following day, with a small tear in my stocking tights. I'd showered and dressed and was just about to set off for Carpentras on errands when he zeroed in on it.

'How can you wear those tights?'

'Why, what's wrong with them?'

'You haven't seen the rip?' he pointed to it with an accusatory finger. '*Putain*, it's an obvious indication of how you take care of yourself. Or rather how you don't. *Tu es une catastrophe*.'

He stalked off.

A catastrophe, this time said in seriousness. Me a catastrophe. I felt the ribbed thread on bare skin and cursed the tights as if they'd knowingly played me a dirty hand. I went upstairs, took them off and threw them in the bin. I felt bewildered and ashamed. But this was only the start.

'Why haven't you lit the candles yet? It's starting to get dark. Honestly, can't you even remember that?' Alain admonished that evening.

Unbelievably, he took me to task for gesticulating with my hands.

'You express way too much emotion with your hands. It doesn't become you and it's annoying. Learn to talk without making all those distracting movements.'

Since when had this innate trait become a no-no?

Whereas before I'd had no trouble pleasing Alain, now it seemed there was nothing I could do right. When the next morning I came downstairs in a pair of sweatpants, he lambasted me for looking dishevelled and frumpy, displaying a sarcasm that I'd only seen him direct at Marc (he told me to throw away the item of clothing, which I didn't do).

'Your left eyebrow, it's not straight,' he hammered. My hand flew to the offending brow and I rushed to the mirror. Looking closely, I could detect only the slightest jag, nothing I could fix or that warranted fixing, at least for any sane person. Alain issued a constant stream of invective over the state of my appearance in general, even though I had become fastidious to a fault—at least in my perspective—about body maintenance. Yet, by his exacting standards, I was a failure.

If this was a rebellion, it took a different form from before. He wasn't ignoring me, treating me as invisible. Quite the opposite, he was scrutinising me, watching my every move and unleashing criticism after criticism. A bit of dust on a shoe was a prelude to an orchestral attack, most of it conducted at fortissimo pitch, encapsulating the disregard I obviously had for myself, and how much I needed to have a greater sense of responsibility about my body.

'You just don't know how to make the best use of your assets. What a waste,' he scolded, as if it were Mozart's talent that was at stake.

With every day that passed, I felt more and more battered. And the kind of shame and humiliation I remember feeling when I was five years old in the first year of primary school and was ridiculed by some boys—who'd lifted up my skirt—for wearing a pair of old knickers. He poured out his scorn on me and I took it without any comeback, like a dog who licks his master's hand after being beaten by that hand. It didn't matter that I knew Alain was being deliberately cruel. He knew my weak points, my proclivity for self-doubt, and he exploited these masterfully. The worst of it was, I started to believe him, that I was a catastrophe. I questioned the very essence of who I was and what I was capable of. Couldn't I do anything right?

The anger that I couldn't direct to him turned inwards, attacking like an auto-immune disease. You're pathetic. How can you be so submissive? He's verbally abusing you and you do nothing? Where the hell is your strength and courage?

Speak. Up. Don't. Take. Shit. Fight. Back. But I didn't fight back because of the cavernous need I had for him. I was afraid that if I spoke out Alain's love for me (whatever was left) would dissolve as fast my self-esteem was doing now. Besides, at least once a day he'd catch himself and say, 'I didn't mean to upset you. I'm doing this for your own good, to improve your sense of self-worth and self-care.' And we still made love, although much less.

In any case, I couldn't upset the boat now. I was leaving for Hamburg shortly to interview more than a dozen people for a report on German shipping. Now wasn't the time to fall apart. I promised myself I'd sort things out when I came back. It was remarkable, nevertheless, to observe how in the space of two weeks a crack in the wall of my confidence had turned into a demolition job. A day before my departure, Alain let drop: 'When you leave for Hamburg I'm going to Carrara. Vicenzo is going to meet me there. We're going to scout around for an apartment.'

'What? You promised we'd go together. The two of us. You promised when you left for Paris you'd take me,' I heard myself plead.

'I know, but the timing is perfect. You're away, so I can kill two birds with one stone. It seems silly to waste this opportunity. And when you do come to Carrara, with any luck I'll already have a flat.'

Alain dropped me off at Avignon station for my overnight train to Hamburg before heading off himself to Italy. Hamburg was cold, grey and sober, in perfect synchronicity with my mood. I did what I had to do—thankfully Annie Leung had set up all the interviews so I had only to show up and do my job. At night, I hibernated in the flat that belonged to some friends of hers. After seven days in Hamburg, I took an overnight train back to Provence, arriving at around nine in the morning. Alain was supposed to meet me at the station, but instead, I caught sight of Danielle.

'Alain couldn't make it, he had an appointment so he asked me to collect you. I hope you don't mind.'

Provocatively dressed as usual, chirpy and chatty, she filled me in on her week as we drove to Carpentras.

'Alain got back last night,' she informed. And the clincher: 'He's found a flat in Carrara.'

My blood boiled. I had to learn about this from her? When we arrived at La Belle Cuisine, Alain was affectionate, hugging me tightly. We gathered in the office, Alain busy at his desk tying up a few administrative odds and ends,

Danielle and I sitting opposite. I felt as rumpled as a used sheet, my clothes and hair wreaking of the stale odour of the train. I glanced at her, her lips so enticing to watch—what must they feel like to kiss? Then for the ostensible purpose of explaining something she rose up, went around the desk and stood over Alain, one hand on his shoulder, the other on her hip, her body close to his—a posture so brazenly flirtatious it belonged to a Hollywood sizzler.

'Well you two, have a good night,' Danielle waved us off when we left the shop. We got into the car.

'*Alors*?' I said.

'Oh Ravinia, I've found a dream flat in Pietrasanta. It's perfect. But it's only available from September.'

He described at length the fluke by which he and Vicenzo happened upon an apartment in that small, medieval Tuscan town, 'a magnet for artists from everywhere'.

'We'll be able to spend weeks, maybe months at a time there.'

I noted the 'we'. The inclusive talk buoyed my spirits. My mood rode on the coat-tails of Alain's, buttressed by the success of his trip and the progression of his marble Buddha. He'd almost finished the lower torso, splayed out into a basin-like lap symbolising the lotus position.

While he sculpted, I wrote my report for Annie Leung, the major distraction the view from my window, the magnetic pull to the rolling vineyards and olive trees, topped by expansive sky. The day after I faxed it to her, Alain's evil alter ego reared up. The verbal whippings began anew, with fresh vehemence. I was a 'catastrophe' for having a bit of dirt on the sole of my shoe or failing to look sexy enough. Apropos of which, the barbs now reached into the bedroom. We were coupling doggy-style on our bed one night when Alain abruptly pulled out.

'I can't do this,' he fumed. 'I just can't do it. It's her fault.' He pointed to my pussy. 'I've told you that sensuality is vital to me. We're not sexually compatible.'

It was an echo of our last night in the Amazon, only much more of a sexual put-down. Tears spat out of me.

'What are you talking about?' I was nearly hysterical. 'After all we've done together, at the club, at the beach, partner swapping, you're telling me you're not happy? That I'm not sensual enough for you?'

He went to the sink and washed his face, disdain flowing from him like waste discharge during a colonic He's thinking of Danielle. I know it. Why can't I just say her name. Call him on it…Danielle. The white elephant in this room.

'You're comparing me to Danielle, aren't you? The sex bomb,' I added in English There, I'd done it. Now I waited for the 'yes, that's right, the best I've ever had, much better than you in bed.'

Alain froze for a moment, then forced a laugh.

'So that's what you think? I'm comparing you to *one* woman?'

The way he emphasised one.

'It's broader-based than that. Maybe a cultural thing. I need a woman who's sensual, wild, a real tigress,' he said, implying I was none of these things.

He began to talk about some of his past lovers as if they had created the Kama Sutra—the subscript being that I was below par to any of them. So every one of these women had climaxed solely through the act of intercourse, needing no other stimulation than his mighty organ? They were presumably always multi-orgasmic too. Ha. Probably they'd simply been fantastic fakers. But I didn't say that. In a twisted way, I was glad he hadn't singled out Danielle, but I didn't buy it. She was still the barometer against which I was measured only he would never say it. He disappeared downstairs to hunt for some whisky, ostensibly to calm me down but it was probably more for his own sake since he couldn't bear female tears or histrionics.

That night we slept back to back, although slept is a misnomer, the shattering realisations like electric prods, preventing me from switching off. Now I knew the hideous error I had made in leaving Hong Kong. Ditching a dream job for a demented artist who acted as if marriage were a form of torture. For a narcissist, an extremist, a perfectionist bastard. For a man who was the opposite of the partner I'd yearned for. How reckless I'd been, how blind, to throw it all away on a whim, led by my hankering for love, my fear of being alone. How, I lambasted myself, had I been so hoodwinked? His vicious, sadistic outbursts were impossible to reconcile with the man I'd fallen for, the gentleman jester in Vietnam, the laid-back lover in Hong Kong, the compassionate hand-holder during those initial months in Provence. It seemed inconceivable that once upon a time he'd come across as so comedic that I couldn't take him seriously. I'd been blinded but the omens had been there right from the start, beginning with my arrival on April fool's day. A fool indeed is what I was. Fool. Fool. Fool. You brought this on yourself.

And yet, the epiphanies hardly mattered.

I was, I was loathe to admit, addicted to him, attached to him like he was the last man on earth. I was hooked on him, all of him. Leaving was impossible, no matter what he said or did. I craved him. I needed his touch, his physicality, his approval. Without it I was sunk, broken, an empty vessel. Nothing else was important. He, or rather his moods, called the shots. If he was nice to me, I was happy. If he was mean, I was miserable. My mental state depended entirely on how he acted and reacted to me. I knew that my yearning for those early days was nothing but a dead end, but yearn I did for the time when he was full of love, when he prefixed his phrases with 'darling' and 'my beauty', when I felt desired, prized, adored, idolised. When he was his charming, magnetic, luminous, resourceful, poetic, squeezing-the-most-out-of-life self.

Alain was out most of the following day. In the evening, I slipped into something slinky, lit the candles, and put chicken and mushrooms in white wine sauce on the stove to simmer. The smell of the food turned my stomach, that and the lead-ball tension I carried. When he walked into the kitchen, he barely nodded. We ate wordlessly, that is, he ate. He was as taut as a tightrope, eyes like drills.

'Talk to me Alain, tell me what's going on.' I knew the moment had come.

He exhaled a tank-full of air.

'I'm miserable. I can't pretend anymore. I'm not cut out for marriage. I feel trapped, in a place where I don't know who I am. You and I—it doesn't work.'

'So, you don't want to live with me any longer, you want us to split?'

'Yes. I want to be on my own.'

I swear I would have preferred a bullet to my head at that point.

'Why did you marry me Alain? Last time I checked, you told me that you didn't feel forced into it.'

'I admit that wasn't entirely true. I did it because I owed you the right of residency here for giving up Hong Kong and your job. I thought, mistakenly, that it would be different. That I would feel different.'

'So, you were honest with your mother and not me.'

A terrible quietness and then, 'What did you want from me Alain?'

He reflected for a minute, his eyes closed.

'Passion,' his eyes sprung open. 'That's what I wanted from you. Passion.'

PASSION? I had passion enough for the whole of Provence. I had more of it than blood. But passion, that ephemeral, transitory intangible? The stuff that blazes hot and puckers out with a pathetic whimper? I wanted more than passion. As a basis for a relationship, a marriage, it was like playing Russian roulette every week…now you're here, now you're not. I tried to explain all that to him.

'Well, I need passion, and if that means changing a woman every six months, then that's how it will be for me.'

Alain went up to bed. I crawled up the stairs to my study and lay, tormented, on the sofa. My world had collapsed. I'd failed. All Fs in the subjects I'd signed up for, sexuality, sensuality…*la vie à deux*. Is this what cold turkey felt like—the chilled skin, the shivers, the twisted gut? Worse than anything were the heart palpitations, the sweats, the beginnings of a panic attack. The more I tried to calm my breathing the more my heart raced. I only know that at some point, as I began praying to something out there, numbness took over. My head seemed to separate from my body and hover in space. I looked down at myself from above, saw myself picking up the phone and dialling my father in America.

'It's over, Dad, it's over with Alain.' The words came out zombie-like.

'What? For god's sake what happened?' I'd heard his nail-hard tone of voice only rarely in my life—during moments of family crisis. My father had no inkling of the rift in our relationship.

'He doesn't want to live with me anymore. He says we're not compatible. I bore him.'

I gave him a brief chronology of events, shorn of all references to sex.

'Leave Provence. Come here, you need to get away from there, get some help.'

'That's good of you Dad, thank you, but I don't know, I don't know what to do.'

My dad kept on with his reasoned talk and solid arguments as to why I should hurtle to the paternal home, but I couldn't commit to any action because I wasn't capable of making a decision. I'd reached out to my father instinctively—when in dire straits I could always count on him, he was my rock and fortress after all. But now I wanted off the phone for with each word he spoke the numbness retracted and the pain returned and my doppelgänger gazing down from above vanished. My mind started flipping around like a car without suspension, my breathing once again punctuated by palpitations.

'Please. Think about what I've said. Sleep on it,' he finished with.

But sleep was elusive. There was no respite from the despair and desperation and there was nothing to blank out my feelings. In the morning, in a state of wrung out delirium, I confronted Alain.

'How can you say it doesn't work, that we're not compatible? You never hinted you weren't happy with me before the marriage, sexually or otherwise.'

But was that true?

'Now that I'm settled in Provence, made a life for myself, you sabotage the relationship. You haven't given this a chance. You don't know who I am. You've never bothered to find out.'

'Look, maybe I'll give this another go after we take a break from each other,' he said, raising my hopes. But the next hour he recanted.

'I'm no good at marriage. Can't you see, this isn't fair to you? I'm thinking about you. What's the point of continuing? You want children. And I don't.'

'You made it seem like you did when you proposed to me, and when we talked about it afterwards. Children. You lied to me about that too.'

'I lied to myself. Listen, I want you to meet someone who can give you that. There are plenty of men who would be keen. And I want to be free, to sculpt without any burdens or barriers.'

And to fuck women with passion. The truth was out but I clung on like a creeping vine. I would have sacrificed everything, motherhood included, to reserve a place in his bed. We went back and forth, my objections to his rejection, his counter-objections. It was Julia who, that same day, broke my paralysis and persuaded me to get on a plane to America, alarmed by my hysterical sobs on the phone.

'Get yourself out here or I'll come and get you myself.'

'So, how much time do I have before you kick me out?' I broke through my Dantesque fog to ask Alain as he drove me to Marseille airport an excruciating day later.

'Find yourself a job first, then move out.'

At a café in the airport, he downed an espresso.

'Put some new ideas into that head of yours,' he waggled a finger at me, my mind circumnavigating madness.

I felt bad for my father. He'd earned enough merit points in his life to enjoy a bit of tranquillity, to see his children settled and decided on a path. As a mellower septuagenarian he wasn't too particular about what that path was, so long as it wasn't harmful. That said, he had high hopes for me, the youngest daughter, the globetrotting adventurer who he forever tried to protect. So the gaunt, emotional mess that walked through his front door—bearing no semblance to the strong woman who'd left Hong Kong—wasn't easy for him to behold.

'Your daughter's a failure,' I repeated over and over again. 'I couldn't please him.'

He cringed at such words. However, in the ten days I stayed with him he never once lectured me. He never once gave me the 'I told you so' speech that I richly deserved. Instead, he treated the whole escapade as an aggravating but not uncommon mistake—a mistake that wasn't the fatality I was making it out to be. I could quickly recover if only I'd file the past and move on. I was still young—young enough at any rate to begin again, meet a good man and have children. He was fatherly and masterful in soothing and reassuring, but below the stolid surface I could detect his feelings of helplessness. He suffered, seeing my pain.

'Stay here for a month, for as long as you want, to sort things out and get your bearings,' he urged.

'I'm grateful for the offer Dad, I really am. But I have to go back to France, make a new life.'

'Why there? Why not go to London where you have family?'

'Since I married in France, I might as well make use of the residency permit I'm eligible for.'

The truth was, I just wasn't ready to let France go. I'd gone so far as to whittle down the options to Paris, where the jobs were, and la dolce vita Nice in the south, my much-preferred choice. My next stop though was Manhattan and Julia, who took a tough-love line with me.

'Where's your anger at Alain?'

'I don't know. I can't get to it. I can't feel it.'

'You need to. You've got to see him for what he is. His kind of mental cruelty has a deep dark foundation. Don't tell me it's just a little allergic reaction to marriage. The man's a menace. He blatantly lied to you, leading you to believe he married you for love. I don't think he's capable of truly loving a woman. I saw that he was a perfectionist and a bit of a narcissist on my first visit, though I couldn't tell you that. And now it turns out, he's mentally abusive, a misogynist. It's disgusting. Wake up, I want you to see this.'

'How can someone change so much?' I spewed ad nauseam.

'The signs were there, you just didn't pick up on them, or didn't want to pick up on them. And maybe there's something going on which you're not seeing.'

But no matter what she, my father or anyone else said to me, I felt I was to blame for the destruction of the relationship. It was my fault that I couldn't please Alain. If only I hadn't done this, that and the other. If only I had done things differently, then maybe I would have been good enough.

'It's you he doesn't deserve. Can't you see that?' she tried to drum into me. I knew it intellectually, but emotionally I was nowhere near to feeling it. As for Alain's accusations that I wasn't up to par in the bedroom—I finally told her about the partner swapping—she didn't swallow it.

'It's all an excuse for his inability to deal with intimacy. How convenient to make you the scapegoat for what's wrong with him.'

Julia was my Florence Nightingale in New York. She had a gift for helping others to see their blind spots, not that I was able to make much progress in dealing with mine. Bastard, sadist, narcissist, toxic misogynist, psychotic perfectionist, screwed up son-of-a-bitch—whatever he was, I couldn't let go of him. We discussed my plight for hours on end, Julia trying to inject some levity.

'So Mr Hyde, which side does he come from, the Basque or the Venetian?'

'More Basque I imagine—although no reflection on his mother. The Italian bit is mostly crazy about Carrara and sculpting, although come to think of it, that goes hand in hand with his extreme perfectionism.'

I was no psychologist but it seemed evident that Alain's relationship with his mother was pivotal to the origins of his misogyny. I couldn't figure out how or why though. She didn't come across as either a nagger/castrator or a Virgin Mary type. I couldn't detect any monstrosities in her make up that might have warped her son's vision of the female sex. Maybe, on the contrary, it was because of this: she had showered him with such perfect love as a baby that when the necessary psychological separation happened—a crucial part of her launching him into independence and manhood—he subconsciously never forgave her for it. Henceforth he had taken this primal 'rejection' out on others of her sex. It was Julia who provided this seemingly logical and technical explanation about his psyche, or rather a psychologist friend of hers who she'd rung up for an opinion.

Even so, I wondered if the contempt he had for women was somehow linked with his father who he had cherished. I thought of Valérie's words: 'It's possible he holds a grudge, blames Josephine for his father's death—on an unconscious level of course.' But he hadn't treated Brigitte or Danielle with such contempt, had he? Then again, they hadn't been so dependent on him, they hadn't moved halfway across the world, given up their life for him as I'd done. They spoke his language. They were French.

I was pleased to see how clear Julia's facial complexion was and to hear that she was controlling her stress levels better. She and Doug lived in a decent-sized, two-bedroom apartment on Third Avenue and 21st street. You could feel the abundance of good feng shui as soon as you entered. The bed in my room was perpendicular to a mahogany chest on top of which sat an assortment of Buddhas, both gifted to Julia and bought. Normally I would have found them soothing, but now they just reminded me of Alain's marble Buddha. The smaller ones I put in a drawer. One night, my impulses getting the better of me, I phoned the house. Danielle answered.

'Ravinia? Where are you?' She sounded curious.

'I'm in New York. What are you doing at the house?'

'I'm cleaning up. We had a wonderful party last night.'

And she launched into a line-by-line account of it, mentioning names. Vicenzo was there, of course. He'd driven over for a week with a car full of iron castings for a gallery in L'isle-sur-la-Sorgue. The gallery had signed him up for a two-month exhibit, a veritable coup. His presence had coincided with the late spring fete at the house that I could never have faced. Danielle hadn't yet finished when I cut her off with, 'I'll call Alain later' and hung up, fearing I might have a mental breakdown.

'For the love of god please don't go back to Provence, don't go back to the house,' Julia pleaded with me.

'I have to. All my stuff is there. I can't just abandon it.'

'Can't you get someone to pack it up for you?'

'That's a huge ask. And anyway I need to know where my things are, my personal papers and all that.'

'Then do it fast. Box it all up and then scoot. Don't stay a single night in the house with him.'

Staying in New York was not an option and Julia knew better than to suggest it. I had a visceral dislike of the city I had lived in for seven years after England. It bore tragic memories of my mother, who died in the apartment where we'd lived on 83rd street and Third Avenue, not yet forty-six years old. In the face of her spreading cancer, the doctors had given her at most a year to live but four months after their diagnosis she got pneumonia, was hospitalised, and then released at her insistence under a nurse's care. A day later she slipped into a coma and soon after stopped breathing. I never got to say goodbye.

But my dislike of the city wasn't only due to my mother's death.

Another bone of contention was something much more prosaic: the hardness and harshness of its contours; the slim slivers of anything blue and breathable between the towers of glass and concrete that made me feel like the air and sky were rationed. Against everyone's protestations I headed back to Provence, to the Minotaur and his lair, but the elements—the spectral sky, Mont Ventoux and the vines—were not inconsequential lures.

Chapter 24

Alain was waiting for me at Marseille airport, a demon decked in a black leather jacket, scalding blue eyes in a darkly, irreverently irresistible face sizing me up. It was all familiar, the shaky gut, the sweats, the dry mouth, my utopian hopes for immediate salvation encapsulated in a smile from him that never came, humdrum conversation only enlarging the importance of the torrent left unsaid.

'I hope Julia and your father didn't speak too badly of me,' was his riskiest one liner, which I met with silence. This time, however, the pastel colours of Provence seemed to taunt me beyond the car windows as if to say: Now that you're leaving, we've just received a fresh coat of paint and we're more beautiful than ever.

This I already missed: pulling into New Delhi Drive, the peachy exterior of the house looming up like some Greek temple; opening the kitchen door to imbibe the earthy scent of the white-washed walls mixed with the faint odour of fresh vegetables in the pantry and the smoky remains of a doused fire in the three dogs room; the timeless gaze of his sculptures, so confident-looking in their niches.

Once inside I went upstairs to unpack, take a shower and change, determined to keep a distance from Alain while I hunted for a job and made plans. My intentions were good, but how naive I was to think I could honour them. The most obvious thing to do—apart from never returning—was to move into my study, steering clear of the house's owner. But no. After changing, as if yanked by an invisible chain, I gravitated to the three dogs room.

He was sitting on the sofa reading a book, shafts of rays through the windows creating playful patterns on the cushions. I sat down at the other end of the sofa, knowing I shouldn't, knowing he was a magnetic field, knowing that in his presence rational behaviour was impossible. His eyes diverted from the book to me. I was expecting him to say buzz off but he said nothing at all. Was I interpreting it right—the suggestion of a smile, his blue eyes gentler, an inviting spark? I moved towards him, tentatively touching an arm. There was no rebuff but an automatic, atavistic response, his touches a lightning rod.

When he penetrated me that was it—the hit I craved, the craving crushing all the defences marshalled from the sensible talking-tos by family and friends. All my nous, and nothing had changed. So what if I couldn't meet his 'pleasing' criteria, so what if those criteria were jaundiced, the go-to narrative of a narcissist.

Now that the ice was cracked, the formality between us funnelled into something softer, even if we spoke little. It was only later, in the candle-lit aftermath of a home-cooked dinner that he said decisively, though not unkindly, 'Listen Ravinia, I want our relationship to be purely on a friendship basis, okay? Forget about being husband and wife. All that is over. *Nous sommes amis, c'est tout.*'

Friends. Just like that. Ha, as if I could ever be that with him. Never mind that he was much nicer to his friends than to me. Never mind he wasn't cut out to be a husband of any kind, let alone the kind I had dreamed of. His statement that now we were just friends was no lifeline but a casting loose to a sinking. For therein lay my Hades. I still wanted him and wanted him to want me even though I knew he never would. It was my own little Shakespearian tragedy. *For where thou art, there is the world itself, and where though art not, desolation*—a quote from Henry VI.

The blind hope that had infused me during our brief coupling disappeared into nothingness and I felt despair and anger at myself for acting like a woman with no self-respect. But that's exactly what I was, a woman with no self-respect. Pathetic and deserving of his disdain.

But miracle of miracles. I hadn't reckoned on the effect that Alain's proclamation would have on himself. Like a spell, it magically removed the matrimonial chains, leaving in their place a renewed sense of freedom and sparking a dramatic change in behaviour that was utterly unexpected. The next morning, he morphed back into Cupid. Our 'friendship' was very nearly a replay of his courtship. '*Ma beauté*,' he once more mouthed, complete with the salivating looks and the precious-porcelain handling. Back in his good graces, restored to my perch, the fog of misery evaporated, replaced by something akin to joy. It didn't matter that it was temporary. The momentary fix, his momentary attentions, were all that counted. Talk about living in the present. At dinner that night he even proposed a deal:

‘You take me to London so I can see where you grew up, in exchange for a visit to Carrara.’

I knew that the offer was pure fantasy, but even so, his words were more resuscitating than an intravenous drip. Sexually I was desirable again, the energy flowing into his loins. No more did I use my fingers. I couldn’t bring myself to do any faking, but I did go heavier on the vocals. The sex felt both more urgent, knowing every instance could be the last, and yet more impersonal because of my self-consciousness. To further compensate for my shortcomings I played the more sexually adventurous, luring him to places where it was risqué, such as on the balcony in broad daylight. I was turning into his ideal, a zealous exhibitionist, just perhaps a year too late.

And then came the olive branch Alain extended one balmy evening. We were enjoying the quiet after a raucous lunch in the garden with a dozen friends. Franco, Nadine and her three children had spent the previous night with us, and the Scottish couple Lillian and Glen were there with their baby. For once, Danielle and Jacques were absent. For a portion of that lunch, basking in the warm air rippled by a gentle breeze amid blossoming vines and dappled fields, all my cares in the world seemed as somnolent as the bees whose nest lay high up in one of the plane trees. Until, that is, Franco and Alain started trading quips about how men were really not manufactured to be monogamous and required a constant replenishment of young females in their stable, their tone suggesting many more grains of truth than gibberish. At one point Lillian, the Scotswoman, leaned over to me, rolling her eyes skyward and whispered, ‘Honestly, what a bunch of macho idiots.’

After everyone had left and we’d cleared up, I went for my daily walk to Mazan, a blend of exercise and walking meditation. When I returned, Alain, lying in the Indian corner, told me to go upstairs and take a shower.

‘When you come down, I want your royal jewels on display.’

I appeared according to his instructions and he began to choreograph:

‘Walk this way, turn a bit more, bend down, that’s good, that angle there. Don’t move.’

Well after the sex, as the sun bled its sleepy red, as we sat sipping a glass of rosé in the three dogs room, he asked how the book was coming along.

‘Not well Alain. I can’t concentrate on the research when I’m in emotional turmoil.’ Given Sylvie’s objections I’d all but decided to abandon the book, but there was no point in mentioning this now.

'Friends or not, I still love you.'

'And I don't? Listen,' he said, taking my hand. 'I have a proposition to make. I invite you to spend the summer here. Relax, we'll have a good time, then we'll re-evaluate the situation in September.'

Oh to be able to freeze that moment like autumn-picked truffles.

On a Saturday night when Christophe was staying at the house, Alain proposed we go to Aphrodite. The last sizzler we'd spent there was in February, a lifetime ago. For the first time since my initial visit, I was reluctant. No, I flat out didn't want to go. I knew it would be different, no matter that his love tap was turned on. How would I feel to see him pairing off now that we were no longer a secure couple? Exhibitionism apart, I no longer wanted the sexual whistles and bells, to play the game. Just being with Alain was enough. It was everything. But I knew if I refused he'd turn sour and the cruel Alain risked returning. So I agreed. Anything to please him.

Entering the foyer of the club, Alain put his arm around my waist. He ordered champagne, asked me to dance, caressed me—all as usual. He followed the script, leading me up the stairs where spider-like, bodies entangled in the dimness. It wasn't long before a woman caught his scent and slithered onto him, the cue for me to switch to automatic pilot and select a nameless monsieur. As we partner swapped, Alain kept me in his sight. *He's still looking at me*. It was only after he returned to me and we made love, that I finally started to relax. The tension bunched in my stomach dissolving. It was then that he said, 'Do you see that couple over there?' He indicated the corner where they were caressing each other on large floor cushions.

'I've seen them here several times before. What do you say we approach them for a *soirée* at home?'

I couldn't recall their faces but even if I'd been able to, so what. I didn't want strangers, threesomes, foursomes or couple-swapping evenings at home. But what I wanted, in my state of fear and insecurity, was beside the point. If Alain wanted it, we would do it.

'Yes, okay, go ahead.'

If he caught the negative inflection in my voice he ignored it. He went over to the couple, discretely interrupting their intimacy. When he returned, smiling, I knew it was a deal. We left the club that night with their telephone number.

On the scheduled evening of our 'date', a buffed and beautified Alain preened, as usual, over my outfit and the hors d'oeuvres of pâté de foie gras, smoked salmon and goat cheese arrayed on a pewter tray in the long room. When our guests arrived, I immediately sensed trouble. The bad news was the woman—or more accurately how desirable she was and how much she damn well knew it. She was Eurasian, with glossy black hair to the midriff and facial features that surely turned heads. It was just as well that under the dim lighting I hadn't been able to observe her closely at the club. But now here she was, furiously pretty and nymphic on the sofa, her nipples showing through the thin fabric of a short, sleeveless red dress fastened by a neck strap. There was a fragility about her, perhaps because of her slight frame, but this was evened out by piercing cat eyes and a strain of petulance, contrasting with the placid, self-possessed manner of her husband. He wasn't much taller than her, had bushy brown eyebrows, a wide smile and a carpet of upright hair that looked as if it was trying to defy gravity. I could see that the tiger woman's frosty, tart sensuality was a turn-on for Alain.

If I hadn't wanted to partake before, now I positively felt like bolting. Having to play this shimmying-up role, knowing clearly that Alain just wanted to fuck her, seemed like my penitence for returning to Provence. But I had to go along with the show.

And so the *soirée* started, with a clink of champagne glasses and polite nibbles, napkins held aloft. When the husband launched conversationally into the story of how he and his wife first met, I assumed this was a prelude to a pair-off.

'She came to see me at my practice, a patient with an ailment. I'm a doctor. I was then recently divorced. Another entanglement was the last thing on my mind, but she stole my heart. There was nothing much wrong with her, but I told her to make another appointment.'

'I was charmed by him too, right away.' She threw him a foxy look. 'That first time he kept me talking in his consultation room for a good hour. I got the dirtiest looks from patients in the waiting room when I walked out,' she grinned.

It was easy to see who wore the pants in that relationship, the husband admitting that his professional life was one thing. It was quite another story at home, where his job was to cater to his wife's whims, sexual and otherwise. Ten years on they were as happy as doves. So happy, in fact, that the woman had no interest in partner swapping with a man. That much became clear when she opened the bag of sex toys she'd brought and fished out a large black rubber dildo. Wordlessly, she removed her dress, revealing cherry-nipple breasts, lace-trimmed silk panties and stay-up stockings over her long thin legs—the star of the show. I watched in morbid curiosity as she strapped on the belt to which the dildo was attached.

'Come on, let's have some fun.' She looked at me. That's when I realised where she wanted to put that thing. That, inside me? How ridiculous. Dildos didn't do it for me. Both Alain and I passed on sex toys, preferring flesh to plastic, rubber, leather and metal. Yet I was so relieved she hadn't zeroed in on Alain that I offered no resistance, indeed I put pillows on the floor and went on all fours, back lowered, behind raised. Alain was miffed by this unexpected turn of events, choosing to sit it out in a sulk. I wondered why he didn't just throw himself in, like he did during our threesome with Monique. Bending over me, tiger woman tried to insert the dildo, which must have been over ten inches long and plenty wide. Too wide, because even with a good dousing of lubricant gel—produced from the bag—the head wouldn't go in. Maybe my subconscious scuppered it. After much huffing and puffing and feeling my private parts stretched to the limit, I withdrew, apologetically.

'How about you fuck me then?' She was prepared to forgive. Removing the waistband she handed me the sex toy. I'd never worn one of these things but it was easy to put on, just a matter of adjusting and fastening the belt. What was it like to have a bulldozer penis protruding from me? It was hilarious, that's what. Try as I might, I couldn't suppress it. My laugh came in waves, a giant release of tension. Unfortunately, though, it was a mood killer, not the kind of thing to increase the erotic temperature. She looked at me with a kind of disgust, packed up the dildo and sought solace in the arms of her husband. What a faux pas I'd committed. I stopped laughing.

This played out well for Alain, who found a new opening in the scene of wife and husband copulating on the couch. He moved in close, kneeling to fondle her smooth white buttocks, rising and falling as she rode her man. It was after Alain unzipped his trousers to reveal his excitement that she whispered to her husband. Withdrawing from the sofa, he shot her a look that I knew very well—of complicity. Alain quickly took his place. Tiger woman kissed him coquettishly, then hungrily. His tongue slithered over her engorged nipples and down into her cockle-shelled vulva. At her bidding, he entered her.

That's when I began to sweat.

Every so often she caught the eye of her husband, draped on some cushions taken from the Indian corner. But Alain—he was completely engrossed in this sultry, petulant madame. I wanted to break them apart. Instead, I had to sit there and pretend I was hooked in. There wasn't the slightest hint of collusion from Alain and from the husband, only indifference. He rejected my advances, keen only on watching his wife, touching himself as the spectacle unfurled. This wasn't proper partner swapping but a duo with a masturbator. The minutes ticked by, Alain and the woman building into a crescendo, the husband quickening his strokes as I sat tense and useless on the floor, wishing that I'd never agreed to this evening, or at least hadn't laughed at the dildo. The woman screamed her pleasure—real or fake who knows—and the two men followed suit, the husband's spurts dribbling onto my favourite sequined patchwork cushion cover.

It was he who, after a heads-together with his wife, suggested before the goodbye pecks, 'How would you like to do this again some time?' Alain nodded vigorously. He didn't ask me if a repeat performance would be to my liking but I had my say after they'd left.

'Alain, the husband isn't interested in being with me, only in watching his wife. I feel left out.'

That was beside the point. I couldn't tell him I was no longer a game player. Partner swapping was fine if you were confident about your relationship status. Now, every female contender for a swap was my enemy.

Reluctantly I set off for the Côte d'Azur in my car on a look-see mission that I had hoped Alain would ask me to cancel, but he didn't. I had a hazy idea about sniffing out job opportunities and flats on the Riviera. However, the four days I managed to stay away from Alain were hardly enough for serious scouting. I looked at a few studio apartments in Grasse, an inland town nine miles from Cannes nestled amid velvety hills thick with jasmine. Its charm and mouth-watering views just made me more morose, reminders of the bounty I was forsaking in the artist's house I still considered my home.

The silver lining of that trip was connecting with Brigitte, who had insisted I stay with her in Cannes while I explored the region. How deceptive it felt walking into her flat. The bigness and radiance of her beauty warranted a poetic country cottage with a concupiscent garden, not the claustrophobic box she lived in with her son and lover. The kitchen had the most character. A jungle of flowering plants hung from baskets amid dangling bunches of garlic, the effect rather like a greenhouse.

After she dropped her toddler off at pre-school and before I set off on my wanders we sat at the kitchen table, finally able to chat in private.

'He's much worse than I thought,' she said in response to my account of Alain's three-week bout of 'post-traumatic stress disorder', the dismissal of our marriage and the loving comeback after the proclamation we were just *amis*. Even as she opined I couldn't help wondering, as I breakfasted on toast and coffee, if she'd come like clockwork with him and had the right kind of orgasms. I couldn't ask her about that. However, she did reveal that she'd grown tired of being a sexy siren every night, which I took as a cue to tell her about our sexual sorties, and she did set one record straight. With her, there had been no partner swapping.

'I think it must have started with Danielle,' who'd been a close friend of hers since their Bac days. I took the risk of unveiling my feelings about Danielle and was relieved when she empathised.

'When Alain and I were together, we often hung out with her and her boyfriend at the time. Danielle was my confidante. I told her all about my relationship problems. When she and Alain embarked on their frenzied affair I was really surprised, to put it mildly, and frankly, quite hurt. You should have seen them together. They were terrible to be around. They inflamed the air with their selfish, egotistical energy. They're so similar to each other.'

'What was it like when Alain and you broke up?'

'I was in a terrible state for a whole year. I didn't know who I was anymore, or what I wanted. I felt completely incapable, robbed of all confidence. Alain made me stop working when I was with him because he wanted me at home, which really set me back. It meant I lost years of job experience.'

'I'm really sorry for you that it's turned into such a mess with Alain. And to think that you came from so far away. He should live alone,' Brigitte concluded. 'He will never find a woman who satisfies him.'

The morning after my return from Cannes, Alain put both Christophe and I to work. His son sallied back and forth shifting the entire wood stack in the garden to the shed that Peppo had just finished building on the outside wall of the pantry. I gathered all the scraggly branches and lined them up neatly into piles at the garden's edge. We laboured while he sculpted. Peppo himself came over for lunch, joined by Danielle and Jacques. Afterwards, Alain took out the chessboard and the men hunkered down to an afternoon of pawns and castles.

'I have to go over to Benoit's to feed their cat while they're away. Why don't you come with?' Danielle offered. I accepted off the cuff. However, minutes after we'd left, I was furious with myself. Why had I said yes? I knew no good would come of her company. What was it with me? I had to admit a part of me wanted to have her on my side even if that meant swallowing some bile. Keep your friends close but your enemies closer. But did I really want to hear more lurid descriptions of her sex life with Alain? Not with any functioning part of my brain I didn't, but then my brain wasn't functioning properly, was it?

Angry and anxious, I followed her into Benoit's house. Danielle sat down on a grey leather pouf next to a low wooden table, took out a small paper pouch from her bag and carefully opened it.

'Want some?' she offered.

It was cocaine.

'No thanks.'

I was stuck. She'd taken her car. If I walked out, I had no way of getting back to the house. There were no buses or taxis where we were.

'I splurged on this stuff for Jacques' sake. I wanted to make him talk.'

She began to cut a long line on the table with a razor.

'Jacques isn't terribly communicative at the best of times but recently he's become totally tight-lipped and refuses to express any feelings whatsoever. I'm tearing my hair out over it.'

The white powder had worked wonders during their holiday in Costa Rica two winters before. A French friend of theirs living in the country had supplied them with copious amounts of coke and for a month, Danielle told me, 'We snorted and hardly slept. Jacques opened up to me as never before and seemed to blossom. It was amazing.'

But when she'd tempted him with the drug this time around he'd shown no interest and so she was finishing it off herself. It certainly activated Danielle's tongue, not that she had any need of a vocal diuretic.

'You seem to have patched things up with Alain.'

The coke now up her nose, she fished in her bag for cigarettes.

Control yourself, don't tell her anything. Not a word more.

'Yes,' I said tersely. I needn't have said anything.

'Listen Ravinia, this whole thing is not your fault. Look at me. I did everything possible to make him happy and the relationship still didn't last.'

And so began her monologue, where what tumbled from her overactive mouth was a jumble of contradictions. One minute she laid the blame for her infidelity with Jacques on Alain, saying that catering to his pleasure, dressing to his delectation had initially been immensely exciting, but then it had become exhausting. In the very next breath, she would lament how murderous it was when he walked out of the Carpentras studio they'd shared and how stupid she'd been to cheat on him.

'It was hell when he left. I suffered incredibly for months. Sexually it was hard, you know. I missed him. After all, Alain is talented in bed. He's the best I've ever had. After the break-up, I was very confused. I had a hard time accepting that the boundaries had changed, that there was no more physical involvement.'

Here we go again. Just what I'd feared. But even worse, for this time she was expressing emotions that were alive, current. The coke was betraying her. It was as clear as daylight that she still missed him, wanted him, maybe even craved him. I felt like strangling her, crushing her nubile neck and temptress torso with my bare hands. Again, I wondered if this was deliberate annihilation or just supreme insensitivity. I was too enraged to open my mouth. Maybe I should have had some coke. It would have made me talk.

Finally she stopped, looked at her watch and said, 'I think it's time we go.'

'Shouldn't you feed the cat?'

I wouldn't have reminded her only I felt bad for the cat.

'Ah yes of course,' and she rushed to the kitchen.

Back at the house, the men were still playing chess, a few joint ends in the ashtray and an empty bottle of wine on the table. Alain pulled me onto his lap, a gesture I wanted to flaunt in Danielle's face. See, he's still mine. Keep your paws off, even though I knew it wasn't true, he would never be mine, and she knew it too. It was all self-destructive delusion. The fury, jealousy and hurt that set me off against Danielle may well have been misdirected. But in the moment, being angry at her and fooling myself was my coping mechanism.

The following day, Alain left for Carrara to finalise the details of the flat he and Vicenzo had their hearts set on. Before driving off, he caressed me hungrily.

'*Tu es toujours ma chérie.*'

Waving me kisses from the car, he added, 'Be good. I'll be back next Sunday.'

I set off immediately for Paris, where this time I rolled up my sleeves, picked up the telephone and knocked on doors. Provence had leached out of me any desire to live in a capital city, ever again, even one as pretty as Paris, but I needed a job and this was the place I was most likely to find one. I had some professional contacts of my own as well as some names and numbers from friends.

'You want work? Then go back to Asia,' I was told by the three or so French journalists I met with, doomsters about the moribund national media market. I had better luck with a major French news agency. A boss I managed to cadge a few minutes with told me to come back in several weeks for a full-day test translating French news copy into English.

My bed was the sofa in the scrunched-up living room of a flat conveniently opposite Les Halles, rented by a good friend of mine. She and I had met at the office in Hong Kong where we had both put in long hours, the same one where Annie Leung had worked even harder—different businesses owned by the same Greek shipowner. My friend had relocated to Paris for a new job. I liked to think she found something titillating—rather than just serially tedious—in my apocalyptic outpourings about Alain and his dogmas about sex and the holy grail of the vaginal orgasm. No matter how often I heard her say, 'He's crazy, he's definitely got problems,' it didn't re-message the recording in my brain of *I don't sexually measure up* that she and Julia, my two biggest arm-props, tried to engineer.

Obsession, like everything else, is relative. As big as they seemed, my relationship woes appeared tepid next to those of Yvette, who I agreed to have lunch with in Paris the day before I was set to return to Mazan. Lunch is perhaps a misnomer to describe the sandwich she barely pecked at in her fourth-floor office, her eyes riveted on the window by her desk that looked onto a busy avenue. She was hoping to catch a glimpse of the object of her adoration, who worked in the same building.

Had Yvette not moved to Paris several years ago after tragedy struck, she would have been part of Alain's tight clique. As it was, we saw her quite frequently, whenever she popped back to the Vaucluse where her mother lived. She was always with Danielle. The two of them were like sisters, hardly surprising given that Danielle's boyfriend of eight years, he who'd been addicted to drugs and had died of AIDS, was Yvette's brother. Around the same time as her brother's death, Yvette's partner of a decade, the photographer father of Isabelle, left her for a younger woman. She became not just depressive but suicidal. The move to Paris was financially motivated: slung out on her own, she needed to work, her fragile mental state notwithstanding. She was making a meagre living as a photographer's agent and having a clandestine affair with a married man who had made it abundantly clear to her that he would never, under any circumstances, leave his wife.

It was evident in the Vaucluse by the way she coddled her brick-sized portable phone that she was always on tenterhooks about hearing from him. The hour or so I spent in her office was proof of how her daytime existence had whittled down to watching him leave and enter the building from her corner-room bureau, waiting for his phone calls and arranging their next undercover rendezvous.

A hardness, perhaps born of loss, had sunk into her eyes, giving them a weather-beaten look. Creases above her cheekbones and mottled tan skin reflected too many hours spent in the sun. There was a gauntness to her face. These elements made her appear older than her forty years; not that she wasn't still appealing. She was tall and angular, donned chic clothes and wore her dirty blond hair fashionably short. She sat on the edge of her chair with her back straight and legs crossed, toes pointing down. If you didn't know she was a wreck you might just have remarked on her air of caustic sophistication. I knew from Danielle that she still had thoughts of taking her own life.

'Yvette, why are you monitoring his movements?'

'I want to know when he leaves and how long he takes.'

'But why? Do you suspect something?'

She shrugged.

'You're going to destroy yourself over him. You said yourself he'll never leave his wife. So what hope is there? Is this how you want to live for the rest of your life, as the other woman always in the shadows? To run to him like a dog and suffer when he doesn't phone?'

I hadn't planned to be quite so personal with her, but it was hard to ignore her eyes darting back and forth to the window and the half-eaten sandwich we had bought at a nearby boulangerie. Yet what hypocrisy! There I was telling her to end the affair to preserve her sanity, when my friends and family were clamouring for me to scram Provence to preserve mine. I was expecting her to turn on me and say, *putain*, what gives you the right to lecture me? In a roundabout way she did.

'Let me tell you something. In France, there is always another woman in the picture. You just have to accept that your husband or boyfriend will have other lovers. This is the way things are here, like it or not.'

'That's a bit fatalistic, isn't it?'

'It's the reality. And it doesn't have anything to do with happiness. I have a guy friend who just got married. He adores his wife, but he still takes his pleasure on the side.'

'So what does it have to do with? Do French men have specific genes that make them incapable of monogamy?'

A sardonic look and an infinitely weary sigh should have kept me quiet but I ploughed on.

'Why do you collectively let the men get away with it? Why do you do nothing?' What was I saying? I couldn't have stopped Alain from straying if he'd wanted to—I didn't count Aphrodite or the sauna as such. But I refused to swallow such mass servility over infidelity.

'You're so naive. It's not so simple. And don't think the women are all innocent either.'

'That's true,' I said, thinking of Danielle and Eliane. 'But still, this attitude of men are just like this drives me crazy.'

She was probably thinking that's your problem even if at present it was very much hers. Mean it was, but I couldn't help comparing and concluding that her insanity was greater than mine. I was feeling good, or at least better, at her expense.

We'd said our goodbyes and I was already at the door when she burst forth:

'Oh shit I almost forgot. Alain won't be returning tomorrow from Carrara. He's decided to stay on another week. Danielle told me to tell you.'

'Thanks for the message,' I said and left.

I was glad that she didn't see me wilt like an overripe stalk—punishment for my haughty thoughts. I knew his staying on didn't presage well for me. There was no point now in rushing back to the Vaucluse so I slept on my friend's sofa for another six days and continued with my job search.

When I did return, Jacques came to collect me from Avignon train station. I'd seen a lot more of him recently since Alain had hired him to plant a row of Cypress trees in the garden, on which mission he worked fastidiously, often staying for lunch. In contrast to his tortoise tongue, his body was lithe and elastic. The way he played squash, diving for balls with speedy prowess, was amusing to watch.

'There's a surprise in store for you,' he said as we drove to Mazan.

'Oh, okay.'

Maybe he wanted me to ask questions or was relieved when I didn't, for I had no desire to confirm my suspicions. The surprise turned out to be a dinner party that Danielle had organised for about half a dozen friends in the garden of our house. She'd used the kitchen and all the facilities as if they were hers. Furious, I thought about disappearing indoors as I yearned to do, but a strain of civility held me back and I joined the cluster. By degrees, the glow of that warm June evening soaked up all the stresses of Paris and thawed some of my anger. I even half forgave Danielle.

We had just finished eating when Alain's car unexpectedly rolled into New Delhi Drive. It came to a stop on the gravel just outside the kitchen door. My pulse raced through the roof. As evenly as I could, I walked over to him as he lifted his bag out of the boot and kissed him. Wordlessly he looked straight through me as if I was air, and in that moment I knew that the second honeymoon was over. His proposition that we spend the summer together and re-evaluate things in the autumn was as if dust. His verbal assurance before he left for Italy, *tu es toujours ma chérie*, was null and void. What had transpired in Carrara? The truth was that the brief, happy interlude had been an anomaly. I stood rooted to the spot as he strode into the house to deposit his bag, unsure of what to do next. Welcome back, agony. I dragged myself back to the table. He joined us a few minutes later.

'We thought you were coming back tomorrow,' Danielle said. 'I hope you don't mind. I invited a few people round to the house, for Ravinia's sake actually. So, how was the land of marble?'

Danielle grinned broadly as she poured him some wine. I knew she'd seen our brief interaction, or rather, his lack of interaction.

'*Alors*, I've been spending all my time with Athena.' His smile was tinged with pride. 'I miss her already, my warrior goddess. Such exceptional qualities she has.'

Warrior. He'd once called me that.

'I hope she doesn't mind sharing you,' Danielle said, winking at him.

Alain looked disconcerted for a moment.

'That won't be necessary,' he said quietly, before continuing his Flaubert-like rhapsody about the marble phenomenon he was bringing to life.

'Wasn't divine Athena a virgin?' I blurted out, bent on injecting something into the conversation.

'Well mine won't be when I've finished with her.'

Later, when everyone had left, I tried to break through the wall of ice he'd erected, asking why he'd returned a day early.

'I came back because of the party, to help get things rolling,' certainly not because of you, he left unsaid. The enigmas of Carrara…encapsulating why I was no longer *chérie*.

The party was held two days later, a last hurrah that Christine staged in a bid to make money for her hat association. Alain had given his blessing for her to use the empty atelier to display her eighty concoctions, arrayed on stands and racks that she, Benoit, Gregoire and others lugged up the stairs. The hats were simple affairs, mostly fashioned from colourful bits of cotton, velveteen and paper sprinkled with trinkets, baubles, feathers and costume jewellery. The entrance fee was fifty francs, which bought you the right to select one item of merchandise.

In the early afternoon, Vivienne came over to help prepare the food. She and I had seen each other on innumerable occasions but had never really exchanged more than small talk. Alain was fussing about in the kitchen, a taskmaster directing myself and Christophe, who had come over for the festivities. I was washing some lettuce in the sink when Alain noticed that the gauze drain cover was not in place. He flew into a rage.

'How many times have I told you to keep the gauze in there.'

And for the thousandth time he brandished me a catastrophe and stalked off. Vivienne was a witness to the scene. She looked aghast but said nothing while I fought back tears. From that moment on, something clicked between us, as if we were seeing each other for the first time.

I can't remember exactly how many people showed up for the hat party but the following afternoon when Christine returned to pick up her inventory (after staying till eight that morning to clean the house) there was very little of it left. No wonder she beamed. I'd made a heroic effort at the fete to pretend that I was just fine thank you although I needn't have bothered. It was obvious to everyone that my relationship with Alain was in decomposition. For the next two weeks until I returned to Paris for my writing test, members of the clique avoided the house, sensing the contaminated atmosphere inside; all, that is, except for Danielle, who couldn't manage to stay away.

This distancing seemed to feed Alain's frenzy.

'I'm not cut out for a couple's life. What good does it do me when I take care of everything—cooking, cleaning, making social arrangements—better than any woman? No, what I need is the sexual nirvana minus the pettiness of a shared existence.'

His facial expressions while thus venting would accentuate the heat of his words. Eyes opaque, lips pinched at the sides, his voice—his normally disarming baritone voice—haemorrhaging hostility.

'You should live alone since that way you won't make women suffer so much,' I threw back at him. 'In any case, you have nothing to offer a woman. You cannot love, you have nothing to give, nothing to share. What sensitive, caring person is going to tolerate you?'

'How dare you say that. You can be sure I'll continue to look for a woman who suits me after you're out of here. It's YOU YOU YOU I don't want to live with. It's you you you I'm not happy with.'

In bits I would race up to my study, close the door and call Julia.

'Don't you understand, he knows how to harm you,' she'd talk me back from the brink. 'You touch on the truth and bang, he attacks you. Don't give him the chance, walk out of the room.' If you can't walk out of the house, she left unsaid.

But one thing I couldn't admit to anyone was the begging bowl I put out for sex. Even as his tongue whipped, my hands sought his flesh and he, indifferent to my body, nevertheless gave in, never quite managing to tame his animalistic instincts. These were particularly fired up at the beach, the only place he was demonstrably different. On several hot, windless days we drove to Saintes Maries de la Mer. Reclining like an emperor on a mat on the hard-packed sand near the lullaby waves he would bask in the halo of the sun, feeding on the sight of naked women's bodies and couples in intimate postures. And when the sun sank, he would turn his attention to me, sating his ineluctable lust between my legs, the contact washing over me like a rainstorm in a desert.

I left for Paris and an intense day of translation at the beehive bureau in Place de la Bourse. I had prepared for the test as best I could but had no idea if I'd scored more than mediocre. All the news agency would divulge at the end of that gruelling trial was, 'We'll get back to you in September.'

Meanwhile my prospects on the Riviera were looking up. Through a friend of a friend I'd made contact with a manager of a financial services company in Nice. Would I be interested in selling life insurance and savings plans to wealthy expatriates on the coast? There was no monthly salary, only commissions on sales, but these could be considerable. Yes, I most certainly was interested. So I'd never sold a thing to anybody. So I didn't have an ounce of mercantilist smarts. The man wasn't concerned. Determination and tenacity are more important than experience he told me. I doubted I had the temperament for sales and I knew no one apart from Brigitte on the coast, but I was prepared to eat a lot of humble pie and learn new tricks to live in Nice.

As soon as I returned from Paris, Alain announced immediately:

'I'm going to Pietrasanta for a month, to sculpt.'

A month. A month. A plunge into blackness.

'You promised to take me with you to Carrara.'

Even as I spoke I shuddered at my words and at the response I knew they would elicit. There was more chance of going to the moon than with him to Carrara. He looked at me in horror, his eyes like flints.

'Pietrasanta is my refuge, my escape from everything. It would be impossible to bring you.'

Carrara, so close, yet completely out of bounds. Once, in another life, around six months ago, he'd vowed to take me to my mini mountain in Tibet.

I didn't want to be around when he put his bag in the car and set off for his 'refuge'. No, it was better to be out and return to an empty house where I could whisper or wail to the stone walls. When I tried to hug him before I left on my walk he flinched, grimacing as if I was tearing him away from the clutches of Athena, rival to the mighty Aphrodite, and his erstwhile love.

Chapter 25

In the sun-blanched days of July I truly became mistress of the house, abandoning myself to a ruleless rhythm. I wandered around unkempt, and showered, ate and slept when I felt like it. I caterwauled at the drop of a hat and stared for hours at Alain's carvings, trying to decipher the hidden messages I thought were crafted in their curves and curlicues. These, his creations, were above criticism. They alone attained the perfection he sought in women, or at least in me.

I walked to Mazan, sometimes twice a day, crystallising the countryside in my memory like an archivist storing old manuscripts. I swung in the hammock Peppo had strung up between the plane trees, dined outside as the sun was dying and after dark, snuggled into bed with a book. I had overcome the challenge of sleeping alone in the house. There was no question of asking Pierre, or anyone else, to baby sit. My saviour was the radio. The constant, low-volume strum it emitted next to my bed drowned out creaks and provided reassurance. I still kept the house lit up at night, so brightly it was surely visible from Mont Ventoux. I thought about the hefty electricity bill that Alain would get. *Tant pis*.

As the days rolled by I began to unwind, to such an extent that my anger at Alain finally exploded. Oh the fury, of being picked up, played with and discarded by a viper whose deep-rooted hatred of his mother he was pouring out on me; by a man incapable of loving, a man so tormented with himself that he damaged the human psyche of others; who thought that because he was an artist he was special and different. He was special and different all right, in the field of mental cruelty.

But it didn't feel good, this anger, even if it had to be unleashed outwards and not turned destructively within. Which it still was for I couldn't keep from self-flagellating. Each nasty accusation I heaped on Alain felt like a cigarette stubbed out on my stomach. If he was bad, if he was a bastard, if he brought only ruination then I was stupid, gullible and immature; guilty of serious missteps.

Funny how my Australian friend had intuited the truth during that 'what's he like?' drink at the Hong Kong Foreign Correspondents Club all those months ago. Was I sure Alain wasn't a closet FUFO?

Yes ma'am. Not closet. The encyclopaedic definition of.

My complicity in allowing myself to be manipulated led only to regret for what I'd done. And regret was cyanide for my soul. I couldn't remember what it was like to wake up in the morning feeling positive about life, that there was a point to it all. Anger and regret. These were but the strongest identifiable emotions, the ringleaders for the emotional mass that jostled inside, quiet only during sleep. And yet I felt empty, a stranger to myself. Unknowable. I knew what had happened. I knew what I'd done. But I couldn't understand it, my reaction that is.

This craving for a damaged man didn't seem to fit my psychological profile. I didn't have a so-called addictive personality. I'd never been hooked on any substance or thing—not cigarettes, alcohol or drugs, not gambling, shopping or food. Just goes to show there's no full-proof armour, no guarantees against getting this lurgy. I'd read before about Stockholm Syndrome—sympathising with your captor. Was there a pinch of that in my predicament? Of course, Alain wasn't my kidnapper. Just the opposite. He was booting me out the door. I was the one clinging on, grovelling at his feet, desperate for his love, sick without it.

I yearned for the person I'd been before Provence when I was intact, knew who I was. The before and after...Would any of my friends in Hong Kong recognise me now? Convinced I had nothing to offer, wallowing in self-pity and victimhood, I wanted to shut myself off from the world. But a few brave women refused to let me.

Not long after the kitchen sink episode Vivienne phoned to ask how I was. Had I sat her down for a one-to-one months ago I might have picked up on her own problems, principally, her faltering relationship with Mathias, the hot-blooded electrician. I might have sensed the pain behind the poker face. She and Mathias lived in a weeny house next to a furniture shop in Carpentras. They slept in a shelf-like alcove in the living room. Vivienne's eleven-year-old son with a previous partner and the five-year-old daughter they conceived together shared the single bedroom. Vivienne had little money to spend on luxuries, but she always managed to dress freshly and stylishly. She was a thrift shop connoisseur, able to walk in and sniff out the pearls amid the offal. At thirty-two, she was two years older than Mathias.

One afternoon she came around, white-faced.

'Mathias has finished with me. He told me he doesn't love me anymore. He wants his freedom. He's moving out once he finds a flat.'

Her face bore the signs of sleeplessness but there were no tears.

'For the ten years we were together I did everything for him.'

It was the usual story, Mathias out playing with his friends, neglecting the children, coming back just for 'a hot meal and sex'.

Six months before, they'd been on the verge of separating. But then Mathias broke his arm in a motorbike accident and she did the decent thing, if not much more: she became his personal slave.

'Now his arm's fine, he no longer needs me and he wants to split. And you know what? Let him. I'm sucked dry. I have nothing more to give.'

Vivienne was strong and stoic, but she suffered, mainly because of her children. She wouldn't get a centime out of Mathias in child support and was worried about how she'd manage. No alimony: this was the flip side to having children out of wedlock when the man walked out. Vivienne had two sisters, who, in addition to her children, were the bedrock of her existence. One of them, Marianne, lived in a sunny house in Perles les Fontaines. Besides parenting, she painted furniture, trussing up tables, cupboards, chairs, anything wood-based, in her outdoor work shed. Everything about her smacked of wholesomeness.

'How can you still love that man, he's such a bastard?'

Referring to Alain, she didn't mince her words. A coffee with her and I'd walk away feeling as bright as the colours on her palette.

I had always thought Vivienne was close with Danielle. Yet although they used to spend an evening together from time to time—and had been co-workers at Alain's kitchen shop—Vivienne told me she didn't trust the woman for a second.

'Once, Danielle popped over when I wasn't there and paraded her charms around Mathias. I was furious when I found out. I told her in no uncertain terms to lay off my boyfriend, or else.'

Cristelle was another stalwart, a woman with as much fortitude and grit as Vivienne. And as enterprising for she was the sole provider for her child, a five-year-old son whose father was a builder—the main muscle, in fact, behind the smashing and rebuilding of walls in Alain's abode. The pair had lived together for a number of years but it was a stormy relationship characterised by his bouts of brutish, even violent, behaviour. At first, I'd had trouble imagining him in that vein. I'd seen only his downcast face when he'd come over to commiserate after she'd left him, more than a year before. Now the two were on good terms and Cristelle, who was thirty-one, said he was a loving father to his son although he didn't contribute to his upkeep.

What was it with these men, who fathered kids but were feckless about financial responsibility? I had to admit that Alain was different in this respect; he coughed up for Christophe, but then again he'd been married and was legally obliged to pay child support, an obligation that he nevertheless honoured without any nudges or grudges. Luckily, Cristelle's rent was modest. I would drive over to her split-level flat in the sleepy village of Mormoiron that would have cost a fortune in Paris. At other times, she'd come to me and we would sit under the plane trees, sipping water or wine, cursing or celebrating depending on the day.

Valérie's links to Alain dated from childhood, which gave her an historical take on him that was always revealing ('I never dreamed as a child he would turn out to be a serial seducer.') But more than that, she was philosophical, her curiosity about language, psychology and the human spirit spurring her to pose questions. She liked to dissect, rather than draw simplistic conclusions.

'We all of us search for an alter ego…we often make mistakes but we need to continue to search because he also is looking,' she wrote to me.

'Naturally, there is the mystery of these hearts of marble who don't want to open themselves up and condemn themselves to solitude…In your saga and the separation from Alain the ball is in his court, and in his alone, because it is he who always repeats the same schema. He would do well to truly reflect upon this to avoid destroying other women in the future, but he won't take the time because he is already elsewhere…he is both as taut as a bowstring and as closed as a fist. Can he be happy living thus?'

I was sure that Alain was screwing the damsels of Carrara in great numbers. Yet each day I spent away from him, with my supportive friends, I felt a tiny bit stronger.

It was a Saturday afternoon. I was lazing in the hammock when I heard the sound of a car motoring up New Delhi Drive. I sat up and squinted. It was Pierre's Citroen. It drew to a stop near the hammock.

'Pierre, what a surprise. What brings you here?' I manoeuvred myself out. It was the first time he'd come over spontaneously.

'I heard Alain was in Carrara. I thought I'd drop by and see how you are.'

I hadn't seen or spoken to Pierre in more than two months, in fact since his babysit at the house. As far as I was aware, he knew nothing about the situation between Alain and I. What point was there in telling him? I doubted Josephine and Sylvie were any the wiser, but I couldn't be sure about that. I was certain Pierre wouldn't have heard anything through the gossipy grapevine since he kept well out of it.

'Did Alain call you?'

'No, Christophe did. He told me he's coming to stay here in a few days' time on his father's orders, even though Alain's away. Driving lessons in Mazan. I know he can't wait to get his motorbike license.'

'Yes, true.'

'You must have conquered your fear of sleeping alone in the house.'

'Enough so I don't need to bother you. Come and sit. I'll get you a drink. What would you like?'

He gulped down half of the citron pressé I brought, looking fit and energetic.

'You look well. How's the running going?'

'Good. I've got into a steady rhythm. Two days on, one day off. Seems efficient.'

'And work?'

'It has its stresses, but I can't complain. I'm lucky to like what I do,' he smiled.

'Still not drinking?'

'No, and I don't miss it but I'm planning to celebrate the run with a bottle of my best Chateauneuf du Pape. I've been saving it for a special occasion.'

'The marathon certainly counts as one.'

'*Ça va toi*?' he asked lightly.

As matter-of-factly as I could, I enlightened him.

'Life is not too wonderful at the moment. Alain doesn't want to be married anymore, he wants to be alone. He's asked me to move out as soon as I find a job, which I've been looking for.'

Pierre picked up his glass and looked at it as if it could talk. Then, still clutching it, he pronounced three words, slowly. 'Are. You. Sure?'

I nodded, thinking his response strange. But stranger was to come. His face turned the colour of the ice in his drink. His hands detached from the glass and covered his eyes and brows before digging into his bountiful hair. His neck was inclined like a penitent.

'Pierre, are you okay?'

'My god I'm sorry.' His voice was choked. 'What a shock.'

He looked like he'd emerged from the trenches. It was utterly perplexing. Was this shock and sorrow for my sake or was it something else? It was almost as if he had been jilted. After some minutes Pierre seemed to recover, pulling his hands out of his hair. He looked at his palms and then at me.

'But you were just married. What happened?'

I described Alain's verbal attacks, his vile behaviour and unbelievable personality change following the marriage. I told him everything, save for the sexual slurs, highlighting how he wasn't cut out for monogamy but sought only nirvana and passion from women. Despite my efforts at control, I couldn't keep out the bitterness.

'Marriage?' I shrugged. 'Far too banal for the likes of a genius sculptor.'

'Why did he marry you then?'

'Out of a sense of obligation. To give me the right to live in France. For practical reasons.'

'Ravinia…I don't know how you're…'

'It's devastating,' I interrupted, determined to keep the tears away. 'I can't even begin to describe, well, you know what it's like. But I'm trying to be strong. To cope one day at a time. I thought I'd collapse over his going to Carrara for a month. But I've found a way to manage on my own. It's ironic, isn't it, that I should be the one to break the news to you. Not your brother.'

His eyes flickered at this.

'Oh I know, you're not close, you're very different.' I'm not sure if he caught the sarcastic tone. 'And he keeps things private. I suppose your mother and sister don't know either.'

'To my knowledge.'

'You can tell them if you like, but please not Christophe. I'm not sure exactly what he's been told but in any case I don't want to drag him into the drama.'

'Of course not,' he murmured. 'So what are you going to do?'

'I've been to Paris to look for work, spoken to some people, had interviews. I'm waiting to hear about a job with a French news agency. There's also a possibility of moving to Nice, selling life insurance, can you believe?' I forced a laugh. I explained about my contact in the business.

'I've never done anything like that before, but Nice, I'd rather move there than Paris. At least it's by the sea,' my voice trailed off.

‘So you’ll stay in France.’

‘Yes. I gave up a lot to come to this country. I want to try and make it work here. But it all depends on being able to make a living.’

‘With your skills and experience, you’ll find something.’

‘We’ll see. Luck and timing are important too. And persistence.’

‘But a good resumé is a door-opener.’

‘Yes.’

My mind detoured for a moment, thinking how I never expected to need urgent door opening at this point in my life.

‘Life is so completely unpredictable.’

At this simple statement Pierre looked at me as if seeing a ghoul. Again I felt that my predicament had unleashed a storm in him that didn’t have to do with me but something in himself. I was going to question him but then thought better of it. He seemed vulnerable, a funny thing to think given how vulnerable I felt. We talked for a few more minutes before he left.

‘Let me know if you need anything.’

He got into his car a changed man from the one who had breezed out of it.

Shortly before Christophe arrived, I decided to deal with something that was long overdue. It was while scrutinising Alain’s agenda, which he’d left behind, that I discovered, tucked in an inner pocket, a postcard. On it was written ‘an ode to love’ by Khalil Gibran. The card was addressed to ‘a special knight, from a damsel’. The handwriting was Danielle’s. The post-marked date was so faint I couldn’t tell when it had been sent. That incriminating evidence was the final straw: using the poet’s words to steal back Alain, as if her flagrant flirting wasn’t enough. Gibran had been our philosopher, Alain’s and mine. The fact that he’d kept the postcard was damning.

Danielle was her usual lively self as she bounded through the kitchen door that morning, arms jangling bracelets, trailing a sweet-spicy scent. She kissed me thrice and sat down at the table, ready for relaxed girlie gossip. I made her an espresso, my nerves too ramped up for a dose of caffeine.

‘Danielle there’s something I need to tell you, something that has greatly upset me for a long time.’ I forced myself to look her in the eye.

‘I’ve found it hard that you haven’t given Alain and I some space to lead our own lives. I’m sure you can understand, given your past relationship with him. Why haven’t you respected our privacy? Why have you come to the house so often? The truth is, I think that you still desire Alain. You seduce him all the time.'

Danielle stared at me, eyes round like saucers.

'Why didn't you say anything to me before about all this?' Her muted tone was a first.

'I don't know. It wasn't easy. I didn't have the courage.'

She looked thunder-struck. Her eyes welled up, her lips formed a tremor, her arms, normally active, hung slackly by her side.

'I had no idea you felt like this,' she kept repeating. 'I came around to see you also, you know. I'm not a mind reader. You should have told me this before. I certainly had no intention of hurting you.'

We talked a bit more. I held back, failing to mention the thousand and one instances of her provocation, sticking to generalities. Without pressing her for explanations, she offered no insights. Limply rising to go, she said:

'Well, it's up to you. If you want to see me, you contact me, okay?'

As she drove off, I felt a mix of emotions. Relief was there, certainly. I'd finally aired what had been eating away at me for aeons. But so was disappointment. I hadn't pressed hard enough. I didn't have the satisfaction of an admission of love or lust, and certainly no apologies for her behaviour. My approach had been too tentative. And yet, I also felt aggrieved at how hurt she'd seemed. But all traces of this were eviscerated the following afternoon when Cristelle came over. The first words out of her mouth were how abominably Danielle had behaved the previous night at a party thrown by Gregoire in Bedoin, which I had studiously avoided.

'She tried to seduce Benoit in the presence of Christine, going up to him and sitting on his lap. She flirted with him as if Christine didn't exist. And Yvette was just as bad, throwing her body around like a slut. They were intolerable, the pair of them.'

I thought my confrontation with Danielle had perhaps been a catalyst but Cristelle wouldn't hear of it.

'You did well to talk to her yesterday. She needed to hear what you had to say. But your conversation had nothing to do with her antics I can assure you.'

Over the next two weeks, the more I gleaned about Danielle the more I regretted how meek I'd been with her.

'That woman will throw herself at Alain once you're gone,' said Vivienne's sister Marianne. 'She had a nice thing going when she was with him, having

Jacques as an amusement on the side. You can imagine how sorry she was when her arrangement was discovered.'

I could barely sleep for several nights after that, planning on how I would confront her anew with the weight of a bulldozer, bearing in mind Christophe's presence. The dad was gone but the son was pressed into staying at the house for part of the summer. Nearly sixteen, he was avid to get his hands on a motorbike license that would expand his sense of independence. All he needed were the lessons Alain had arranged for him to take in Mazan. He was also advised to notch up hours of solo practice using the motorbike Alain had bought for himself several months before, which lay idle against the woodshed wall. Staying at the house, bereft of friends and father, with a sort of stepmother who was on the way out was probably the last thing in the world Christophe wanted. But it was the path to that precious piece of paper.

There was no escaping the awkwardness of the situation. Yet, from initially dreading his presence, I came to enjoy it, and there was a payoff for him too. He had free rein over my television, which he installed in his bedroom. Often, I would drive him to Mazan for lessons with the same instructor I had driven mad. I would prepare healthy meals and we would take turns rocking in the hammock.

One evening, not long into Christophe's stay, Pierre showed up. We'd just finished dinner and were lounging in the kitchen, a pack of cards on the table.

'Hi Pierre.' I adopted a light tone. 'What perfect timing, we're just about to start a game, come and join us.'

'How are you?' he asked casually. I suppose he'd been digesting the substance of our last talk but with Christophe around he had to self-censor.

'Great, busy here with your nephew.'

'Have you come round to check on me?' Christophe said. Pierre ruffled his hair and enveloped him in a great bear hug, which he pretended not to like but you could see he was tight with his uncle. Pierre was in a pair of cut-off denim shorts and a white t-shirt that night and I couldn't help but notice the well-defined musculature of his limbs. The contours of his face had grown sleeker, which rubbed off some of his boyishness, no bad thing in my opinion. His looks were pleasing in a holistic kind of way. I couldn't imagine him hanging out at the sauna, preening on the Camargue beach or partner swapping at Aphrodite. He seemed too earnest, simply not cut out for those types of specialised games—at least from what I knew about him. I was sure he was the monogamous type, once with a woman always and only with her. I assumed he was still not dating but what did I know? His sex life wasn't my business.

Over glasses of raspberry grenadine we played multiple rounds of Polignac, a French version of knaves, and Lanterloo, both of which Christophe had taught me. We were also playing at happy families—at least Pierre and I were, Christophe blissfully unaware (I hoped) of the emotional storm unleashed by his dad. When Christophe bade us '*bonne nuit*' and went up to his room to watch TV, Pierre, frowning, asked how I was doing.

'Status quo.'

'Has Alain called?'

'He phoned just once from Italy, to speak to Christophe. But I have to admit, just the sound of his voice broke me.'

'I thought maybe he'd changed his mind.'

I shook my head. 'He is not…' I wanted to say he is not one to backtrack. 'No. There is no question of that.'

I wanted to be proved wrong of course.

Christophe was away at a friend's house in Montelimar the weekend that Alain came back from Carrara. That day loomed like a trial. A trial of my newfound strength, of the serenity I'd attained in his absence. Vivienne and Cristelle tried suasion.

'The worst thing you can do is to stay at the house. Don't do that, stay with me,' they each begged. I was tempted but couldn't tear myself away. That being the case they were unanimous in their instructions.

'Do not have any physical contact with him. Try to be indifferent, to maintain a minimum level of civility, but apart from that, no conversation,' Cristelle counselled.

'Ignore him as much as possible, and whatever you do, no sex,' Vivienne's sister Marianne insisted, regarding which I swore an oath to myself.

The sun was drooping and I was just about to set off along the back lanes to Mazan when I heard his car pull up. I hesitated, procrastinating. The next thing I knew he was in the kitchen, enfolding me in his arms. He smelt of the car and of sweat, mingled with his natural scent that was even more dangerous than his charm. I wiggled out of his grasp.

'How are you Ravinia?' he asked softly.

'*Ça va*, I'm just about to go for a walk. I'll see you later.'

I sprinted off. When I returned forty-five minutes later, coiled with tension like a spring, he was sitting under the plane trees, a joint in his hand, the last vestiges of the sun casting his face into a bronzed mould.

'Come join me.'

We sat in silence, looking towards the fields beyond the clumps of wild grass where last summer we'd made love, his sperm dripping onto the ground. Distant. Be distant. This was all new for me.

'It would be nice if you smiled.'

'Look Alain, while you were away I did a lot of re-evaluating. I've accepted that it's finished between us.'

I was proud of the words I'd prepared, but already felt a sliver of self-doubt. He looked at me studiously, took a long toke of the joint and exhaled slowly.

'Ravinia, I'm very sorry for everything.'

Sorry? At that moment he sounded it, but was this mini mea culpa supposed to whitewash him?

'It's a little too late for that.'

Silence again.

'I still haven't made up my mind where I'm going, whether it's to Paris or Nice. The news agency will let me know whether I have a job in September.'

'Look, you can stay here for as long as it takes to decide. There's no hurry.'

I understood the dynamic. I was being rejecting, which made him contrite and sparked his desire.

'How was Carrara?' I finally asked.

He'd frequented an atelier in Pietrasanta, where, he said, the delights of the food and the dialogue made it a veritable paradise for sculptors seeking to mingle with like-minded artists. I allowed the thought of how he had spent his nights to linger for only a few seconds.

'I brought Athena home. Come look.'

We walked to his car. He flung open the boot and there she was, a waxen nymph springing meteorically from the head of Zeus, supreme creator. Her profile conjured up Amazonian goddesses, her breasts and hair, which cascaded outwards in a sea of waves, Botticellian beauties. Hewn from white marble, she was perched on an iron tripod in the form of the god-king, her father. I wanted her to be ugly, I wanted to feel nothing, but instead I felt rage because she was so ethereally exquisite and far beyond the realm where I could compete. He carried Athena lovingly into the long room and placed her next to the fountain, from where, mounted on her feisty father's head, she swept up like a vortex all who gazed upon her.

That night while I prepared dinner, Alain followed me with ingratiating eyes. I kept mine averted. At bedtime I quickly undressed, slipped under the quilt and turned my head away without a single word or gesture. I congratulated myself. Alain lay beside me, motionless, biding his time. This was a game, after all, whose odds of success were on his side. The manipulation started in earnest the next morning, another glorious summer's day.

'Let's go to the beach,' he suggested after breakfast, the defences I'd erected still standing but a notch lower. I accepted, determined not to give in to his fantasies or my appetites. Armed with water and fruit, we stopped at our customary charcuterie in Sainte Marie de la Mer to buy a roast chicken. Parking the car, we cut across the dunes to the beach proper, chose a spot near the water, dug in our umbrella and laid out our mats. He stripped naked, while I kept my bikini on.

I could almost taste the erotic tension effervescing in the sweltering air. Even with my eyes closed I could sense Alain gazing at my body, gulping me in. But he did not touch and I held strong. There was something delicious about this power I wielded, however warped it was, in the face of those devouring eyes. These continued their vigil at an outdoor café at Avignon station, where we went to collect Christophe on the way back from the beach. I decided I wouldn't spoil things by revealing my bust up with Danielle—not yet anyway.

I was *chérie* that night at dinner, after which I disappeared to my study, leaving Alain alone to play his guitar and sing his solipsistic songs. Christophe had disappeared to his room. When later I came downstairs I found him lying in the Indian corner, gazing at his sculptures lovingly in the candlelight.

'I'm going to bed,' I announced.

'I'll be up soon.'

'I'm sleeping in my room.'

'Oh.'

Difficult, but a victory.

That Monday morning I was the first to arise, the heat already settling in as I brought my breakfast outside. Alain joined me at the table, still treating me as an object of desire. A little later, just as I was about to get in my car, he stopped me.

'Where are you going looking so beautiful?'

'To the market in Bedouin.'

It was a sacrilege to miss the weekly market, so splashed with colour you felt like you were stepping into a rainbow.

'Wait, I want to come with you. Then we can go to the beach.'

The blinkers in my head screaming danger danger, I nevertheless accepted his proposition. I could feel my discipline draining like water from a bath. Inevitably, the more I was in his presence the weaker I became. It was typical of my compulsion, any compulsion where the object of one's downfall is in sight. At the beach, under the irradiating glare of the sun, we lay still. My breasts were bare, my vulva covered. Alain stared at me with undisguised lust. I caught his look.

'You're a treat for strangers passing by,' he said.

As at the sauna, there were always more single men than couples on this spit of the Camargue, and they were not shy about parading their bare torsos, no matter the state of their physiques, for this was no Copacabana where only the toned and bronzed were showcased.

The minutes ticked by. His manipulation was working. My willpower was wilting…and then it was gone. As the sun slid low, I gave in and we pressed together, bodies bucking in a breathless, blind fusion, sublime and slime. Afterwards, as we walked back over the dunes towards the car, I bitterly castigated myself for giving away all of my power for what, ten minutes of pleasure?

'That's the last time,' I told him, knowing perfectly well it wouldn't be. He gave an embarrassed laugh. Predictably, from that point onwards, his interest in me puckered out like a spent bulb. The next night, when Christophe had gone up to bed and with stars set like pincers in the sky, we swung into action in the hammock. But after a time he drew away and climbed out. The challenge had gone. He knew he had won and there was little point now in being courteous. Back came the contempt, the cold shoulder, the cutting responses, the clipped tone which inflected what a drag I was on him. And back came my physical, torturous need of him. Hooked again after my rehab.

'How's it going with Alain?' Vivienne asked over the phone.

'It's hard, very hard,' was all I revealed, far too ashamed to mention our coupling. She was stressed to the extreme because even though Mathias had finished with her, he hadn't yet moved out and unbelievably, he still wanted to have sex, a thought that she now found repellent. The next evening Mathias himself swung by the house, desperately needing to talk. Alain served drinks in the garden, where we sat together in the twilight, the two men conversing.

'It's terrible feeling chained to a woman, losing your independence,' Alain told him at one point, unmindful of my presence. Mathias nodded his head in agreement.

'I was miserable with Vivienne for so long. I should have ended it way before. Freedom is something I want to taste again, being with a woman only when I feel like it.'

Livid, I left them after dinner, stewing in my study as they continued long into the night. I knew what they were saying, these men of like breed, who felt that women owed them the world, or at least the right to use their bodies whenever they wanted and to hell with the rest. When Mathias left, Alain went upstairs. I burst into the bedroom. He was brushing his teeth at the sink.

'Mathias doesn't deserve Vivienne at all, not one bit. It's good that he finished with her. She'll meet someone far better.'

'How dare you criticise him like that,' he barked. 'He's my friend. He came over in obvious pain, wanting to talk. You have no right to go flinging accusations around like that.'

Fury blinded me.

'You know, if I'd known your true nature, what you were really like, I never ever would have come to Provence. Had I known you were an egotist, a narcissist, a misogynist…'

'How dare you say that. Don't you ever call me those things again, do you understand? You have no idea what you're talking about. I'm exactly the opposite of that. I constantly give to people. I'm always helping out. And let me tell you something. I knew soon after you arrived here, way before we were married, that it wouldn't work out with you.'

He spit it out, you you you.

Alain knew how to spear me. He saw me crumple like a house of cards.

'Come here,' he held out his arms. I went towards him. Every ounce of strength and determination I'd had when he'd returned from Carrara had vanished, all that hard work for naught. In bed, he kept his arms around me but his tone was chilling when he said. 'You must never again call me a narcissist. You mustn't talk about what you don't know.'

It was no use. With Alain, it was as if I had a cutting machine in my head, shearing sense into nonsense. No wonder I always ended up in pieces after any confrontation.

'Enough anger,' he softened his voice. 'Let's try and have some fun. How about an outing to the club on Saturday night?'

The thought of him using me as a conduit to screw other women was repugnant. But on the other hand, it might butter him up. He might be nice to me. We would drink champagne, I would dance for him. He would fuck me. I would satisfy, for a moment at least, my endless craving. It was grasping at thin air, I knew, but anything was better than nothing.

But all was torpedoed by a little scuzz. On Saturday afternoon, he started to sweep; and kept on sweeping as his anger mounted. I thought I'd kept the house reasonably tidy, never leaving a dish in the sink or crumbs on surfaces, but in truth I hadn't given the floors a proper scrubbing or the place a dusting since Alain had left for Italy.

'You may be able to live in this filth, but I can't,' he thundered.

I joined him in cleaning. With every movement of the broom and brush, his mouth turned fouler. For the first time I feared he'd strike me. Mechanically, I started to make dinner, shaking from the putrefaction of his glare.

'This fish is overcooked. How do you expect me to eat it? You can't do anything right. Take it away.'

I removed his plate, but in my slippery hands it dropped. Shards went flying across the floor. I picked up the bigger pieces, put them carefully in the bin and fetched the broom, willing myself to sweep up the remaining fragments. He extended a threatening hand, in which I sensed violent intent. I dropped the broom and ran up the stairs to my study, the hysteria rising in me like bile. I tumbled downstairs and fled the house, telling Alain, who had gravitated to the long room, only that I would be back later.

It was still light when I knocked on Cristelle's door, even though I knew she wasn't in because her car wasn't parked in its usual place. I waited for fifteen minutes in the hope she'd nipped out briefly, but she didn't return. I got back in my car and found myself heading along the Route de Caromb to Baumes-de-Venise. I didn't bother ringing the bell. His vehicle wasn't in the driveway. I sat on his doorstep in the expanding darkness and cried. And when the tears ran out I continued to sit there, my head between my knees, feeling the lick of cold limestone through my skirt, the darkness now complete. I don't know how long it was before his car pulled in and the driver's door opened and closed.

'Ravinia, *mais qu'est-ce que tu fais ici*? What's happened?' The alarm in Pierre's voice brought back the tears.

'Please can I come in?'

He opened the door. I followed him into the living room and sat down mechanically on the sofa.

'I'll get you some water.'

'Something stronger if you have.'

'You're driving.'

'Just one glass.'

He returned with a bottle of Bandol Blanc and two glasses.

'I don't want to corrupt you.'

'I can handle it,' he grimaced. 'Ravinia, what on earth is going on?'

I couldn't describe Alain's anger with the nuance I wanted, fault of a tired, unclear mind, so it came out in childish bursts, the dirt, the sweeping, his reaction, my fears.

'You can't let him do this to you. He's not worth it.'

It was what Cristelle and Vivienne would have said. Coming from him it sounded strange, anarchic even, but somehow more reassuring.

'It's terrible to see you like this. He's not worth it,' he repeated.

Great bear sobs shook my shoulders. He didn't hug me as my girlfriends would have done. Instead, he proffered a hand, which I gripped. The comfort of being there, where there were no spectacular sculptures, nothing to which I felt inferior. There was a television on a black stand, books and videos stacked on shelves and a pile of engineering magazines spread over a glass-topped coffee table. The wall-to-wall beige carpet had thick springy strands. The metallic blinds on the windows were raised, the blackness reflected back in. Tasselled cushions feathered the creamy leather sofa. The sobbing stopped, replaced by a kind of stasis. I let go of his hand, embarrassed at how hard I'd pressed it.

'I'm sorry to put you in a difficult position. Here I come crying to you about your brother…'

'You're not. Don't apologise.'

'How can you two share the same genetics?'

I didn't blame him for not answering. To shift the focus away from my drama, I asked Pierre how his evening had been. He told me he'd come back promptly from a dinner with friends, turning down an invite for drinks at their place because he wanted to be up early to run. As he talked, I noticed the animation returning to his face, his hair combed to one side, a mouth with even upper and lower lips that I could never imagine in a snarl, hazel eyes warm like a comforting duvet. I wondered if he resembled his father. I asked about his circle of friends, his favourite places to eat, what he was reading. The minutes passed. But then, as if under curfew, I suddenly jumped up.

'I've got to get back.'

'Are you okay to drive? You can stay here you know.'

I thanked him but shook my head and headed to the door, now bone-weary.

'You're sure you're okay?'

'No, but I have to go.'

'Why?'

I shook my head again and left. It was around midnight when I pulled up at the house. There was no sign of Alain. I went up to my study, collapsed on my sofa bed and tried to sleep. Around two in the morning, I heard the crunch of his car in the driveway. After that my eyes must have closed, awakening to a fiery sun. I worshipped the heat but that morning the weather seemed impertinent, too at odds with my jellified guts. Unable to eat, I brought my bowl of café au lait into the garden. Perhaps half an hour later Alain came outside.

'I hope you've pulled yourself together and gotten over whatever it was that made you act so strangely last night,' he reprimanded, hands on hips.

An astounding statement. I just laughed.

'Where did you go last night?'

'To see Cristelle.'

'No you didn't. I phoned and no one was there.'

'She had her answering machine on.'

'Well, I was so furious at you that I drove to Avignon and bought something to smoke. You behaved terribly, going off like that. We were meant to go to the club.'

Was I dreaming? Was he really serious, or just pretending not to understand?

'It's a fine day, let's go to the beach.'

'No. I have things to do here.'

I ended up caving in. But at the beach I punished him by covering myself with a sarong and he punished back by ignoring me. I slept in my study that night. But the next morning, driven by insanity, I went into the bedroom before he'd arisen, the light pouring in from the glass-partitioned atelier with its through-views of Mont Ventoux. I slipped into bed and waited. When he stirred and saw me he was silent. I offered myself and he responded to my roaming hands and mouth even though the sex was as if nothing to him, if not just proof of my utter contemptibility.

'I think it's best you move out now. I can't go on like this any longer. And I'm sure you feel the same way,' he said perfunctorily at lunch. 'Go and look for a studio. I'll pay a few months' rent, just like I did when Brigitte moved out.'

'Okay, but I need a bit of time,' I stalled, wondering how many different levels and layers there were to feeling destroyed.

Chapter 26

It was Alain who left, a day later scooting off to Pietrasanta like a piston released from its spring, throwing some francs on the kitchen table for Christophe, who was still pinioned to the house. I just had to bide my time, having planned an escape for the beginning of September when Alain said he'd be back. Telepathically, Annie Leung had rung in late July to see if I could make it to Hong Kong for a few weeks of editing work at the end of the summer.

'Annie, I now believe in miracles. I was going to ask if you had any work for me.'

Once again, the house became my refuge as I scrabbled to resurrect blown away bits of fortitude, only this time it was with a less breezy Christophe. He was greatly relieved to have passed his theory exam, which left only his driving test at the end of August. As it happened, Danielle had sat with him in the same theory class. She did so in a bid to master Jacque's powerful motorcycle. She and Christophe were good pals who had a certain shared history together. Perhaps she'd broached the subject of our feud in class. For when he asked why she never came around anymore and I replied 'we had a disagreement,' he accepted the explanation without any comment. However, he became less communicative, more distant with me after that. And I wasn't through with Danielle. Shortly after Alain left, when Christophe was out, I rung her up in an unforgiving mood, meting out the treatment I'd fantasised about.

'Listen, I just want to remind you to stay away from the house. I can't bear to see you. I don't think I made my point clear before. You've acted outrageously, constantly flirting with Alain, like a dog in heat. It's clear how you feel about him. You want him back. How stupid I've been not to say anything to you. I just want you to know I'm sick and tired of it. And I'm not putting up with it any longer.'

'Well, you don't have to worry about my coming over. While you're still around there's no chance of that. I've done a lot of thinking since that day we talked, and I'm furious about what you said. You're just jealous of my relationship with Alain.'

True.

'Huh, what don't you understand? Are you really that stupid? You need to stop and analyse your actions. And, just so you know, I am not the only one to think this. You have a reputation as a slut Danielle. Do you realise that? Trying to steal the boyfriends of your so-called friends while living with your lover. Everyone around you sees it…and so does Alain,' I couldn't help saying. 'He's always said you're just a party animal, all show and no substance.'

What did I expect after this coup de grace? Grovelling? An apology?

'You're just insanely jealous, especially now that your relationship is over.'

'And you're using my jealousy as a way to excuse your disgusting behaviour.'

On the phone, we were two degrees away from a vicious catfight. In person, we'd have clawed. It was sickening, but in no small part liberating.

'Before I hang up, there's something you need to know,' Danielle sprung. 'Alain only married you to get back at me. His revenge for my cheating on him. He wanted to teach me a lesson, make me suffer. But in fact it had the opposite effect. I know him better than he knows himself. I knew the marriage was doomed. He's not cut out for it. It was guaranteed to end your relationship. You're so naive. He didn't get you to move to Provence out of love. It was only payback.'

'Payback bullshit. You can't take the fact that I was in his bed and not you. Because that's where you want to be isn't it?'

'Actually,' she said breathing fire into that word. 'If you'd been better in bed he might have kept you around a bit longer, not dumped you so quickly. But I heard it from the man himself that you're a lousy fuck, he even asked me for advice about what to do. It's probably a British thing. I mean you lot are not exactly known for your specialities in sex are you? You overcooked slabs of rosbif can't possibly compete with us in the art of love and you've just proved it again. While screwing you, he's been thinking of me. He still wants me. And as soon as you're gone we're going to…*Oh ma pauvre*.'

'You're diabolical, a real piece of shit.'

'And you're a fucking catastrophe, you English bitch.' And with a 'ciao', she hung up.

I wanted to smash the phone. Instead I screamed out expletives, the stream of invective from my burning throat falling on deaf ears. Alain's sculptures were indifferent, or were they silently laughing at this spectacle of my defeat? I could just imagine the smirk on Danielle's face now, the ebullient taste of victory. She had scored the jackpot, won the lottery. The humiliation sweepstakes. How good it must have felt to fire off what she'd probably been salivating and rejoicing over for weeks if not months. I'd opened the valve for her to divulge what Alain had despicably divulged to her. Automatically I phoned Vivienne, babbling hysterically. I think she just managed to make out 'Danielle… Alain… Sex… Catastrophe…'

'Listen to me,' she directed in a firm voice. 'You've got to get yourself over here. Can you handle the car? I'd come and get you but I can't drive, I've broken my arm.' She'd just returned from a weeklong trip to the beach but I was too destroyed to ask how she'd broken it.

It was one of those times when the car seemed to understand my state of mind and miraculously drove itself. Vivienne answered the door with her left arm in a cast and sling. The right arm gave me a hug, took my hand and led me to the kitchen table. She pointed to a small glass bottle.

'Bach flowers. Rescue remedy for shock. Put four drops onto your tongue,' she instructed. 'And take the bottle with you. You need a repeat dose every few hours.'

She'd prepared a pot of chamomile tea and half a pear tart made by her sister lay temptingly on a plate but I could barely swallow my saliva, tinged now with the rescue remedy. We went to the sofa. She waited for the sobbing to stop before asking what had happened, her good arm protectively around me, my head against her shoulder. Sitting up, I vomited it all out, the war of words over the phone that I had launched. I had to provide a bit of background to Danielle's barbs, explaining how I could never measure up to Alain sexually, Danielle's rhapsodising about their sex life together and how I'd always felt inferior to her. It was excruciatingly embarrassing. Vivienne was a warm and wonderful friend, but being French, a part of me thought she'd judge me too. But there I was totally misguided, blinded by my own prejudices. She was nothing if not absolute grace and solace.

'You know what, it's only to be expected that that *pute* would mess you over. You sprang some home truths on her. Deep down she knows she's pathetic, she has a lot of self-loathing going on, which is why she acts out. She'll say anything she can to put you down. Anything. The more humiliating the better. And she's achieved her goal. She's got you feeling exactly how she wants. And Alain…if you ever needed proof of his character, this is it.'

Vivienne had the courage of her convictions. Alain had hired her to work in his kitchen shop when she'd needed a job, they'd known each other for years, but she didn't feel obliged to take his side or try to justify his behaviour. She was consoling and defending me, an outsider.

'His betrayal is what hurts most. Telling her how awful I am…and she must have been ecstatic to hear it. They've been laughing at me together. Making fun of me. I'm the big joke, the boring-in-bed English girl…' I trailed off, crying into my cup.

Vivienne's good arm took hold of mine.

'Well, you don't know for sure that Alain said all that to her. She could've made it all up. It's easy to do. Sex is Danielle's weapon and she wields it with power. She's used it from the start to cut you down. Believe me, she's calculating, she knows what she's doing. Getting caught having sex with Jacques was what ruined it for her with Alain, so of course after you called her out on her game she does what she knows will hurt most. You've had something she wants, just as you told her.'

'She used the word catastrophe. It's what Alain has called me so many times. You even heard him doing it in the kitchen, remember?'

'Exactly, and maybe she heard him slinging it at you too. Or maybe it's one of their pet words. Maybe he did describe you as a catastrophe to her. But whether he said anything or not doesn't change the facts. Alain's dangerous and detrimental to your health. You need to be free of him.'

It was the cringing simplicity of this and my inability to follow through that was the crux of everything. We both knew it.

Even so, I hadn't finished. 'What if it's true that Alain brought me here only to punish Danielle. That he never loved me. That he still loves her. I know she's dying to get back with him. That's always been obvious. And I think, I really think…Alain still wants her.'

I broke down again. Vivienne touched my hand. She spoke softly.

'I saw the way Alain looked at you in the first months after you moved here. How he couldn't keep his hands off you. That wasn't faked. He was into you, no matter what he or Danielle says. And you know what?' she continued more forcefully. 'If they are hatching something together, if there's more mileage to go in their seedy business together, good riddance I say. They are twin sides of the same bad apple.'

It was only after an exhaustive back and forth, when I was spent of force and free of tears, that I could finally turn my attention to her.

'Vivienne what happened to your arm?'

She explained how she'd dislocated a bone below her elbow when a huge wave pummelled her onto her arm in the sea during a camping trip with some friends at a beach in Bordeaux. She was told the injury would take weeks to heal and the handicap was a real hindrance. But instead of looking depressed about it she was all radiant.

'I'm in love,' she confessed as I boiled water to make more tea. The new man in her life was an old acquaintance whom she'd rebuffed when she was with Mathias. He'd learned of their split and approached her anew. Romance had blossomed behind tent flaps, for he'd been a member of her camping contingent. This man was everything Mathias wasn't: attentive, mellow, genuinely caring, and blond and blue-eyed.

'He wants to move in with me, but I've told him it's out of the question right now. I'm not ready to make that commitment. I don't want to confuse or hurt my children again with someone else.'

Love? Move in? That was quick, I thought, not without a measure of envy. Good for you, I told her. She was owed big time on happiness.

Fortified by friends and Bach flowers, I made an overnight trip to Nice for an interview with the regional manager of the financial services company that I'd been in contact with for a job. After a two-hour talk, we shook hands on my acceptance of his offer to be a financial consultant, aka insurance peddler. The deal didn't amount to much. There was no salary or office and I had to pay for all my business-related telephone calls. Finding clients was my responsibility. If I didn't sell any products, I didn't earn. I cared little for the work but it was a means to an end. At least now I had a destination and a starting date: first of October. I'd be gone for most of September, on a mission for Annie Leung.

In Alain's absence, I made sure to regularly sweep and scrub the floors, removing mites of dust and dirt from every surface, including his sculptures. It wasn't love or fear that drove me to dust his works of art. It was the mystery they held for me, as if by handling them they would reveal insights into Alain's odiousness and genius by osmosis.

Once I was so engrossed in the task I almost missed the phone when it rang, finally picking up to a voice I wasn't pleased to hear. It was the tiger woman who had come over with her doctor husband for the partner swap that wasn't.

'How are you?' Without waiting for an answer she said, 'I'm calling to invite you both over for an evening of fun. What do you think?'

'That sounds great but in a few days we're off travelling for three months. We'll call you when we get back.'

I was surprised at how readily the lie came.

The following evening Vivienne's sister Marianne invited me over for dinner. In the salubrious setting of her dining room, over lamb casserole and glasses of Tibouren rosé, she once again pinned labels on Alain as she tried to wrestle with my malediction.

'He's your Achilles heel. Achilles didn't recover from his wounds, but one day you will.'

Driving back to Mazan in the blackness, my thoughts kept me company. Cancer, he's like an inoperable cancer that I let grow and fester. It's not that I let him or have a choice. He's invaded me, he pulls my strings, he's my keeper in Hell. I laughed into the silence. That 'H' word jogged a memory. '*Hell is empty, all the devils are here*'. A quote from the Tempest. I could always count on Shakespeare for a bit of veracity.

Pulling into the drive, my headlights illuminated a bulk. His car. Jesus. Shit. I panicked. What to do? Head back to Marianne's? To Cristelle's? But I stayed put, the craving stronger than my quaking at seeing him again, the masochist in me feeding on the certainty of what lay ahead: self-sabotage after the separation.

The house was dark save for a light on in Christophe's room, which I saw from the driveway. Inside, candles were lit the length of the long room, which heaved with fragmented shadows, Cathedral-esque in the chiaroscuro.

He was sitting on the piano stool playing his guitar, a lyrically musical Heathcliff. He looked up at me and smiled as I approached him.

'*Salut.*'

In that simple greeting, everything coalesced: his overpowering magnetism, my compulsion, his emperor-like domination, my capitulation. He lay the guitar down carefully on the floor. Danielle's phone revelations changed nothing. Instinctively, unfathomably, I sat down on his knee. He held me there, one hand on my bare leg, spreading its warmth. It was a gesture more intimate than the whispering of honeyed words, yet it was a trickster, promising nothing. I saw follicles of stubble around his mouth and chin. I imbibed his smell. He launched into details about Italy.

'This time around I slept in a tent in a campsite near Pietrasanta. It was the only accommodation available since the place is packed in the summer and I hadn't reserved anything.'

That would explain the stubble, I thought, and also his early return home, to terra firma and a proper bed.

'I've discovered iron. Look.'

I saw the silhouettes positioned next to Zeus' tripod. A row of small, genderless bodies in movement, mounted on white supports. The iron looked stiff and unyielding. I didn't much like his figures but his brilliance was indisputable, his ability to create in a totally new medium.

I stayed straddled on his knee, the identity I'd walked in with minutes before vanishing as if someone was rubbing me out like a pencil drawing on paper. I didn't mention my upcoming travels to Asia or the decision I'd made about Nice. To do so would break the illusion of what, union? When he rose to go to bed, I followed him up the stairs and into the bedroom, not even trying to maintain a distance.

'You're sleeping here?' was all he said.

Naked, we lay on the bed, alert to the silence. Waiting. I knew he was willing himself not to reach out and touch, aroused though he was, but I couldn't hold back. The effort was too agonising. I turned towards him and touched his face, the protruding stubs of growth around his jaw. I made to kiss his mouth but he didn't allow this, instead taking hold of my waist, easing me onto my back then lowering himself onto and into me. With him inside, I would have gladly extinguished myself.

I woke up the next morning with just one thought in my head, a repeat of the previous night's performance, which I initiated as soon as he opened his eyes. It was your standard sex that didn't seek anything beyond the male orgasm. For me that was enough. But it was too much for Alain, who, after he'd finished, growled, 'We shouldn't do that.'

He showered quickly and went downstairs, his exasperation lingering in the bedroom like a smelly sock. When I joined him in the kitchen, he didn't waste a second. 'You've got to leave. I want you out out out. Now. Have you found a flat yet?'

‘I was going to tell you. I’m leaving in a week for Hong Kong. Working for my Chinese friend. When I get back I’m moving to Nice. October first.’

It was at that point that we began to bicker about money.

‘*Mon amour*, I make enough to support us both,’ Alain had been swift to assure me when I’d moved to Provence. ‘I want you to keep what you have so if you want to leave me, you won’t be constrained by a lack of cash.’

He paid his mortgage and the utility bills, plus food. ‘Room and board’ is how my father articulately put it. I’d covered all my own expenses, the driving and French lessons and doctors’ bills. I’d bought my car and the furniture for my study. That was my due and there was no argument. Now, however, when I wanted Alain to cough up two months deposit on a flat and a month’s rent, not knowing if I would earn a penny in Nice, he was being a philistine, pleading broke. He harped on about his now shuttered-up shop in Carpentras, ‘a noose around my neck’. Several people had viewed it, but so far there were no takers. Cash flow was tight. He hadn’t worked the entire summer and had monthly payments outstanding for Christophe, on the house, his car and life insurance. But he had spent unstintingly in Carrara and always seemed to have enough money to do exactly what he wanted.

I reminded him of his promise.

‘You told me you’d pay a deposit and rent on a flat, just like you did for Brigitte.’

He countered with, ‘If I don’t get any work now, and there’s no guarantee I will, I don’t know how I’ll make it through to Christmas.’

We sparred back and forth. I felt he hated me more with every mention of money, but for me it was about principle. I’d given up a well-paying job in Hong Kong to mould into his way of life. He was shoving me out. What had he sacrificed? In the end he wrote me a check to cover the deposit on a studio, promising to send me money for two months’ rent (which I eventually let drop). His face was sketched with but one desire: to turn the page on the English woman and start anew.

It was another four days before my flight to Hong Kong. Knowing Alain couldn’t hack anymore, I needed an immediate exit strategy and settled on Paris and my friend’s couch. The night before I left, Alain invited Vivienne over for dinner. She’d said yes, thinking I’d welcome the support. She was right, but I wondered at Alain’s motives. He could have asked her over any evening after I’d gone, in less emotionally charged circumstances (and when she was sling-free. A friend gave her a lift over but Alain drove her home). I don't think Alain realised just how close she and I had become or maybe he didn't care. It was treading on eggshells, this social soirée, for what do you talk about when so much is forbidden territory? Perhaps he didn't want to be alone with me but in that case he could have gone out. Maybe he was impatient to show off his latest works and those he couldn't wait to create, for he spent the evening regaling Vivienne with tales about Carrara and the 'incredible' iron forge he'd found, which awaited him along with the apartment he was due to take up shortly. Maybe it was good, for I didn't have to say much. Speaking risked an avalanche of tears. It also spared Vivienne from having to make big small talk.

Alain showed me photos of the forge the following day when he stopped to pick up the film he'd had processed, en route to Avignon train station to drop me off.

'Here it is, it's just outside Pietrasanta.'

He had been offered the run of the place by a sculptor who'd rented it for several years and was now returning to Rome. 'It's perfect for me,' he stressed, as if I was worried that it wouldn't be good enough.

After depositing me at the station he sped away quickly, like the Road Runner leaving behind wreckage. The first thing I did in Paris was to phone the chief of the English-language section at the French news agency. I intended to let him know I was moving to Nice. But before I could utter a word, he interjected, 'Ah, I'm glad you called. I want to sound you out about something. Would you be interested in a reporting job in Geneva?'

Geneva? I knew nothing about Geneva.

'Yes.' I was intrigued. 'But I'll be in Asia for the next month.'

'No matter. Can you come to Paris when you're back? I'll let the Geneva bureau chief know you're interested. When you get here you can do the interview.'

It was good to have more options even though I was all set on Nice, but a reporting job…yet nothing was confirmed so best to let it go. My friend in Paris welcomed me with open arms but a limited quotient of patience. If I was hoping for sympathy, I'd come to the wrong place. She—like my family—empathised with my situation, but there was no endless supply of compassion. Everyone was mystified as to why I hadn't beaten a retreat and fled the Frenchman months ago.

Speaking on the phone from London Lilly said, 'Why don't you just get the hell out of Provence, finished, done, dusted? I really don't understand you staying. He might have made a pact with the devil, but so have you.'

I understood her impatience. Common forms of addiction, to drugs, alcohol or gambling, say, tend to be treated as clinical diseases that produce brain altering bio-chemical reactions. They have their own established support groups in cities and towns across the globe where, thank god, you can walk in from the street to a warm reception and the solid structure of a twelve-step programme. I'd heard about something called Co-dependents Anonymous but I hadn't checked out whether they had a branch in Provence or anywhere else in France. But was that the right venue for me? What I wanted was an imaginary Addicted-to-Toxic-Males Anonymous. Might as well have support that was tailor-made to the diagnosis. Given a choice, though, I'd have much preferred to be hooked on heroin than on him. At least I'd be understood. How I saw it, enslavement to another human being was viewed through a different lens. It was a softer, fuzzier area where will and willpower were still seen as the determinants. I was weak, I was self-destructive, I was my own worst enemy. These were the things I was told. And they were true, but why was I like that? Why was I so weak? Why, in the face of so much suffering, couldn't I simply say ciao to Alain and move on? I couldn't seem to communicate, to make people understand, the abyss I'd fallen into, the torment that glued me to Alain, the psychological need to persistently and consistently be around a person who was noxious.

The withdrawal effects fit the dictionary definition too (I know because I looked it up): 'The syndrome of often painful physical and psychological symptoms that follows discontinuance of an addicting drug' (in this case person). I despised him. I detested him. Yet still I craved him, adored him. Still I was shattered by his rejection. Still I felt I had failed him and that I was the one at fault. I was sunk in self-loathing.

As if that wasn't enough, could you also, I wondered, be addicted to a village, to Mont Ventoux and to an old stone house?

Chapter 27

'Like it?' Annie Leung asked as she led me inside her latest acquisition, the air conditioning blasting away the mugginess of the hazy September day. It was on the twenty-first floor of a brand-new skyscraper complex in the New Territories. The apartment was about seven-hundred square feet, with mock-gold doorknobs, teak floors and marble-topped sink and surfaces in the bathroom. The walls were punctuated by windows that looked out over hills bathed in green, other residential towers cascading up like needles on a pincushion, and a railway line.

Annie considered herself fortunate to have quarried the flat, which cost considerably more than Alain had paid for his Provençal house. She'd financed the down payment from the sale proceeds of her first apartment. Given the prestige of owning property in Hong Kong, one could say that this ex child labourer had hoisted herself up a very exclusive ladder. She proffered this lovely little nest to me as home for the duration of my stay in Hong Kong. As before, I tapped on my computer during the day, in the evenings taking the underground train to Hong Kong Island, where I mingled with more than just friends. I didn't realise it at first, but I was on a mission, a sexual mission to prove I could still please.

I met the first man through some mutual friends at an Italian restaurant, all dark panelling, smoky mirrors and earthy lights. He was a thirty-something Greek banker from London temporarily residing in Hong Kong, a pleasing mix of gentlemanly and jaunty. We sat next to each other and fell into a conversation that led to an after-dinner invitation to his flat, which I unhesitatingly accepted. We made love most of the night, his determination to please me more confusing than clarifying, given the objectives I had set myself. Neither of us pursued it beyond a second night, he almost surely sensing my yawning need for reassurance or simply how broken I was, although I mentioned nothing to him about Alain.

The second man I already knew. He was someone I used to sleep with occasionally during the year or so before I left Hong Kong. We'd met at Mother's Choice, a refuge for babies awaiting adoption located on Bowen Road. Both of us had been Sunday afternoon volunteers. This six-foot-five-inch, bushy-haired, moustachioed American loved infants. He was pining to be a father but couldn't stomach a regular girlfriend let alone a wife. Not that I wanted that from him but no-strings-attached sex suited us both.

'Come on over,' he propositioned when I phoned him, surprised by my reappearance. He lived in a spacious flat on a high floor in Causeway Bay where natural light didn't penetrate (at least when I was there) because the thick curtains were always drawn. This was mainly for the sake of the movies he watched in the miniature cinema he'd concocted with state-of-the-art equipment.

'I want to know your honest opinion, how am I sexually, do I please you?' We were lazing on his king-sized bed after a fairly acrobatic session. He smiled at my bluntness.

'I have no complaints at all. Can I ask why you're asking?'

With nothing to prove to him and thinking this would be our last encounter, I told him an abridged version of the truth: the man I'd left Hong Kong for, who I was still married to, who'd now finished with me, thought I was boring in bed.

'Can I ask why he thinks that?'

'Well…I wasn't enough of a roaring, kittenish, enticing, seductive, tigress, always coming at the stroke of his penis, etcetera.'

'He's French isn't he? Figures. Maybe it's a good thing you've split up. Frankly I find his insults funny.'

And thanks to the American so did I—for the next half hour or so until I left.

There was no avoiding the personal questions about Alain that my friends in Hong Kong posed, although there is something about the walking wounded that prevents people from pressing too hard and in fact keeps some away altogether. Would I move back to Hong Kong? several asked. To that, at least, I categorically answered no. The city still felt like my second home but the gravitational pull was within Europe, but to where, Nice or Geneva?

Monsieur Baudin, the Geneva bureau chief, was a gentleman of the old school, formal, entirely civil, a tad awkward, but no-nonsense. After querying my background, he described the substance of the job—I would be the bureau's sole English language correspondent—and the salary and benefits. When, an hour later, I walked out of the interview at the French news agency's Paris headquarters it was with an offer and the request to 'please let me know your decision by Monday'.

I phoned him with my response later that day from my friend's flat, having made up my mind on the spot. The only thing we still had to negotiate was the starting date. Then I phoned Alain, the act of punching in the number like the lead-up to a bungee jump. I fought to sound calm.

'*Bonjour* Alain.'

'So, you're back in France.'

'Yes, in Paris. I need to get back to Provence to pack up. I'm taking the train tomorrow.'

'What time do you arrive in Avignon? I'll pick you up.'

The adrenaline rush was a flood. I hadn't seen him in almost five weeks. Five weeks clean.

I hardly noticed the landscape as the train consumed the kilometres, the destination approaching like a missed deadline. I had lost count of the times he had brought and collected me from Avignon station over the past eighteen months. But on every occasion when the TGV drew in, I voyaged back to the fairy-tale moment on that first day of April, when, feeling weightless, I'd practically somersaulted into his arms, ablaze with something far stronger than hope. I could taste the spring breeze and smell the lively scent of sprigs combined with the sour odour of the platform. I felt the force of his kiss that'd crushed doubts. That was the first time. And this was the last.

A pall hung over the early October sun but there wasn't a ripple of wind. He was waiting for me at the platform exit, arms folded stiffly like a tin soldier, roving eyes and a stern expression the visible face of thoughts I could only guess at. He kissed me gingerly on the cheek, this man who I adored and abhorred, craved and cursed in equal measure, a measure that was off any chart.

'I'm not going to Nice. I have a job offer from a French news agency. The job is in Geneva and I've accepted.'

I disgorged these facts as soon as we were in the car. Alain was impressed and, I immediately saw, vastly relieved. I would be earning a stable salary, which let him off the hook, and I was leaving the country—a more definitive barrier between himself and a clingy 'catastrophe'.

'When will you go?'

'In eight days.'

From one second to the next, his blue eyes became less bluesy and the ends of his mouth unscrewed. The end was at hand.

'Let's go eat,' he proposed.

We headed to Carpentras and Chez Serge, a bistro opposite the main market. Alain led me to a table on the terrace, where flower pots and trellises reduced run-off noise from the street. Menus were brought and orders taken. Alain waited till the waiter placed a carafe of rosé wine on the table before leaning forward.

'I've got some news for you,' he announced. 'I've decided not to take up the flat in Pietrasanta. The trips there and back would cost me a fortune in petrol alone and besides, there's no one around in the winter. It's impractical.'

Impractical because now I was going, he had no need to abandon the house.

'No, Pietrasanta is out,' he drew out the words pleasurably. 'I'm building an iron forge at the house.'

How typical of him. An idea that had galvanised him just a few months earlier was now tossed into the garbage, replaced by a new venture. The words that Valérie had written to me came to mind:

'He's a man who drops everything sooner or later—jobs, houses, women. He's only happy in desire, discovery, conquest, change. I doubt that he will ever in his life stop, for something or someone.'

The hunter needed a new target, and today it was the outdoor workroom that Peppo, master of the *tarte tatin*, had been hired to construct. Alain was already tired of the vast indoor atelier that artists far and wide would have murdered for, the reason he'd bought the house in the first place. He'd hardly used it, preferring to sculpt in the open air.

I saw the outlines of the edifice as we entered New Delhi Drive—a sidelong extension of cemented brick abutting the woodshed. Jumping out of the car I walked over to the site, the details that Alain had greedily divulged over lunch running through my mind like a ticker tape. The forge would be encased in floor to ceiling windows, providing an uninterrupted view of Mont Ventoux. He would spend hours in there, sweating in front of the red-hot furnace, fashioning figures and god knows what else out of inert matter. I would never see the room completed. He must be doing okay financially I thought. This can't be cheap. Piles of stacked-up bricks lay nearby on the grass together with wheelbarrows containing cement.

I went into the house. The long room teemed with his wooden carvings from an earlier era, with works of marble and stone, and now with his latest iron creations. It looked like an exhibition hall. Inside, regal Athena was the undisputed matriarch. Outside, the white marble Buddha held sway, acting as watchdog of the property. The more crowded the space became with his art, the less habitable it was for humans.

The familiar smells of the *mas* teased my nose; the old stone walls, only weeks ago like protective shields, seemed to have withdrawn their allegiance, now whispering: It is time to go. There is nothing left for you here. You are history.

That night, Alain grilled lamb cutlets on the embers and filled our glasses with champagne, the well-worn routine. He was civil that first day and even the second, before the veneer vanished, replaced with open hostility. He didn't attempt to barricade himself from me at night though. Now that I had a departure date, he could tolerate sex. As for me, it was essential, the only way I could put one step in front of the other. I was just like an addict facing a forced stint in rehab, using as much as possible before the cut-off date, or as much as I was allowed to. My physical need for Alain—well, any junkie would understand—the rush of the hit from coitus followed by the calm followed by the need again, and the pain body when it wasn't immediately satisfied. The thought that he was picturing Danielle as he thrusted, his constant slurs about my sexual performance—these were jingles I repeatedly heard in my head but the cravings were louder. I knew I was deferring withdrawal, I knew my thinking was deranged even as I told myself that as long as he still touched me and penetrated me, at some primeval level he must still want me.

In that final week, with sex as my crutch, I managed to box up my possessions without breaking down—that in itself was something. Apart from clothes, almost everything I owned was in my room at the top, my refuge with its sloped, wood-beamed ceiling and Alice-in-wonderland windows looking out onto vistas that had invited sumptuous dreams. My room, where we'd made love, more often than not with the shutters open to the stars. Into a box went the wedding gifts, all apart from the sharp-edged carving knife from Lilly and Nick, which Alain had claimed.

'If we split up I get the knife,' he'd said months beforehand, covering the tracks of this early bid with attempted humour. I had agreed, but when a day later I mentioned to Lilly on the phone that I was leaving it behind she cussed.

'Take it. He doesn't deserve a thing.'

So into the box went the knife. A few hours later Alain noticed its absence.

'It was supposed to stay here.'

'Well, I'm taking it. Orders from the family.'

'So they're Indian givers are they? We had a deal.'

A deal. The spiteful pettiness of separation. 'Indian givers' Alain repeated in such a derisory manner that I unpacked the knife and put it back in the kitchen. Appeasement.

Among my most precious possessions were the research notes and letters from Tristan plus some photos of him that Alain had given me for the book. I was brooding over the photos before packing them—marvelling again at how much Tristan resembled Jesus—when the insight struck. Tristan was a saint. Yes, he was truly a saint and Alain was the arch opposite. The sadist and the saint the sadist and the saint the sadist and the saint, how pleasing it sounded to the ear. Tristan was the ultimate altruist, giving up all worldly things and connections in the pursuit of spiritual enlightenment and service to the poor. Sex had not been a part of his existence. Alain's existence was dominated by sex. They were polar opposites, extremists in their own way, absolute juxtapositions representing evil and good in a simplistic way because of course few things on this planet are categorically black and white. One day maybe I'd be able to examine the brothers from a more detached vantage point and come up with more sophisticated descriptions but for now, the monikers provided some crumbs of comfort, a symbolic act of rebellion against the sadist.

While I tied up loose ends, Alain drove off to meet clients. I no longer asked whether and how many kitchens he was selling for third-party retailers. I assumed he was doing brisk business because he was funding his pet projects. Not just the new forge, whose construction he surveyed with a hawk's eye. He had also taken on a dossier that had once, always, been verboten.

'I'm having a professional photographer take photos of all my sculptures because I've decided to put together a portfolio and approach the big galleries in Paris.'

For him, this was not just radical but heretical. Alain had attacked anything that smacked of commercialism as a sell-out and contrary to his philosophy. How many times had he sworn with bull-headedness, 'I will never mix my art with money-making. Sculpture will always be on my terms and never for the lapdog interests of outsiders.'

The bastard. Now he's going to woo the big guns in Paris. What a hypocrite. God damn it. I bet he does. I bet he gets them. He's certainly good enough. I struggled to digest this newest about-turn. Another slap in the face.

To him I only said: 'That's a huge change. Why?'

'There are too many sculptures in the house now.'

He waved an arm around his collection.

'I've got to do something with them and I feel it's time for me to progress. Yes, it's time to make a move, to take this to another level.'

He'd obviously put the wheels in motion long before his revelation to me because the next day the photographer, an acquaintance of his, showed up. She lived most of the year in South America, returning to Provence every so often to see her parents. It was a physical undertaking, involving as much manoeuvring and heavy lifting as shooting because each item had to be carried to, and snapped against, a white background—in this case a giant white board. Now I understood why Alain had mounted all of his sculptures on supports. It was a specialist's task, the material, shape and elasticity of the base pivotal to the overall artistry. A support can just as easily detract from a carving as embellish it. On occasion, Alain would spend hours in montage, only to discover that the base—wood, stone or metal—didn't work.

The photographer, who I guessed to be in her late thirties, laboured methodically for several days. One by one she captured his works on film, her considerable height useful in hoisting up heavy objects, her long limbs bending into position to capture the light from a particular angle. In the early evenings, she and Alain would unwind over a joint, their easy amiability contrasting to the frigidity he displayed towards me. I naturally wondered if they'd made love or were planning to. There was a sensuality about her stage-managing his sculptures that had only to be transferred to flesh.

The single outing we made together was to a Notary in Cavaillon, where I was asked to sign a document making me a non-beneficiary in Alain's will. For we were still legally husband and wife.

'We have to get a divorce you know,' Alain said on the way back.

'Can't I first apply for French citizenship?'

'You don't need it now that you're going to Switzerland.'

'Don't need but want,' I said, to rile Alain. Through the car window I gazed at the long line of deciduous trees slowly shedding their cover, the sun squinting through the furry leaves like golden haloes.

'Impossible. I want to get things moving as fast as I can.'

Of course. How inconvenient to have a marriage dangling around your neck, as if a boarded-up shop wasn't enough.

And so it was that week, the last of everything, including a meal with the Scottish couple who, disgusted with Alain, had invited me round to their place without him.

'You know, Alain treats his animals better than you,' Lillian spoke bluntly.

With Bianca, the four-month-old addition to the household, that wasn't difficult. Alain had a soft spot for this bundle of white feline fur, according her privileges he had denied Bali, her predecessor, who had wandered off one day never to return. Bianca had her own bed in the kitchen by the fireplace. Alain prepared gourmet titbits, which he served to her on a proper plate. He spent ages playing with her, as if she were some kind of purification. He still didn't allow her in the bedroom but she had a habit of creeping up when the doors weren't closed and napping on the bed. I doted on her too.

No friends braved a call at the house. No, I lie. Jacques came by once and I read in the limp nod he addressed to me the full weight of the injustices I had heaped on Danielle. Alain made sure I knew about it the two times he'd headed over to their place, miffed that Danielle wouldn't step foot in his house while I was still there. I'd told him we'd rowed, given him a bare bones story minus the bits about the bedroom and his backfiring act of vengeance against her—I couldn't stomach actually hearing him confirm it. Had she filled him in on the details of our verbal fisticuff? Had she trashed me to him in the full blaze of victory? I couldn't be sure. But I knew whose side Alain was on, even if, bizarrely, he sought to reassure me.

'Listen Ravinia, I want you to know that I won't go back to her when you're gone. It's out of the question, you can be sure about that.'

Sure about that? His ego had taken a giant thrashing from being cuckolded by her. I was sure about that. And that a part of him, consciously or otherwise, hadn't let her go, all those derogatory comments about her be damned. I'd had the evidence all along. The previous day, riffling through my personal papers, I came across Alain's initial letter to me in Hong Kong. It was the missive following Act One of the opening of Pandora's box, when I'd written to him out of the blue three years after our fling in Vietnam. I thought of the day I'd read it, chuffed not only that he'd remembered me but seemed genuinely happy to hear from me. Finding that letter again, I should have binned it. Instead, I re-read it.

And stopped cold. There, on the second page, in his beautiful bold-stroke handwriting were the words that I couldn't remember seeing, words that had never registered. He was talking about his passion for sculpting in marble:

'I find as much pleasure from this as from the love of a woman. The difference is there is no suffering in return, no thoughts of making another suffer.'

He was referring of course to Danielle. His suffering as a result of her infidelity—suffering he'd repackaged and gifted to me. The damning realisation kicked me in the teeth: Danielle had disgorged the truth to me that day on the phone. When Alain had asked me to come live with him he wasn't over her. He still loved her, still desired her. His pressing me to come to Provence was nothing more than an act of vengeance. The two of them had unfinished business to settle and I was an unwitting pawn in a sickly drama that went way over my head. This was it, the twisted, hideous key to the whole saga.

One day, I thought, playing devil's advocate, I'll look back and see how privileged I'd been to experience a side of Provence that you didn't read about in books. Not the banalities, the narrow-mindedness, the focus on food and fetes, not the lack of curiosity about what lay two feet beyond. But the fact that behind all those pretty facades, among such stunning scenery and surface perfections, there coursed a putrefaction of sexual one-upmanship that sought to harm. Provence wasn't supposed to be like that. Not that it negated the idyllic side, because if it had I wouldn't be so ravaged about being cut loose.

Danielle, Jacques and Yvette—she involved with the married Parisian—were now rolling around in a threesome according to Vivienne. Her left arm now mended, my friend was bouncing on air, her new relationship rapidly evolving into fixity. I could already visualise her and her lover having a baby together. As for Mathias, I hadn't expected him to grow disenchanted with bachelorhood quite so quickly. He'd come knocking on her door one afternoon with a bouquet of flowers in hand and a measure of contriteness. He wanted her back.

'Can you imagine the audacity? We have to remain cordial of course for the sake of our daughter, but what must have gone through his brain to think I'd take him back? Maybe that'll teach him to treat the next victim better, although I doubt it.'

When I drove over to say goodbye, Vivienne was making lunch, spaghetti with strips of sauçisson, her children bent over a game on the living room floor, a household of happy disorder. I declined to stay for lunch. Although an invisible string was holding my emotions together I didn't know how durable it was and besides, I wanted to pay last calls on Cristelle and Valérie.

'Listen you, Alain is not worth anymore of your suffering. You'll find what you want, don't worry.' Her parting words.

Josephine happened to ring the house that week to speak with Alain, who was out. I'd not seen her for months.

'How are you?' she added as an afterthought, as if nothing was remiss.

'Not terribly good actually.'

I told her about my imminent departure, the reasons for which I knew she already knew.

'Well, what can I say?' she replied and I thought lots of things, like sorry it didn't work out, I wish you well, good luck in Geneva. Instead she rang off abruptly and I thought, those are her true colours. Perhaps her revelation to me about Alain feeling forced into marriage hadn't been an innocent slip of the tongue after all. At base, for her and her daughter, I was just another casualty to add to the heap.

Another call came in, from Monique, the woman we'd had a threesome with at the house ten months before.

'I'm going to be passing your way and I wondered if I could come by.'

'You'll have to talk with Alain. He's not here at the moment. Can I get him to call you back?'

'No, I'll ring another time.'

I wondered how quickly they would rendezvous after I was gone.

I shied away from calling Christophe, lacking the nerve for a final *au revoir*. His mini Calvary of spending the summer at the house had paid off. From what I gathered he was now scooting happily around Miramas. I just hoped he had more of his mother's genes, psychologically speaking, and was not cursed with extreme misogyny—a diagnosis I'd definitively pinned on his father.

I finished packing and sealed my boxes, which would be trucked to Geneva in a few weeks. My study, now bare apart from the boxes, seemed to have gained a size, although maybe it was just the contours of my own grief that I saw. I had made barely a mark in the rest of the house, probably exactly as Alain had wanted.

I had just one more mission in mind.

Chapter 28

Sunday morning, a day before the exile, I headed to Beaumes-de-Venise, having phoned Pierre beforehand to make sure he was at home. I found him pottering in the kitchen, twiddling with the entrails of a broken toaster.

'Let's sit outside, it's a beautiful day,' he put the gadget down.

His garden was of a size to allow a decent game of football. Trees and shrubs circled it off from a lengthy run of neatly planted vines that gave onto low foothills. A gentle October breeze floated over us like cream on top of milk. Gazing at the vista, I thought…you have your own corner of paradise.

Over peppermint tea, we talked about my summer trip to Hong Kong, his projects, the Paris marathon, evading the obvious for a time. Finally reality inveigled when he asked whether I'd found work.

'I've accepted a job in Geneva, as English correspondent for a French news agency. I'm leaving for Switzerland tomorrow. A new life in a new city.'

He frowned, his hazel eyes sooty. He seemed to remember himself and smiled.

'That's fantastic for you. Congratulations. So what does it involve?'

I explained my role, omitting to mention the stabs of fear I felt about resuming pressure-cooker work and being able to deliver to deadline. My face must have given these fears away or perhaps he read my thoughts.

'Don't worry. I'm sure you'll do well. You'll be back in an environment that you know, where you've proved yourself. When do you start?'

'Tuesday, the day after I arrive.'

The bureau chief had originally wanted me to begin three weeks from the date of the interview, but there's no way Alain would have allowed me to stay that long at the house and so I pushed hard for an earlier start.

'They're putting me up in a hotel for two weeks, which gives me a bit of time to find an apartment.'

'Have you been to Geneva before?'

'Once, when I was about eleven, but I remember almost nothing about the city. About the only thing I do know is that it has lots of banks.'

'And mountains.'

'But not Mont Ventoux.' I blinked back tears. Don't you dare cry.

'The Alps. They're something. Do you ski?'

'No, not snow ski. I water ski.'

'Well, now's your chance to learn. I love to ski. As a university student I went every year to La Colmiane in the Alps Maritime, and…'

I stopped listening, a single question invading my brain. I needed to know.

'Why have you been so good to me Pierre,' I interrupted. 'You've been my ally against your brother. You stayed at the house with me when you didn't have to. You've been there for me when I needed, when it wasn't normal. Why?'

'No, not really, I haven't.'

He sounded alarmed. He leaned his head back and shut his eyes. I guessed he was debating with himself. All at once he sat forward, galvanised.

'Do you remember I told you that my former girlfriend left me for someone who I knew?'

'Of course.'

'Well, that person…'

I shuddered. The cortisone pumped. I knew what was coming.

'That person was Alain.'

Deep within I had known it. Why else had Pierre not been more specific, revealing who had betrayed him? Why else had I not asked him? But the avowal was sickening. I felt dizzy, as if cut off from gravity. When I closed my eyes, the dizziness got worse.

'Can I get you some water?'

My nod sent him to the kitchen. I willed my guts to settle so I didn't have to get up and go to the toilet, fearing I might fall. Pierre returned with the water. The dizziness ebbed and my bowels obeyed.

'Do you want to hear about it?' The alarm had gone, replaced with a kind of grim determination.

'No, no…Yes. Everything.'

'You see,' he began, 'Alain and I used to be close. When Tristan left for India, we saw each other a lot. He'd often take me out for dinner in Marseille when I was a penniless student and he even took me skiing. It wasn't long after I met Flore that he started living with Brigitte in Aix-en-Provence. In a nice little cosy cottage. It was good to see them so much in love. Flore and I would drive to their place on a Friday or Saturday night, or for Sunday lunch. Brigitte and Flore seemed to get on well together. When Brigitte and Alain split up, we continued our trips to Aix. I never suspected anything. I never sensed that something was going on under my nose. I never would have believed it.'

'Flore started to see Alain, in secret. To give him credit, Alain wasn't the instigator. That's what Flore told me and I believed her. She said she'd made the first move, knowingly jeopardising our relationship. In court she might have argued that there were mitigating circumstances. Her exact words were, "it was an attraction I had no control over". But Alain didn't stop it. He had broken up with his girlfriend so he was free. After I lost Flore, they saw each other for oh, maybe eight months…until she discovered she was pregnant.'

'And that's when he finished it? And you don't know if she had the baby?'

He shrugged his shoulders.

So Alain might have another child somewhere. A child conceived in lust but dumped before birth, never to know its father. The crime, the crime and there had been no punishment.

'When you told me about Alain's rejection, that he wanted you gone, I wanted to ask if you were pregnant,' Pierre continued. 'If that was the reason why. But how could I say anything? I knew that would have given it away.'

'Did you confront him, get angry with him? Did he apologise to you, express regret or shame for what he'd done?'

'Right after Flore confessed I drove over to see him like a madman. It's the first time I'd ever felt violent. I accused him of stealing my fiancée. He echoed Flore, telling me it was she who had initially come onto him. I asked him, "so you're going to continue with her" and he said yes, he hadn't stolen her but he loved her.'

'I don't understand why you moved to Beaumes-de-Venise, so close to him.'

'It was my ex-wife's idea. She took a great fancy to Beaumes, of all the villages in the Vaucluse. And I couldn't say no. Ironic, really, since she's the one who then left. I've thought about moving many times. But I'm fond of this house. And he and I don't run into each other, mixing in different circles as you know.'

'You never confronted him about Flore being pregnant?'

'No. I was too torn up. I couldn't face him. I was also, I think, afraid of doing something stupid, something I'd regret. So I kept away, had nothing more to do with him for years. But with time, the anger lessened, turned more into sadness.

There was a rapprochement to the extent that I could be around him at family gatherings and so on and he's reached out to me, even asking for a helping hand in emergencies, like picking you up at the station and asking me to stay over when he went to Lyon. I talked it out and understood that if I hung on to my anger it could ruin me. My mental health.'

'Talked it out. You mean you saw a therapist?'

'No no. I talked with myself.' He shook his head as if to clear the memories. 'When you appeared I thought Alain might have changed, learned a few lessons. That whole episode with Danielle and Jacques, well, he got a taste of his own medicine. It was quite a comeuppance, some might say divine retribution, though I never wished that on him.'

I thought of Pierre's reaction the afternoon he'd come by the house, when I'd laid the facts bare. Now it all made sense.

'When I told you at the house about him wanting to end the marriage, it brought it all back to you didn't it, the betrayal, the anger?'

He nodded. 'Yes, but it was more than that. It was the shock that Alain hadn't changed, hadn't learned a thing. That he'd done it again, with a woman who was also good, also intelligent, much too good and intelligent for someone like him. Not that I don't understand the attraction. Anyway, I wanted to believe it would work out with you.'

'Just so you know, he wanted me here in Provence as a way to punish Danielle for what she did with Jacques, not because he loved me. It was Danielle herself who told me. She said it was payback and I believe her.'

He looked incredulous.

'How can you trust what she says? But either way, he's gotten worse.'

I steered him back to his revelations.

'Your mother and Sylvie, did they find out about Alain and Flore?'

'I said nothing to them. I didn't want to create a rift, force my mother to take sides. They know something happened between Alain and I. But they are not ones to pry, especially if they suspect they will not like the answer. We're a family that shelters in silence and denial. And I think Alain was grateful that I kept quiet.'

I wondered if Brigitte and Danielle knew any of this. Brigitte might have kept this from me to spare my feelings, although she'd been pretty up front in Nice. Then I realised that Alain must have dumped Flore not that long before I'd met him in Vietnam. I couldn't make sense of it. How can you behave so badly one moment and so gentlemanly the next? Maybe it was a case of different places, different personas. Neither his comedy nor his civility had seemed like an act. Then I thought how stupid it was of me to think this way. As if his behaviour and motivations could be so easily deciphered at every step. And yet, wasn't that precisely what I was trying to do? Decipher and label? The psychology of it—a minefield of nothing but confusion. Bafflement.

'What he did to you. It's despicable. And to Flore.'

'I told you so you have no illusions. So that maybe it will be easier for you to leave tomorrow.'

If only.

There seemed nothing left to say, if not just triteness. I felt wrung out. I wanted to be alone.

'I should go.'

'Won't you at least stay for lunch?'

'I'm not hungry but thank you.'

I sought the toilet off the hallway. When I came out, Pierre was waiting for me by the front door. There were no polite pecks this time but a clasping hug that conveyed the acknowledgement of mutual pain. And then a funny thing happened. As we drew apart, he brushed my lips with his. This turned into a tentative kiss, which turned into a full-fledged kiss, which drew in arms. I pulled away.

'Pierre! *Qu'est-ce qu'on fait*?'

'I'm sorry,' he sounded aghast. But quick as a whippet I brought my lips back to his. I couldn't bear him feeling guilty or bad about it but it wasn't only to placate. There was a comfort in that kiss, a beauty, a letting go. For several more seconds, we embraced before I disengaged.

'Pierre, this can't go further. It wouldn't be fair to you. But don't apologise. In another context…'

'You don't have to explain. It wasn't planned, but it was dreamed.'

Which made me want to know more. I wanted him to describe his feelings, reveal a story. But he held his tongue. He'd been brave enough already. Why should he go further when I couldn't? Though my head wanted it, my legs refused to walk out the door. Instead, they went to the staircase.

'I've never seen the second floor. Would you show it to me?'

I followed him up the pine wood stairs. The door to his bedroom, across the landing, was open. Inside I was amazed to see a four-poster bed made of solid oak. Over it hung a huge mosquito net, the sides tied to the pillars like curtains. A brown leather sofa took up a large chunk of one wall. Above it hung a tropical landscape—sky, mountains, palm trees—the style distinctive.

'A reproduction of Gauguin?' I pointed to the painting.

'Yes, by an artist in Toulouse. Like it?'

'Gauguin's one of my favourites.'

I walked to the window, which looked out onto the garden, the sea of vines and the foothills beyond. Pierre joined me.

'Why the mosquito net? Surely there's aren't mosquitoes here?'

'The occasional one in summer. But that's not the reason for it. Once—I must have been eight or nine—I read a book about a boy in Africa who said that curling up under his mosquito net at night was like being in the cave of his ancestors. I liked that.'

I stood gazing outwards, engulfed in thoughts of betrayal, rocked by the kiss. Why had it happened? It wasn't planned but it was dreamed. So, he liked me in that way. Only he'd never shown it before—of course he hadn't, I was a wedded woman. And yet. There had been signs. I thought back to his stay at the house for a week, the way he'd sometimes looked at me, his kindnesses above and beyond call. I stared at the open vista. Who knew what Pierre was thinking. We were idling, together but far apart.

'Pierre, would you mind untying the mosquito net?'

He went to the bed, untied the white strings and unfurled the mesh.

'May I go inside?'

'Of course.'

I took my shoes off, slipped under the netting and beckoned for him to do the same. Both of us lay on the bed for a moment, not touching. Then I put my head on his chest, hands bunched against my cheek, permission for him to drape an arm loosely around my shoulder. There we stayed, wrapped in that mosquito-proof space. For a long time, I didn't feel compelled to say anything. When I did it was for small talk.

'As an engineer, it must make you feel confident to know how things work. How they're put together, bridges, tunnels, escalators.'

'On the contrary, it lowers your confidence because you know all the mistakes that can be made, the human error that can weaken the strongest steel struts if corners are cut.' His voice came through muffled and I could hear his heart beat.

'What's the best thing about your job?'

'Well…Projects have a beginning and an end. And a long middle,' he laughed, 'which is where I mostly come in. Still, there's a sense of achievement when a technical challenge has been worked out, when you can see it all come together.'

'The fruits of your labour, visible, permanent. Quite like art.'

'Hopefully, but not always permanent. What's the best thing about being a journalist?'

Chasing an unfolding story, writing, being on the front lines of big events. No. Not only.

'Being able to ask questions. And if I'm honest, to hide a certain lack of self-confidence and reserve.'

'You, a lack of confidence?'

'I'm glad it's not obvious.'

'Actually, you're not the only one. I also use my work to hide behind, as a kind of shield for not having to think and go after what I want or think I want. I'm a terrible procrastinator. It's a big character defect. I play it safe, let life slide by. I don't grab it head-on like my…'

'Brother'?

'Yes.'

It never occurred to me that he might envy some traits about Alain. Maybe he'd always felt in his shadow, just as I'd done with Lilly.

'And what would you choose to do, if you didn't have to work and earn money?'

'Go to India, explore ashrams, study sadhus.'

'Come on, be serious.'

'I am serious.'

'What else?'

'Learn the tango.'

'But you don't have to quit your job for that. You could learn here.'

'I could. In Avignon. But I don't. And it's not the same as doing it in Argentina.'

And on we went for an hour or so, following drifts, not budging, my head on his chest. In that bugless place, I recognised a feeling I had just about forgotten—calm.

Driving back to Mazan in the afternoon, I had a powerful sense of déja vu. I'd known in my soul the truth about Alain that Pierre had revealed. Ha, the good brother. Why couldn't I have met him first? Tristan may have been the real saint but Pierre warranted a good half title. Demi-Saint Pierre. He wouldn't like that at all, humble as he was, and he'd probably take issue with Alain and the sadist label, but maybe not. He'd stayed clear of him after the treachery but they were still brothers. You couldn't change that. Alain's betrayal was odious. But it meant I now faced a new dilemma. How could I keep the information inside? Pierre hadn't asked me not to tell Alain. In fact, I think he wanted me to. But if I let the cat out of the bag, Alain wouldn't touch me that night, my last night, and I needed the sex to sleep. In that moment, I almost hated Pierre for spilling the beans.

I thought back to our second round of goodbyes—a brief, tight hug. I didn't expect he would make himself any more vulnerable, but then he said, 'Will you phone me when you get to Geneva? To let me know you've arrived safely? I could come visit.'

For an instant, I thought of playing along.

'Pierre, he's toxic, he's poisonous, but I still love him. I have to get over him. I don't want you to be my rebound man.'

A moment of indecision and then I added: 'I'll phone you in…say six months. Maybe by then I'll be okay. And you'll probably have met someone.'

'Keep asking lots of questions,' he waved me off, his feelings tucked inside.

I was halfway along New Delhi Drive when I spotted Danielle's car, parked symmetrical to the Fiat. My spot. I felt like ramming it but instead, manoeuvred my car onto the grass, just about avoiding a collision with the plane tree. They weren't in the kitchen or anywhere on the ground floor. I tiptoed upstairs. No one in our bedroom or in the rooms on the top floor. That left the atelier. I opened the heavy wooden door. Empty. I returned to the bedroom and sat on the bed, ears pricked for sound. Maybe they were doing it in the hut in the field where Alain and I had fucked. 'I won't go back to her when you're gone. It's out of the question.' The diabolical curse of jealousy. Now I understood how it could happen, a crime of passion, how you could pull the trigger.

I heard the crunch of footsteps on gravel and voices in the drive and bolted to the window. Alain and Danielle were talking under the smaller plane tree. I couldn't hear what they were staying. He was gesticulating, pointing to the path behind the house. Danielle looked cat-womanish in tight jeans, a black jacket and black boots. She touched Alain's arm, they kissed each other's cheeks, he disappeared inside and she drove off. I shot downstairs.

'Danielle.' I gagged on her name, unable to string a proper sentence together.

He gaped at me. My pallor must have been something for he appeared to take pity.

'Not that I owe you an explanation, but she came round to help. One of the neighbours came here this morning to tell me he'd found a wrought iron table in the field just beyond his farm. He had no idea how it got there or who it belonged to. He wanted to know if it was mine and if not, did I want it. It was too heavy for me to carry myself and Peppo and Jacques weren't around.'

But of course Danielle was. I could have helped you, I wanted to scream. But I'd been at Pierre's.

'You can have a look at it if you like. It's by the woodshed.'

He didn't ask where I'd been.

The brief interlude of calm under the mosquito netting now seemed eons away.

The last supper. A medley of chicken, olives, tomatoes and onions cooked in thyme and oregano accompanied by basmati rice, a menu not out of the ordinary although like everything else that last week, I stapled it to my brain. We sat at the table in the long room, dark apart from the flickering candles, once the very essence of beauty and intimacy, now reminding me of a wake for a corpse. With a mean gleam, Alain began to describe the holiday he was planning to Colombia that winter, making it clear he was going largely to savour the women, in other words, to fuck his way across the country.

'I've had it with European women. I'm fed up with the lot of them, all wanting commitment and long-lasting relationships. Babies. Boredom.'

'That's what most women want, Alain, a sense of security, a commitment. Don't think that women in Colombia are any different.'

'Well, I'll never give stability to any woman, ever,' he said, hatred reverberating through every rotten syllable. 'What suits me best is to stay with a woman for six months, maximum a year, and then move on.'

Did he really mean his words, or was this just his parting gift for an amalgamated eighteen months of misery?

'It's impossible to believe you're brothers. You're from different planets.'

'And what brother might you be referring to?'

'Pierre, although the same could apply to Tristan.'

'You leave Pierre out of this.'

'Why? He's a good friend and an honourable man, unlike you.'

'Meaning most likely you've slept with him. He stayed in this house with you for a week while I was gone. You think I'm blind? But neither do I care. If you're playing the jealousy card, it doesn't work.'

'Only a misogynist would think like that. No, sex is not what it's about with him. It's about something much stronger, much deeper.'

Intrigued, he put his fork down and leaned forward, his neck extended like a rubber band.

'Honesty. Pierre told me what happened. How you were the one who betrayed him, being with his fiancée after she left him for you. It was you who dumped her when you found out she was pregnant.'

These were facts. Not interpretation, but facts. How would he twist them? He pushed his plate away and finished off his wine.

'Would it have been better if I'd married her, been a father to her child, keeping her around to torment Pierre?'

Well blow me away. So he'd acted quite the chivalrous knight. Well well well.

'You were her lover. You. Had. An. Affair. With. Your. Brother's. Fiancée.' It deserved to be screamed from the rooftop. But I could barely go beyond a whisper. 'Despicable. Is that what you're teaching Christophe? Are those your morals?'

'Morals?' He laughed. 'Since when do you have morals? You want me to fuck you still, right? Are those your morals, when you know you mean nothing to me?'

The bastard. Hoisted on my own petard.

'It's not the same thing and you know it. I'm not harming anyone else. Especially not my sibling.'

'Women, always trouble.'

He rose abruptly, went to the three dogs room and returned with his bottle of snake brew. I cleared the dishes, fury, hurt, despair and disbelief coated in a thick shell of numbness.

He looked straight ahead as he downed—not sipped as was usual—two shots of the stuff. Then he stretched out arms and legs, glided off the chair, and with that decisive mien of his, picked up jacket and keys and headed for the kitchen door. I shouldn't have asked him where he was going. It was long passed being my business. But because I did, he shot me a sardonic look that said, 'almost free,' without answering.

I refused to give into paralysis before I'd cleaned up. Only then did I collapse onto the kitchen floor, eyes screwed shut. Eventually, sluggishly, I wheedled myself to the three dogs room and slumped on the sofa, staring at the fireplace. Oblivious of everything but the canyon of pain. Too deep to ever climb out of. Silence all around. Then the hailstorm hit, pellets of vengefulness. His sculptures. Destroy his sculptures. But how, with what? A pen might do it. I could deface Athena and his Angel, but ink came off didn't it? Paint would be better. Just pour it over the marble and stone. But then I remembered there was no more paint in the woodshed. I could take Athena, Diva, Cleopatra, the Three Sisters and Bali II and throw them out of a high-up widow. Or smash them right here with a hammer. Yes, I could do that. Athena ruled the roost but…the three dogs. Yes, the fireplace—his *pièce de résistance*. But how do you mangle stone that is immovable?

The solution was suddenly obvious. Heart racing, I rushed up the stairs, pushed open the door to the atelier and switched on the light. I'd never been in the room alone at night before. The unbroken blackness seeping through the glass gave the vast space an eerie aspect, like a calm sea before a violent storm. The trestle table was in a far corner by the window, in front of some metal shelves. His work overalls hung over a chair. His sculpting tools were placed neatly on the table, chisels, stone-carving knives, hammers and mallets, all of varying sizes and weights. *There it is.* I ran to the table and picked up the drill. It was heavier than I'd expected, with its circular disc that cut through stone, spewing forth grey mushrooms of dust. The long electrical cord was attached. Handling it carefully, I hurried back down. I inserted the plug in the electrical socket nearest to the fireplace and holding the drill as far away from myself as I could, turned it on. I almost toppled backwards from the force of the whirring disc. It was all I could do to turn it off, realising not only that I had no clue how to wield the instrument but that I could very easily lop off a few fingers or a hand in the process. I cursed out loud, dashed to the atelier, put back the drill, seized the largest of the hammers and sprinted once more to the fireplace. Thunk thunk thunk. They were strong my hammer blows, but useless against the unbreakable canine flanks.

Athena. I honed in on one of her perfect conical breasts, thinking this the most vulnerable spot. But the marble also resisted the blows. Plan C then. In the bedroom I lifted Shiva off his stand and carried him up to my study, eyes averted from the chiselled mass. I had to lay the sculpture on the floor so I could open the shutters, which were just above the radiator. Leaning forward, I looked down to the driveway, obscured by the dark, imagining the head splitting open and Shiva's wooden brains spilling out. I dangled him outside in the crisp night air. *Drop it drop it.* The seconds ticked by, my arms sagging from the weight. *It's easy just drop it.* The hands were defiant. I pulled Shiva back inside and slumped to the floor, head bowed, arms crossed, shivering from the cold, the exertion, nerves. It wasn't that I wanted to save Shiva, although god knows this piece of wood had been an icon of sorts. It wasn't the thought of Alain's anger or violence at the discovery of ruin. It was something so vile that, coming from someone else, I'd have thought they were beyond redemption. No fix. If I do this there'll be no fix, this, on my last night.

I was in bed when he returned, sometime after midnight. I heard the sound of footsteps on the stairs and the bedroom door being opened and closed. He brushed his teeth, removed his clothes and slid into bed.

'You're not asleep.'

It was a rhetorical question.

'Well, I suppose you were waiting up for me. I had a good time tonight. She was wild, this one—*fofolle.*' He laughed like a throat clearing. 'What a mouth, what legs…Elodie, no need to give her any lessons.'

He drew up to me, his face close to mine. I smelled the alcohol on his breath through the toothpaste, and a cloying scent on his body. That still didn't prove anything. But then, why shouldn't what he said be true? He was a free agent now. I kept quiet—that at least. In the end, he can't have been that sadistic, can he, because he gave me what I needed. Or was it because he understood that the act was so much more degrading for me than for him? That last time, after putting on a condom, he banged into me with his eyes closed and a Marquis de Sade smirk. The last time.

I awoke every hour or so, the finality that awaited rearing up like a repulsive reptile. In the dark I stared at Alain, in a deep, rejuvenating sleep as usual, dreaming perhaps of Elodie or his impending liberty. In the morning, Peppo was at work outside when, showered and dressed, I went into the kitchen, braving the notion of some bread and yoghurt. He'd almost finished the forge, which required only the installation of the windows and the furnace. What more could a sculptor want than this glass enclosure, a temple of creation (and destruction)?

The sun was fully discernible, its rays bathing the garden, the leaves of the plane trees and the still-vibrant vines in its tranquil warmth. Under its perfect prism all human emotions seemed irrational, irrelevant. Mine were anyway on hold, suspended in the lavender-blue sky. I snuck in a last look at the long room, the sculptures on their stands, an eclectic, extended family presided over by still-unblemished and ever-radiant Athena. Bianca was curled up in her corner in the kitchen, Alain's agenda lay open on the counter, a half-consumed loaf of country bread sat on the table. In the three dogs room grey ash covered the surface of the hearth.

Alain carried my two suitcases outside and put them in the boot of the Honda. While I lingered at the door under the guise of ensuring I had everything, he stood on the gravel waiting impatiently, like a horse stamping its hooves. I thought about saying you're a blasphemy to your species, but I wasn't sure how to phrase that in French.

'Don't make any more women suffer,' I settled on. 'No Alain, no cry. Okay?'

He brushed it off, pecking me coldly on the cheek.

'Good luck.'

I got in the car, buckled up and turned the key. It wouldn't start. Shit, not now. This had never happened before. Alain, expecting to hear the sound of the engine, walked over.

'What's wrong with the car?'

'I don't know.'

'Let me try.'

I vacated the driver's seat. He bore down on the ignition like a bullfighter going for the kill, but his efforts yielded nothing.

'I've got to get myself ready to see my accountant. Peppo will help you,' he said tetchily. And with a 'ciao Ravinia', the man who'd told me I was the woman of his life definitively shoved me out of it, disappearing inside to take care of more pressing matters.

Peppo took charge, sticking his head in the engine and tinkering around inside while I leaned against the car door, sweating and praying. In a matter of minutes, though the time seemed endless, the problem was fixed. Peppo, wiping his hands on his faded overalls, left the engine running while I got into the car and shut the door. He waved goodbye rather poignantly, standing in front of the forge. His profile receded as I drove to the end of New Delhi Drive, into Mazan and intentionally past the old Marquis de Sade château. *You've left your mark in Mazan*. Swinging through Carpentras I entered the motorway, snaked around Avignon before heading north, past Valence and Grenoble to the Swiss border.

Chapter 29

He picked up the phone on the fifth ring.

'Allo?'

'Pierre, it's Ravinia.'

'Ravinia?'

'It's well over six months, more like nine, but I told you I'd call.'

'You kept your promise.'

He replied hesitatingly, intimating he didn't believe for a second that I would—or most likely he'd forgotten what I'd said.

'Anyway, I wanted to tell you that I'm alive, that things are okay and Geneva's not so bad, especially after the winter when the sun comes out of hibernation. I understand now why most people are ski-mad. On the mountains, it's another world.'

'Where are you living?'

'In an apartment, a one-bedroom on a busy main road can you believe? The great thing is, it's on the top floor, there are only six floors, so it has a view. I can see lake Geneva and beyond that, Mont Salève in France. If it's a really clear day, I can see the tip of the Alps. I have a balcony but it's too noisy to be outside. I can walk to my office in the Palais des Nations, up a long hill.'

'It all sounds very positive. But it can't have been easy.'

'Easy, no. But I've had good help. I won't bore you with the details.'

'The details, you're not going to deny me all of them, are you?'

'Well, where to start?'

Not with those first weeks and the stark, brutal effects of withdrawal, when whatever had protected me in those final days in Provence did a runner and I cried for hours at night like a colicky baby. It was the sheer discipline demanded by my job, the need to focus under the pressure of deadlines that kept my emotions in check during daylight hours.

The evenings had been the hardest. Finally, after about a month, I'd found a way to neutralise the anguish of the nights. After work, in the wintry darkness, I would scurry back to my flat on the Rue de Lausanne, eat something, then sit down once again at the keyboard, this time to frenziedly record the saga of Alain and Provence. It all came tumbling out on the screen, accompanied by a steady outpouring of sobs.

I told Pierre about the two superwomen who gave me strength. Maude, the irrepressible office manager of the French news bureau had taken me under her wing and insisted I stay with her when, after a fortnight of hunting, I still hadn't found an apartment. A single parent to an adult son, she let nothing stand in the way of her and having fun. Her laughter was intensely therapeutic, complementing the twice-weekly sessions I had with an excellent psychotherapist.

Actually there were four superwomen. My sisters nourished me with their unwavering support. Relieved that I was finally out of Provence and into a good job, they checked up on me regularly, uttering affirming words and strong reassurances that I'd feel good again, whole again, in fact more whole than I'd ever felt because the worst was over and I was dealing with my demons. I was glad they'd both been to Mazan and had a chance to vet Alain, Julia more so than Lilly. Both had borne witness to his outsized charm and magnetism, they'd understood how these had ensorcelled. But both had also divined his dark underbelly and known it didn't bode well for marriage or indeed any kind of relationship.

'I felt like slapping him when he rubbished your dress—the morning you got married,' Lilly said after I'd made the move. 'Remember that?'

How could I forget.

'Jesus, I just wanted to yell at you, tell you to stop, that it was craziness to marry him. I just knew he wasn't…it wouldn't work. But I managed to control myself. I knew no matter what I said, you had to play this one out.'

She was right. Shame had stopped me from reaching out to her at many points during the ordeal but once I got my act together, she and Julia were a loyal sisterhood. If anything, Provence had brought us even closer together.

I didn't reveal to Pierre my sexual suffering. From copious amounts of sex I'd gone into enforced celibacy, at least at first. It was hard to admit to any commonality with Danielle but share one I did.

‘It was hell when he left. I suffered incredibly for months. Sexually it was hard, you know. I missed him. After all, Alain is talented in bed. He’s the best I’ve ever had.’

That’s what she’d said. For months afterwards I also suffered, craving him physically, but no, he wasn’t talented in bed. Quite the opposite, he was egotistical in bed, the woman’s pleasure important only if it validated the power of his penis. When finally he was purged from my system, I decided to remain on a sexual cleansing fast. I’d break it only when I was ready. I also decided to grow my pubic bush again, a symbolic if not physical act of rebellion for my royal jewels.

‘I suppose you can say I’ve been confronting some home truths,’ I told Pierre.

Truths that should have been obvious before Provence. I knew enough from the drama with my using ex-boyfriend in New York to realise that addiction was fundamentally about escape from the self, low self-esteem, feelings of unworthiness and shame. At least that was a part of it because there were surely a million different reasons for something so complex.

That my enslavement to Alain had been completely out of context made it no less painful or excusable. Yes, I’d had my share of ‘FUFO’ men before Alain. But I didn’t have a track record of courting or tolerating abuse or destroying myself for the sake of a man. I’d been the one to leave my junkie boyfriend. Those women who handcuffed themselves to bastards, who were strung up, quartered and tortured by another’s tongue or hand, they could never have been me. A preposterous thought. But now I knew. I’d been one of them, afflicted with the ‘I’m not good enough’ virus. And to think I’d believed I’d expunged it from my system; not just through therapy but with a virus eradication tool kit containing things like meditation, life development courses, books and the wisdom of ancient philosophers. But this bug is extremely tenacious once embedded. It enjoys longevity, can lay dormant for ages and lunges unexpectedly. Plus it has variants.

One of the hardest things about my present therapy was coming to terms with this: What happened with Alain wasn’t a zero-sum game where me the self-hater was the great big loser. There were gains to being a victim, although I was still trying to figure out what exactly these were. Any attempts with my therapist to monologue about Alain’s awfulness and cruelty led not to any affirmation of how terrible he was but to a shift of the focus back to me and my messy emotional landscape. For every instant that I'd degraded myself with Alain I and I alone was responsible. The thing about dealing with such slippery issues was that they were a work-in-progress. I'd had bouts of therapy well before Provence. And I was still in therapy.

'Tell me about you Pierre. Did you run the marathon?'

'It was a close call because of a torn tendon but yes I did. In just under three hours.'

'That sounds respectable. One life ambition achieved, bravo.'

'I ached for two days afterwards, but I'm already prepping for the next one.'

How good it was to hear his voice, firm and steady yet inquisitive, and to imagine him sitting at the kitchen table with the glass figurines nearby. Or perhaps he was upstairs in his bedroom, lying on his comfortable duvet under the mosquito netting, a book by his side, the eight o'clock twilight illuminating the colours of the Tahitian landscape. In the past few months I'd thought about him a great deal. I'd thought about his kindness, his empathy, his being there for me. I'd thought about his sportiness, his reading about saddhus, his curiosity about things, his self-admitted tendency for procrastination and playing it safe. I'd thought about his understated sense of humour. I'd thought about the suffering he'd been through with Flore and the betrayal at the hands of his brother, about his wife's infidelity and his divorce. I'd thought about how calm I felt in his presence, how easy he was to be with and talk to. He had the qualities that I cherished, a solar system away from the extremism, perfectionism and narcissism of his brother.

The more I'd thought about Pierre the more I'd realised that yes, he was a man whose values I shared, he was built of something solid and stable and good and worthy and honest and loyal and dependable, he was able to truly love and give to a woman. I'd thought about my head lying on his chest and how safe I'd felt with him nestled on his bed and about our long kiss, his tongue tasting of fresh mint. I'd thought about his wholesome face and tall, fit physique. I'd thought, or rather fantasised about his touching me and us making love. And I'd thought that maybe I was romanticising things with him because I was lonely and missed the connection with a man and was in the process of recovery. Which is why I hadn't called him sooner.

He filled me in about his work and I told him about mine, and about cross-country skiing and my car getting stuck in the snow. Then he said, 'I want you to know I came down hard on Alain. It got a little ugly. I even told my mother and Sylvie, knowing that…'

'Pierre, stop,' I interrupted. 'Please stop. I don't want to hear anything about him or know how he's doing.'

But I was the one to then elaborate.

'He contacted me once, to tell me he'd started divorce proceedings. He wanted me to come to Provence for the judgment but I told him that was impossible. I said he would have to do it without me. And he has.'

'When will the judgement become final?'

'I'm not sure exactly but it won't be long. There's nothing complicated about the divorce, nothing to contest.'

A long pause. And then the plunge.

'Do you remember what you said when we said goodbye at your house? That you could come visit me? It would be lovely to see you, if you're still up for it. You don't need to come all the way here. We could meet half way, in Lyon for instance.'

I'm not on the rebound anymore, I wanted to say. I've been through hell and made it out to the other side. I'm not needy. I'm ready for…

'Ravinia,' he breathed out. 'I've met someone.'

It hit me like a boulder. But it shouldn't have been a surprise. I'd even predicted this would happen when last I saw him.

'That's good Pierre.' I forced a phone smile. 'You deserve it more than anyone. What's her name? Is she from the Vaucluse?'

'She's from Montpelier, a buyer for a big retail chain. It's been about five months…we shall see.'

'Well, may it all work out well for you and her.'

'I'm really happy to hear you're okay, that you've come through and are building a good life in Geneva.'

'Thank you. Take care of yourself. Keep up the running.'

I put the phone down and stared into space, the tears cool against my cheeks. Nine months, what had I expected? Of course he'd met someone. Of course of course of course. So that was it then, closure. Closure not just with Alain but with Pierre and Provence. I'd been a fool to think I could cultivate a friendship—or more—with him. Now I had to consign all of it to the past, let it all go. Pierre was not to be and so be it. It was for the best. I would get over it. It was a lesson I still needed to learn.

The joggers were out in force that Saturday morning, running along the smoothly paved path by the lake's edge. I was on my weekend constitutional, a brisk walk in crisp conditions, not a cloud in sight and the lake and mountains like cut-outs from a Hans Christian Anderson epic. The jet d'eau was spouting and a few sailing craft were bobbing along in the direction of Lausanne. The beautiful scenery further buoyed my mood. Not that it needed much buoying because I was in a pretty good place, feeling strong and good in myself—the self who I was coming to know again after my various bits and pieces had been picked up off the floor, washed, spun, dried and reconstituted. I could genuinely laugh at jokes. I could even make them. And I could laugh at myself. There. That was progress.

After fifteen months in Geneva, I felt settled in the city and my French was fully fluent. I could think about Provence now—Pierre included—without a catch in my throat, indeed with a grin. But I took nothing for granted, least of all my wellbeing. I still marvelled, when I woke up in the morning, about the absence of all those familiar feelings: of rejection, hurt, pain, anger, shame, self-loathing, a huge, dense mass of emotional agony. I marvelled about what had replaced them. Gusts of brightness, peace, pleasure. It was like I'd peeled off a layer of pustulous flesh, finding in its stead healthy, breathing skin. I intended to keep the odious memories alive though, as a reminder of how I needed to nurture myself, work to maintain self-like and if possible self-love as the default setting. My self-esteem was still a fragile thing. Probably it always would be. If a self-esteem barometer existed, it would surely show a leap from its cratering in France, the absolute bottom when it wouldn't have shown any measure at all. But I had to remain vigilant that it didn't swing back into negative territory again.

I'd started dipping my feet into the dating waters, enjoying dinners with a Swiss man who worked for the International Federation of the Red Cross. We were slowly getting to know each other and there was a mutual attraction. I felt ready again for sex, non-addictive sex where I didn't have to pretend to be what I wasn't. There was good news on the family front too. Julia was four and a half months pregnant and Lilly and Nick had bought a five-bedroom cottage in Gloucestershire.

Opening the door to my apartment, I thought only of a restorative glass of water and a laid-back coffee. But first the toilet, which is where I was when the phone rang. I'll just leave it, I thought. But whoever it was, was insistent for it kept on ringing. I finished up and dashed to the cordless phone.

'Ravinia, it's Pierre.'

'Pierre?' It took me a moment to register. 'How did you get my number?'

'A bit of detective work. It was easy to track down your bureau, but hard to convince your friend, the woman I spoke to, to give me your home number.'

'Well, I should hope so.'

'Luckily she knew who I was. Finally I was able to convince her, threatening her that if she didn't give me your number you might never forgive her. And I swore her to secrecy.'

'I shall have words with Maude on Monday.' I laughed, nervously. That had been bold of him.

'How are you?'

'I'm good Pierre,' I said, beginning to feel not so good. 'Growing to really like Geneva. And you?'

I wasn't going to ask why he'd called.

'Up and down,' and then, 'the relationship has ended. I ended it, actually.'

'Ended?' Oh Jesus, I didn't want to know. 'I'm sorry to hear that.'

It was the polite thing to say and I realised I really meant it. He paused, waiting for me to ask what had happened but I didn't, not even to break the awkward silence.

'I realised she wasn't right for me,' he went on. 'I think I was hit by an early mid-life crisis.'

'At thirty-five?'

'I said early. What I do know is, I want to see you. In Geneva, if your offer still stands.'

Stands? He must be kidding.

'Pierre, I'm going to be totally honest with you. I'm in a different place to when I spoke with you last time. I've had realisations…Provence is over. It's all behind me now and I don't want reminders of it. I…I…seeing you, no. It's not a good idea. I'm sorry,' I whispered.

'When I said I was hit by a crisis, I also meant the desire for change. Do you remember my telling you during our dinner in Mazan one night how I'd always longed to live abroad? Well, the time has come. To get out of the Vaucluse, out of France.'

He paused. And then, calmly:

'I've moved to Geneva.'

'You've what?' I cried, wondering if I'd heard correctly. 'You've moved here? You can't be serious. I can't believe you'd do that.'

The hostility of my response was clear and intentional, conveying the bombshell of it. I mean, what a difference two seasons make. If he'd have told me this six months ago, I would have celebrated the news. But now? I felt as if the ground had cracked open, the solidity I'd so painstakingly re-erected, suddenly in peril. Always quick to register shock, my bowels turned watery. Legs unsteady, I flopped to the floor, very nearly colliding with the sharp edge of a low table. There I huddled, one damp hand around bunched-up knees, the other holding the phone.

'You didn't move here because of me I hope.'

'No, not because of you,' he said in the same even tone. 'Not at all. Well, okay, a little. I can't lie. You were, let's say, a motivating factor. But there's no obligation on you. Absolutely none. I want to be clear about that. I had to make the move for myself. Soon after I ended the relationship I contacted several engineering companies in Geneva and a job sort of fell into my lap. I didn't expect it to be so easy. I guess that means it was meant to happen.'

'What about your house?'

'I've rented it out.'

'When did you move?'

'Three weeks ago. I'm renting a furnished flat in Carouge.'

Maybe he's had a breakdown.

'Do you know when I first started to…?' He left the sentence hanging. 'It was during that same dinner in Mazan. When you asked about my divorce and I found myself telling you something I wouldn't normally have done to a person I hardly knew. Especially', he emphasised that word, 'my brother's girlfriend.' He paused. 'The diplomatic but persuasive way you have of asking questions. Your curiosity.'

It struck me that a facet like this would never have earned a compliment from Alain, so blind-sided by things sexual.

'And when you said you were digging into Tristan's life, writing a book about him, I thought that takes guts. I loved you from a distance and I expected it would always remain that way. It wasn't going to stop me from meeting another woman. I loved you but I wanted you to be happy with Alain. A very odd situation I agree.'

Odd didn't bother me. It was the treacherous timing.

‘I’d just like to see you. For lunch. Or a coffee or a walk if you prefer. I know it’s not fair to put you on the spot. You need some thinking time. I’ll phone you back Saturday mid-morning, if you’re free then.’

That was three days away.

He was true to his word, calling just after eleven. I sat on one of my straight-backed kitchen chairs, as tense as before a school exam. There were no preliminaries.

‘So, the moment of truth?’ His voice contained a leap of hope—and anxiety.

‘I’m sorry Pierre but the answer’s still no. It’s not that I don’t like you—you’re a good…wonderful man. You’ve been incredibly kind to me. I’ll always be grateful to you. But it’s about self-preservation, being through with the past. You couldn’t know it, but when I phoned you months ago, when you told me you were in a relationship, I went through an agony. You see, I’d dreamed up this fantasy of you and I together. That wasn’t your fault of course. It’s just that…that’s when I decided enough was enough. I’ve worked so hard on myself these last few months to purge myself of Provence, you included. When you rang three days ago it was a shock. I never expected to hear from you again and I felt really angry. I’d put you in the past and here you go, showing up practically on my doorstep.’

This is my terrain, not yours, I wanted to say.

‘Anyway,’ I took a deep breath. ‘Just for argument’s sake, let’s imagine what would happen if we did meet up and it went well and we wanted to see each other again, then what? The truth is, it just wouldn’t work. You and me. It’s not meant to be. Too much baggage from the past.’

I hadn’t wavered from the speech I’d prepared, my decision final.

‘Am I just a reminder of Provence to you? A reminder of him? Is that all I am?’ He spoke quietly, the leap of hope extinguished. ‘Do I not exist in any other realm, as a person without this label, this baggage of Provence? This baggage my brother dumped on you? If that’s the case then you don’t know me, you don’t know who I am. You’re not giving me a chance, you’re not giving yourself the chance to find out.’

His words were an uncanny echo of what I’d said to Alain when he announced he wanted me gone. ‘You haven’t given this a chance. You don’t know who I am. You’ve never bothered to find out.’ I put myself in Pierre’s shoes. How well I understood him. How well I knew the feeling of another person's purposeful blindness, of not being seen or appreciated for who I was, the very core of me. But I couldn't…I wouldn't change my mind.

'The timing's all wrong. The past is the past.' Tell him you're dating someone. You've met a man. 'I'm truly sorry.'

'Are you afraid of rejection?'

'Yes, but that's not it. Come on, let's face it, the reality of us together…because of the history, your family and yes, your brother, how could there be a future? Too much has happened. It's impossible. And as individuals we're not compatible.'

I didn't believe that last bit but threw it in for emphasis. He ignored it.

'I've been rejected and I'm afraid of being rejected again. I've told you. I'm not a risk taker. I've always lamented that about myself. But I've taken more risks recently than I ever thought possible. Facing my fears. But I also feel strong. Strong enough to have realised a dream, and that's thanks to you.'

'How is that?'

'You left Hong Kong for Alain. It was a disaster but you tried it. There can't be regrets about that.'

'Not true, there are. I wish I'd stayed in Hong Kong. I wish I'd followed my head instead of my heart and stuck with the job in television. I made a terrible mistake.'

'No. You would have always wondered about Provence. Anyway, there's another way of looking at all this. It's because you've been through so much that you know that life is rarely about absolutes. That would be too easy. It's chaotic and we have to sort out what's right and good for us at any one time, because everything changes. If we don't take risks, make ourselves vulnerable again after pain, then we're closing the doors to…who knows what wonderful possibilities. I wish I'd followed my heart more, not married someone I didn't love, been more adventurous. I can't turn the clock back on the decisions I've made but I can do things differently from this point on. I don't want any more regrets.'

His words, reaching inside me, opening the spigots.

It is not in the stars to hold our destiny but in ourselves. Shakespeare knew a thing or two about psychology and what really counted. The quote had squirmed its way into my brain, as if summoned by Pierre.

'Okay Pierre. We'll meet once for old time's sake.'

I thought quickly.

'How about next Saturday. There's a café called La Clemence in Place du Bourg-de-Four. It's a café in the old town. Can you note that? Is two o'clock good for you?'

I hung up, already upset with myself for caving. My anger at Pierre kept me awake that night and stalked me for the next few days and I had a hard time concentrating at work. Just like that, from one moment to the next, I was jolted, my recovery from all things Provence feeling as wobbly as broken ice skates. How dare he move here. What gall. I didn't want Provence in Geneva. This was my turf. And how presumptuous of him to think I'd want to see him. And why had I agreed? Mainly I'd felt sorry for him, and a sense of pressure. Not valid reasons for a reunion. Now I saw only the negatives, the uselessness of starting a dialogue that couldn't possibly lead anywhere. Why do this to myself? How dare he put me in this position. And round and round my head spun, taking me further and further down. I was no longer seeing my therapist – a crutch I now sorely missed. Finally I called Julia and told her about Pierre, wanting her to coddle me in my crankiness, but, in character, she did something far more valuable.

'Why are you giving your power away again? You know your anger is just misplaced fear,' she said.

'I guess so. But why am I so freaking fearful?'

'Maybe it's about being sucked back in, feeling things you don't want to feel,' Julia said. 'But you know what? You have a choice, remember. You don't have to hold onto your anger or fear. You can let it all go or let it ride with you, keep you company. In any case that's your stuff. And Pierre, he's no threat. You can't be goaded into anything.'

She was right. Not now. Never again.

'And maybe, just maybe, you should be proud of him for what he's done and let him know it.'

Touché again. The conversation with my sister set me straight. It was my choice to be angry and to hell with that, to hell with playing the victim again. I felt a weight lifted. Alleluia. I realised how brave Pierre had been, breaking through his own barriers, choosing to exit his comfort zone. He'd taken a stupendous step and that deserved acknowledgement. I didn't want a relationship with him. But I did want to congratulate him in person. A one-off coffee would do it.

Chapter 30

Saturday dawned cold, but with a pale sun managing to poke through the clouds and spread some rays. Not bad for a mid-winter's day. I set off from home, decided on taking the bus to avoid parking hassles in town. I'd chosen to wear monochrome: black leather boots and a shin-length skirt under my black wool coat, a white cashmere polar-neck sweater and silver earrings. Once on the bus, they kicked in, sweaty palms, dry mouth, heart thumping like I'd drunk five double expressos. Nerves. How annoying.

I saw him as soon as I entered the café, sitting at a corner table. He rose up, smiling. With each step forward I felt more on edge. Then, stopping just short of him, indecision. Do we cheek-kiss two times Swiss style or three times the southern French way? Or hug? He quickly broke the impasse, lightly placing his hands on my shoulders and kissing me twice before pulling away just as I went for a third. It was a stumbling moment, but then it was over and my nerves calmed. After carefully draping my coat over the back of my chair, I settled into my seat. For a few seconds, silence reigned as we each took stock of the other.

There it was, the face I'd yearned to see then spurned to see: fresh but no longer boyish, the thick brown hair cut shorter, the chin smooth, ah, but with a shaving nick just at the underside. The hazel eyes, earnest and firm. The familiar scent. His smartly casual black jumper and jacket I hadn't seen before but I recognised the brown corduroy trousers. All as I'd logged it yet totally different. Maybe it was just the context—the fact that I was seeing him so very out of context. A turning of the tables. He was in my corner, which he'd now made his.

I wondered what his thoughts were about me. I expected him to say something along the lines of, it's so great to see you, thank you for agreeing to meet. I'd answer truthfully, that it was good to see him too. But he surprised.

'Nice place this,' he remarked, as if we'd seen each other yesterday. The lamp-lit interior was a little dark but the café was spacious and quiet enough for conversation. The draw was the large terrace, packed in the summer.

'You found it okay?'

'I knew where it was. I spent last weekend exploring the old town. Very charming.'

He spoke lightly, still smiling.

'I happened to discover this gem of a bookshop, about a ten-minute walk from here. Les Recyclables. Do you know it? It has a large section of foreign-language books. I walked out with the complete works of Shakespeare—in English.'

It certainly was a curious conversation opener. Then it struck me.

'In English? But Pierre, you don't speak English.'

'No, but I can read it, and I'm going to start learning to speak, from the playwright himself.'

I laughed.

'You're going to learn Elizabethan English? A lot of good that will do you in twenty-first-century Switzerland.'

'Ah, but then I can quote the original passages from his plays.'

'Eez ziss a daggAIR weech I zee beforrr me, zee ANDel towards my And?'

I recognised the quote from Macbeth. *Is this a dagger which I see before me, the handle towards my hand?*

It was the first time I'd heard him say anything in English and it was hilarious. I laughed even more. His accent, it was priceless. And the movements he made—hands out, eyebrows raised—were used to great effect.

'I apologise,' I tried to rein myself in. 'I don't mean to make fun of you,' and I broke up again, saying a silent 'sorry' to Shakespeare for having a laugh at his expense.

'Eez ziss a daggair…'

He began again, clearly enjoying my reaction, oblivious to the stares from curious onlookers. I laughed so hard the tears rolled down my cheeks, and he joined in, which brought on more fits. Alain had minted humour out of Shakespeare, yes, but the funny prize went to Pierre.

'Well,' I said, finally recovering, 'all that laughing has given me an appetite. How about you? Shall we order?'

I was in the mood for sweet and asked for my favourite dessert, *tarte tatin* and a tisane. He opted for a croque monsieur maison.

This Pierre was delightfully funny and I wanted to stay in that lightness of being zone around Shakespeare. But needs must. I had a purpose for seeing him.

‘Pierre.’ I tried not to sound rehearsed. ‘I should have said this to you before but…congratulations on your new job, on moving here. Getting out of France. You’ve done it. You’ve realised a dream. That’s enormous.’

I aimed for a neutral, unemotional tone. He raised his brows.

‘Does that mean you’re not angry with me anymore for my fait accompli? For springing up here unannounced?’

‘It means I think you’ve got guts. You went after what you wanted, to leave Provence and experience something different.’

‘You didn’t answer my question.’

‘No, I’m not angry with you anymore.’

Even if I’d still been mad when I walked into the café, I couldn’t have stayed in that state with someone who’d pushed all my giggle buttons.

‘You did what you needed, wanted, to do,’ I told him. ‘It’s your decision and your life. I can take care of myself and do what’s best for me. That much I’ve learned. Just curious though. Why didn’t you tell me before that you were thinking of moving to Geneva?’

He studied his fingers for a moment, resting on the table, then raised his head, his expression more serious now.

‘I thought of contacting you many times. I imagined the conversation, but I just couldn’t do it. I had to do this on my own. To be honest, I didn’t want you to influence my decision. And I didn’t want to put any pressure on you.’

Good of you, I thought.

‘I was drawn to Geneva, following in your pioneering footsteps and…it just seemed like a good place to start my little foreign adventure. And if we see no more of each other after today, it will at least be a closure…’

No more of each other. That’s right. That’s what I’d vowed and there would be no volte face. No matter that he was a good man, that we still had an easy rapport with each other. Time had moved on. Pierre was a closed chapter and that’s where I wanted him to stay.

‘So tell me, how did you make it all happen?’

‘Well, I sent out my CV to a bunch of firms in Geneva and followed up with calls. I guess the timing was right. Ingeni, a structural engineering group, got back to me. They happened to be looking for someone with my background and skills. They asked me here for an interview. I flew in from Marseille.’

‘You obviously impressed them.’

'Not sure about that, but I did do my homework on the company and brushed up on my interview skills. I hadn't had one of those in what, ten years?'

I could imagine him methodically preparing, doing his research, making lists, responding to imagined questions.

'When did they offer you the job?'

'Two days after I got back.'

'So then, what do you actually do?'

'They hired me for a new design unit they've set up. Just six of us at the moment, with a team leader. But with a lot of growing room, I hope.'

'And do you like it? The place, the people?'

'I'm just cutting my teeth right now. Getting to grips with these strange Swiss accents. I'm sure they think the same thing of mine,' he laughed. 'But the work is much more interesting than what I'd been doing, design-wise. A new set of structures to focus on. And the team, a very ambitious bunch but welcoming I'm glad to say. And I have whiter, brighter walls to stare at. Actually, I don't have a minute to stare, but if ever I do.'

'Sounds good. I'm glad for you Pierre. Did you drive over? And what about your flat? Seems you found a place pretty quickly.'

'I have my car here, yes. I live in an apartment in Carouge, as I mentioned. I love the area, though the parking is tricky. I'm told I'm very lucky to have found a place so fast. Thanks to the company really. They put me in touch with a *Regie* they work with.'

'Absolutely you're lucky. Because honestly, the real estate agents here are an absolute mafia. They make it so hard to find anywhere to live in this city. Must be strange for you to live in an apartment after your house.'

'It takes adjusting to that's for sure. But it's temporary.'

The waiter arrived with our food, setting the plates down carefully.

'Bon appétit,' I said, anticipating that first bite.

'This is delicious,' Pierre said after a few forkfuls of his croque monsieur.

'So is this, although not as good as Peppo's *tarte tatin*. His is unbeatable.'

He looked askance at that, surprised, I think, at my alluding to Provence. So was I. But once I'd started, I kept on theme.

'You know, the divorce came through. I received the final judgement in the post.'

'That's good. Completion.' Said matter-of-factly.

'How is your mother?'

I was testing the waters, speaking about his family. But it didn't evoke pain. It was liberating.

'She and Roland, they're both fine, enjoying the simple pleasures of life. Thanks for asking.'

'She must have been pretty shocked by your move here. Did she try to talk you out of it?'

'She didn't take it particularly well, that's true. I told her only that I'd been headhunted by this company in Geneva and that it was too good an opportunity to pass up. I didn't tell her I was on a mission to leave.'

Or that I was in the picture, I thought.

'And of course you living in Geneva didn't enter the conversation,' he said, seeming to read my mind. 'Maybe she thought it an odd coincidence, your moving here and then me. Or maybe it never occurred to her. In any case, she didn't try to change my mind. She knew she couldn't. And Switzerland isn't India.'

'Apart from apparently being stubborn she's resilient your mum.'

'She had to be, as a young girl exiled to France on her own.'

'And to have raised you single-handedly. Having to work for the first time in her life when she was what, over forty? I never asked you this before Pierre, but what was it like for you as a child after your dad died, when it was just you and your mum?'

He smiled, not from the question but, I suspected, the way I asked it, reminding him of how I'd grilled him in the past.

'After my father died I remember my mother telling me we couldn't eat beef anymore and the sauçisson disappeared and things like buying comic books, actually any books, were out of the question. Luckily we had a good library near us so I could keep reading, and I read voraciously. When I was fourteen, I started working at a bakery on the weekends, stacking shelves and making some deliveries and the like and most of what I earned I gave to her—and I got some free bread in the bargain. She didn't force me, I wanted to help and she was grateful.'

His taste of poverty had dictated his choices.

'I studied hard at school and I was rewarded with top marks. I was driven. Because of all the hardship and struggle, I intentionally chose a career that was stable and predictable, where I could count on making a good living.'

'I don't know if you remember it—the time we had lunch at your mother's flat. You told me you went into engineering because you didn't inherit the artistic genes. I never thought that was quite true.'

'I didn't have the same chances to be as happy-go-lucky and carefree as my brothers, to live in an imaginary world. I was always very aware of lack and limitation. But it's true. I didn't, don't, have their strain of genius.'

You're better off, I thought. Genius comes with a hefty price.

'Sounds hard, your childhood.'

'It was. But with all her stress and unhappiness, my mother gave me a lot of love. In that area, there was abundance. And if I have kids of my own one day, I'll know what really matters—love and bakery rounds,' he joked.

If I have kids of my own…A world away from Alain.

'Now, change of subject. Tell me about your life. Today. Now.'

I told him about my work as a journalist, the friends I'd made, playing the piano, going for walks in the surrounding forests and hills, seeing films and concerts, shopping at Migro supermarket and at markets across the Swiss-French border in Ferney Voltaire. I told him about my cosy apartment, furnished with the new and the old, including the sofa bed, the desk, the art-deco lamp and the TV I'd bought in Provence. I'd invested in a queen-sized bed, quality kitchenware and a glass-topped dining table with chairs.

But I said nothing about the Swiss man. I was seeing him tonight as a matter of fact. A date with sex I'd decided. I was more than ready, fairly drooling with the anticipation of it. Was something of that ionised in the air? Was it written on my face, that tonight I was going to make love for the first time in, how many months was it? Go on, come clean about the man, ready steady go. But the words refused to come out. What was the point of telling if I wasn't going to see Pierre again, I rationalised. If he'd have asked me straight out whether I'd met someone, I would have told him the truth. I suppose he had his reasons for not asking.

'And the book about Tristan? What's happened with that?'

'Nothing. I'm not pursuing it. Actually, I'd made that decision in Provence because your sister hated the idea, which I understand. An invasion of privacy. But maybe, who knows, one day I can resurrect the project as fiction, about an Italian or Spaniard or Englishman who went to India and became a sadhu and guru and did extraordinary things, like walking to the Himalayas and back and living among wild animals in the jungle, becoming a mythical, revered figure.'

In fact, I'd had another idea for a book—a book whose contours had taken shape even as Provence receded into the past. I'd thought of calling it *The Sadist and the Saint*, about two brothers born under the awning of Mont Ventoux, one a genius artist, utterly narcissistic and a destroyer of women, the other, a Gandhi-like figure who gave his soul to India's villagers. Yes, I'd had a determination to write this tale—at some point in the future—of diametrically opposite siblings, a subject I found fascinating. But then I'd dropped the idea. I had no appetite for revenge. But what a pity, for what a tale it had the potential to be.

'You know, I wanted Tristan's story to be told by you,' Pierre said.

'Thank you for that. But whether it's written or not I want you to know I'll always be grateful for what your mother revealed to me about Tristan. I understood her need to find out anything she could about her son.'

'She will never understand why he left France for India and never once returned. The rules about sadhus having to cut blood ties with their own families don't register with my mother or sister.'

We spent hours conversing in the café and as we did so, the words spoken became a smokescreen for my own inner dialogue as I analysed him and myself. I'm sure he was doing the same with me. Was I okay? Yes. Were old feelings for him starting to surface? That's where things were becoming a little muddy. I'd consciously turned the lights off on him but despite everything, flickers arose, glimmers of warmth, of wanting. His eyes focused on mine, his folded hands resting comfortably on the table, his upper body leaning slightly forward at times, then back, his bearing relaxed and carefree. He seemed genuinely happy. Yet I suspected that the feelings were there, ready to surface if I'd said it's great to see you, I've been re-thinking…and deployed a body language of desire. No, I told myself. Cannot. Must not. I steered my thoughts to my date tonight. The excitement of what lay ahead.

And yet…Pierre's identity was dissolving and re-evolving by the second. In this café he was no longer the younger brother, the baby sitter, the serious one. He was no longer in the shadow of. He was a new Pierre, or rather the old one minus a certain angst. Distance from Provence seemed to suit him. Or was it simply the confidence that comes from realising a dream? I reckoned he'd made peace with our one-off catch-up, his new life and untold adventures stretching enticingly before him. That was his future. And mine? Tonight, at any rate, it was the Swiss and I—newly lovers.

Finally, I looked at my watch, suddenly aware of the darkness outside.

'Quarter to six already,' I said. 'I've got to go.'

'Of course.'

He caught the eye of the waiter and signalled for the check, in the next instance taking a pen and business card from his jacket pocket, scribbling something on the back and handing it to me.

'My card and home number, just in case you ever need to get in touch. If you ever need help with…engineering or technical things,' he smiled.

'Thanks.' I put the card in my bag.

'This is on me,' Pierre said, plucking cash from his wallet and leaving it on the table with the bill.

We walked out in silence, standing a few metres from the glass café doors.

'I drove here. My car's in a garage in the Quai de Rhône. Can I give you a lift?'

'No, but thanks for offering. You go on.'

We stood, hesitating. I shivered.

'Well then. It was good to see you Pierre.'

'You too.'

This time we hugged each other properly—if only briefly—me on tiptoes, he bending down an inch, coat against jacket, hair touching hair. We drew away simultaneously.

'So, be well. Go strong. Good luck…with everything,' I said.

'Keep writing all those stories for the world to read.'

And like that, we parted, heading off in different directions.

As I walked, I felt that strange, out-of-skin sensation like when I emerged from the dark entrails of a movie theatre into bright sunshine. And then, what kind of mind twister was this? Every certainty vanished. I swivelled around. He was in his stride, about to turn right into the Rue de la Fontaine. Quick, I thought, and began to run.

'Pierre,' I shouted out, a few metres behind him. He stopped and turned, caught off-guard.

'Listen,' I said, catching my breath. 'How about some homework to help you with your English? Some quotes from King Lear.'

He laughed.

'Okay, I'll recite them to you next time.'

Next time, I thought. And the thought was pleasing.